Leaves
of the
Banyan Tree

TALANOA
CONTEMPORARY PACIFIC LITERATURE

Vilsoni Hereniko, General Editor

ALAN DUFF *Once Were Warriors*

EPELI HAU'OFA *Tales of the Tikongs*

HONE TUWHARE *Deep River Talk: Collected Poems*

Leaves
of the
Banyan Tree

Albert Wendt

TALANOA

CONTEMPORARY
PACIFIC
LITERATURE

UNIVERSITY OF HAWAII PRESS
Honolulu

For my father Tuaopepe Alualu
and
Filia and Tupuola Efi
and
Lynne and Tuala Karanita

Copyright © Albert Wendt *(Leaves of the Banyan Tree)* 1979
All rights reserved
First published in New Zealand by Longman Paul Limited 1979
Published in North America by University of Hawai'i Press 1994
Printed in the United States of America

02 03 04 05   6 5 4 3

Library of Congress Cataloging-in-Publication Data

Wendt, Albert, 1939–
Leaves of the banyan tree / Albert Wendt.
p.   cm. — (Talanoa)
"First published in New Zealand by Longman Paul Limited, 1979"—
T.p. verso.
ISBN 0–8248–1584–X (pbk. : alk. paper)
1. Family—Samoan Islands—Fiction. I. Title. II. Series.
PR9665.9.W46L4   1994
823—dc20   93–41685
CIP

University of Hawai'i Press books are printed on acid-free paper
and meet the guidelines for permanence and durability of the
Council on Library Resources.

www.uhpress.hawaii.edu

Contents

Editor's Note

Leaves of the Banyan Tree, which took twelve years to write
and was first published in 1979, is the most ambitious of
Albert Wendt's works to date. It is an epic that spans three
generations and explores on a grand scale a number of uni-
versal themes that include greed, corruption, colonialism,
exploitation, and revenge. In *Leaves,* Wendt creates a work
of art that fuses all his various talents and experiences: the
result is a powerful and impressive banyan tree that towers
above the young saplings.

Wendt has said that one reason he writes is to correct the
inaccurate images of his people that have been created by
early explorers and anthropologists like Margaret Mead.
More than his earlier novels, *Sons for the Return Home* and
Pouliuli, Leaves probes deep and wide into the Samoan
psyche, with a colorful cast of characters so convincingly
drawn that one can easily forget they do not exist except in
Wendt's imagination. Samoans in this novel live, breathe,
fight, engage in double-dealing, love one another, hate one
another, and die, just like any other people whose lives are
complex and complicated.

As a Samoan, Wendt understands the aspirations, fears,
hopes, and dreams of his people. As a leading intellectual
from the Pacific, he straddles many worlds and is conversant
with many traditions: the old and the new, the local and the

global. As an artist and committed writer, Wendt cares deeply about the plight of the oppressed, irrespective of who they are or where they live.

Since the publication of *Leaves*, Wendt has written two other novels: *Ola* and *Black Rainbow*, which is being made into a feature film with Wendt scripting the adaptation. He has also published two collections of poetry: *Inside Us the Dead* and *Shaman of Visions*. A collection of short stories, the novella *Flying-Fox in a Freedom Tree*, and *Sons for the Return Home* have been made into feature films.

Wendt has lived and worked in New Zealand, Samoa, and Fiji where he has been instrumental in the encouragement and promotion of Pacific literature. Currently he is professor of English at the University of Auckland, where he teaches post-colonial literatures and creative writing.

In 1992, Albert Wendt was awarded a Senate Certificate by the Senate of the Sixteenth Legislature of the State of Hawaii in recognition of his talents as a writer and his contribution to Pacific and world literature.

Talanoa is honored to publish this classic by a literary giant.

Vilsoni Hereniko

Book One
God, Money, and Success

1   The Price of Copra

It had rained nearly all day, and Tauilopepe Mauga had remained in the main fale plaiting sinnet. Now it was evening, time for prayers, and the throbbing chorus of cicadas ached through Sapepe village. Masina, Tauilopepe's mother, came in from the kitchen fale where she had been helping cook the evening meal, opened the large wooden trunk, got out the Bible which had been in her aiga since the missionaries came, and sat down at the front of the fale, facing her son. Tauilopepe stopped plaiting and put on the shirt that was lying beside him. The rest of the Aiga Tauilopepe, his wife and three children and numerous other relatives, entered and sat down at the back posts of the fale.

Masina coughed, put two fingers to her mouth, and through the gap between them spat a thin streak of spittle out into the falling dark. She began to sing a hymn. The others joined her, but a moment later Tauilopepe was neither singing nor listening. Head bowed, he sat mentally adding up the profits he hoped to make from the copra he was going to sell at Malo's store the next day. He broke from his thoughts when his only son Pepe sat down beside him. Sensing that Pepe was going to speak, he placed his hand over the boy's mouth gently. He could feel Masina looking at him, so he started singing again.

Should get twenty pounds, he concluded, as the hymn faded into the amen. Masina began to read from the Bible. Tauilopepe remembered that they owed Malo fourteen pounds; it was a man's duty to pay his debts; all that work for nothing; all to Malo. Pepe moved up against Tauilopepe's side and put his head on his father's knee. Tauilopepe tried to concentrate on the reading but failed. The bitter thought of all that money disappearing into the steel drawer in Malo's store defeated him. And at least two pounds had to be donated that Sunday to the upkeep of

3

their pastor Filipo. 'Keep us, O Lord, from straying into the sinful ways of the world', Masina prayed. Immediately he felt guilty, and for the rest of the prayer he repeated every word to himself to try to distract his thoughts from the debt. He'd leave it to God, he decided, as Masina said amen and closed the Bible.

He still kept his eyes shut. He'd been cheated. By whom he didn't know or want to know; he'd been cheated, that was all. When he heard the crunching sound of bare feet coming towards him over the pebble floor he opened his eyes. His wife, Lupe, loomed above him in the gloom. She placed the kerosene lamp in front of him, gave him a box of matches, and waited for him to light the lamp. He pushed the box open, pushed too hard, and the matches spilt into his lap. He cursed under his breath, picked up a match, and struck it furiously across the box. The match exploded with light. He glared up at Lupe. Seeing how angry he was, she looked away quickly and lifted the lampshade. He stabbed the burning match at the wick. The lamp spluttered, then its light ballooned across the fale. He looked across at Masina; she looked away from his anger too. He looked at the other members of his aiga. They got up silently and left the fale. Lupe put the lamp on the floor near the massive centre post and went to the kitchen fale. He watched her go. Pepe jumped up noisily to follow her.

'Don't ever do that again!' Tauilopepe warned him. Pepe looked questioningly at him, sat down again, and started to jab his fingers into the floor. Tauilopepe cuffed him across the head. Pepe jumped up again and ran out of the fale.

'Where's the meal?' Tauilopepe called to the kitchen fale. Masina sat gazing out into the darkness.

Soon his two daughters entered with foodmats laden with fried fish and taro. He didn't look at them. Vao, the elder girl, with bowed head, placed the foodmat in front of him, retreated, and sat down at a back post. The rest of their aiga, except Pepe, entered with basins of water and baskets of food and arranged themselves beside Vao, all ready to serve Tauilopepe and Masina. They remained silent and avoided looking at him.

Tauilopepe didn't wait for Masina, who usually said

4

grace before this main meal of the day; he mumbled a short prayer and dug into his food. Masina glanced at him, then started to eat also. They ate in strained silence.

Moths and tiny beetles danced round the lamp, safe from the wax-coloured lizards watching them from the rafters, as the crying of the cicadas faded into the night which now drenched the village. From the neighbouring fale, pockets of light in the darkness, came the clatter of dishes and the muffled sound of conversation and laughter. The tide was surging in over the reef. It would soon be licking the crablike roots of the mangrove trees behind the Tauilopepe home.

Tauilopepe finished eating and pushed away his foodmat now littered with fish bones and taro crusts. Vao brought him a chipped enamel basin of water. He washed his hands and mouth and dried them on the hand-towel she gave him. She returned to her place. The rest of the aiga started their meal. Tauilopepe watched them and picked at his teeth with his fingers.

He suddenly noticed Pepe wasn't there. He was going to ask why, when Pepe slipped in from the darkness and sat down between Lupe and Vao. Lupe placed a large fish, which she had reserved specially for him, on his foodmat. Pepe ate eagerly.

The track to the pool was a wet snake with its head buried somewhere ahead in the darkness and the lapping of waves. The mud was slippery under his feet. He usually bathed at night, a habit he had acquired from his father when, as a boy, he had accompanied him to the pool. The stench of pigsties veined the still air. He stopped, blew his nose into the end of his towel, coughed and spat, and continued on his way.

He looked down at the pool. It seemed to have snared the last traces of light. Beyond it the sea and sky were an invisible murmur of water shifting and stirring. He picked his way down to it over the rocks and boulders. They felt smooth and warm.

His skin prickled, anticipating the cold that would shock it. He dived into the water. The cold stung him; he sur-

faced, gasping, and swam swiftly to the bank. He lathered
his body with the piece of soap he had brought with him
and tumbled back into the water to wash it off. After a
while the cold didn't bother him so he floated and gazed
up at the few stars blinking in the black belly of the sky.
Dogs barked from nearby fale. He didn't think of the debt
until the cold seeped back into his bones. He flipped over,
swam to the bank, clambered up, got his towel, and dried
himself quickly. His bladder ached. He urinated into the
rocks. He heard a crab scuttling under the rocks and
remembered he hadn't urinated by the pool since that time
long ago when his father had caught him and slapped him
again and again on the back and shoulders. The memory of
those painful blows reminded him of the debt, and his
frustration and anger returned.

When he entered the fale Masina was reading to Pepe
from the Bible, and his daughters and Lupe were hanging
up the mosquito nets. They paused, briefly but noticeably,
when they saw him. He went to the wooden trunk where
most of their clothes were kept, got a bottle of coconut
oil, and rubbed oil into his body until it glistened. He
wrapped his sleeping sheet round himself, flattened down
his unruly hair with his hands, sat down a short distance
from Masina and his son. Lupe and the girls left for the
pool.

The mosquito nets stirred lazily in the breeze that was
beginning to blow in from the sea. Masina's voice flowed
into his mind but the words were the blank flimsy whiteness of the mosquito nets, the flicking of the beetles
against the glass lampshade, the shadows crouching at the
edge of the light.

Pepe yawned. Masina told him to go to bed and to
remember to say his prayers. Tauilopepe glanced at his
son. Pepe smiled back, got under the sleeping net, said his
prayers loudly so Masina and Tauilopepe could hear him,
and, ending with an extra loud amen, stretched out on his
mat and pulled his sleeping sheet up to his neck.
Tauilopepe looked out at the darkness, and because some
of his anger had gone the shadows no longer seemed hostile.

'Is the copra ready?' Masina asked. Tauilopepe flicked the remainder of his cheroot out of the fale and watched it fizzling on the damp ground. Masina began to speak again. He got up and left the fale.

Flying-foxes screeched from the mango trees which divided his land from that of the Aiga Toasa. He walked towards Toasa's fale. Always, when he had nothing else to do at night or when he was feeling troubled, he visited Toasa and played cards, the old man's favourite occupation.

His father and Toasa had grown up together. They had spanned fifty years before his father died in 1928. In his memories of them Tauilopepe could never quite separate one from the other. They had both brought him up, nurturing him as one father, yet they were so different: Toasa full of laughter and vigour; Tauilopepe Laau, his father, aloof and silent, almost unapproachably cold. He had thought of them as making one complete human being — Toasa the flesh and bone and his father the calculating mind, the real power behind their leadership of Sapepe. But when his father died Toasa absorbed unto himself the being of his father, as it were.

Tauilopepe stopped outside Toasa's fale and looked in. Toasa was sitting in the middle of the fale, scrutinising the rows of playing cards in front of him on the floor as if he was studying a difficult puzzle. One of his sons, a few years older than Tauilopepe, was making a fish-trap at the far side of the fale. A large mosquito net, shivering in the breeze, stretched across the fale behind the old man, its harsh whiteness heightening the colour of his darkly tanned body which was bare to the waist. His abundant belly hung in folds over the thick leather belt that held up his lavalava. Periodically he slapped at the mosquitoes which settled on him, but his eyes never left the cards. Tauilopepe entered.

Toasa looked up. 'Have you come, Tauilo?' he said. Toasa was the only man in Sapepe who didn't address Tauilopepe by his full matai title but then Toasa didn't address the other matai by their titles either but called them by their ordinary names. Grinning broadly, Toasa waved Tauilopepe down to sit opposite him. 'Just what I've

been waiting for—a fish to snare!' he said. Tauilopepe
didn't really want to play cards but Toasa, as usual, was
intent on beating him at Suipi, the game he had started to
teach Tauilopepe on the day he proved to Toasa's satisfaction that he could shuffle a pack of cards properly.

Before Tauilopepe was comfortably settled Toasa collected the cards and started shuffling them. He squared the
pack and banged it down in front of Tauilopepe, who cut
and handed it back to him. 'Now, watch the champion
move!' Toasa said, dealing out the cards faster than anyone
else Tauilopepe had ever seen.

Toasa won the first game easily, quickly.

The women of the aiga entered and strung up more
mosquito nets. They and the children got under them, and
the oldest woman started to tell the children the legend of
Sina and the Eel.

'Those papalagi have got aeroplanes now,' Toasa said
during the second game.

'Aeroplanes?' his son asked.

'Flying machines,' replied Toasa, taking another point
with a loud whoop. His son looked puzzled for a moment
but then returned to his work.

Tauilopepe wondered how Toasa knew about the aeroplanes, especially as he hadn't visited Apia for over a year.
To most of the people of Sapepe the outside world was
something heard about but never quite believed, a world
as mysterious as those aeroplanes, those flying machines
that Toasa had mentioned so casually as if he knew all
there was to know about them. Apia was a place to be visited perhaps twice a year, marvelled at, and returned from
with bewildering tales of mechanical marvels, ice cream,
big stores that sold everything a person could want, and a
picture theatre where cowboys (brave heroes) and Indians
(villains)—in true stories, mind you—killed one another
without any thought of Jehovah or of moral consequences.
But beyond these tales and the familiar and secure world
contained within the coral reefs lay a fairyland ruled by
papalagi, the builders of those aeroplanes and the messen-
gers of Jehovah, the papalagi who, after establishing Christianity in Samoa, had themselves reverted to pagan ways.

As he played Tauilopepe thought of the first time that Toasa and his father had taken him to Apia. A group of Sapepe rowers rowed them in a fautasi because there were no roads to town then. When they arrived the two men dressed him in his best clothes. Then his father held his frightened hand as they led him from the jetty to the main street. Only a few impressions remained: how the men took him to the town market — the biggest and noisiest and dirtiest building the boy had ever seen — and to the milk bar where he had his first thrilling taste of ice cream; how he tried to make the ice cream last as he walked between his father and Toasa through the town and they named the main sights for him; but how the sweet cold thing melted quickly in the heat and he cried as his father wiped his hands and clothes clean from it; how, tired and hot from walking, they rested in the market-place packed with people and, eating bread and butter (a luxury he had never tasted before), watched the carriages and wagons swaying past, while he wondered why the weird contraptions and horses were in such a hurry and where they were hurrying to: how Toasa unconsciously blocked the path of a young papalagi — dressed in white trousers, white shirt, and tanned shoes, which the boy could see his reflection in — who pushed Toasa off the footpath; and how Toasa didn't rebuke or hit the papalagi for his rudeness as he usually did when a Sapepean was rude to him; and how he, Tauilopepe, wondered why and was ashamed for Toasa, ashamed and embarrassed for Toasa and his father, who in that moment of frightened humility ceased to be the giants they had always been in his thoughts; how, after the papalagi had humiliated Toasa and his father they bought some things to take back, got into the fautasi, and were rowed home, with neither man speaking to the other, and with the boy vowing that he would some day kill that papalagi and noticing how the two men were avoiding having to see their shame in each other's eyes.

'Aeroplanes have two wings and an engine.' Toasa interrupted Tauilopepe's thoughts.

'Wings?' his son asked. There was a noticeable break in Toasa's play.

9

'Yes, wings,' Toasa said, covering up his lack of knowledge by playing enthusiastically.

Tauilopepe suddenly remembered the small wireless at the pastor's house. That must be where Toasa had got his information about aeroplanes. The wireless, which had been given to their village by the government, kept telling them about 'Progress' — a mysterious but evidently very important thing because the wireless always emphasised it — which was being established in Samoa by the New Zealand Administration. 'Progress', which most Sapepeans were suspicious of chiefly because they didn't understand what it meant, was something that would lead to a higher standard of living; it was a force and blessing which would benefit their children and future generations, the wireless claimed. And Tauilopepe, who had experienced more than most Sapepeans of this 'Progress' in action in Apia and at the theological college he had attended, believed in it and wanted to possess it not only for his children but for himself.

'There, beat you again!' Toasa announced. Tauilopepe tossed in his cards, hoping Toasa had had enough, but he gathered them up and began to shuffle them again. 'Two more games,' he said. Most of the lights across the road had gone out. Tauilopepe cleaned his left ear with a drilling motion of his forefinger.

Someone in the mosquito nets started snoring. Toasa reached behind him for his bamboo ali and hurled it at the net. It landed with a dull thud on the someone's head; there was a yelp of protest, then silence again.

'Your copra ready yet?' Toasa asked. Tauilopepe nodded as he fanned his cards. 'Should get quite a bit for it, eh?' Toasa said. 'Knew a man in the old days. Worked till his back was bent like a camel's to make a fortune in copra. Know what happened? He collected about ten tons. Wrecked his wife, children, aiga, and horse doing it. The palagi trader gave him all the credit he wanted while he was slaving to get his copra, and when it was ready told him the money it brought was just enough to pay the debt he'd run up at the trader's store. Poor ignorant fellow! He tried to kill that palagi trader. Was arrested and charged

10

with assault and put in jail!' Toasa stopped playing and laughed. Tauilopepe looked at Toasa's son; they smiled at each other. Toasa laughed on, his spraying spittle peppering Tauilopepe's face, and, as he laughed and repeated parts of his story, a very upsetting thought seeped into Tauilopepe's mind: Toasa was laughing at *him*. Feeling hot, he pushed his sleeping sheet down off his shoulders.

Toasa swooped up the last two points and won again. Tauilopepe collected the cards to shuffle for their last game.

As the game progressed, with Toasa chuckling and joking about fools and copra and unscrupulous traders, an accusing thought clogged Tauilopepe's head. He had always known that Toasa cheated at cards. In the past it had been something to laugh about for it had meant nothing; but now — feeling that Toasa was laughing at him — when he caught Toasa's right hand sweeping up a card he had hidden in the folds of his lavalava, 'Stop cheating!' he heard himself say loud and clear. 'Every night you insult me by cheating!'

Toasa stared at him in disbelief. 'Is it *that* important?' he said.

Tauilopepe flung down his cards, sprang to his feet, and stamped out of the fale.

Tauilopepe got under the mosquito net and lay down beside Lupe. She rolled on to her left side, turning her back to him. He moved against her back and embraced her. 'Don't come to me because you want to use me to lose your fears and anger about everything,' she whispered. He clutched her shoulder and turned her over on to her back. 'Don't!' she said but she didn't push him away. She lay still.

'You're my wife,' he muttered, his face buried in the softness of her neck. Her body was like unforgiving stone. 'Don't do that to me. Hold me!'

'Don't just use me,' she said. But he ignored her.

So she tolerated him.

11

2   In the Rain

Tauilopepe watched the skeleton of his conscience glowing rib by rib as the grey morning light filtered through the fale blinds and dispelled the dark trapped in the net and the fale dome. He gazed at Lupe for a long while, reached out to wake her and apologise to her, but didn't; he rolled out of the net without waking her, put on his stained singlet and working lavalava, and taking his bushknife from the thatching of the kitchen fale crossed the road and walked between the sleeping fale. Only a few pigs and hens were about, foraging in rubbish heaps and puddles. Everything was covered with a fine layer of dew. He climbed over the high rock fence behind the village on to the track that led to his plantation. Grey clouds gripped the mountain range to the east. No birds. Nothing to break the monotony of grey sky.

When he reached his plantation he immediately started to slash the creepers off the banana trees. He worked with a furious intentness. Ants and bugs stung his arms and face, and he was soon soaked to the skin. The bushknife got tangled in the creepers and was wrenched from his hand. He paused, gazed up at the mountain range stretching like a storm cloud right across the centre of the island, sighed, and wiped the rain and sweat off his face with the end of his lavalava. It started to drizzle.

Near noon, the light drizzle having stopped, he stretched out in the shelter of a clump of banana trees and for the first time that day felt pangs of hunger tugging at his belly. He ignored them stoically. A spider dangled from the banana leaves towards his face. He reached up and crushed it.

His plantation, part of the aiga land that went with his title, was not very large but it had been cultivated and handed down from Tauilopepe to Tauilopepe for generations. Most of the men before him had been content

12

merely to cultivate enough land to feed their aiga daily,
even though the Aiga Tauilopepe could have developed
the largest plantation in Sapepe because they controlled,
by right of rank and tradition, the major part of all Sapepe
land. His father had done nothing to extend the plantation
and, when Tauilopepe asked him why, he said that he was
satisfied with what he had. This had infuriated Tauilopepe,
especially as Malo, the chief rival to their aiga's leadership
of Sapepe, was at that time pushing his plantation further
and further inland. The only things his father had
cherished of this aiga land, Tauilopepe now concluded,
were useless bits of history connected with it: how his
great-grandfather, Tauilopepe Mosooi, who was head of
their aiga when the papalagi missionaries arrived in Sapepe,
refusing to become a Christian, had died there from spear
wounds he received in a skirmish with the neighbouring
district; how, even before Tauilopepe Mosooi, two sons of
Tauilopepe Mauga, after whom he was named, had killed
their father and then fought over the aiga title and slain
one another, thereby allowing the Aiga Malo to dominate
Sapepe for a generation, until Tauilopepe Uputoa,
Tauilopepe Mauga's grandson, had defeated the Malo faction, using warriors of his mother's aiga; how, even before
that, in the dim past, the sons of one of the Tauilopepes
(a famous war priest) had used war clubs fashioned from a
tree of this land to repel the fiercest invasion Sapepe had
ever experienced; how, right back to the Sapepe fountain-
head, this land had always been the refuge of the Aiga
Tauilopepe in times of war; how, when the first Aiga
Sapepe was shattered by internal strife, the Tauilopepe faction from which he was descended had found sanctuary
there; how, above all else this part of their aiga land was
the shrine of the Aiga Tauilopepe god, the Owl.
Tauilopepe remembered how one afternoon, when they
were returning from the plantation, his father had found a
dead owl on the track and, forgetting his son was there,
had knelt down beside the bird, which was already alive
with maggots, and bashed his forehead with a stone until
his blood flowed down his weeping face, and when he
asked his father why he had done this he did not answer,

but Tauilopepe had found out from Toasa that every member of the Aiga Tauilopepe performed that ritual whenever he saw the body of a dead owl, the aiga god. A history of birth and sudden brutal death, Tauilopepe thought: whole generations bursting into the world only to die swiftly, forgotten in the profusion of the unchanging bush. The people of earlier generations had superstitiously believed that the land had an identity, that it was to be revered and loved for what it was. His father had been one of those men without vision or education; men who were also ignorantly lazy.

Although the arrival of the papalagi had brought changes to the bush they too had been slow. Even when men used the more efficient papalagi tools the bush sooner or later crept back over their feeble clearings. The tempo of change had quickened in Tauilopepe's own lifetime. But out of recent attempts to conquer the bush only Malo, the first Sapepean to realise the rich profits to be made by using papalagi implements and knowledge, seemed to be succeeding.

Tauilopepe yawned and uncurled to his feet. Raindrops slid into his eyes; he blinked and looked around. The sight of the small plantation shocked him back into the inescapable realities of his life. He picked up his bushknife and wandered through the banana trees, not knowing what to do to defeat that dread feeling of inadequacy which over the years had become as real as the flesh on his bones.

An owl fluttered high above him. He looked at it for a moment, then dismissed the disturbing associations with superstitions and the ancient religion which the sight of it had conjured up in his mind.

He cursed silently as he swung with an effortless sweep of the bushknife at a banana tree, and cut it to the ground. He cut more bunches, stacked them into two large baskets, shoved a yoke through the baskets, lifted them to his right shoulder with one jerk, and headed for home. The massive load bent his huge frame and made him look like a squat beast of burden.

Half an hour later he was over the high rock fence

behind the village. Smoke was spiralling up from nearby kitchen fale: it swirled and twisted up into the heads of the palm trees, and was finally swallowed by the grey sky. People greeted him. He ignored them. Ahead the fale that were his home steamed in the rain. He rounded the main fale and dumped his load outside the kitchen fale where Lupe, his daughters, and some of the young men of his aiga were preparing an umu.

Pepe ran to him but stopped a few paces away. They gazed at each other awkwardly. Tauilopepe picked out the ripest bananas and handed them to his son. Pepe peeled one and extended it to him. He took it and Pepe smiled at him.

He avoided looking at Lupe when she came to pick up one of the baskets and carry it into the kitchen fale. From the corner of his eye he caught his daughters staring at him and he suddenly felt foolish standing there, so he retrieved his bushknife and went to cut the grass in front of the main fale.

His body was a shivering bundle of cold fatigue as his arm curved in an arc, forward and back, the bushknife slashing at the soggy grass that flew up and over his shoulders. Pepe stood behind him and watched, all the time stuffing ripe bananas into his mouth. A purple-coloured bus, shiny with rain and packed with people, fruit, and pigs, clanked past, kicking up the water on the road. He stood and watched it disappear down the road towards the town; then he attacked the grass again. The light rain drifted across the fale and trees, lapping his wet lavalava against his legs.

Someone called to him. He looked up and saw Toasa waving from the warmth of his fale. The old man looked unreal behind the screen of rain. He waved back reluctantly: he wasn't going to apologise for last night! Through the gaps at the heads of the mangrove trees he saw two canoes floating like discarded logs near the reef which was capped with swirling foam, and he wondered who the foolishly courageous fishermen were. It started to rain heavily. He would have to seek shelter in the main fale where

Masina was weaving mats, but he lingered in the rain until he saw Pepe rushing round with outstretched arms, then he turned and Pepe raced him into the fale.

He gathered the towel which hung from the sinnet strung across the fale and dried Pepe. Then he dried himself and hitched on a dry lavalava. The rain lashed at the fale thatching, sliding down off the eaves in a thick screen and breaking on the paepae with an endless clatter. For a short time he watched the water splitting on the stones and disappearing in rivulets down the crevices between them; then he sat down on the thick layer of mats behind Masina.

'Are you going to sell it?' she asked, without turning her head.

Pepe, who was sitting facing her and watching her weaving, looked at him. 'Tauilo's going to sell the copra,' he said.

'Don't forget some money for the pastor this Sunday,' Masina said.

The rain drummed in his head. He opened the tobacco tin and rolled a cheroot. Pepe came and sat beside him. 'You know something?' Pepe said. 'Toasa told me a good story today. A story about a prince who changed into an eel, then back into a prince, and then back into an eel. You know why? It was to win the love of Sina.'

'Did he win her love?' Tauilopepe asked, lighting his cheroot.

'Don't know,' Pepe said, picking up a piece of dry banana leaf and rolling a cheroot minus the tobacco.

'Why not?' Tauilopepe asked. He sucked the smoke in and blew it out quickly.

'Toasa wanted to eat; he didn't finish the story,' Pepe said, blowing an imaginary stream of smoke from his mouth. 'I don't think people can change into eels, do you?'

Tauilopepe didn't know what to say. Anyway, once Pepe made up his mind about anything, there was no changing it. 'I think it was just a story,' he said.

They sat and smoked.

A group of children ran by, shrieking with laughter as the rain whipped down. Tauilopepe looked at the reef.

16

The canoes had disappeared; he hoped the fishermen had returned home safely. Behind the reef the tossing sea tumbled over the horizon, taking his breath with it, leaving only a yearning to return to that state of innocence when one believed that princes could change into eels for the sake of love.

The rain eased. He got his bushknife and went on cutting the grass. His whole body ached but he refused to stop.

A shadow fell on him. He glanced round. It was Lupe. He continued working.

'Are you going to sell it?' she asked.

With his back still turned to her, he said, 'Leave it to me.'

She turned to go. 'You know we won't get anything after the debt is paid,' he said. She stopped. 'All that work for nothing,' he said. He faced her, wanting to apologise for the previous night, but she lowered her eyes and walked away. He stabbed the bushknife into the ground and watched her go, then spat into the grass, pulled the bushknife out of the ground, and sat on the paepae, gazing out at the grey horizon. The rain had washed the sky clean of clouds; a few birds skimmed across the waves, swooped up into the air, veered off, and streaked towards the horizon until they were mere dots. He picked up the bushknife and ran his fingers over its cold blade.

As a youth he had dreamt such dazzling dreams of a papalagi house just like Malo's down at the other end of the village, a plantation as big and as profitable as Malo's, a store, and enough money to send the children he would have to town schools where they would graduate and get jobs in government offices. But now, he was thirty-five years old and those dreams had vanished for ever, shattered by his aiga's and Toasa's opposition to papalagi ways.

His father and Masina had wanted him to fulfil the aiga wish that at least one son should become a pastor, a man of God. This wish had been an aiga tradition ever since Christianity first wove itself firmly into the fabric of Sapepe life. Toasa wasn't the devout Christian he verbally pretended to be, but he had supported Tauilopepe's father

17

and Masina in their wish for Tauilopepe to be a pastor.
Both men and Masina had made sure he didn't falter in his
religious training. For him, evenings and week-ends were
lengthy sessions of Bible reading and prayers. By the age
of sixteen he was the pastor's favourite pupil, thoroughly
conversant with the Bible, with Jehovah's way from Adam
and Eve down to the Revelation and the Apocalypse. At
eighteen he gained entrance to the London Missionary So-
ciety's Theological College at Malua, the youngest student
ever to be admitted.

During his first year at the college he studied diligently.
He had to succeed: the prestige of Sapepe and his aiga was
at stake. But more enticing dreams began to undermine his
diligence. All the students had to work every afternoon on
the college plantations to grow their own food crops. It
was here, as he watched with utter fascination the papalagi
missionaries using the implements of their world to tame
the land, that a new enthusiasm began to submerge his
desire to be a pastor. He soon mastered the use of these
papalagi implements and became the best student at
agriculture. His missionary teachers were pleased; but
when he started to lose interest in the religious instruction
and to spend much of his time in the plantation they grew
alarmed. When they discovered he was selling the college
crops to neighbouring villages and at the town market they
whipped him and told his father who, while whipping him
also, told him he was doing it for his own good and, above
all else, for the good name of the Aiga Tauilopepe. He
accepted the beating, blamed his own human weakness,
and returned to the college vowing to succeed.

He was a model theological student for about another
year. Then he started to take a keen interest in the motor
car, one of the first in Samoa, which belonged to the
papalagi missionaries. He befriended the afakasi mechanic
who took care of the college machinery and was soon helping him. He watched and learnt. Engines were to be
respected because they contained the mystery of the
papalagi world, the mechanic told him. Engines were good
people, better than real people because they left you alone
and only did what you told them to do. Women were the

worst people — they lied, cheated, and used you. (The mechanic, Tauilopepe found out later, had been married twice but had always found it difficult to retain any woman. He was a bitter, ugly man who drank secretly.) Soon Tauilopepe knew enough to help mend the car's engine, and every time his hands delved into the metal intestines of the mystery a strange power seemed to flow from the engine into his body. It was a feeling close to reverence. A few months later the mechanic started getting drunk more often, all the time mumbling obscenities against all women, and in particular against the Savaii woman who had been his last wife. He sat by while his now able disciple catered to the car's whims. One day he told Tauilopepe that unless he got him a woman he wouldn't allow him to touch the car. So Tauilopepe seduced one of the girls who worked for a missionary family and persuaded her to sleep with the mechanic. From then on he had complete freedom to work on the car.

This episode ended like the first one, with his teachers enraged, because, while the mechanic was on holiday, Tauilopepe dismantled the car engine and couldn't put it together again. They whipped him again and called on his father who, while whipping him until blood oozed from the welts, reiterated that their aiga needed and was going to have a man of God even if it killed him.

A few months after Tauilopepe had been readmitted to the college for the third time the mechanic was dismissed from his job and Tauilopepe was expelled: the girl he had procured for the mechanic had got pregnant and confessed all to her missionary employers.

Tauilopepe's aiga wept and wailed when he returned home. He had humiliated them, had disgraced the name of Tauilopepe beyond repair. His father whipped him with a yoke, breaking it to pieces on his shoulders and back. But he just sat there, waiting for the storm to abate so he could start to develop his plantation on the aiga land, the plantation that would lead to the fulfilment of his new dreams.

Now, however, as he sat on the paepae, picking at a sore on his arm until the blood ran, he felt that he had returned to failure. When he glimpsed Pepe playing with some of his friends behind Toasa's fale his bitterness deepened because he believed he had failed to give his son all the good things he had hoped to.

His father had refused to let him work the aiga land, and Toasa didn't help him either because to Toasa his father could do no wrong. Ridiculed by most of his aiga, he served them without showing his bitterness. Manual work and the monotonous ritual of daily living soon made a coffin to lock his bitterness in.

Three years after his return home he had met Lupe. She was from another village but was staying with relations in Sapepe. When they met at night on the beach or in the bush he escaped into the warmth of her flesh. She got pregnant and they were married in church so as not to disillusion his aiga further. In time he fell in love with her, if love was the painful feeling that he could no longer do without the magnetism of her presence, her unquestioning loyalty, and her promise of a future through their children. When Vao, their daughter, was born, an extension of Lupe (and proof of his masculinity), she deepened his need for Lupe. For the first time in his life there were two people who owed the continuation of their existence to him, two people to console and be consoled by. Vao and Lupe became the spiritual centre of his existence, the sanctuary he withdrew into. He had no other friends and he preferred it that way. Most of his aiga and the other Sapepeans grew slightly afraid of him, of the circle in which he enclosed himself and his wife and daughter and into which no one was allowed to trespass. Then came a second daughter, Niu. And later, Pepe.

Tauilopepe speared the bushknife into the ground at his feet. He could do nothing to alter what was and what he dreaded would always be. His father, by living on, had forced him to wait too long. When his father died the aiga title came to him and he was free to do what he liked with the aiga land. But he found he had grown afraid to change what was: change might prove disastrous for him and the wife and children he loved; it was safer to remain part of the ritual, part of the tradition, like everybody else.

20

You want too much, be content with what the Lord has given us, Masina always said to him.

He stretched his arms high above his head as if he was trying to reach out to God, only to snap them down to his sides when Pepe tugged at his lavalava and told him to come out of the cold. At that moment a red truck loaded with people swished past on the road. When Tauilopepe saw Malo waving to him from its front window he pushed his son away.

3 Traders

Tauilopepe stopped in front of the church and shifted the sack of copra from one shoulder to the other. (Some youths of his aiga had already carried the other three sacks to Malo's store.) The church was a massive concrete building, with three large pillars at the front above the twenty steps, fin-like protrusions on either side of the pillars, a rusting corrugated iron roof, and two steeples housing bells. He glanced at it, veered off the road on to the village malae, and headed for the store. Pepe skipped along beside him, shattering his reflection in all the puddles he could find.

Malo's store was a box-shaped cell with steel bars over all its windows. It nestled against a two-storey house extravagantly blinking row after row of windows. The red truck which Tauilopepe had seen earlier that afternoon was parked under the bread-fruit trees beside the store. Pepe ran on ahead over the malae and up the steps into the store. An aimless group of youths were perched on the veranda railing; they watched Tauilopepe as he approached. He acknowledged them with a curt nod and went into the store.

The strong smell of kerosene and copra and the stifling heat hit him. He dumped the sack on the floor beside the other sacks, looked up, and found Moa, Malo's wife, gazing at him. He retreated to the far corner where Pepe was sitting on a drum of kerosene.

'A lot of copra you've got there,' someone said. A middle-aged couple he knew stood against the counter at the far end of the store. He just smiled. There was no one else in the store.

To his right were two windows. He looked at them, at the steel bars outlined against the dust-covered panes, at the large X which someone had traced in the dust. Then, from the corner of his eye, he watched Moa. She sat behind the counter in a leather-padded chair, noisily chewing gum and scribbling aimlessly with her forefinger on the counter's varnished surface. Her gaudy dress blended with the myriad-coloured background of shelves filled with rolls of cotton material, stacks of tinned corned beef, pilchards and herrings, packets of salt, sugar, and flour, and lavalava that hung down from the ceiling.

'Is your mother well?' she asked. He nodded. 'And your aiga?'

'They are well too, thank you,' he had to say. She scratched her cheek and smoothed down her hair. He lowered his eyes, knowing from experience that the harmless dialogue would eventually lead to a discussion of his debt.

'May we have some kerosene and some sugar?' the other man asked. Moa looked at him. The man shrank visibly under her gaze. 'Please,' he added.

Moa took the account book and thumped it dramatically on to the counter. She licked her thumb. Skipping quickly through the pages, she stopped with the usual flick of the wrist, the usual pursing of lips, the usual short cough. The man and his wife avoided looking at her.

'You already owe fifteen pounds,' she said. 'Better pay it soon.' The couple mumbled something Tauilopepe couldn't hear. Moa reached behind her, got a small packet of sugar and a bottle of kerosene, and pushed them across the counter. The man's wife clutched them, mumbled her thanks, and scuttled out of the store; her husband followed her, trying not to hurry.

The account book remained open on the counter. Moa made no move to shut it. She tapped her forehead with one hand as she examined the nails of her other hand. Tauilopepe couldn't take his eyes off the book. He wanted to flee from the store as the other man had done. Pepe moved against him and smiled to him. He heard Moa drumming with her fingers on the account book.

'Tauilo, may I have some lollies?' Pepe asked. He glanced at Moa. 'May I?' Pepe repeated. Moa pulled a liquorice strap out of the jar beside her and tossed it to Pepe, who caught it eagerly and put the end in his mouth.

23

'Have a cigarette,' Moa said to Tauilopepe, holding out a
packet. He went over to her. His hands trembled as he
pulled out a cigarette. She gave him a box of matches. He
lit his cigarette hurriedly while she gazed at him. As he
inhaled the smoke he smelt her perfume. Lupe's face
flicked into his mind. He moved away from Moa. She
leant forward on to her arms folded on the counter, and
her breasts flopped over her arms into her loose blouse.

'Tonight,' she whispered before he could safely put himself beyond her reach. He half-nodded his head. The door
behind her to her right swung open. Malo entered. She
straightened in her chair.

Malo, who was much older than his wife, shuffled up
and stood beside her. He greeted Tauilopepe.

'He has some copra,' Moa said.

'Good,' said Malo. 'Someone's been working hard in
Sapepe. Pity most people here don't work as hard as we
do, Tauilopepe. But then laziness is the vice of every
Sapepean man, woman, and child.' Tauilopepe tried to
smile. Malo was a small stringy man. Dressed in a white
shirt and navy-blue lavalava, he looked more like a pastor
than a shrewd business man. A pair of horn-rimmed spectacles and two fountain pens protruded from his shirt
pocket. 'Where's the copra?' he asked. Moa pointed at the
sacks. Malo immediately placed his hands flat on the
counter and hurdled over it to land in front of Tauilopepe
and Pepe.

'Still fit. Nearly sixty and still fit and strong,' he said.
'Now let's see how much copra we have here.' Tauilopepe
moved to the hefty sacks to lift them on to the scales. 'No,
I can do it,' Malo stopped him. 'Still tough,' he added. He
flexed his arms, hugged the first sack, and wrestled it on to
the scales with a series of exaggerated grunts. Hugged the
second sack. Lifted. Dropped it on to the floor. Tauilopepe
glanced surreptitiously at Moa. She was staring at the windows. Malo took a deep breath. Hugged the sack again.
Lifted. Whooped when the sack thumped on to the scales.
'Told you I could do it!' he gasped. Hugged the third sack,
with a less enthusiastic ugh. Lifted. Dropped it. Lifted.
Dropped it. 'Getting old. Must be!' Laughed. Coughed.

24

Lifted. Pepe whistled in admiration when the sack dropped on to the scales. 'Told you. Could...could do it!' Sweat on his face. Facial veins pulsating. Suppressed coughing. Now the last sack. They all watched him. Hugged. Heaved. Dropped it on his right foot. Embarrassed face-saving chuckle. Wheezing cough. Tauilopepe stepped forward. 'No,' Malo said. Heaved. Desperate waddling towards the scales. Face a contorted mask of pain. Triumphant whoop. Leant against the counter, panting, arms shaking. 'Told you! Still tough! Still strong!' Tauilopepe looked away politely. Only a boastful old man trying to impress his young wife.

A decent period for Malo to recover. No one saying anything, no one looking too closely at him, not even Pepe who, after expecting a spectacular fit, had returned to munching his liquorice strap.

'Fifteen pounds and ten shillings,' Malo announced. 'Good at arithmetic.' Stopped, remembering something. Took the spectacles out of his shirt pocket and put them on. 'Good at arithmetic,' he repeated. 'Do it all up here.' Pointed at his head. 'That's the secret of my success.' Punched Tauilopepe playfully in the stomach. Tauilopepe glanced at Moa. She smiled at him. 'Why do you think the papalagi is rich and powerful? Why do you think he's got cars, skyscrapers, and bullets? Why is he running our country?' Tauilopepe looked at the floor. 'Because he's got brains. And he uses them. Why do you think I got where I am now? Because I copied the papalagi. I used my brains and I worked hard.' Malo noticed the silence, chuckled, and, placing his right hand on the counter, hurdled back over it to stand beside Moa.

'Now, do you want the money?' he asked Tauilopepe.

'He hasn't really got a large debt,' Moa said. 'He can pay us some other time.'

'Good, good,' said Malo.

Tauilopepe gazed unbelievingly at Malo as he opened the drawer and counted out the money for the copra from a fat roll of soiled notes. He placed each note in front of Tauilopepe with a flourish. 'Any time you want a job, come to me,' he said. He put the roll back into the drawer,

25

locked it, and wiped his face and hands with a red handkerchief. Tauilopepe continued staring at the money lying
on the counter. Malo refolded his handkerchief meticulously, placed it in the pocket of his tailor-made lavalava,
took off his spectacles, folded them, and sheathed them in
his shirt pocket, coughed, and said, 'Well, back to work.'

'Thank you,' Tauilopepe said.

'Good,' Malo replied. He slapped Moa's buttocks,
turned, and left.

Tauilopepe watched his right hand reach forward and
clench round the money. Slowly he became aware of Moa's
presence. Her perfume eased comfortably into his nostrils.
He accepted.

'May we have some sugar, soap, and two tins of corned
beef?' he asked. It was more a command than a request.
He looked directly at her. She filled the order quickly and
pushed the groceries across the counter. 'And some lollies,'
he added. She put handfuls of sweets in a paper bag and
tossed it to Pepe. Tauilopepe placed some money on the
counter, all the time looking into her face. She shook her
head and looked away. He hesitated, then picked up the
money.

'Tonight,' she said, without looking up at him. 'On the
beach behind your fale.'

He turned and walked out the door.

Pepe followed him with the groceries.

The sky was a glittering dome of healing yellow. Across
the malae, on which a group of children were now playing
cricket, the church seemed to beckon to him. He hesitated
when he saw the youths on the store veranda, then he
waved to them with the hand which held the money. He
heard them sigh enviously as he marched down the steps
on to the malae.

Once on the road, his reflection trapped clearly in a
large puddle, he stopped and looked back at Malo's house
and store. They no longer seemed beyond his reach.

Pepe trailed him home.

4 Games

Lupe refused to speak to him when he crept under their mosquito net. She lay gazing up into the darkness. He placed his hand on her shoulder. She shrugged it off. A mosquito buzzed round inside the net, trapped.

'What's the matter?' he asked.

'You leave me alone every night,' she said.

'Is that all!' he sighed. 'I've been down at the pastor's house, playing cards,' he lied finally. It was the first major lie he had ever told her and he was surprised to find how easy it was to lie to her.

She turned towards him and put her arms around his chest. Her breath was warm on the side of his face.

'Wasn't it good I got all the money for the copra?' he said. She nuzzled her face into his neck. 'Maybe we'll be able to send Pepe to a town school soon.' She pushed her body against him. 'I'm tired,' he said. She left him alone, obediently.

The trapped mosquito buzzed louder above their heads. He suddenly found himself on his knees, slapping at it. 'Got it,' he said, rubbing his hands together and feeling the blood on his palms. He settled down again beside Lupe, and they lay listening to the dumb roar of waves breaking on the reef. Occasionally flying-foxes screeched from nearby trees.

Moa had demanded; he had complied. It had been easy, too easy — something would go wrong. To him she had been only a tangible shadow of flesh and pulsating bone, the odour of seaweed and the breeze clapping through the talie tree they were lying under, the murmuring of the sea dying in her throat. After she left he dived into the waves and washed himself clean of her, but the taint of their bargain still lingered in him. Lupe moved against him. He embraced her. He was doing it all for those he loved, none of it was for himself, his pride and dignity were still intact.

This thought calmed his fears, and together with Lupe's healing warmth drugged him to sleep.

He spent the rest of that week in his plantation planting more crops. He always took Pepe with him: Pepe's presence seemed to protect him from his fears. At home he pretended that nothing was troubling him.

Their aiga had unlimited credit at Malo's store. No one in his aiga asked him why.

He met Moa twice that week on the beach at night. His initial feelings of guilt gradually vanished in a darkness free of village gossip and suspicion. The third time they met, after he had performed what she expected of him, she asked if he needed anything. He didn't find it difficult to ask her for money to feed the Sapepe men while they worked on his plantation.

He recruited thirty men. As was the custom he didn't need to pay them wages but only to feed them. For nearly two weeks these men worked alongside all the men of his aiga. They cleared new land and planted cacao trees, taro, and bananas. This successful expansion of his plantation began to restore his self-confidence, and he talked again of sending Pepe to a town school, of building a papalagi house and store, of how, after all these years, the Aiga Tauilopepe, under his leadership, was going to regain its true position as the leading aiga in Sapepe.

Lupe grew strangely silent. He didn't notice.

'So you're going to be rich, eh?' Toasa said, as he shuffled the cards. Tauilopepe grinned and picked at the blisters on his hands. He had spent all day in the plantation and the sun was still throbbing in his head and on the skin of his face.

The fale blinds behind Toasa were swept open and Lafo and Pologa entered. Toasa told them to sit down and get ready to be beaten. He dealt the cards.

'And how is the rich man?' Lafo asked. Tauilopepe just smiled. Lafo was nearly as wide as he was tall and wore an almost permanent impish grin. Pologa was much taller and his body was weighted heavily towards his left leg which was fat with filariasis.

28

'Some day you'll be able to buy a seat on that papalagi aeroplane,' Toasa said. Lafo laughed. Pologa cupped his hand over his mouth and wheezed his laughter into his hand. 'Play!' Toasa said.

Lafo opened the game by taking two points. His partner, Pologa, slapped his balloon-like leg gleefully. 'Don't worry, it's only the start,' Toasa said.

Lafo was an even more boisterous player than Toasa: each throw was slapped on to the mat, every point taken meant a resounding slap on the thigh, a whoop, a jiggle, a chance to comment loudly on the weaknesses of his opponents and his own brilliance. Pologa was more restrained, restricting his joy to tongue-clucking and loud giggling. Soon the whole neighbourhood reverberated with the noise of their game.

Half-way through the first game Tauilopepe glanced up at the lamp dangling from the rafters. When he saw the lizard's tongue flick out and catch the moth he tensed and looked at his cards.

'Concentrate,' Toasa said. (Their partnership was losing the game, and Toasa hated losing.)

'One plus one equals two,' Lafo said. Bang went a card on to the mat and up came two aces, two points. Lafo's filariasis-ridden partner giggled. Toasa glared at his cards. 'Five plus four equals nine, eh?' Bang. Another card. Further giggling and laughter. Tauilopepe misplayed. Toasa fumed.

Tauilopepe and Toasa lost the first game badly.

'Not your night tonight,' laughed Lafo, collecting the cards for his deal.

'Deal!' was all that Toasa said. The women had raised some of the fale blinds. A half moon had edged into the sky, and Tauilopepe suddenly wanted to be out there away from Lafo's gaiety and Toasa's sullen silence.

As Lafo dealt he commented breathlessly on why they had won the first game and why they were going to win the next one. ... 'Luck is with us tonight,' he said. 'Luck makes the world go round. Luck makes some men rich and others poor. If you've got it you can't help but get what you want. Like a wife, for instance. Look at Pologa here.

You can't say he was ever lucky. No wife. Only a sad leg he can't be proud of and a weapon he's never once used!' While he laughed and Pologa giggled Toasa and Tauilopepe tried to smile.

They played the second game. Lafo and Pologa won again.

'The rich man can't beat the poor man if the poor man's got luck,' said Lafo. 'Perhaps Pologa and I will get seats on that papalagi aeroplane before you do, Tauilopepe.' Tauilopepe's hands trembled as he picked up his cards. He looked out. The half moon glittered like a sharp knife-blade above the palms. 'Pologa here may even get to use his weapon!' Lafo and Pologa went on laughing. Toasa glared at them and they stopped immediately.

Toasa and Tauilopepe lost again.

'What's the matter with you?' Toasa asked, blaming Tauilopepe for their defeat.

Tauilopepe got up and left the fale. He went walking along the beach. In the moonlight everything was the colour of shiny metal, even his body. They knew about Moa, he thought.

The following morning he retreated into his plantation where he wandered about observing the banana trees which were now bearing fruit. He returned home soothed by the promise of profit he saw in his crops. As he ate his evening meal, sharing his foodmat with Pepe, he remembered he had to meet Moa that night. He called for a basin of water. As he washed his hands he overturned the basin; he made no attempt to prevent the water from seeping into the mats. Pepe picked up the basin and took it to Lupe. Tauilopepe resolved that when he had sold his first crop of bananas he would stop seeing Moa — she would be of no further use to him.

After the meal he sat smoking with Masina. She asked what was worrying him. He shook his head.

'The papalagi world is not for you, not for us,' she said.

'I want our aiga to have the new things,' he said. 'The papalagi world has come to stay. Like the Church. Look at Malo. He was like me once. He couldn't do much for his aiga because he didn't have money. Look where his aiga is

30

now.' He waited for her to reply. She refused to say anything. 'You'll never understand,' he said finally.

'It is enough to have God,' she said.

Her mention of God frightened him. Like her, he did not question the basic assumption of their way of life: God was the giver of all blessings, all life, the reef round their world. A man was a good man only if he had God. He remembered Malo. Malo had reconciled money and God so Malo had everything. He was going to tell Masina this but she opened her Bible and began reading to herself.

On the reef — a swishing arc of white waves in the moonlight — three palm-frond flares spluttered and blinked at him. As he watched, one of them, obviously thrown up by a fisherman, arched high into the air, curved down, and died instantly on hitting the water. The stench of coral was heavy in the air. Malo possessed that wonderful blessing called 'Progress'. In his thoughts he wove the scattered strands of his information about Malo and Moa into a coherent pattern.

When Tauilopepe's father, Tauilopepe Laau, was alive, Malo Malie, the older brother of the present Malo, had been a weak opponent. Consequently the Aiga Malo was easy to subdue in Sapepe affairs. Malo Viliamu, Moa's husband, had disappeared into the town, where he worked for a trading firm. He worked and saved, not only his meagre salary but also, some Sapepeans maintained, safe amounts of company money. When he had enough money and enough knowledge of trading he branched out on his own with a small store. He waited and saved. A few years later his brother suffered a fatal heart attack, brought on, so Toasa diagnosed, by overeating. Malo Viliamu immediately sold his store in Apia and prepared for his triumphant return to Sapepe. He was over forty and still a bachelor who, too obsessed with making money, saw no profit in having a permanent wife. However, knowing his aiga and Sapepe would ridicule him if he returned without a wife, he proposed to Moa whom he had occasionally paid for catering to his modest sexual needs. Moa told Tauilopepe during their third meeting on the beach that

31

she had been born into an aiga with no money, no status, no love. So what else could she do when she was old enough but turn to sailors, taxi-drivers, and other men in order to make her way in the world? And what else could these sources of revenue do to her over the years but turn her into a fast-aging, desperate young woman? Malo Viliamu was the answer to her prayers, she boasted.

So Malo Viliamu returned to Sapepe and the aiga title with a wife nearly twenty years younger than himself. Five years after his return he owned the biggest plantation in Sapepe. By 1932, four years after Tauilopepe's father died, he owned the only store in Sapepe, and the only papalagi house and the most magnificent double bed. In this house he installed Moa, who soon after, so Malo's numerous enemies said, found her miserly husband unenthusiastic in bed and consequently sought fleshly satisfaction elsewhere.

Tauilopepe heard a baby crying from a nearby fale hidden from view by the mangrove trees. He got up and strolled along the beach. Moa emerged out of the darkness ahead like some creature from the sea. He waited for her. She came and without speaking took his hand and led him into the dark under the sprawling talie tree where they had met before.

'What's the matter?' she asked. He rolled off her and sat up. She reached over and caressed him but he remained unresponsive. 'Be honest with yourself,' she said, sitting up. 'I'm not ashamed because our relationship is only a bargain.' He remained silent. 'I'm not ashamed because I've seen it all my life — the buyers and the sellers. In the store I enjoy buying other people's pride, especially those women who look at me with scorn. Enjoy humiliating them, watching them sell their hypocritical dignity. The price is high but they sell. They despise me but they sell to me. The same thing I had to do when I was a girl and men bought me.' She stopped. 'With you it's different. I'm beginning to despise myself. You have a lot to sell — your unbelievable masculinity and your indifference to me. But you sell at a very low price — money. I learnt much from the men who bought me. Or thought they were buying me. There are dishonest sellers and dishonest buyers. Both

32

suffer from what is commonly known as guilt after the bargain is consummated.'

'What category do I belong to?' he asked.

'You know. I don't need to tell you. As for me, I'm honest down here.' She took his hand and placed it there. He pulled it away.

'Malo has organised a meeting of all the matai in four days' time,' she said after a while. She ran her fingers over his belly. 'Don't you want to know why?' he maintained his silence. 'It's a meeting to divide the uncultivated land of the district, the land that doesn't belong to any particular aiga. Toasa has agreed to it.' She caressed him. He tensed at once. 'Knew you'd be interested,' she said. 'With your title, you're entitled to a very large share.' He was strong. 'Now pay me,' she said.

He held her roughly and pushed her back on to the sand. She sighed triumphantly.

'A woman should never lie down there. Am I lying? Feel it talking honestly?' she whispered as he stabbed furiously at her flesh.

5 Orators and Gold

All the ceremonials were over. God's blessing and protection had been asked for, and the kava had been pounded, mixed with water, shared out, and drunk, as was the custom. Because Toasa, Tauilopepe, and Malo held the three most important Sapepe titles, Toasa occupied the middle post at the right-hand side of the fale, Tauilopepe the post directly opposite Toasa, and Malo the middle front post. The other matai, the heads of the other twenty or so Sapepe aiga, occupied the remaining posts. On the back paepae were gathered a large group of untitled men who had come to listen, observe, and learn from their elders. In Toasa's kitchen fale, half-hidden from view by a thick hibiscus hedge, many people were busy cooking food which would be served to the matai at the end of the meeting. A silent crowd of children sat in the shade of the kapok trees beside the main road. The late morning sky was webbed with luminous strands of white cloud.

Like the untitled men on the paepae, Tauilopepe had rarely missed these important meetings when his father was alive. Through them and through Toasa's expert tuition he had become a proficient orator. But, even when he had received the aiga title and hence become a member of the matai council, he seldom spoke at the meetings. Now, however, he had to speak because he wanted a major share of the uncultivated land; he knew that the importance of his title gave him a right to such a share, but he needed Toasa's support because Malo was manoeuvring for the same thing.

Malo, dressed in khaki, with expensively sandalled feet, brilliantined hair, and bespectacled face, sat fingering the account book in which all the matai's debts were recorded. Toasa was plaiting sinnet; his lavalava had slipped down, exposing the tattooed lower half of his back and top of his buttocks. He appeared not to be listening to the speeches, but everyone knew that he wasn't missing anything.

The matai spoke one after another. They all agreed to the land being brought under cultivation but no one discussed the question of when and how it was to be divided. For the most of them the meeting was just another opportunity to display their verbal brilliance; to a few of them the food at the end was most important. All of them knew that Malo was after a major share of the land and they resented him for it but were afraid to challenge him openly because of their debts to him. Once again they were waiting for Toasa to stop Malo from getting an unfair share by using their debts to frighten them into supporting him. Only Toasa seemed impervious to the tense silence that fell as soon as Malo started speaking. Malo's oratory was the style of the town: a glib, crisp mixture of almost colloquial language and often inappropriate poetic phrases and proverbs. The sharp light reflecting off the stones of the paepae was trapped firmly in the rims of his spectacles.

'Business is business,' Malo said. 'And land is now good business. We must wake up to this fact and cultivate our land *now*. Use the money to build a new school and hospital. If most of you are too weak to cultivate the land then you must leave it to those who can. And, with God's help, the strong will conquer this land for the benefit of Sapepe!' Tauilopepe fidgeted uncomfortably. Malo explained that their forefathers had come out of the sea, driven by war and the godly desire to find peace; they had claimed all this district for their heirs and had defended it against others so that all Sapepeans could lead prosperous lives. Their forefathers had known nothing about making profits out of the land. Can we blame them? he asked. No, because their beloved fathers hadn't gone to school, hadn't known what money was; the papalagi hadn't arrived with the marvellous blessings of education, the Bible, and money. He wiped his face with his handkerchief. He was the only Sapepean who used handkerchiefs. They were living in a predominantly papalagi world, he continued, and, even if papalagi were greedy and arrogant, Samoans could no longer do without them and what they had brought, were bringing, and would continue to bring. He paused for a few seconds and scrutinised his audience. If they wanted to be equal to the papalagi they had to use the papalagi's weapons. Paused again, dramatically. If their land was well planted and looked after it would yield them the necessary money, the necessary *dough*, to give their children a good life. (Malo, the other matai knew, was well acquainted with town slang. They also believed he was the only Sapepean who could speak English fluently.) When he stopped speaking this time they thought he had finished, but when he picked up the account book and put it in his lap they knew he wasn't going to stop hunting them. If they didn't want to cultivate the virgin land they had to allow the stronger members of their peaceful community to do so, he told them. Then, smiling benignly, he declared that he had never cheated them in anything, that he paid their teacher's salary and most of the money towards the upkeep of their pastor and church. Paused. Coughed. If they couldn't carry out the back-breaking job of clearing and cultivating the land they had to say so — it wasn't a sin to admit one was weak. He reminded them of the parable of the talents and said that it was the duty of the strong to protect their less fortunate brothers.

Toasa coughed. Malo stopped speaking.

They all looked at Toasa. The old man had stopped plaiting and was gazing at Malo. They sighed in thankful relief. 'Yes, the land must be divided fairly,' Malo continued valiantly. Toasa's cough had broken the spell of fear which Malo had cast over the matai. 'This land bequeathed to us by our forefathers to be cared for as we care for our children. Soifua!' Malo ended his speech.

They all expected Toasa to speak then but he didn't. He coughed loudly again and looked at each matai in turn. When his gaze settled on Tauilopepe he nodded, and Tauilopepe realised, with his heart thudding loudly, that the old man wanted him to speak. Half a lifetime of trying to master the awesome skill of manipulating language and the massive and intricate heritage that went with it were now to be demonstrated in his first major speech before the council, before the expert, critical scrutiny of Sapepe.

He spoke and, to his surprise, the words came easily. When he sensed that Toasa was listening attentively he knew he was displaying his thoughts in the right words in the right way. For method was everything to Toasa: style and technique were the justification for almost everything. If you had to do something, anything, you had to do it better than it had ever been done before. Even when you shat you had to do it with style, he remembered Toasa joking once.

'. . . The land is our greatest blessing from God, our most precious inheritance from our forefathers. Without it we would have no roots, we would be a canoe without a secure anchor, birds with no permanent and safe nesting-ground. The land defines us, gives meaning to our titles and history. And besides our titles and the memories we will leave behind us when we die is the only worthwhile possession we can bequeath to our children. Therefore it must never be alienated. Our forefathers—and they were far-sighted, valiant men—made sure our land was not lost; they knew that without it we would be nothing.' He paused and looked at his listeners. 'Not all that the papalagi has brought and is bringing has been good. Our way of life, our precious faa-Samoa, is changing—some say for the worse, some say for the better. This humble person for one believes that some of the changes, such as the new education and medicine, have been very beneficial. This humble person, who has no right to speak so loudly and at such great length before you today, wants these benefits, these blessings, for Sapepe. This unworthy person believes too that we can acquire these blessings with God's guidance.' Lowering his voice, he explained. 'For a long time now I have, in my own stumbling way, searched for the best means of acquiring these blessings for our beloved district. I have gone to God and asked Him in prayer. And in His Wisdom and Grace the Almighty has whispered to my heart that we, His beloved children, must now use the most valuable gift He has bestowed upon us. And what is that gift, Dignity of Sapepe? As I have already stated, it is our land. Yes, the land and the wealth it keeps locked in

37

its body. . . .' He continued elaborating on this point, immersed in the poetic flow of his own imagery. A little later he was saying: 'This person agrees with Malo, who is the most able and generous and hard-working among us, that the land must be cultivated and its wealth used to educate our children, build a hospital, construct a tap-water system, and — most important of all — used to build a more beautiful church to glorify our most generous Father in Heaven. Malo himself has shown us through his efforts how the land can be cultivated using the new implements and knowledge of the papalagi, cultivated so efficiently that it will yield a limitless bounty. Malo has shown and is showing us the way. Let us follow him.' Another dramatic pause. Malo's eyes were shut and he was smiling. Tauilopepe looked away from him to Toasa and said: 'We must divide the uncultivated land among all the aigá and we must divide it *equally*. That is my unworthy opinion. Even if one aiga is weaker than another it should still get an equal share — that is the true faa-Samoa, the true way of justice which God and our forefathers laid down.' He noticed that the other matai were trying not to look at Malo who was now staring at him. 'However, in my humble opinion Malo was correct to remind us of the parable of the talents, and we should now agree that we all believe in using our talents to the fullest and we must exhort our children and aiga to do likewise. Nevertheless, how an aiga chooses to use its share of the land should be left to that aiga. That is this humble person's advice. You may choose another way. This humble person, whose mind is still young like new grass, will accept any decision you make.' After another brief pause, he concluded, 'Dignity of Sapepe, this morning will be remembered in our history as one of the great mornings, second only in importance to that morning when Jehovah and His story reached our shores. This morning will be remembered as the morning the Dignity of Sapepe chose to heed God's advice, which He has so wisely put into our hearts, and to reap the rich promise of our land. . . . Soifua, and may God's blessing be always on our council!'

When Tauilopepe finished speaking Toasa slapped his

thigh and laughed. 'Our young friend has an eloquent tongue,' he said. 'I haven't heard such good oratory for a long time. And he owes it all to me, his gifted teacher!' Except for Malo everyone laughed.

When Tauilopepe got home late that afternoon, after he had helped Toasa eat a whole suckling pig, he hurried into the fale and told Masina what the council had decided. She simply nodded her head and went on smoking.

'What do you think?' he asked.

She looked up at him. 'Why don't you become a deacon?' she said, ignoring his question. 'The pastor has been wanting you to be a deacon for a while now.'

'All right,' he replied without much thought.

The full implications of his commitment to Masina dawned on him as he strolled towards the kitchen fale where Lupe was fanning a fire over which a pot was boiling. He stopped. Ever since he inherited the aiga title Masina had wanted him to become a deacon. It was her way of showing Sapepe that her son (and the Aiga Tauilopepe) had not failed, that the disgraceful episode at the theological college was well in the past, something to be forgotten. He had refused her, convinced that Sapepe would never let him forget his disgrace; but, as he stood there in the blazing heat with Lupe watching him, he experienced a dizzying feeling of freedom. He was sure that God had intervened on his behalf that morning at the meeting. Becoming a deacon would be one way of repaying God.

'What's the matter?' Lupe called. He shook his head and went into the kitchen fale. He sat down on the log beside her, picked up a piece of firewood, and jabbed it into the fire. The fire spat sparks. They watched it. 'I am with child,' she said.

'What are we going to call him?' he asked, as if he had known all along that she was pregnant. She grinned at him. He laughed and drummed the stick against the side of the soot-coated pot as the breeze shuffled through the eaves and folded blinds and played in Lupe's hair. He saw Pepe walking towards them. Behind their son some youths were sticking wickets into both ends of a cricket pitch they had marked out. He was sure that their unborn child would be a boy. And the future was a dazzling vision of a huge plantation and two male heirs. Nothing was impossible. The flames danced in his eyes. With Toasa's support at the council meeting he had been given the right to cultivate the largest portion of the land: a wide well-watered valley that stretched from the end of his aiga's land right up to the foothills and the rim of the range, all virgin bush, but in his mind's eye he saw it transformed into a lush profitable plantation.

Vao and Niu approached the kitchen fale, with buckets of water hanging from yokes across their shoulders. When he saw them he realised they were developing into comely young women, especially Vao. His daughters went round to the back, put down their loads, sat down on the paepae and began to talk. He vowed he would pay more attention to them.

A pig darted across Pepe's path as he neared the kitchen fale. His hand curved down swiftly to a stone and, in one sweeping motion, threw. He missed. Tauilopepe laughed, and before the pig disappeared into the taro patch behind the kitchen fale he pushed it out of sight with a stinging stone. Pepe whooped. Then he came and leant against the fale post beside Tauilopepe.

'Where've you been?' Lupe asked.

'Helping some people with their umu.'

'You spend most of your time helping others and not me and your sisters,' she said.

Pepe shrugged his shoulders, knowing she was only pretending to be angry. 'Do you believe in aitu?' he asked.

'Who's been talking to you about aitu?'

'No one. Did you know there's a headless, wailing, weeping, ferocious aitu living in Toasa's plantation?'

'So it's Toasa who's been telling you that?'

'This aitu eats bananas and rats and owls and missionaries,' Pepe said. His parents laughed. Pepe watched them sceptically. 'Toasa's going to take me to see him some day. I wanted Toasa to take me right away but he said some day. It's always some day. Even the lions.'

40

'The what?' asked Lupe.

'The lions,' said Pepe. 'Toasa reckons there are lions right on top of the mountains. You know, where all the rivers in Sapepe start from. He's the only man who's seen the lions.' His parents struggled to suppress their laughter. 'I believe Toasa even if you don't!' he said. His parents tried to look serious. 'Do you know the valley behind our plantation?' Tauilopepe nodded. 'Well,' continued Pepe, 'Toasa believes if you burn down all the trees in the valley and dig up the ground you'll find gold there.'

'That's our valley now,' Tauilopepe said. 'Toasa made sure we got it.'

'Does that mean we can burn down the bush and dig up all that gold?' Pepe asked.

'But there's no gold in Samoa,' Lupe said, trying to look serious.

'There *is* gold!' laughed Tauilopepe. 'Gold that grows out of the fertile ground.' He sprang up and danced mincingly round the fire while Pepe and Lupe laughed and Vao and Niu watched them from outside the kitchen fale.

That night Tauilopepe didn't go to meet Moa; he spent a long time beside the lamp, reading the Bible.

6 To Market, To Market

They were travelling straight for the morning sun. The truck groaned on, its wheels crunching at the unsealed road and kicking up a cloud of dust. It was Malo's truck; Moa had got it for Tauilopepe. He glanced through the rear window at the baskets of bananas. Five young men of his aiga sat on the baskets, guarding them. (All the men of his aiga had spent the previous day cutting down the bunches and packing them. The work had been arduous for they had to carry the heavy baskets on their shoulders three miles from the plantation to the village.) A clinging heat started to stir in the compartment.

The driver was Malo's fat brother, Timu. He was dressed in baggy khaki trousers and a tattered T-shirt with a faded picture of Superman on the front. Because of his enormous belly Timu looked as though he was finding it extremely difficult to steer the truck and change gear.

'Hot, isn't it?' Tauilopepe remarked.

'Yes, very hot,' Timu replied. Tauilopepe lit a cigarette and gave it to him. 'Thanks,' said Timu. 'Got a big load of bananas there. Going to sell them at the Apia market?' Tauilopepe nodded. 'Going to make a lot of money,' said Timu. Tauilopepe lit a cigarette for himself.

Pepe, who was sitting between them, all the while watching Timu's actions and the dials on the dashboard, bumped against Timu when the truck hit a deep rut. 'First time you've been in a truck?' Timu asked. Pepe nodded quickly. 'Liking it?'

'Don't know yet,' Pepe replied.

Timu chuckled, his numerous chins wobbling. 'Always good to be on the safe side. Never know what might happen. Might get stuck in a ditch, run into a tree, hit another car. Or run over someone. Would you like that?' Pepe shook his head. 'Don't you want to see someone who's been squashed flat by a truck?' Pepe shook his head more emphatically. Timu winked at Tauilopepe. 'Saw a dead man once,' Timu said.

'When?' asked Pepe.

'When I was your age. They had to drag him out of the surf. Had no legs or arms left.'

'Why?'

'A shark got him. He went fishing but he got fished instead.' Noticing how scared Pepe was, Timu laughed uproariously. Tauilopepe looked out of the truck window, wishing Timu would stop telling Pepe such gruesome stories.

They were passing through a government plantation: unbelievable acres and acres of palms under which cattle grazed, orderly, neat, and profitable — the type of plantation Tauilopepe was hoping to have.

'They spent a week searching for that fellow's arms and legs,' Timu said. 'They even tried to snare the shark that did the job. They gave up and buried only half a man.' Pepe wasn't listening any more; he had decided that Timu was a liar, and liars, so Toasa had told him, were worse than sharks.

Tauilopepe hadn't made the trip to Apia for nearly a year, and he was rediscovering the villages that lined the road winding along the sea-shore. Villages just like Sapepe although they were smaller: rows of fale neatly arranged under palms, mango, and bread-fruit trees. Sometimes the fale were spaced over white sand that sloped down to beaches and a sea dancing away in brilliant shades of blue and green. In the middle of each village, usually at the edge of the malae, stood a concretê church and a pastor's house that dwarfed the people's homes. Every village had a store very similar to Malo's, but nearly all of them were owned by trading companies. On the beaches of most villages many latrines, made of rusty corrugated iron and scrap timber nailed together haphazardly, stood on fragile stilts. As they passed through one village Tauilopepe glimpsed a man sitting in one of the latrines, indifferent to the fact that the door was wide open. Timu waved to the man, the man waved back, and Timu and Pepe laughed. When Tauilopepe was at the theological college he had twice used a flush toilet in one of the missionary's houses. He now resolved he would have one attached to the papalagi house he was going to build. The truck slowed down unexpectedly. Tauilopepe and Pepe bumped against each other, and Tauilopepe saw a dog scurrying away from the road, tail between its legs.

'If I had my way I'd have all dogs drowned. And all horses as well!' cursed Timu. 'Did you hear about what happened to me? I hit a horse last year. Split its guts open. Should have seen the mess on the road. Blood and intestines and horse-shit. Split it wide open.' Stopped, licked his lips. 'I had to pay for the horse. The horse's owner took me to court. Told the police I'd killed his horse deliberately. Me of all people. You'd think I was mad or something. The palagi judge fined me. Threatened to send me to jail if I did it again. I had to pay for the horse as well. Ten pounds for a thin carcass of an animal. I nearly told the judge where to go. Don't know why I didn't.' Timu continued analysing his reasons but Tauilopepe didn't listen any more.

They were travelling through a dense area of bush by then, and the tall trees shaded them from the sun. Tauilopepe sighed softly, relieved that they were free from the heat. For the first time that day he heard the shrill crying of birds above the roar of the truck. The men on the back of the truck started to sing. Timu joined them.

Pepe had persuaded himself that he had nothing to fear from the truck his father had enticed him into with promises of ice cream and lollies. He edged over to the window and looked out. He saw a mound of rocks beside the remnants of a fale; he recognised it as a grave and wondered what it was doing in the middle of all that bush.

The truck broke from the shade of the bush and rolled down to another village. The singing stopped. Timu, drenched with sweat and peppered with a thin layer of dust, wiped his face with a dirty rag and spat out of the window. Tauilopepe lit another cigarette for himself.

At the next village a couple of children ran to the edge of the road and waved to them. Pepe waved back. The

44

children lifted up their lavalava, bared their backsides towards them, and, with wild shrieks, ran off. Pepe shook his fist at them. At the end of the same village a gaggle of women and girls were washing clothings in a pool. Some of the girls waved, their wet, half-naked bodies glistening in the light. Timu and the men on the back of the truck waved back furiously.

Slightly bored with looking at the villages, Tauilopepe scrutinised the dashboard. He vowed he would some day own a truck and he thought of the theological college and the afakasi mechanic who had taught him about engines. The mechanic was probably dead from too much drink and loneliness. He watched Timu's driving and judged that he, Tauilopepe, was a better driver and mechanic. He hoped vaguely for the truck to break down so he could demonstrate his superior knowledge of car engines. But the truck roared on.

Pepe struggled to stay awake but couldn't. Tauilopepe nestled him into his side. The heat and dust and the smell of petrol fumes throbbed in the compartment. Timu yawned repeatedly. Then the Tauilopepe's eyes ached and his back felt stiff. Then the men on the back started singing again. Timu's spirits revived at once and his baritone boomed in the compartment. What began as a harmless children's song was soon turned, mainly by Timu, into a bawdy parody. Tauilopepe tried not to listen to the words but they were as inescapable as the heat. He hoped Pepe was asleep.

> Went hunting the other day,
> saw a pig in the trees,
> sent my dog after it
> but he sat down,
> shat on the ground,

sang Timu and the others.

> A moetolo crept
> into the pastor's house,
> tried to out-creep the pastor's daughter,
> got stung in his creeper
> and two long years in prison. . . .

45

Timu blew the horn and laughed, but when he saw Tauilopepe looking sternly at him he stopped singing. The others stopped also when they heard that Timu had stopped.

As they drew closer to the town Tauilopepe counted more and more papalagi-style houses. Some of them were corrugated tin shacks with only front doors. None of the children they saw waved to them. One boy hurled a stone and, missing the truck, fled into the trees behind a ramshackle house. The villages began to look more disorganised and unkempt, dirty. It was as if some strange aging force, which Sapepe hadn't yet experienced, had penetrated slowly and deliberately into everything. In some villages four different churches — all massive structures caked with dust and rust — were spaced throughout. Tauilopepe also noticed wire fences and hedges dividing aiga from aiga, and groups of youths, dressed in dirty lavalava or trousers or shorts, lounging on the verandas of the trading stations. He felt light and elated for he was drawing deeper into the heart of the vision, his world. Even the heat felt mellow on his skin. Passing cars became more numerous, swishing past them in a fury of exhaust fumes and deepening his sense of wonder.

Half an hour later, with the sun a throbbing pain in the empty sky, they were on the outskirts of Apia, among houses, shacks, and fale huddled together like a defeated army or a swarm of large sea-crabs which had crawled out of the sea to die on dry land to the sound of mechanical marvels and the stench of swamp rising from the deep ditches beside the road. And Tauilopepe knew he was *there* in the glittering eye of 'Progress', and he forgot the heat, the sun.

'Can you play billiards?' Timu asked.

'Billiards?'

'That's the new game everyone's playing. You'll see it at the market,' said Timu. A bus crossed in front of them. The truck swerved and Tauilopepe caught the terrified faces of passengers flashing by. 'You use long wooden sticks and three balls. One red, two whites. It's a very good game.'

They turned into Taufusi Road, arrowing straight down towards the high town clock and the heart of Apia. The road ahead was a flashing blade on which a noisy stream of traffic bustled and shoved. Both sides of the road were lined with stores; behind them straggled dilapidated fale and shacks occupying land rented from the Roman Catholic Mission to which the first converts had given it. Most of the area had once been swampland; now it was the most valuable land in Samoa. Timu, swearing under his breath in a mixture of Samoan and English, sounded the horn constantly to clear the way of pedestrians and vehicles. Tauilopepe couldn't understand why Timu was cursing so. Surely one had to tread with awe in the domain of the papalagi!

His father and Toasa had told him something of the history of Apia. They had explained that it had been carted from across the seas and nailed on to the shore with copra profits. A horde of settlers and transients — uncouth beachcombers, sailors, remittance men, and drifters from Europe and America — had come in search of adventure and women and quick profits. All these papalagi banded together and turned Apia into a bastion of papalagi arrogance and greed, into a small Europe, notorious for its bars and political intrigues. The British, the American, and the German groups fought among themselves and tried to get their respective governments to take control of Samoa. The foreign governments, with mutual suspicion as their constant bed companion, played the Samoan political factions off against one another. Anarchy, which was extremely profitable to traders gun-running to all factions, resulted. Then came partition, the only solution, and among Samoan leaders bitterness because they could do nothing to stop it. The papalagi had come to stay in a town over which Samoans had no control but which ruled all Samoa. The two men had told Tauilopepe that the papalagi was a greedy double-dealing animal. Before he went to the theological college he had believed them. However, his experiences at Malua, and Toasa's and his father's treatment of him when he failed to become a pastor, led him to believe that they were just bitter old men who were igno-

47

rant of the true worth of the new ways. What they saw as a
curse on Samoa he saw as a blessing.

He woke Pepe when they neared the town clock.

'Look!' he said to his son, sweeping an arm over the
shops and stores, as if he was showing Pepe a treasure-
house.

Pepe gazed out. 'Look, there's a papalagi!' he exclaimed.
Tauilopepe saw a lanky papalagi striding along the footpath
under a large black umbrella. 'Is that where he carries all
his money?' Pepe asked, pointing at the papalagi's satchel.
Tauilopepe wasn't sure. He expected Timu to answer
Pepe's question but Timu said nothing. So Tauilopepe said
yes and left it at that.

At the end of Taufusi Road the truck, directed by a
traffic policeman sprucely starched in a white uniform,
turned right and ran along the waterfront. Department
stores walled off the right side of the street and pedestrians choked the footpaths. Pepe watched them. On the
shore stood pulu trees trimmed to look like gigantic
umbrellas; a mob of people milled under one of the trees
which had strings of fish and octopuses hanging from it.
On the reef lay the grotesque wreck of a warship which
had died there during the Great Hurricane of 1899.

Tauilopepe's breath quickened when he saw Mulivai
Cathedral — it seemed to anchor the whole town to the
soil. He knew this was the most imposing building in
Samoa. Towers preaching awe in the air. A few children
were playing in the cathedral courtyard; a white soutaned
priest watched them from the second-storey veranda of an
adjoining building. Although Tauilopepe was prejudiced
against what Toasa haughtily called 'the Church of the
Roman's' he bowed his head as the truck thundered over
Mulivai Bridge. On the other side of the bridge, sprawled
behind a row of low pulu trees, was the Marist Brothers'
School, famous in Samoa for the champion boxers, civil
servants, and male typists it produced.

'That's where I'm going to send Pepe to school,'
Tauilopepe said. Timu nodded.

The truck shot past the wide entrance between two
buildings that led into the neighbourhood known as the

Vaipe. The Vaipe, so Tauilopepe had heard but refused to believe because some of his relatives lived there, was notorious for loose women and the illegal home-brewing of faamafu.

Then they were at the market. The truck turned off the main street and stopped beside it in a cacophony of protesting metal. Timu got out with a series of grunts and waddled off towards it. After straightening their clothes Tauilopepe and Pepe got out too. Tauilopepe told his relatives to unload the bananas. When the baskets were safely stacked on the ground he guided Pepe into the market.

There were numerous holes in the roof of the large building; mud and dirt caked the floor; vendors squatted at the front near the main street, peddling fruit, seafood, and vegetables; noisy customers swarmed round them and round the cooked-food counters behind the billiard saloon. The crowd outside the saloon, looking into it through a series of low windows, was thinner. Tauilopepe eased his way through, pulling Pepe after him.

The spacious but stuffy saloon was brightly lit. Against the walls sat male spectators on benches, and, at the largest table Tauilopepe had ever seen, a table which was covered with soft green material, two men were poking sticks at three balls which shot smoothly and swiftly against one another and sometimes dropped into the pockets at the corners of the table. Tauilopepe saw Timu in the far corner, eating peanuts and gazing at the game as if hypnotised. He waved to him but Timu didn't see him. A thin old man occupied the highest bench; beside him was a small blackboard on which he was recording the scores. Tauilopepe watched him. His movements were slow, almost mechanical, his spindly arm rising from his lap to the blackboard, writing, then falling back again to his lap. Every few minutes he called out the score in a toneless voice, only his lips moving, his thin emaciated face remaining still, his eyes dead. For a time Tauilopepe couldn't take his eyes off him.

'What are they doing' Pepe asked.

Tauilopepe watched the game again. 'Playing billiards,' he replied.

49

A little while later Pepe tugged at his hand and whispered that he was tired of watching. 'It's a good game, isn't it?' Tauilopepe said as they walked away from the saloon. Pepe didn't answer.

A large group of customers surrounded the baskets of bananas. Tauilopepe got behind the baskets.

Alone for the first time in the town, Pepe got into the truck and watched. The customers pressed closer to the baskets. Tauilopepe waited. One of them would eventually ask the price. From the size of the crowd he knew that few other vendors were selling bananas that day.

The woman who stepped forward was massively solid, with thick legs which seemed to grow out of the ground. 'How much?' she asked. She had no front teeth and this destroyed the threatening appearance she was presenting to him.

'Six shillings each,' he said, loud enough for most people to hear. They murmured in protest because the usual price for a basket was four shillings.

'But that's too high!' she said.

'Take it or leave it,' he replied.

She hesitated for a moment, then stepped forward, grabbed a basket with both hands, lifted it to her shoulder, and tossed the money at his feet. She turned, and shoved through the crowd, loudly telling everyone that all these people from the back were thieves who'd strip a poor woman naked if she didn't watch out.

The others surged forward and, stuffing their money into Tauilopepe's eager hands, lifted baskets and hurried off, grumbling that someone from the back (so they called the outer villages) had got the better of them, yes, they the sophisticated, educated inhabitants of Apia. Soon all the baskets were gone.

Tauilopepe leant against the truck and counted the largest sum of money he had ever earned; Pepe watched him from the truck window. When Tauilopepe noticed his relatives gazing wistfully at him and the money he handed one of them a ten-shilling note. 'Don't spend it on useless things!' he said as they moved off towards the market.

He rolled the notes and sheathed the roll in his shirt

pocket, the pile of coins he put in a paper bag and then into his small suitcase which Pepe handed him. He locked the suitcase, called Pepe out of the truck, unpinned a safety pin from his shirt and used it to pin down the shirt-pocket top over the roll of money.

The milk bar to which he led Pepe had steel bars over its front windows, steel bars over its display shelves, steel bars round the small compartment in which the cashier sat, and steel bars, so Tauilopepe started to imagine, round the room where the milk bar's owner probably slept away the day while the money came rolling in. He too would have steel bars all round his store, he decided, as he took Pepe up to the milk bar counter. You never know who will rob you.

A girl sat behind the counter reading a comic book. 'Ice cream two,' Tauilopepe said. The girl glanced up, then continued reading. 'I said, "Ice cream two",' he repeated. The girl, ear-ringed with small metal skulls that rattled whenever she moved her head, glared at him, slammed the comic book shut, opened the refrigerator, took out two ice creams and shoved them under his nose.

He banged a two-shilling coin on to the counter, snatched the ice creams out of her hand, and said, 'I want my change!'

She rummaged in the money-box behind her, and banged the change down on the counter.

'Eat shit!' Pepe said. A stunned pause. A stunned look on her face, the skull earrings still for the first time.

'Yes, you do that,' Tauilopepe said. He wheeled with the ice creams. Pepe followed him out.

'Ignorant Samoans!' she called after them.

As they sat in the truck eating their ice creams Tauilopepe said nothing about what had happened at the milk bar. It was the first time he hadn't punished Pepe for swearing. He patted his shirt pocket often to make sure the money was there; the suitcase lay under the protection of his left hand.

'Can we buy some coconut buns for Toasa and Lupe and Vao and Niu?' Pepe asked. Tauilopepe gave him some money and Pepe went to the market and bought the buns.

51

When their relatives returned, clutching ice creams and packets of peanuts, Tauilopepe told one of them to fetch Timu. Timu came reluctantly, annoyed with Tauilopepe for calling him away from the arena where gladiators poked sticks at religious balls in order to make money. And they returned to Sapepe.

One Saturday a week or so later, unaccompanied by Pepe who had disappeared mysteriously while they were loading the truck, they sold another load of bananas at the market. The baskets were smaller but the town people bought them. They sold two more loads the next week. On their third trip Tauilopepe bought a new hurricane lamp (the latest model, with two wicks), pieces of cotton material for Lupe and the girls, a Bible for Masina, a crisp pack of cards for Toasa, a white T-shirt for Pepe, a pair of American sandals for himself, and three large tins of cabin bread that were shared among all the members of his aiga in Sapepe. He didn't tell anyone how much money he had earned; he kept the money in his suitcase and the suitcase under his pillow at night.

When the taro crop was harvested Tauilopepe again got Malo's truck. This time he hired it. Three loads to market fetched him another large sum of money. He now had enough money to feed the Sapepe men and his aiga if he got them to start clearing and cultivating the valley, his new estate. To keep his money safe he dug a hole under a bread-fruit tree near the main fale when everyone was asleep, stuffed the money into two empty corned-beef tins, and buried them in the hole. He examined the spot every night to make sure the money was safe.

During the following weeks he spent most of his time on the plantation supervising nearly all his aiga as they pruned the cacao trees and planted bananas and taro. He returned home each evening tired, and after his meal and bath fell into a dreamless sleep. He neglected village affairs and his aiga. Some of the matai began to refer to him as 'the man who was after a seat on the papalagi aeroplane'. Beneath this light-hearted ridicule, however, they admired him as someone who was trying hard against weighted odds. They were sure he would fail as he had failed at theological school; he didn't stand a chance against Malo.

When Tauilopepe stayed away from church two Sundays running, Filipo, the pastor, preached a fiery sermon about certain men who were selling their souls to the Devil for money. Hell and eternal damnation was to be their just reward. Masina sat through Filipo's sermon feeling that her son was again disgracing the Aiga Tauilopepe (and her) before Sapepe (and God). After Sunday toonai she began to weep into the end of her lavalava. 'You promised me,' she cried. 'All my life I've tried to bring you up as a God-fearing man, Now you do this to me, to our aiga, and the memory of your father!' Tauilopepe, who had heard about Filipo's sermon and was angry, had vowed never to set foot in the pastor's house again, but he relented as he listened to Masina's loud grief. 'How do you think I felt when Filipo, the faithful servant of God, told the whole of Sapepe about you, about selling your soul?'

'I'll go tonight and see Filipo and apologise,' he said. 'And I'll ask him to accept me as a deacon.'

Masina picked up her half-smoked cheroot and relit it. 'You won't be sorry being a deacon,' she said. 'Look at what the Almighty is doing for you now. Soon we'll be the wealthiest aiga in Sapepe which in the first place was founded by *our* aiga. A man close to God.'

Masina's attitude to her son had changed subtly over the previous weeks as she observed him successfully amassing what she called 'worldly wealth'. (He was her only son. God, whose justice was beyond all human understanding, had willed away her other four sons and her husband during the series of influenza epidemics.) She attributed his recent success to God, so she was no longer against his drive towards what she termed 'godly power'. Secretly she was proud of him because Sapepe was again taking notice of her aiga (and her).

7   Pastor's Advantages

Tauilopepe stopped at the bottom of the front steps. The pastor's spacious house, which had been built by the village, was made of concrete and corrugated iron and was open on all sides. Two hurricane lamps hung from the centre roof beams; Filipo sat reading a newspaper under the lamps. As Tauilopepe looked at him he felt envious of the spectacles that gave Filipo his solemnly learned air. Chairs ringed the concrete posts of the house — they were made of cheap timber carefully camouflaged with varnish. Behind Filipo, against a blood-red partition, stood a large bed; on it was a fat mattress covered with a silk sheet, with tassels all round its edges; beside the bed, with the swirling light trapped in its rectangular mirror, stood a tallboy in which Tauilopepe knew Filipo stored his two suits and ties, his Bibles and notebooks, and a large world map which he had won in his student days. A curtain with hand-painted pictures of the apostles on it was half-drawn behind Filipo. Tauilopepe debated whether to go in or not. He had never quite liked Filipo: it had something to do with his condescending manner and the way he used the pulpit to condemn anyone who offended him. Tauilopepe was also — and he didn't want to admit this to himself — slightly afraid of Filipo.

Aiga photographs were displayed on the posts. Most of them, as Tauilopepe had carefully noted before, were of Filipo — a whole pictorial history starting from the day he won that world map at the age of twenty-two to only a few weeks before when he had delivered a lengthy sermon at the annual meeting of the LMS church in Malua. Second in number were the photographs of Taulua, his wife: the first photograph showed her as a nurse clutching a baby she had helped to deliver at Apia Hospital; the next photograph showed her in a flowing white wedding gown, looking like a healthy adolescent, beside a birdlike Filipo, stiff in his white suit; in the next photograph she was sitting on a box, holding her first child, already a buxom matron with fat jowls and a contented cat-like smile; the rest of the series portrayed her as increasing in weight, still beaming, still holding babies—a truly prodigious breeder. The remaining photographs were of Taulua's and Filipo's children displaying the certificates and prizes they had won at school. Tauilopepe walked up the steps reluctantly, deciding that his papalagi house would also have a collection of photographs of his aiga.

Startled by Tauilopepe's unexpected entry Filipo whipped off his spectacles, stuffed the newspaper behind him, and smiled up at his guest. Tauilopepe bowed his head and sat down opposite the pastor.

'Have you come? May God bless this auspicious meeting of brothers,' Filipo said, then closed his eyes and said a short prayer. Tauilopepe noticed he was sitting on a brand new mat. Filipo's eyes flicked open at the amen, and he began to describe how well the services had gone that day, how heart-warming it had been to see so many people at church, people who had found joy and comfort in his humble words. (He did not mention his fierce attack on Tauilopepe and Malo.) 'And how is your aiga?' he then asked.

'They are well, thank you,' Tauilopepe replied.

'The Almighty has been kind to us this month. No deaths or suffering, and the weather has been very good,' said Filipo. Tauilopepe nodded. 'Here, have a cigarette.' Filipo handed him an American cigarette.

Tauilopepe mumbled his thanks, and—awkwardly—started the long speech he had prepared. 'Sir, I have come to apologise for my behaviour during the last few weeks,' he said.

'You don't need to apologise to me, Tauilopepe,' said Filipo. 'We all have moments when Satan leads us astray. All we need is faith in God. Too many people have lost their faith and are copying pagan papalagi ways, pursuing money and wordly possessions and pleasures. These people are selling themselves for Judas's forty pieces of silver.'

Now feeling more at ease, Tauilopepe asked what true faith was. Filipo said no one could fully explain what it was, one could only *experience* it, like St Paul and the flash of heavenly light which had changed his life utterly. 'How is your plantation?' he asked.

'All right,' Tauilopepe replied cautiously.

'Good, but we must be careful — too much wealth can destroy a man's soul.' Filipo had one of the most productive plantations in Sapepe, a plantation which his congregation had hacked out of the bush, on land given to the church by Tauilopepe's grandfather. As was the custom the plantation was maintained by the congregation, especially by all the young people who attended the pastor's school. 'Satan tempts us with many enticing things,' Filipo went on, 'money, power, drink, books — you ought to see some of the books they're selling in Apia! A sad pity because, as you know, I love reading.' He paused and ran his tongue over his lips. 'And, of course, women. Those beings who bear our heirs, clean our homes, cook our food, and wash our clothes. The flesh is weak. Remember Eve and the snake. Only the other day I heard a tragic story of a husband leaving his home, his children, his wife, his mother and sisters and brothers for another woman. And, this is confidential' — he lowered his voice and whispered — 'the woman had spent years in Apia on the waterfront.' He looked at Tauilopepe.

'Doing what?' asked Tauilopepe, the dark connotations of the word 'waterfront' having escaped him.

Filipo didn't pursue the point. 'And how is your mother?' he asked.

'She is well, thank you.'

'A devout woman; she'll live to be a hundred.'

Filipo then chose to explain again what faith was. As he rambled on Tauilopepe gazed up at the largest photograph of Filipo, which was crucified to the front middle post of the house. In his mind he replaced Filipo's face with his own. The same smile, confidence, power! The spell broke when Filipo said, 'Faith, yes, faith in the Resurrection is all we need.'

56

Tauilopepe nodded repeatedly and stubbed out his cigarette butt on the concrete floor. 'Do you remember your offer?' he asked. 'Well, I'd like, with all my heart, to accept it.'

Filipo's eyes lit up. 'The Lord has triumphed again,' he said. 'I am glad.' He gave his guest another cigarette. 'The ways our Father uses to guide men along the right path are known only to Him. I am so glad.' He stopped and lit Tauilopepe's cigarette. Then he described his own conversion. He was only eight years old when God had called him, he said. It was during a fierce storm when the wind howled and the seas rose up and pounded the shore. Right in the middle of that storm, as he lay in his fale, shivering and shaking with mortal fear because he knew the Devil was out there, he heard a voice. It was a wonderful voice, sweet and soothing, like the spring water Moses had got out of the rock to quench the thirst of the fickle Israelites, melodious like a church organ. It sounded like his mother's voice. (His mother, a devout woman, much like Tauilopepe's mother, had died the previous year.) The voice which surely belonged to his mother told him not to be afraid because he had been chosen. It didn't tell him what he had been chosen for. But he knew, just as he knew there was a storm out there with the Devil trying to wreck his home: he knew he had been chosen by God to do His work. Filipo ended his story and gazed at the floor.

Tauilopepe was impressed. Filipo's conversion was like something out of the Bible, genuine proof of the existence of God and His love, and Tauilopepe regretted not having made the most of theological college.

Soon after, members of Filipo's aiga brought steaming mugs of cocoa and plates stacked with cabin bread with thick layers of coconut jam on it. 'Eat,' Filipo said to his guest, after he had said a short prayer of thanks to God for guiding Tauilopepe back to the true path. Then, without waiting for Tauilopepe, he broke a biscuit of cabin bread in half, put it into his mouth, and crunched it noisily. 'Don't forget God and His Church when you succeed,' he said through a bulging mouth, 'because it will be He who will open the treasures of this world to you. We'll accept you into the church as a deacon two Sundays from today, the Lord willing.'

Tauilopepe picked up one biscuit of cabin bread and started to eat. Being a deacon had definite advantages, he thought, feeling the sweet pulp of well-chewed cabin bread slipping smoothly down his throat. As he lifted the mug of cocoa to his lips he looked up at Filipo's photograph. Then he raced Filipo through the cabin bread and cocoa.

'I'd like you to take the sermon the first Sunday next month,' Filipo said when they had eaten everything. 'If you need any help in preparing your sermon remember I'm always here, always available.'

Tauilopepe had never felt so complete as now when he pictured himself up there in the pulpit telling the people of the mysterious ways of Jehovah. He would have to buy a new suit and a black tie, and he must remember to wear his new sandals.

8 Lions and Aitu

The sound of the sea faded as they penetrated deeper into the plantations, about a hundred men in single file meandering over the track, all carefully avoiding the puddles. It was early morning and some of them were still half-dazed with sleep; they were hungry also for they hadn't eaten. They carried bushknives and axes. Dew dripped off the vegetation, and a few birds streaked over the trees, heading for the sea and the village the men had left behind. Ahead, a blanket of mist covered the bush-clad range. The sun was not yet visible over the barrier of trees to their left, and they hoped that a kind shield of cloud would keep it off them while they worked. The night before, Tauilopepe had summoned about half the Sapepe matai to his fale, and after a heavy meal had told them of his plans for clearing his new land. Toasa had immediately offered to allow the men of his aiga to work for Tauilopepe. Most of the other aiga heads offered also.

Some of the men started to sing a sea chant: the stirring rhythm of paddles and sea, of taut muscles, and the promise of a large catch rose up to the waking sky. Tauilopepe didn't join the singing, he was busy thinking up methods of getting the most work out of the men. In front of him shuffled Toasa leaning on his walking-stick. He had insisted on accompanying the work party despite Tauilopepe's warning that the heat and distance might prove too much for him. Tauilopepe was glad he had come though. With the old man watching them, the men would labour conscientiously. Tauilopepe hoped that Lupe and the women of his aiga were starting to cook the food to feed the men in the afternoon. The tinned food had cost him over half the contents of one of his money-filled corned-beef tins.

Cacao trees, burdened with scarlet fruit, lined the sides

of the track; among them were gatae shrubs and sometimes sugar-cane, taro, and taamu; beneath them lay a carpet of cacao leaves. He heard Toasa's laboured breathing and wanted to help him but he knew the old man would refuse help. He was stubborn and vain, boasting often of the times he had lifted hefty loads twice his weight and walked miles with them, swum oceans, knocked out men with one punch. No idle boasting either. All the old people could vouch for Toasa's strength.

The sun emerged from the trees, sucking the mist off the range and the dew off the bush. The murmur of the sea had ceased. A flying-fox circled above them; then, when someone shouted, it curved off and disappeared into the trees. They came to a stand of pawpaw trees, yellow with ripe fruit; some of the men picked the fruit and distributed them. Tauilopepe accepted some slices. The thick sweet juice dribbled down his chin as he ate. No one sang now. It was going to be a hot day. That night they would sleep deeply, with aching bones and muscles, and with the ferocious sun still pulsating in their heads. But before sleep they would listen again to the healing sermon of the sea.

They were climbing now, knowing that over the hill lay the valley and, a few miles further up, hard grinding work. Sweat. Strained muscles. Fearless insects stinging their bodies. Wood dust in their eyes. And hunger.

The plantations grew fewer, looked more impermanent and neglected after they passed Tauilopepe's plantation and began dipping into the valley. There were only a few banana trees and taro, smothered by creepers, and stands of massive trees became more numerous — wild defiant barriers against the wind — and silence, always the green threatening silence. The track was harder to follow. Bushknives slashed at the undergrowth blocking their way. The dank smell of rotting wood and leaf and wet earth pervaded everything.

Then came the clearing, stretching for a hundred yards or so — a carpet of tenacious creeper over lava rock. Beyond it, virgin bush confronted them. They stood and stared at it in silence: they had been away too long, had become men of the easy shore lands: this gigantic wall of tree and liana and creeper they had combated only in their nightmares; now it was real, and they felt puny, helpless. Some of them looked at their bushknives and axes and shook their heads. This work needed fire, blazing hungry flame. Tauilopepe stood beside Toasa, not knowing what to do to restore the men's faith in themselves. He stabbed his bushknife into the ground.

Only Toasa broke from the line and started to make his way across the clearing, his walking-stick stabbing footholds into the creepers, like a blind man painfully searching his way across unfamiliar territory. The men watched him. Half-way across the clearing he stopped and turned to face them. Somehow he no longer looked ridiculous set against the background of bush — this lone figure of an old man who had come home to the aitu and lions and legendary creatures he insisted on filling the children's imaginations with. Suddenly they saw his body shaking. His face contorted in a strange way and they thought he was weeping. But the sound which issued from his mouth and echoed across the clearing was laughter.

One by one they made their way towards him. Tauilopepe was the last.

'There she is,' Toasa said, sweeping his walking-stick across the bush. 'No one has touched her before. Anyway no one who's alive to tell us, eh? She has remained pure since God created these islands. Line up!'

All the men except Tauilopepe, who remained beside Toasa, formed a line at the foot of the green wall. 'Remember, no one has touched her before!' Toasa shouted. The men advanced cautiously. 'What are you waiting for, eh? You don't want to deflower her? You scared of her?' A few of the men laughed. Tauilopepe advanced to a short tree and chopped it down with one blow of his axe. 'There, see that?' called Toasa. 'It's easy. She won't scream and charge you in court with rape!' Many of the others followed Tauilopepe's example. 'Good! Come on now, raise your baby-sized manhoods and chop, cut, burn!' The line advanced; the axes and bushknives started biting into the flesh of the living wall.

61

When the first big trees thundered to the ground, tearing and levelling all the small vegetation before them,
some of the men cheered. Their axes and bushknives took
on greater fury. Soon the snapping chomping sound of
iron biting deep shattered the silence and chased the birds
like wood chips into the air and away towards the range.
Toasa moved from group to group, encouraging them to
hack and chop. 'Prove your manhood!' he said.

As the men advanced, leaving behind them fallen trees
and cleared undergrowth alive with bugs and gnats and
ants, Toasa tired of what he had turned into a game. That
walk across the clearing had reminded him of a previous
journey he had made across a similar clearing. (Or had it
been the same clearing?) But, when had he made that
journey, walking ahead towards the bush with other men
watching him, stopping, turning, and laughing for no
reason at all? Had he only dreamt it? A nightmare
perhaps? Or was it just a trick his imagination was playing
him? An old man's mind wandered, forgot things, made up
things. Only one thing was not a trick: he had felt as he
walked across the clearing that this would be his last journey into the bush. He sat down on a boulder in the shade
and smoked and studied Tauilopepe.

To Toasa the bush had always been a mystery —
impersonal and aloof yet always there watching, like the
sea. His ancestors had taken from it, after appeasing it with
prayer and ritual, only what they needed; had cleared only
small areas for food gardens. They had learnt through the
centuries to live with the mystery and the gods in the mystery. They had believed that the gods and the land and the
bush and the sea and all other living creatures were indivis-
ibly part of that perpetual cycle of birth, life, death, and
rebirth. They had drawn boundaries over the land from the
shore to the mountain ridge, but it had been for ownership, not to burn and clear the land for farming and profits.
Ownership of land gave meaning to their way of life, to
the titles and status of their aiga. Disputes over land had
often resulted in open warfare, but when the feuding
ended the victors left the land as it had been — bush-clad,
proof of one's mana, the scene of one's valiant deeds.

When the papalagi came they outlawed the bush. They bought land, bush-free land, in other districts, with guns, cheap goods, and lies. Then with fire and steel they drove the bush and gods inland, and erected barbed-wire fences. All for copra. With the missionaries, these papalagi settlers shattered the tapu that had ensured the survival of that cycle in which man had respected all other living things. Now Toasa was witnessing his own people continue that process of destruction. Even the mosquitoes seemed agitated; he counted four on his arm but left them alone. In that slow walk across the clearing he had finally accepted the inevitable. He had looked at the bush, then back at Tauilopepe; he had realised he was standing between them and had decided to make way. That was why he had laughed. To Tauilopepe the past had no real meaning. He had seen that often enough in Tauilopepe's eyes after he had returned from theological college. The deck of cards had been cut years before, even before these men were born, and he, Toasa, had lost. Luck, as Lafo said, was either for you or against you. You either had it or you didn't. And he didn't have it, not any more, the papalagi had made sure of that. The world he was trying to prop up would sooner or later collapse completely.

When he was a boy the changes introduced by the papalagi had bewildered him. He thought again of Tauilopepe Mosooi, Tauilopepe's great-grandfather, the only matai who had resisted missionary penetration into Sapepe, and who had died in the last pre-Christian battle, hurling himself at the enemies' spears, yelling, 'I'll die a man!' One last defiant gesture. After him Sapepe had accepted totally, relinquished the old religion, and everything else which offended the missionaries, to gain the mana of the new God. The years accelerated the establishment of the Church. He, Toasa, growing up with Tauilopepe Laau and conditioned by a faith which had become a vital part of the Sapepe way of life, he too had accepted Christianity, even though the pull was strong in him of what the missionaries and pastors condemned as 'a pagan past without light'. But this had not meant the adoption of papalagi values and ways. When he assumed the

63

aiga title his leadership was rooted firmly in tradition and the values of the faa-Sapepe, the Sapepean way, or in what he believed these values had been. Together with Tauilopepe Laau, the other half of what he called his 'private aiga', he had successfully curbed the missionaries and traders, prevented wholesale radical change. Even Malo, he had believed, through whom the threat of the town was growing stronger, could do little to alter the balance of power in Sapepe. The Sapepean way of life could not be changed, he had believed then, for had it not been given to them by Jehovah who alone could change or destroy it? Most of the matai of his generation had believed this also, so that Christianity had not weakened their way of life but strengthened it. He had encouraged this belief. But now most of those men were dead.

A male child came into his life, his friend Tauilopepe Laau's youngest son. He loved him more than his own children and he helped Tauilopepe Laau to bring him up. Toasa had hoped that the boy would continue their system of leadership, and he hadn't really wanted to take part in Tauilopepe Laau's and Masina's relentless attempt to make their son a pastor. But he did; and he felt hypocritical for having done so. The boy returned from Malua Theological College a failure to his parents who felt he had disgraced their aiga, and a failure to Toasa who felt he had turned into a stranger, a man of the town. When Tauilopepe Laau died only he, Toasa Faaola Matagifa, was left, the last of a generation. Eccentric. Cantankerous. Obsolete. A quaint card-sharp who no longer fully trusted the younger matai, especially those like Malo and Tauilopepe, because to such men loyalty to anyone or anything was barterable; integrity was a commodity which could be sold and bought. So now, as he watched the men working, as the trees crashed to the ground, he concluded that, like the bush, he had become obsolete. His one inconsolable regret was the fact that Tauilopepe, the son of his friend, of the man he had loved so much, would be responsible for the final destruction of his world. At the meeting of matai, by allowing Tauilopepe the best share of the land, he, Toasa, had chosen Tauilopepe as his executioner.

64

Slapping at the mosquitoes on his arms, he flicked his cheroot into the creepers and watched it die slowly. The desperate hope came, that perhaps the strength of the past which encompassed Sapepe would absorb the new changes, would subtly modify them as it had absorbed and modified Christianity. He squinted as he looked up at the sun now near its zenith. At least the sun would never change.

The trees kept on falling.

When Toasa saw Tauilopepe approaching him he straightened up and was again the old man whose sole preoccupation in life was card-playing and the acceptance of whichever way the cards fell.

'The work is going well,' Tauilopepe said. Toasa nodded. Tauilopepe sat down beside him. They watched the men working.

'Going to be a deacon, eh?' Toasa said. Tauilopepe grinned. 'That's good. Your father was a very good deacon despite the fact he could hardly read or write.' Tauilopepe cringed visibly, and Toasa wanted to hurt him. Why? He didn't know or care. 'Neither could I. Never bothered to learn, never saw the use for it, eh. But your father had a prodigious memory. Like a book centuries old. He could remember far more than I could of Sapepe history. Even a storehouse of songs, chants, and rituals that went out when the missionaries came in. But I suppose you knew that about him?' Tauilopepe nodded. Toasa knew Tauilopepe was lying — Tauilopepe Laau had revealed almost nothing of what he knew to others, and especially not to his own son. Toasa had never understood why his friend hid behind an impregnable mask of secrecy, especially from his own wife and children. But he had never asked him. There had been an unwritten pact between them — there were to be no questions; they had each to accept the other as he was and to trust each other to the point of death. It had proved a lifetime trust which neither of them had ever broken or doubted. 'Your father was a great fellow,' he said. 'I would have given my life for him, and I'm sure he would have given his for me.' He saw Tauilopepe shift uncomfortably. 'But I suppose you know what trust is. Honour, integrity, and all that ancient excrement, eh?'

65

Tauilopepe tried to smile. 'Did you know we were the only people who ever reached the top of the mountain range?' Tauilopepe shook his head. 'The only two since the missionaries and traders nailed us to the sea-shore. Do you know what we found?' Paused, and looking steadily at Tauilopepe said: '*We found lions and aitu and important memories.*'

For an instant Tauilopepe looked stunned. Toasa thought, ah, he's afraid I've gone mad. So he went on. 'We were only twelve years old — foolishly brave because we didn't know what fear was. One night we dared each other. Later we'd have liked to break the challenge, but we didn't want to admit to each other we were still without hairs, eh.' He laughed. Tauilopepe didn't laugh. 'We stole out early in the morning and I can still remember the barking dogs, the cold feel of the dew, the noisy pigs, and the fear. We pissed over the rock fence and watched the steam rising as the water slapped into the ground. Your father's back was turned to me. He was a prude; he never discussed sex or farted openly or told bawdy jokes. A bit like you!' He glanced at Tauilopepe and saw the downcast eyes.

'Well, we hurried through the trees, carrying our basket of taro and bottles of water. No one knew we had left. We thought we'd be back the same day. At first the going was easy — we knew the track well. But two hours later the track ran out and we were scared. We looked at each other and knew we couldn't break our bargain. "Come on," said your father. He always led when the going got tough. I was his shadow, tagging along because a shadow can't do anything else. We didn't take the trail we came on today: we dipped into the valley from the western side. He stumbled. I caught him, straightened him up. "Shall we go back?" I asked. Without speaking he crawled ahead through the undergrowth down towards the valley floor and into a clearing where we rested and gnawed at our dry taro and gulped down the water. Afterwards I pulled up my lavalava and shat. He looked away. And he laughed, eh. The first time he'd ever laughed at anything like that. And I had to laugh too. And our fear started to disappear.

66

Going up the valley on to the foothills was easy. We pretended we were warriors stalking enemy troops.

'It was late afternoon when we reached the top of one of the hills half-way up the range. We rested under the wild trees and watched the wood pigeons and remembered what Tauilopepe Faiga, your grandfather, had told us about the great pigeon hunters of the ancient days. War and pigeon hunting were the sport of alii; something gone now, forgotten. Anyway I shouted, and in a clatter of wings the pigeons were gone. I've never seen any as free since then. Free. Keeping to the range away from the rifles. It's slaughter to hunt with guns. No skill or art about it. In the old days a hunter would even wait for days to snare a pigeon, using a live trained decoy to lure it into a trap. That was art. All gone. Today, it's aim, fire. Beauty exploded in a brutal instant, eh!' His voice reached a passionate intensity. Then he remembered where he was and who he was talking to, blinked, and laughed.

'We got up and went on. Always up and ahead, with the sun sinking and our fear returning because we'd heard of the aitu the missionaries had exiled to the bush and range. Ancient aitu, gods who'd fallen from grace, out of date yet still believed in when the dark fell. Over lava boulders we crawled, scratched and bleeding. Helping each other up towards the sky and the wind curling through the trees. Then we were there, on the top, under the highest trees. And the ocean was before and behind us, slipping away into nothing at the ends of the world. Below us the ridges and valleys and the plains lay blue and still, as peaceful as our forefathers must have seen them when they first settled here. Anyway we sprawled out and fell asleep. The aitu didn't haunt us. We didn't even feel the mosquitoes.'

He stopped again and saw that Tauilopepe was looking at the range. 'We woke at dawn, wet and cold and hungry, our bodies blistered with mosquito bites. And our fear returned when we realised where we were, feeling the aitu and the gods watching us from the trees, from the mist. Your father got up, saw I was crying, and said, "They won't hurt us. *I know.*" Your old man was always a strange fellow. I never once saw him afraid of the supernatural. I think he actually believed in the ancient gods. Not that it stopped him from being a good Christian deacon. One god isn't so different from another. It all depends on the man. When he said that, I suddenly felt free — the mist, the shadows, the wind, the bush, and the gods — or whatever they were — weren't against us but were *with* us. Do you understand? They were our friends.' He sniffed hard and spat. 'Then we saw the rock platform under the highest tree, facing the east. We went to it. You know what we found, eh? ... Two conch shells cracked and brown with age. Nothing else. Nothing to show who'd brought them all that way. Do you know what conch shells were in the old days?' Tauilopepe shook his head. 'In many villages they were symbols of the gods, the voices of certain gods. But I didn't know that then. Up to that moment your old man had always been the brave one, so I thought I'd better prove I had hairs too. So guess what I did, eh? I picked up one of the shells and got ready to blow it. The shell was nearly to my lips when — boom — your old man hit it out of my hands. I just stood there, really angry with him. He picked it up gently and put it back on the platform. "Why did you do that?" I asked. He only glared at me. It was only an old useless thing and there he was looking at me as if I should be dead. "Why?" I said again. I sat down when he told me what his father had told him about conch shells. He sat down too and we stared at the shells for a long long time. When the first rays of the sun hit them your father and I made a bargain: we would never reveal the location of the platform to anyone else. Not even to the people we trusted. Why we made that bargain we didn't know. Only that we felt it was important to make it, to keep the shells a secret, perhaps for ever. It *was* important. Do you understand what I mean, Tauilo? There are things a man — and your father and I became men when we made that journey — must commit himself to, even if most people consider them meaningless. To us, the conch shells *were* important.' His voice broke and he looked at Tauilopepe who was watching the men working. 'Anyway,' he sighed, 'we agreed to keep the shells and shrine a secret. And to make sure we'd never reveal their whereabouts we agreed to refer to them as "lions". Of all the names we could have called them, we called them LIONS.' He laughed lightly but he was feeling tired, sensing that Tauilopepe was far away, lost in the fertile valley. 'When we returned home we got the thrashing of our lives. They'd spent the whole night searching for us. But we never told them where we had been. Never.' He paused. 'I wonder what would have happened if I had blown the conch, the voice of the gods, eh? Do you think they would've returned out of the grave? ... Lions, aitu, and memories!' He slapped Tauilopepe's shoulder and started to laugh. Stopped suddenly and said, 'What are you going to plant?'

'Cacao, taro, and bananas,' replied Tauilopepe.

'And money, eh!' said Toasa. 'Pity money doesn't grow on trees. It'd be a lot easier for everyone if it did, wouldn't it?'

Tauilopepe said nothing.

The sun had clambered past noon and chased the shadows from the two men sitting there impervious to the heat. Toasa gazed up at the range, now a dark blue haze against the blinding sky, and thought of the journey that had turned him and Tauilopepe Laau into men and inseparable friends. When he became aware of Tauilopepe again his heart longed for the boy he had loved who was now lost within the stranger beside him. Then he remembered Pepe and determined to try again. Pepe understood the lions and aitu. Were the lions still up there, waiting to be found, waiting for the human breath that would bring them back to life? Maybe waiting for Pepe? Pepe was *his* son.

At first Tauilopepe had listened attentively to Toasa's tale, eager for a glimpse of the father he had never really known. But Toasa had revealed little of him. He had exaggerated as usual, Tauilopepe thought: they had probably never been up on the range, had never endured that trek, the whole story was a product of Toasa's imagination.

As for the lions and aitu, that was just too much. Toasa was becoming senile. So he had stopped listening, catching only bits of the story and nodding his head.

Not long after Toasa finished his story, Lupe and Pepe and other members of the Aiga Tauilopepe arrived, carrying baskets and pots of food dangling from yokes. In the brilliant light they looked like panting beasts of burden. Pepe, who was carrying a black kettle, broke from the group, ran to Toasa, and handed him a large baked taro. The old man broke the taro in half and they started eating. The others took the food and rested in the shade.

A tree swayed and crashed down. Pepe stared wide-eyed. 'Did you see that, eh?' he asked Toasa. 'Just missed those men. You think they would have got killed? Do you think so, eh?'

'Would've flattened them,' replied Toasa. 'Flattened them like flies.' Tauilopepe winced.

'No hope, eh?' said Pepe.

'No hope whatsoever. Even a miracle wouldn't have saved them.'

'What's a miracle?' asked Pepe.

'A miracle?' Toasa paused and, looking at Tauilopepe, said, 'That's when something comes out of nothing and nothing comes out of something. Like when fish grow legs and walk ashore.'

'Oh,' said Pepe. Toasa laughed. He looked at Tauilopepe and dug him in the ribs with his elbow. 'What kind of fish are those?' Pepe asked.

'Miracle fish,' replied Toasa.

'Can you eat them, eh?' asked Pepe, developing the joke further.

'Only miracle-workers can eat them.' Toasa swallowed the last bit of taro and belched.

Pepe handed him his own piece of taro and asked, 'Are there any miracle-workers in Sapepe?'

'Oh, those. Yes. They're odd fellows, very odd.'

'Why odd?' asked Pepe. Tauilopepe wished the senseless conversation would stop.

'Well, because they're hairless, eh. Every time they perform a miracle they lose ten hairs. So too many miracles result in baldness.'

Pepe laughed and said, 'Was Christ bald then?' A tense pause. Tauilopepe glared at Pepe and Toasa looked at Tauilopepe, amused.

'No, Jesus wasn't bald.'

'Therefore Jesus was no miracle-worker, eh!' reasoned Pepe. Tauilopepe waited eagerly for Toasa's answer, for the heretical declaration, but he hadn't taken Toasa's subtle brain into account.

Suddenly Toasa stood up and said, 'Attention!' Pepe snapped to attention. Tauilopepe was confused, so confused he was angry with being confused. He thought Toasa really was senile but waited to see what he and Pepe were up to. 'At ease, lion!' Toasa ordered. Pepe obeyed smartly. Tauilopepe's confusion became more jungle-like. Toasa was either senile or he had gone mad. Tauilopepe cursed to himself. Another tree crashed down; the sound boomed across the valley.

'Who are we?' chanted Toasa.
'Lions three — you, me, and
the miracle-fish; the mountain,
sky, and bloody sea!' recited Pepe.

Lupe and the people in the shade laughed. Tauilopepe's confusion changed into embarrassed, angry bewilderment. Toasa wasn't senile or insane, he was just plain stupid.

'Who are we?' chanted Pepe.
'Aitu three — you, me, and
Filipo's tea; money,
sharks and Sapepe's pig!' recited Toasa.

Some of the men stopped working and laughed.

Lupe came over and sat behind Tauilopepe. 'Is the food ready?' he asked her in an attempt to stop himself from listening to Toasa and Pepe.

'Yes, she replied. 'How long will it take? The work I mean?'

'Don't know.'

'Lot of work,' she said.

Tauilopepe couldn't take his attention from Toasa and Pepe. They had stopped laughing and were now whispering to each other and pointing at the range. 'Is there enough food?' he asked Lupe.

'I think so.'

'Are you sure?'

'Yes, I'm sure.'

'You don't have to get angry,' he said.

'I'm *not* angry.'

'You are!' he accused her. Another tree thundered to the ground.

'I'm not, but you are!' she replied. They suddenly noticed that Toasa and Pepe were looking at them and they stopped quarrelling. One punch and she'd be out cold, Tauilopepe thought. Would serve her right for talking back. Lupe got up and returned to the shade and the other women. When he felt that no one was looking at him he moved into the shade too. But Toasa and Pepe followed him and sat only a few yards away from him.

'What is your name?' he heard Toasa ask Pepe. The laughter was gone.

'My name is Pepe Tauilopepe, Descendant of the House of Sapepe, Heir to the Estate of the Dead, future Protector of the Living, Guardian of the Unborn,' Pepe recited. It was the same ritual that Toasa had taught him at Pepe's age, a ritual he had responded to whole-heartedly then but discarded at theological college — and rightly so.

'What must you do?' asked Toasa.

'Be a leader, strong and merciful. Be a man, just and ....'

'Be a man just and *fair*,' Toasa prompted. Pepe recited the whole answer again.

'What must you remember always?' Toasa asked.

'That the Dead of Sapepe are with us, and we, the Living, are with the Dead and the yet unborn, for ever and inseparable. Our duty is to uphold what the Dead

72

bequeathed to us to guard and bequeath to the Unborn when we too join the Dead,' chanted Pepe.

Tauilopepe recaptured the time when he had visited Toasa and told him how he had learnt at the pastor's school that Moses was the prophet who had miraculously caused water to flow out of a barren rock. Toasa had started there and then to teach him the oral ritual he was now reciting with Pepe. A few days later he had informed Toasa that the pastor was sure Jehovah had created mankind from Adam and Eve and the snake. Toasa laughed and told him the Sapepe myth of the Creation.

'In the beginning there was only the Void,' Toasa had told him. 'Different colours formed in the Void. These colours turned into solid matter, combined, and formed the world. The gods then covered the world's nakedness with creepers. After centuries of light and darkness the creepers rotted and turned into maggots. Out of these maggots emerged Man, who, on his death and the falling of the dark, turned into maggots again.' Tauilopepe was extremely loyal to Toasa then so he didn't tell the pastor about this heretical story. He even believed maggots were beautiful, and he continued to visit Toasa in the evening to learn the ancient beliefs and history of his people. But now, as he gazed at the land being cleared, he resolved that his son's future was with the land and the promise of profit it held, not with Toasa and his peculiar madness. And yet, as he listened to Toasa and Pepe, he thought of the Living and the Dead and the Unborn, and remembered the maggots, a terrifying squirming mountain, feeding on itself and disgorging mankind. He got up, took his bushknife, and hurried to bury his fears in the ritual of work.

An hour or so later everyone gathered in the shade and the men had their meal of tinned herrings, corned-beef stew, baked taro, and bananas. Swarms of flies buzzed round the food: the women warded them off with small branches while the men ate. Vao and Niu went round with buckets of water, filling enamel cups which the men emptied in long gulps. All the men were streaked with dirt and stank of sweat and wood sap; their hair was brittle dry from the heat and webbed with dead insects, bits of leaves, and wood chips. They ate without talking: there were groaning bellies to fill, cool baths and sleep to think about. But they still had hours of work to do, a taunting sun to tolerate and curse until it fled laughing over the western ridge, and the long dreary march home.

Pepe shared Toasa's foodmat. They were the only ones with enough energy to talk. 'How are your manhoods now?' Toasa asked the men. A few of them looked up from their food. 'Can't stand up, eh? The bush too much of a woman for you?' Some of the men grinned. Tauilopepe gritted his teeth. 'When I was your age I could work all day long. Chopped down whole forests and still had time to snare a shark or two at night.' The grins turned into chuckles. 'Used to eat them raw too. Good for the liver, and the female sharks loved it!' The chuckles changed into lewd laughter. Some of the women giggled. Tauilopepe tried to smile. 'Looking at you tired fellows anyone would think you've been working,' Toasa continued, until he had most of them talking and joking back.

'Were there any trees in your day?' a man asked.

'Trees! Just oceans of them. So tall you couldn't see their tops, eh. The trees you've been chopping are only weeds.'

'What about axes?' asked another man.

'Axes? Who needed them? We used to break trees down with our bare hands!' Toasa said. Except for Tauilopepe, he had them laughing, even most of the women.

Lupe handed round two packets of tobacco. The men rolled cigarettes, and lit them with a smouldering branch that Niu brought. After the cigarettes and a short rest they returned to work, the women started back to the village, and Pepe and Toasa slept in the shade.

Shortly after, most of the men stopped working and looked up, shielding their eyes with their hands. Tauilopepe noticed their silence and looked up too. They had never seen so immense a tree: its sheer height took Tauilopepe's breath away for a moment. He joined the others under the tree — a banyan tree. It looked like a gigantic octopus squatting on the land, its tentacles rooted firmly into the earth, and casting an eerie trembling

74

shadow which seemed to frighten the surrounding bush and the valley itself. Tauilopepe sat down on a tree trunk. Centuries old, the banyan looked as though it had always been there. Men had probably come, looked at it with bewildered astonishment, and passed on into oblivion. The base of the banyan was larger than the paepae of the biggest fale in Sapepe. It would even dwarf the church. Only the sea could match it.

Two men rushed to it and began chopping at one of its roots. The others laughed. It would take a month to destroy it, Tauilopepe thought, a month of strained muscles and curses and perhaps final defeat. A month wasted and his money running out. Fire might do the job, but....

'What shall we do with it?' a man asked.

'We'll burn it down some other time,' Tauilopepe replied.

They passed on to less formidable trees that were more pliant to their vanity. But, as Tauilopepe worked, he stopped often and gazed up at the banyan. He couldn't understand why he was growing angry; it had to do with Toasa's tale of the trek and the lions and aitu and the maggots, and Pepe, and now the banyan, all these made him feel *small*, made him feel he hadn't achieved anything worthwhile and he didn't want to feel that way. He swung his axe, felt it sink into the flesh of the tree he was felling, and enjoyed the sense of power, his power. He suddenly wanted a woman, a big insatiable woman who needed a lot of power to satisfy her.

When the sun squatted on the shoulders of the western ridge Tauilopepe ordered the men to stop working. They woke Toasa and Pepe and started trailing homeward, already feeling the cool water on their skins, the hot food in their bellies, smelling the sea and tasting the salt in the night breeze that would surely rise from the sea, hearing their children. And their women around them like the sea. And sleep.

'Going to call the new plantation "Leaves of the Banyan Tree",' Tauilopepe said. A few of them nodded. The rest were too tired to care.

9 Truly Inspired

Hidden in the mangrove trees, Tauilopepe counted the money he had left in the one remaining corned-beef tin. He compared what he had spent in feeding the men with the area they had cleared and planted, and concluded that every penny had been worth it. Nearly a hundred acres of taro and banana and cacao trees planted in just over a month.

The tangled roots and branches of the mangrove trees were like an impregnable wall around him. Through the gap above him he glimpsed a sky covered with a mattress of grey cloud but he knew it wouldn't rain. He counted the money twice aloud. The tide was out and he was buried to his ankles in mud. Only ten men hadn't lasted the month of exhausting work: five had taken ill, the others had just stopped coming. He peeled fifteen one-pound notes from the roll, debated a moment, then put two of them back. He'd give thirteen pounds to the men; perhaps they would use it for a feast. He squatted back on his haunches. There had been times when the men had nearly given up, but he had challenged them with day-long displays of hacking and chopping, no rest even for food, from morning to sunset, until he could hardly swing an axe. It had worked. The men had kept up. He sighed, his mind caressing the dazzling picture of his new plantation, the crops growing lushly, bearing fruit, and then more money.

A large black pig, caked with mud, broke through a gap in the tangled roots, snout nosing the mud aside. Tauilopepe scratched his genitals and thought of Malo's house and store, and of Moa. The pig grunted and looked warily at him. His hand edged down and round the empty corned-beef tin. The pig turned. Too late. The tin caught it a glancing blow on the snout. A painful screech and away it crashed through the trees.

He again examined the roll of money and suddenly remembered that Filipo was expecting him to deliver his first sermon that Sunday. Warily he glanced up at the sky. God was surely watching him at that moment. He scrambled forward, picked up the tin, stuffed the money into it, and hurried through the trees. When he realised he was running he stopped, telling himself that he had no reason to be afraid of God. After all, was it not God's doing that he was acquiring worldly wealth.

When he was sure no one was watching he reburied the tin under the bread-fruit trees behind the fale. He wiped his feet with a sack and went into the fale where he found Masina and Pepe sleeping. Lupe and the girls were in the kitchen fale preparing the evening meal. He got the aiga Bible, opened it carefully, and read. After reading a few pages he went to the family trunk and took out one of Pepe's pencils and an exercise book. He sat down and read the pencil label and then the company's name on the exercise book cover. He licked the pencil lead. Liked the taste. But wished he owned a fountain pen. (Filipo always wrote his sermons in blue ink, using an expensive fountain pen that his son in American Samoa had sent him.) He had that night and the whole of Saturday to compose his sermon. He folded back the cover of the exercise book and flicked through the pages, licking his thumb before turning each page. He was exhilarated by the smell of new paper: something he hadn't smelt for years, ever since he had secretly burnt all his books the day he was expelled from Malua.

He turned the first page. Caressed it. Fondled it. Lifted it to his nose. Sniffed at it. Ah-h-h. A whole unpopulated world soon to be inhabited by his words, thoughts, knowledge, dreams, visions. His hand trembled as he lifted the pencil and poised it above this virgin world, ready for the creative dive. Licked the pencil point again, then plunged it down. There! Printed his name in capital letters at the top of the page. Examined each capital letter thoroughly. Not bad. Printed his name again on the top right-hand corner. And then again. Sighed. Remembered his father had been illiterate. It didn't matter. Not any more. Printed his father's name three times across the page. His hand had stopped trembling. So, opening the Bible at the very beginning, he copied the first sentence he read, finishing it with a flourish and an admiring sigh. He hadn't lost the gift. He copied another sentence and yet another, all the time humming to himself. Gifted, that's what he was, and it was all God's doing. Remembered he had learnt some English at Malua College, and printed the words CAT, DOG, GOD, MONEY, JEHOVAH, and CAT, over and over again. He spelt each word out loud and then printed WOMAN, MAN, CAR, BOY, GIRL, FISH, and his full name TAUILOPEPE MAUGA NAMAUAIVAO. He concentrated again but couldn't think of any more English words. He coughed, tore out the page that was now filled with words, folded it neatly, and placed it in his lap.

On the top of the next page he printed his name. Licked the pencil point as he pondered hard. Ah! Printed the word PIG under his name. Then CHICKEN. Squinted. Scratched his head. Started sweating. Flicked through the Bible for inspiration. The tide was rushing in over the reef; he could hear the monotonous roar. The page was a blank. His mind was a muddle. Sunday was an empty pulpit and everyone in Sapepe laughing at him. Failed again, they'd say. He shouldn't have hurt the pig, that's why God was punishing him. He daren't think of Moa and their adultery. He prayed a short desperate prayer. Opened the Bible. Closed it. Opened it. Shit! He swore over the Bible without meaning to, and then expected the wrathful bolt of lightning to strike him. It didn't come. God was still on his side. Looked at the blank page. The pencil plunged down again. Printed MONEY. He tensed. Inspiration. Divine inspiration. Printed SUCCESS. Then GOD. Put the three words together in heavier print: MONEY, SUCCESS, GOD. There it was. Yes! How about GOD, MONEY, SUCCESS? Not quite. He could feel it coming, as surely as the roaring tide. The pencil descended again, the page opening to welcome it. Yes! GOD, MONEY, AND SUCCESS. The sermon. The text of his sermon. As God had inspired Moses to carve the Ten Commandments on the stone tablets, so God had inspired his unworthy hand to put these words on paper. No other explanation for it.

As the sun toppled behind the horizon's edge in a blaze of purple light he started to compose the body of his sermon. The words flowed on to the paper easily, God inspired he believed. Evening prayers and the meal interrupted his work. But afterwards he continued writing and writing until he had enough material for three sermons at least. He hoped to use it in future.

When the cock crowed in the early hours of Saturday morning he extinguished the lamp, went out and urinated into the grass, returned, and, yawning loudly, got under the mosquito net. Lupe woke when he touched her. He pushed his whole body against her back, reached over her hip and, caressing her belly, pondered the greatest miracle of the Lord — a growing child safe in its mother's womb.

As his fingers moved over her warm fullness he asked her if the baby was all right. She said she was tired. But his hand moved down and he thought of the bush (and of how he was conquering it) and the new crops (and of how he had planted them) and the banyan tree (and of how he was going to burn it down) and Moa (and of how he was the only man who could satisfy her) and then of the silk smoothness and moist heat of the petals under his fingers, and he whispered:

'You love me, don't you?'

She gave in to his demand.

'God, Money, and Success,' he murmured before he fell asleep.

Lupe stared into the darkness. She felt a twitch in the pit of her belly and thought of their unborn child. She started to cry but there was only the dark to comfort her.

10 The Day of the Sermon

Under the supervision of Faitoaga, Lupe's brother who had returned from Savaii the day before, Tauilopepe's aiga worked hard at making the Sunday umu. Tauilopepe, who usually made the umu, watched from the main fale. The wood-smoke rising from all the kitchen fale in the village hung over everything like a light fog. A while later Tauilopepe got his starched white shirt and new black tie, placed them carefully on a clean mat, and sat down again to begin reading his sermon.

Vao brought him some soap and a basin of water. He hummed as he shaved, and examined his face in the small hand-mirror—the only mirror they owned. After shaving he went to bathe in the pool. When he returned he found that the umu was already covered and Faitoaga was smoking a cigarette in the shade. In the fale Pepe handed him his white lavalava. The last things he put on, slowly, delicately, were his new sandals. He had never worn sandals before. Then he slicked down his hair with thick brilliantine and took his pandanus fan, Bible, and sermon.

As usual he stopped under the kapok trees in front of Toasa's fale and waited for him. He had never felt better in his life. This was a new beginning.

'Going to let them have it today?' Toasa asked as they walked along. Tauilopepe just grinned.

'You don't look well.'

'I feel well,' Tauilopepe said. The fog of wood-smoke had lifted but the air was still dizzy with the pungent smell of burnt wood. As they went through the village, people, all dressed in white, emerged from their fale and headed toward the church. Many of them greeted Toasa and Tauilopepe.

'When I was a boy,' Toasa said, 'we used to look forward to Sundays, not because of religion but because we didn't have to do so much work. We weren't at the beck and call of adults all day long, eh. I suppose children today like Sundays for the same reason.' Tauilopepe remembered that as a boy he had sometimes been allowed to go swimming in the Sunday sea after toonai. But it had had to be in adult silence. Once, in their joyful splashing and games, they forgot that rule and yelled and screamed. God's wrath descended on them in the form of his father's fierce hand. 'Are you sure you're well, eh?' Toasa asked again. Tauilopepe nodded.

A short distance ahead, looking as if they were floating a few inches above the road because of the heat waves, shuffled a woman and a boy — the boy was leading the woman by the hand.

Toasa and Tauilopepe caught up to them. 'Are you well, Nofo?' Toasa greeted her.

'Very well, thank you,' she said. Toasa took her hand; the boy ran on ahead. Tauilopepe tried not to look at her blind face.

'Isn't Taifau, that good-for-nothing who calls himself your husband, coming to church?' Toasa asked.

She shook her head and said, 'He is very sick.'

'What he needs is a good spell of hard honest work,' said Toasa. Nofo's aiga was the poorest in Sapepe, and as Tauilopepe looked at her shadow he vowed to help them; after all the Aiga Taifau were a minor branch of his aiga, having originated from a couple who had fled from another district to find refuge with the Aiga Tauilopepe.

'But where would he get work?' Nofo asked.

'He can come and work for me,' Tauilopepe said.

'I'll make sure he comes tomorrow,' she said. 'Thank you.'

When they reached the church, Toasa led Nofo up the front steps. Tauilopepe made his way to the rear door where Filipo was waiting for him. The church bells tolled loud and metallic.

'Ready?' Filipo asked, waving a feathered fan across his sweating face. As he followed Filipo into the church Tauilopepe felt disappointed because he didn't have a wristwatch and a tie-pin like Filipo, but he healed the hurt by telling himself he'd soon have all these things and more.

Once he was in full view of the congregation his heart struggled like a hooked fish and he didn't even hear the organ playing or see Filipo take a seat immediately in front of the pulpit. He glanced at the congregation and mounted the pulpit steps. The congregation fell silent and the silence buzzed in his ears as he knelt out of sight in the pulpit and prayed.

Then he forced himself to his feet. The congregation started to sing the opening chorus. Row after row of sceptical faces confronted him: most of the people were waiting for him to fail again, he imagined. He looked at the ceiling. Gay paintings of winged angels and cherubim blowing golden trumpets gazed down at him. He looked at the back wall, at the sprawling painting of the Crucifixion, at the tortured figure of Christ nailed to a blue cross, at the anguished expression on the face, at the glittering crown of thorns and the blood trickling out of the wounds. Just below the Crucifixion, in the last pew, sat Toasa. He smiled at Tauilopepe whose fear diminished a little. Tauilopepe sang hesitantly at first; then, as he continued to look at Toasa, more confidently. After a while he found he could look directly at the congregation. Even though they weren't looking at him, they were, he sensed, observing his every move, especially Malo and Moa who occupied the pew immediately behind Filipo.

All the children were sitting on mats on the floor at the front. He saw Pepe among them. Pepe smiled at him. The shaking drained out of his knees as the hymn cascaded through the church windows and across the sun-drenched village. Masina and Lupe were in the middle of the congregation; they looked worried. The hymn ended, the congregation coughed and fidgeted. He clasped his hands together and swallowed hard. 'Let us pray,' he said. He bowed his head quickly and raced through a short prayer. Then he announced the number of the next hymn and slumped down into his chair, his body sticky with sweat. He looked down at Filipo but the pastor was too preoccupied with fanning himself to offer him any encouragement. Every time he placed his hands on his thighs he left wet handprints on his lavalava. He searched again for

Toasa, and found the old man gazing up at him as though saying, You're doing well!

Opening the Bible, he sought the chapter he had planned to read. The hymn ended. He still hadn't found the place. He scrambled up and started to read from Genesis. As he listened to the rich baritone sound of his own voice echoing through the church his self-confidence revived, and he raised his arms, believing he was injecting the congregation with the power of God through the beauty of his own voice and dramatic presentation. '"... And God called the dry land Earth; and the gathering together of the waters called He Seas: and God saw that it was good. And God said ...."' He read and read.

Someone coughed loudly. Toasa. Tauilopepe stopped reading, banged a clenched fist into the cushion on the pulpit, announced the next hymn, and sat down. Fears of failure had been replaced by self-righteous anger, caused, so he told himself, by the hardened indifference of the people he was trying to educate with God's wisdom. Anchored to the pulpit by this notion, he was not afraid of the congregation any more. Filipo was nodding to sleep behind the fan. Tauilopepe stared coldly at him.

He flipped through the Bible and stopped at an appropriate passage that would convey God's wrath to the congregation. He wiped the sweat and hair-oil off his forehead with his hands. The bouquets of frangipani just below the pulpit were starting to droop in the heat, brown spots were spreading across the petals.

One boy yawned too loudly immediately after the hymn, and Filipo's wife, Taulua, cuffed him across the head. The boy sniffed his tears into his hands. Tauilopepe sprang to his feet before the congregation had settled down fully, shouting: '"And the Lord spake unto Moses, saying, Again, thou shalt say to the children of Israel, Whosoever *he be* of the children of Israel, or of the strangers that sojourn in Israel, that giveth *any* of his seed unto Molech; he shall surely be put to death: the people of the land shall stone him with stones. ..."' He didn't hear the words but he felt their weight of wrath descending on the congregation. Even Filipo was sitting up and wide awake. Tauilopepe's fist punched at the pulpit. '"...Then I will set my face against that man, and against his family, and will cut him off, and all that go a whoring after him, to commit whoredom with Molech. ..."' He studied the congregation as he read. Some of the women had bowed their heads. '"...And if a man lie with a beast, he shall surely be put to death: and ye shall slay the beast."' Lupe looked away from him as he continued, '"And if a man shall take his sister, his father's daughter, or his mother's daughter, and see her nakedness, and she see his nakedness; it is a wicked thing; and they shall be cut off in the sight of their people. ..."' He gasped audibly when he saw Moa gazing up at him, skipped the rest of the verses, and ended, '"Ye shall therefore keep all my statutes, and all my judgements, and do them: that the land, whither I bring you to dwell therein, spue you not out."' Slammed the Bible shut. Prayed.

As the fourth hymn was being sung, he spread out his sermon on the pulpit, and studied the congregation again; now even Filipo looked receptive and eager for his sermon. He tried not to look at Moa. The church was flooded with heat. Some of the children were asleep.

He cleared his throat with a muffled cough and intoned, ' "God, Money, and Success".' He repeated this 'text' when he saw that Toasa and Filipo looked deeply interested. To further emphasise its importance he said it a third time, but in English. With that manoeuvre he captured the full attention of everyone who was still awake. 'To believe in and to follow God is to find Success,' he said. 'To be successful is to have found God. To love Jesus Christ is the path to Success and Heaven Everlasting.' He paused. Toasa looked as if he was mentally figuring out an arithmetical problem. 'We all abhor worldly wealth when a man sells his soul to obtain it. Yes, that is the way our Lord wants it to be. But we all, I am sure, would not condemn; in fact, we would admire and praise the man who retains his soul and, at the same time, his wealth, because he has proved by this that he has kept Jehovah's Commandments, that he has respected the Lord's Sabbath and has honoured his father and mother, that he has not committed foul murder nor adultery.' He felt Moa watching him, but he didn't care any more; all that was in the past; God had forgiven him. He went on to praise men who had not stolen or borne false witness against their neighbour or coveted their neighbour's property or wife or manservant. In short, he declared, such men lived righteous and godly lives, and the Lord had rewarded them with worldly wealth and power. Apart from the few who were asleep, he believed the congregation had fallen under the spell of his sermon. Then he saw Nofo: her blind eyes were focused on him. He glanced at his notes. He felt her stare on him, reminding him of his father's uncompromising honesty. But he continued his sermon valiantly. He talked about Job, and how, because he was a righteous and exemplary man, he had been rewarded by God with all the blessings this world could offer. Then God had deliberately tested Job in order to prove his spiritual strength to Satan: his children were killed and so were his herds and flocks, but Job rent his mantle, shaved his head, and continued to worship God. Even when Job's flesh broke out in boils and his fickle wife asked him to renounce God, he kept his integrity. Lowering his voice, Tauilopepe ended the story of Job by saying, ' "So the Lord blessed the latter end of Job more than his beginning", with greater flocks of sheep and camels and oxen and asses, "with seven sons and three daughters. ... And Job lived till he was one hundred and forty years, and saw his sons, and his sons' sons, even four generations." ' He sighed and wiped his nose and face with the end of his lavalava. The congregation was completely silent. Into the silence eased the soothing roar of the surf. 'What more can we ask for?' he whispered. 'What more?' he shouted. Some of his listeners jumped in their seats. He no longer saw Nofo or Toasa; the pulpit was his pulpit; the church was his church; all the people in it were his people. Only his father and Toasa had been able to snare the people's attention this way, he thought. His father couldn't call him a failure now. 'If we preserve our integrity and honesty and faith we too will be rewarded by our Heavenly Father. He has boundless gifts to bestow upon us. If we lose them, eternal damnation will be our just reward. Eternal damnation, my brothers. The liquid fire and the wailing and the weeping until eternity, until the Day of Judgement when our wrathful God will sit on His throne of whirling fire and separate the sheep from the goats!' His voice had reached a passionate crescendo. 'The Fire, my people. The Fire and the Darkness!' Someone got up at the back of the church, someone who had been sitting under the Crucifixion painting. Tauilopepe couldn't believe it: Toasa was shuffling towards the door, mumbling to himself and taking the congregation's attention with him out into the breeze blowing in from the sea. Some of the children started to whisper among themselves. Tauilopepe folded his sermon, shut the Bible, and said quickly: 'God, Money, and Success. To believe in and to follow God is to find Success. To be successful is to have found God. Let us live as Job lived. Amen.'

He called the last hymn, and sat down.

The old fool! he cursed Toasa. Why does he humiliate me? Why?

Seated in the most honoured position in Filipo's house, Tauilopepe took off his tie and drank a glass of orange cordial that Taulua had brought him. As was the custom, every Sapepe aiga donated a basket of food to the pastor's Sunday toonai with the matai. Many of these baskets now lined the back of the house, and Filipo's numerous sons and daughters continued to bring in more. The enticing smell of baked taro, luau, pork, fish, and chicken aggravated Tauilopepe's hunger but he stopped himself from looking too hungrily at the food.

Filipo emerged from behind the curtain, smoking a cigarette. 'Brilliant sermon,' he said as soon as he sat down and started picking at his nose. 'Reminded me of your father's last sermon, the one he delivered a few weeks before he passed away so suddenly. Remember the text? Yes, a man's duty is to serve God, then Sapepe, then his aiga.' As Filipo talked on, his forefinger drilled methodically into each nostril and pulled out dried snot which he wiped off his finger with the end of his shirt.

86

Tauilopepe was back there in the fale, sitting beside his father's body. In death his father had become even more of a stranger—the cold blue face protruding out of the thick covering of fine mats. The flies. The wailing. He had felt no loss, no sorrow, only a gnawing desire to examine the face, every detail and mark on it, for proof that his father had loved him. But death had made the mask more inscrutable. And, for the first time since he left the theological college, he had wept. He knew now that he had wept, not for the man whom he had called his father but for the unquenchable emptiness which had gripped him as he sat there beside his father's corpse.

The first matai to arrive was Lafo, garbed in a gaudy floral shirt with a picture of a hula girl on the back. He sat down a few feet away from Tauilopepe. Filipo greeted him in the customary way. Lafo replied, and then got out a packet of chewing gum, broke it, and slid the gum into his mouth without offering any to the others. 'A very good sermon,' Lafo congratulated Tauilopepe. Lafo was a deacon and had already preached many times; he usually made everyone laugh at his sermons. 'The part about Job was specially good,' he went on. 'It's hard to imagine someone suffering so much and still retaining his faith in God.'

Four other matai entered. Lafo stopped talking while Filipo greeted them and then continued to flatter Tauilopepe, his nicotine-stained teeth chopping noisily at the gum.

Tauilopepe stopped listening and recalled the last influenza epidemic in 1928, which had killed his father. A Sapepe woman who had been in Apia visiting relatives had brought the influenza death to Sapepe. She died the day after she returned. A few days later her husband died. A dark fearful silence fell on Sapepe, shattered only by wailing. A district of neglected plantations fast choking with weeds and creepers, of helpless victims wheezing with fever behind lowered blinds, excreting where they lay, until the final break of breath deep down in their chests. The elders blamed a wrathful God. Prayed. Prayed. But God's anger was not to be appeased until about a fifth of the Sapepe population had died. Tauilopepe had helped his father and Toasa bury the dead, wrapping them in mats and lowering them into mass graves, until he was hollow-eyed and feverish from lack of sleep and fear. But he had continued to pit his strength against Toasa's and his father's. Believed he had won when his father, one morning, told him to go out alone. When he returned home that evening his father was dead.

Toasa yawned as he folded down to the mat, and mumbled something about how hot the day was. Lafo stopped talking. The others looked at Tauilopepe. 'That was a good stirring sermon, Tauilo,' Toasa said. Tauilopepe did not look at him. 'I'm sorry I had to miss the end of it. But old age makes a man less receptive.' A strained silence, punctured rhythmically by the noise of Lafo's teeth grinding the gum. Most of the matai were now seated. They watched as Toasa unbuttoned his shirt and exposed his navel and the top of his tattoo. 'Hungry!' Toasa called to Taulua who was supervising the serving of the meal. 'What this boy needs is food.' The tension eased. They all knew what Toasa was going to say next; he said it every Sunday. 'Put that chicken on my foodmat,' he ordered Taulua. She promptly obeyed. 'And that. Yes, that.' Taulua placed two large baked taro next to the chicken. 'And some fish and three luau, eh.'

After giving Toasa his food Taulua came and sat beside Filipo. The men and women who were to serve the meal entered and sat by the baskets of food. Everyone stopped talking. As was the custom one man opened each basket of food and announced what was in it and the name of the aiga it came from. While the man was announcing the food gifts Malo arrived with two youths carrying a suckling pig. Malo sat down opposite Tauilopepe. The other matai welcomed him in the customary manner. 'Congratulations on a good sermon,' Malo whispered to Tauilopepe. Malo's food gift was announced. The other matai, except for Toasa, thanked Malo.

One of Filipo's sons carved the pig with a bushknife in the customary way. The different parts were distributed on the matai's foodmats according to their rank. Toasa got the highest-ranking portion.

Immediately after the foodmats were placed before the matai Toasa coughed and, closing his eyes, prayed, 'Our Father thank you for this food and for everything else, including the wonderful sermon my son delivered this morning, and also for the protection you offered us this week and last week and for the good health you will surely grant us tomorrow. Amen.' And before the others had opened their eyes he was tearing his chicken apart with his enormous hands. 'Good, good,' he mumbled as he chewed at a chicken leg.

As he ate, Tauilopepe sensed that Malo was watching him surreptitiously, and his appetite died quickly, but he went on eating. Outside the sand between the palms and fale glared white-hot in the sunlight. On the reef the waves shattered into foam while the breeze rippled shorewards and lost its way among the palms. Throughout the village all the aiga were having their toonai, as they had done ever since the missionaries came.

When the meal was over some of the matai accepted cigarettes from Malo. Now that Tauilopepe had identified his real opponent in his quest for wealth, he felt a close affinity to Toasa again. Malo was too powerful to fight alone. He handed the old man his packet of tobacco. Toasa belched, rolled himself a cigarette, smelt it, and stabbed it into his mouth. 'Don't fret too much about what I did this morning, eh,' Toasa whispered. 'I was just too tired, that's all.' Tauilopepe believed him. They smoked and listened to the others talking.

Lafo was elaborating a theory about what he called the true nature of the papalagi's relationship to God: he claimed that the papalagi had magnificent possessions such as cars, guns, and aeroplanes because God had blessed them with these things; it was the papalagi's reward for spreading Christianity to all the dark corners of the earth; but, because the papalagi were reverting to sinful and pagan ways, God was deliberately letting them develop fearful weapons to destroy themselves with. They had nearly done so in one world war already, he pointed out.

Malo agreed with much of what Lafo had said but claimed that papalagi had always been hypocrites, even during the time they spread the Word. Look at what had happened in Hawaii, he argued. While the papalagi missionaries were preaching the Gospel there they had stolen all the land.

Immediately Filipo rose to the missionaries' defence: the honourable missionaries, he maintained, who had come to Samoa and who were still in Samoa had brought the true God and the Light and hadn't stolen and weren't going to steal their land. Their missionaries weren't hypocrites. Except for Toasa, who seemed too busy picking his teeth, all the others agreed whole-heartedly with Filipo. But Malo qualified his agreement by saying that didn't mean the missionaries who had gone to Hawaii and everywhere else in the Pacific hadn't been hypocrites.

'Thieves?' suggested Toasa.

'Yes, if you prefer that word,' said Malo, who then maintained that they, the Samoans, were the only Polynesians who had succeeded in making Jehovah their own, the only ones who had successfully reconciled God, Money, and Success. In fact, he claimed boldly, the Samoans were the only *true* Polynesians left. All the other Polynesians had bowed down to the papalagi; and of course Maoris, Hawaiians, Tahitians, and so forth, had all originated somewhere else, but they, the Samoans, had originated in Samoa.

Filipo couldn't let that go. He interrupted Malo to ask if he was saying that their islands, beautiful and like paradise though they were, had been the original Garden of Eden. Remember Adam and Eve, he cautioned Malo. Filipo's stern reminder of what was in the Bible swiftly destroyed the basis of Malo's contention. Even Malo didn't dare try to refute the Bible.

'Of course Samoa might very well have been the Garden of Eden,' Toasa announced. 'Does the Holy Book say where Eden was, eh? Of course not. None of our legends, myths, and genealogies can be traced to any other country or place, least of all to Jerusalem where some people claim

Eden was situated. Therefore the most logical thing to believe is that Samoa *was* the Garden of Eden.' No one spoke. They avoided looking at Filipo who was attempting to light another cigarette with trembling hands.

Lafo tried to save the pastor by asking if they believed the claim that human beings were descended from apes. He addressed his question to everyone because he didn't dare ask Toasa directly.

Filipo sighed, relieved that the initiative had been wrested from Toasa, and asked Lafo to say who had made that heretical claim. A papalagi who was obviously mad, Lafo said. With the noticeable exception of Toasa, the others laughed. Filipo explained that the Book mentioned nothing about apes, but that God had fashioned Man in His own image. Adam and Eve had looked like Him; it said so in the Book.

Toasa's laughter filled the house. Filipo cringed. The others waited for Toasa to continue his attack but the old man slapped his knee, staggered up, and said, 'Well, I'll leave you to ponder the gorilla. This gorilla's very tired, eh.' He picked up his walking-stick. 'Don't expect me at church this afternoon,' he said to Filipo, and lumbered out of the house while they watched him and felt sorry for Filipo.

Tauilopepe left too and hurried after Toasa.

'The pomposity of gorillas!' Toasa guffawed as they walked. Tauilopepe laughed with him.

As they veered off the road and headed for their respective fale, Tauilopepe remembered Malo. The heat closed in on him again.

In preparation for the church collection that afternoon Tauilopepe got his money from its hiding-place and put five soiled one-pound notes and some loose change into his jacket pocket. Pepe went to church with him.

Filipo conducted the service. Using the impregnable authority of the pulpit, and because Toasa wasn't there, he reiterated that Adam and Eve were the progenitors of mankind, that Man had emerged out of the first original sin, the Fall. Men, he warned, shouldn't believe the Satan-inspired theory that they had evolved from the apes, or the assertion that Samoa had been the Garden of Eden. Such views were contrary to the truths in the Holy Book.

Tauilopepe listened to Filipo for a while and then drifted into an enthralling world of unlimited wealth and charity and love under a just God. When disturbing memories of the last influenza epidemic threatened this fabulous world, he pushed them away. Pepe, who had fallen asleep, flopped against him, jarring him out of his day-dreams. Tauilopepe cuddled his son into his side and sang the last hymn. He fingered the money in his pocket. Unwelcome but exciting memories of Moa infiltrated his defences: nude, sweating, grappling bodies coupling in the darkness, the moist and hot pulse of her organ as he tuned her to the rhythm of moaning sand and sea; her legs wide apart, around him, pushing him deeper into her demanding clutching heat; dead bodies of women he had buried during the epidemic; male corpses with erect members, all cold and pregnant with death; maggots; and the sweet nauseous stench of rotting flesh. His lust subsiding.

The hymn ended. Lafo and another deacon went up to the foot of the pulpit and stood behind a table. Lafo greeted the congregation and then called out the name of each aiga. Representatives of the matai, usually their wives, went up to the deacons and handed them their donations. Lafo read out the amounts while the other deacon recorded them in an exercise book. As yet no aiga had given more than two pounds. Tauilopepe looked anxiously at Malo.

Moa marched up the aisle when Malo's name was called. Tauilopepe waited. 'Three pounds from Malo and his aiga!' Lafo announced. Tauilopepe took out four pounds and, waking Pepe, put the money into his hand. Masina was gazing at him; she was expecting him to give more than Malo; it was a matter of aiga pride.

Pepe hurried up the aisle when it was his aiga's turn and slapped the money down on the table.

'Four pounds from Tauilopepe and his beloved aiga!' came the thrilling announcement. No one had ever outbid Malo before. Tauilopepe was fearfully expecting Malo to

92

send up someone with more money but he didn't.

Tauilopepe waited for Pepe but he went and sat down beside Nofo. The name of her aiga was called. Pepe took her donation to Lafo. 'Two shillings from Nofo and her aiga!' Most of the congregation, knowing that Nofo could ill-afford the money, thanked her.

Tauilopepe felt humiliated. He believed that Pepe, by associating himself with such a miserable gift, had associated the Aiga Tauilopepe with poverty in front of all Sapepe. He motioned Pepe over, gave him some loose change, and told him to take the money to Lafo on behalf of Nofo.

'A further five shillings from Nofo and her beloved aiga!' Lafo announced.

Tauilopepe looked at Nofo. Her blindness didn't distress him any more. Besides giving money on her behalf he was going to provide Taifau, her husband and the most worthless man in Sapepe, with work; the money he was going to pay Taifau would save Nofo and her children from the humiliations of poverty.

'True charity for the work of our Saviour is the true path to eternal salvation!' Lafo proclaimed.

11 Dog

Taifau had disappeared from Sapepe at the age of seventeen, with nothing but a reputation for cowardice and endless boasting. He had returned eleven years later with a blind wife and a guitar which, he liked to boast, had been given to him by a papalagi priest who had *adopted* him (many Sapepeans reckoned he had stolen the guitar) and, he claimed, had rewarded him with the guitar after he had spent two years training and conducting the priest's church choir. He refused, however, to name the priest and his village. He talked endlessly about the guitar but he never talked about Nofo, his wife. If his stories about his numerous and beautiful conquests were so true why, the sceptics asked him, had he taken a blind woman as his wife? Surely he could have done better! Because she was the *best*, Taifau claimed. Best at what? someone asked. Best at *listening*, and she didn't mind him being an ugly coward; after all, she couldn't see him.

In Sapepe, Taifau's cowardice was a household word. It was used as a standard for measuring the cowardice of others. 'He's less of a coward than Taifau,' the villagers would say. The remarkable part of it was that in spite of his cowardice the young men and all the other males who envied his reputation as a seducer and musician viewed him with begrudging respect. The one quality that would destroy a man in Sapepe (and in the whole of Samoa) was a reputation for being chicken-hearted; the main virtue required of any male, children included, was personal courage, especially in physical combat of any sort. The future belonged to those who completely disregarded whether they lived or died. To be taken seriously a man had to react instantly to insult, meet a row head-on, and have captivating tales of personal bravery to relate. Taifau was the exception to this rule. He was Taifau, and Taifau couldn't be anything else but a coward, the Sapepeans contended. They were, one could almost say, extremely proud of possessing the most chicken-hearted man in Samoa (and probably in the whole world). Over the years stories of Taifau's complete lack of courageous intestines, as Toasa put it, became a much discussed aspect of Sapepe history, and of stories which the Sapepeans related with boastful pride to other villagers.

For example, it was related how when Taifau was caught red-handed stealing Filipo's chickens he prostrated his meagre frame before the irate pastor and prayed: 'O Lord, O Merciful Protector of righteous men as well as thieves like this unworthy person, please protect your starving servant from the wrath of men who at this very moment are ready to kill your hungry and helpless creation. Men who, while this thief is praying, are committing sinful sacrilege by not kneeling beside this unworthy person and asking You to forgive them for committing foul murder in their hearts!' While he was praying and weeping profusely he kept an eye on Filipo and his aiga who suddenly grew afraid of Jehovah and started to pray for forgiveness.

Then there was a more recent incident when Taifau organised the seduction of the young taupou of the neighbouring village. One night, after he had boasted for at least an hour about the time he had seduced a pastor's daughter while her parents and a houseful of people snored all around her, his listeners, six youths, challenged him to put his infallible methods to the test. He asked them to name the maiden. They named the daughter of the leading alii of the next village.

Two nights later Taifau and the six youths disappeared from Sapepe. (It had taken Taifau two nights to persuade his cohorts that one of them should have the *privilege* of seducing the taupou. It would be as easy as squeezing coconut cream, he told them, because his plan was foolproof.) Each youth carried a palm-frond basket large enough for a man to hide under. They made their way stealthily through the plantations to wait under the huge mango trees behind the alii's fale. To prove further that his plan was indeed foolproof Taifau didn't have a basket: they wouldn't really need the baskets, he told his disciples. Just wait and see.

The youth who had been chosen to execute the most rewarding part of the operation was a skinny virgin by the name of Fa'atasi. (Naturally he was the only one who knew he was a virgin.) Taifau and the other youths were to hide at strategic points outside the fale to make sure that no one entered or left it and so ruined the caper. Taifau of course allocated himself the safest position.

Sure that the aiga were asleep they crept towards the fale, so the story went. The quarter moon gave just enough light to see by. A favourable omen, Taifau remarked to his disciples. Fa'atasi's chattering teeth suddenly shattered the silence, and four of the gallants had to physically restrain Taifau, who was nearly hysterical with fear, while one clapped a choking hand over Fa'atasi's mouth. An hour or so later, after Taifau had been persuaded that everything was still all right and Fa'atasi's courage had been restored by juicy visions of a juicy maiden, they went into action. But before Fa'atasi started for the fale Taifau altered his foolproof plan slightly: Fa'atasi had to leave his basket with him. It would only impede his progress, Taifau told him.

Fa'atasi's instructions were these: he was to crawl into the fale, creep over the sleepers, find the taupou (according to Taifau, she would be sleeping near her father), give her a short right jab in the gut to knock her out, and then the rewarding rest was up to him. Fa'atasi crawled over the paepae and disappeared into the darkness of the fale. The others took up their positions. Taifau sheltered behind two boulders directly in front of the fale. He not only prayed but he got under the basket to do so, the story went.

It was almost as if the aiga had been waiting for poor Fa'atasi. He came catapulting out of the fale, with a pack of insulted males pounding after him and yelping for his blood. The baskets had been brought for the gallants to hide under in case of such an emergency. (Taifau reckoned they would look like boulders in the darkness and the pursuers would streak by without taking any notice of them.)

96

They were to remain under the baskets until the enemy had passed. But before Fa'atasi cleared the edge of the paepae Taifau was up and away — faster even than his namesake the dog, Sapepeans will tell you. He cleared the high rock fence with a dive and plunged into the safety of the plantations. Fa'atasi was not so lucky. (Not that Fa'atasi had been blessed with luck at any point in his life, the story went.) He hadn't even got within a foot of the taupou. And, as he was scrambling frantically up the rock fence in flight, a couple of stinging stones, hurled by his pursuers, winged him. He was unconscious, bloody, and broken-ribbed when the taupou's aiga delivered him to the village medical station. The other youths had remained under their baskets until Fa'atasi's pursuers whizzed by and had then fled in all directions, eventually returning safely to Sapepe, threatening to murder their leader who had left on the earliest bus bound for Apia Hospital where he was admitted for observation after throwing what the doctors diagnosed as an epileptic fit. He stayed in hospital for over two months: every time he feared the doctors were going to discharge him he threw another convincing fit. Such a lovable coward, most Sapepeans would tell you. Even a scarred-for-life Fa'atasi forgave him.

Just as the Aiga Tauilopepe were sitting down to their Monday morning meal, Tauilopepe sighted Taifau heading towards their fale and remembered he had promised Nofo a job for him. (Taifau was notorious for his perfectly-timed arrivals at other people's homes just before mealtimes.) The enormous silver buckle of his belt glinted in the light. Like the guitar, which Tauilopepe had also heard about, Taifau had a very involved story concerning the belt. It had something to do with how Taifau had saved the life of a schooner captain. As far back as Tauilopepe could remember, Taifau had been a story-teller, a liar. It was almost impossible to distinguish the truth from the tall tales. No Sapepean knew who Taifau's father was, only that his mother, after visiting a village in Savaii, had returned with Taifau in her belly. Tauilopepe's earliest memories of Taifau were of a boy who looked like a plucked rooster. In fact, as children they had called Taifau 'Rooster', not only because he looked like one and could crow inimitably but because he could also make his penis rise with the first flick of his hand.

'Bring our *guest* something to eat,' Tauilopepe told his daughters, as Taifau, even when invited to enter through the front of the fale, made his way round to the back posts.

He came in with bowed head and flopped down cross-legged by one of the back posts near Lupe and the girls. Vao and Niu giggled. Taifau didn't seem to notice. Vao placed a foodmat before him. 'No thank you,' he said, 'I've just eaten.' Vao left the foodmat where it was. Pepe, who had been in the kitchen fale, rushed in, sat down beside Taifau, and started talking to him.

'Greetings to your lordship, the great musician and provider. Welcome to our humble home,' Masina said. The girls giggled behind their hands.

Taifau smiled and, breathing in deeply, said, 'Thank you. This unworthy person feels honoured to be here. Here in the home of the most distinguished aiga in Sapepe, the aiga who not only founded Sapepe but who were responsible for bringing it fame, fortune, and *class*. Without the Aiga Tauilopepe this district and all the people in it would not have become what they are today.' Paused, wiped the mucus out of the corners of his eyes with his fingers, then addressed Tauilopepe. 'Sir, the most noble son of Sapepe and heir to Sapepe, this unworthy person has come to accept the great work you promised my most unworthy wife. ...' As he continued, his flattery became more hypnotic and Tauilopepe gradually warmed towards him.

'Come on, Taifau,' Masina interrupted. 'Stop acting and eat.'

Taifau blinked, smiled, but continued, 'This unworthy person has come to seek your patronage and protection. Not only this unworthy person but this person's sick wife and mother, his numerous and hungry children, and all the ungrateful members of his unworthy aiga. We all seek your generous protection because we are weak and poor. And, as the Good Book states, the poor and the weak need the help and protection and guidance of the strong. We are also the same aiga. This unworthy person well knows and appreciates the fact that your illustrious and kind forbears saved the miserable ancestors of this person. . . .'

Tauilopepe had always been revolted by Taifau's physical appearance. Besides the eyes, milky white with cataracts, and the skin, covered with ugly ringworm, scars of healed yaws and sores spotted Taifau's legs and arms. His teeth were brown and rotten with decay. It was a byword in Sapepe that Taifau disliked soap and water. But, as Tauilopepe floated in the silver stream of Taifau's flattery, he decided that the physically revolting little man was worth reforming, saving, redeeming. The rest of Tauilopepe's aiga also grew enraptured with Taifau's dramatic performance.

'All right!' Tauilopepe laughed. Taifau stopped talking. 'You can start work today. How much pay would you like?'

'Anything, sir. Anything that will be adequate to support this unworthy person's sightless wife, aging mother, six children, and fifteen worthless relatives, sir.'

'I'll think about it.'

All through the meal Taifau continued his captivating monologue, which covered topics from theology to agriculture, the town and motor cars. He would raise his eyes heavenwards from time to time and laugh uproariously, and he never once forgot to flatter his new employer.

'Why haven't you been to church all this time?' Masina asked him suddenly.

As if stung by a hornet Taifau slapped his knee, and said, 'Mother, this unworthy creation of the Almighty, as you can well see from his ugly disease-ridden appearance, has had his full share, and is still having his overfull share, of illnesses. People, gossip-mongers, will tell you otherwise. They will tell you, and incorrectly, that this person is lazy, cowardly, sinful, and hates Filipo, our most beloved pastor. True, Filipo and this unworthy person have had some small differences, but this person, in all sincerity and honesty, can only say that he has been too sick to attend church regularly. Just cast your most worthy eyes on the diseased body of this unworthy person. Is he telling you a lie, mother?'

Masina only laughed.

'Three pounds a week,' Tauilopepe said.

'Thank you, sir. Thank you. As you well know, this ignorant, uneducated person does not possess words large enough to express his heartfelt gratitude.' And he was off again. By the time he had finished this instalment of his performance the food on his foodmat was all gone. He stretched his belly and looked as though he was ready to battle anything and anybody. 'When do we go to work, sir?' he asked Tauilopepe.

'Today. You can take Faitoaga and start pruning the cacao trees.'

'Good. All right. Good,' Taifau declared. 'By the way, sir, may your humble servant have some of your worthy tobacco?' Tauilopepe tossed him the packet. Taifau rolled four cigarettes, lit one with a bit of burning husk that Pepe brought him, sprang to his feet, and backed out of the fale.

'He'll let you down,' Masina warned Tauilopepe as they watched Taifau and Faitoaga strolling across the road on their way to the plantation.

'But it's good you gave him work,' said Lupe. 'His aiga needs the money.'

'I'm going to turn him into a new person,' said Tauilopepe. 'Wait and see. What we need in Sapepe are hard-working people.'

'Taifau's the best on the guitar,' said Pepe.

'That's all he's good at,' said Masina.

'And he's the best at story-telling too. That is, apart from Toasa. You know something, Tauilo? I never tease Taifau like the other children. He's an...an *artist*. That's what he calls himself,' said Pepe. Everyone laughed. Pepe didn't understand why.

That afternoon, when Tauilopepe and Pepe went to the plantation, they found only Faitoaga pruning the cacao trees. Tauilopepe started work without asking about

100

Taifau. Pepe disappeared into the trees.

The sun was burning gaping holes through the flimsy cloud cover; no trace of wind lifted the heat; the scarlet and yellow cacao pods hung down like withered breasts. As he worked Tauilopepe forgot Taifau. Suddenly a long black lizard slid across the lowest branch of the cacao tree he was pruning; he cut it in half automatically. The lizard's tail dropped to the ground, quivered for a moment, and then lay still. He remembered that in the ancient religion some districts had worshipped lizards as the visible manifestation of some of their gods. He quickly picked up the tail, threw it into the creepers, and told Faitoaga to have a rest. Faitoaga strolled away into the plantation.

A baritone voice and the lilting plucking of a guitar flowed through the trees. Tauilopepe stopped working, and as he listened to the music he became acutely aware of the heat and sweat and the aching in his muscles. Stabbing his bushknife into the ground he rested in the shade. The words of the song were clear in the stillness:

> ... What benefits me if I work in the blazing sun?
> My brain will wring out dry, my skin will burn to black.
> I don't want to die from brain dryness,
> I don't want to die from black skin decay.
> But give me a nubile woman with a wild embrace
> and I will gladly die ....

The song ended with Pepe cheering and clapping.

Tauilopepe got up and marched through the trees to the source of the music.

Taifau was lying on a thick comfortable bed of banana leaves, chewing the end of a piece of sugar-cane; Pepe sat beside him clumsily strumming the black guitar. Faitoaga, who was sitting a few paces away from Taifau and Pepe, didn't warn them when he saw Tauilopepe; he just picked up his bushknife and went off to resume work. Tauilopepe stopped at the edge of the small clearing and watched.

'Light my smoke,' Taifau asked Pepe. Pepe lit a match and held it towards Taifau's cigarette. Taifau raised his head, lit his cigarette, sucked deeply, and — collapsing back into the banana leaves — said, 'This is the real life, Pepe.

101

Away from it all. Away from Nofo's nagging and the worries and troubles which give a man grey hairs and stomach ulcers.' He blew out a long stream of smoke.

'Can you start teaching me how to play now?' Pepe asked.

Taifau closed his eyes and said, 'Some other time. It's too hot.'

Tauilopepe moved towards them.

Pepe saw him. 'Here's Tauilo,' he said.

Tauilopepe nearly laughed when Taifau scrambled up, hurled his cigarette into the trees and, turning to face him, bowed his head.

'Is Faitoaga working hard, sir?' Taifau said. 'I instructed him to work hard.' Blinking like an owl peering into a strong light, he looked at Tauilopepe. 'That's the only way to success, isn't it, sir?' He rehitched his lavalava. 'Back to work,' he said. 'Nothing like hard work to keep a man healthy, isn't that so, sir?' Tauilopepe didn't reply; he picked up a piece of sugar-cane and ripped at it with his teeth. Taifau took his bushknife and hurried off.

'Make sure you do work this time!' Tauilopepe called after him.

Pepe, who was running his fingers over the strings of the guitar, said, 'Taifau can really play and sing, can't he Tauilo? Sure wish I could play like him.'

'Those things are for people who don't know any better,' Tauilopepe said. 'They don't feed anyone's aiga. Remember that.' Pepe shrugged his shoulders, placed the guitar gingerly on the bed of leaves, and ran off after Taifau.

Whenever Tauilopepe was there Taifau laboured conscientiously during the next few weeks, but when Tauilopepe was away he reverted to his idle ways, spending most of his time in the shade, watching Faitoaga working. To keep Faitoaga content he sang songs and told ribald stories about his past escapades. He even composed a song in praise of Tauilopepe, his patron. This was its chorus:

102

> He's a man as tall as the sky,
> a God-fearing, Bible-reading man.
> He's a man as strong as David,
> a tough, pulpit-loving man.

The cacao crop was harvested, dried, and sold to a trading company in Apia, and Tauilopepe was once again ready to continue planting his new estate, Leaves of the Banyan Tree.

12 The Wage Battle

'Well?' Tauilopepe asked Taifau. It was approaching noon, but, because of the rain clouds that had gathered, a dull greyness hung over Sapepe. A strong wind was buffeting the lowered blinds of the fale.

'The men...I can't get any of them, sir,' said Taifau.

'Why not?'

Taifau looked as if he was on the verge of crying. The muffled sound of thunder echoed from the mountain range. 'Well, sir, Malo has hired all of them to work on his new land.'

'*Hired* them? What do you mean?

'Besides meals he's paying them three shillings a day, sir.'

The palms were whistling in the wind but a sullen silence had fallen inside the fale. Tauilopepe, who had spent the previous night planning how to continue clearing Leaves of the Banyan Tree, glared at Taifau but saw only Malo. His move had no historical precedent: the men of Sapepe, as a group, had never received wages before; only common labourers on government and papalagi-owned plantations worked for wages. It was a breach of customary practice.

'I did my best, sir, but all the men had already committed themselves to Malo and his money,' pleaded Taifau. The thunder had stopped and they could hear the heavy patter of rain approaching Sapepe from the direction of the range.

'Does Toasa know anything about this?' Tauilopepe asked.

'I don't know, sir. Perhaps Toasa will put a stop to Malo's flagrant violation of customary practice if he finds out about it. Don't you think so, sir?'

Tauilopepe said no more to Taifau but pushed open

some blinds and hurried to Toasa's fale. The rain storm hadn't reached the village yet.

Toasa was cutting grass behind his fale with a taivai. The greyness had deepened and the wind had dropped away to a slow pulse now that the rain was approaching. Tauilopepe stood behind Toasa, not knowing what to say. Toasa's taivai hummed through the grass, kicking it up over his head and shoulders; he seemed oblivious of the breaking storm. All the blinds of his fale were down and there was no one in the kitchen fale. A large fishing-net — a circular white web draped across the clothesline — stirred uneasily in the dying wind. Tauilopepe coughed. Startled, Toasa swung round, acknowledged Tauilopepe with a smile, but continued cutting the grass.

'Something wrong?' he asked a few minutes later.

'Nothing,' replied Tauilopepe.

'Don't lie. I know you too well.'

The sound of the rain had mounted to a loud clatter; Tauilopepe turned and saw it whipping at the trees behind the fale on the other side of the road. 'The rain's here,' he said, hoping the old man would go into the fale where they could talk.

'Let it come. I'm tired of brain-eating sun. Weeks of it.' Toasa came and sat down near Tauilopepe on the paepae, and Tauilopepe handed him a cigarette. 'Might as well,' said Toasa. Tauilopepe lit the cigarette for him, as the first heavy drops of rain fell on them.

'Shall we go inside?' suggested Tauilopepe.

'No. It's a long time since I felt rain massaging my stiff carcass, eh.' Tauilopepe could barely hear him above the rain. Toasa flicked his now soggy cigarette into the grass, stood up, and, chuckling like a child, stretched his arms into the air and caught handfuls of rain which he washed his face and head with. 'It's good. Good!' he shouted. He danced a few steps forward, then back again.

Soaked to the skin, Tauilopepe was feeling foolish at being soaked to the skin and standing there watching a foolish old man dancing in the rain. 'Did you know that Malo's *hired* all the men?' he asked.

'What?' Toasa shouted above the rain's roar.

'Did you know Malo is paying wages to the men to work on his plantation?'

'What men?'

'Our men.'

'I knew,' said Toasa, sitting down on the paepae, his hair streaming water down his face. 'I suppose you're going to tell me Malo's action is against our way of doing things, eh? I thought you didn't hold with our traditional ways. How does it go now? Yes — "God, Money, and Success".' The mangrove trees behind the kitchen fale were swaying under the rain's lash, and beyond the trees the sea was a mist of steaming rain.

'If you don't like my way of doing things, why haven't you told me before?'

'I never said I didn't like them. I'm only curious, interested in the working out of the new ways. Anyway why are you so upset about what Malo's done, eh?' Tauilopepe didn't answer. 'Are you just going to let Malo compete you out of business, eh? What does the wireless say now? Yes — "competitive enterprise". Such a nice-sounding name.' Puddles had formed on the flat rocks at the edge of the paepae. Toasa scooped a handful of water out of one them and threw it at Tauilopepe who jumped back. Toasa laughed. 'Well, I'll leave you to stare into space.' He stood up. 'This boy's going to have some more exercise.' He got his taivai and went on slashing at the grass.

The storm was drifting seawards, leaving behind it steaming fale and trees and a Tauilopepe wringing the water out of the ends of his lavalava and trying not to hear Toasa's infuriatingly mysterious chuckling. Someone started to pull up the blinds of the fale. Tauilopepe saw one of Toasa's daughters looking at him from inside.

'Why don't you come out of the wet?' she called to Toasa.

'It's all right,' he replied.

'Aren't you cold? You know you're not well!'

'Just leave me alone!' Toasa replied.

Tauilopepe got down from the paepae and started to leave.

'Don't let Malo compete you out of a plantation!' Toasa called.

Taifau was fast asleep in Tauilopepe's fale, his open mouth emitting a soft continuous snoring. Tauilopepe nudged him with his foot. Taifau sat up immediately. 'Tonight go and offer the men four shillings a day. No, better make it three and sixpence a day plus one free meal,' Tauilopepe ordered Taifau.

'Brilliant move, sir,' said Taifau, digging the congealed sleep out of his eyes with his fingers.

What the Sapepeans later came to refer to as 'The Wage Battle' had begun.

For the first week the men, who were now becoming aware of their economic worth in terms of what Taifau called 'the mighty penny', worked on Tauilopepe's plantation at three shillings and sixpence a day.

'The men are starting to complain, sir,' Taifau told Tauilopepe on Saturday evening.

'Why? They're getting highly paid for the little work they're doing.'

'I'm free, sir, free of blame. This person, your most grateful servant, would never complain!'

'Neither you should,' snapped Tauilopepe. 'You get the highest wage!' Taifau cringed. 'What are they complaining about?'

'They say you're driving them too hard, sir.'

'What do they think I'm paying them all that money for? Loafing? Tell them I'm not paying them a penny more. They're not worth it!'

Taifau scuttled out of the fale into the safety of the darkness.

At church that Sunday most of the men avoided Tauilopepe, and neither he nor Malo attended toonai at the pastor's house. On Monday the men returned to work for Malo at four shillings and sixpence a day. Tauilopepe spent the day wandering aimlessly through Leaves of the

107

Banyan Tree. He got home in the evening, ate quickly, then, after trying to read the Bible, sat gazing out into the darkness. A small group of children, led by one of Taifau's sons, went past singing a new song. When he heard Pepe singing it from the mosquito net, he asked, 'What's that song?'

'"The Wage Battle". Taifau made it up,' Pepe replied.

'How does the first verse go?' Vao asked.

'Think it goes like this,' said Pepe. And he sang:

> My patron's got the penny
> to pay his workers good.
> Someone else has got the penny
> to pay his workers best.
> But God will choose my patron's penny
> and the men will return to work.

The following morning, Tauilopepe summoned all members of the Aiga Tauilopepe who were in Sapepe to his fale. He promised them a share in Leaves of the Banyan Tree if they worked on it. After all, he argued, the plantation belonged to the whole aiga; and did they want to see their aiga humiliated by an aiga of upstarts? He drove them relentlessly against the bush for about a week. They had to beat the Aiga Malo, he exhorted them. He refused to offer more money to get the men back, until a youth of his aiga broke both arms under a crashing tree branch and Lupe pleaded with him.

The other men of Sapepe returned at five shillings a day. But their enthusiasm for 'the mighty penny' dwindled steadily as Tauilopepe pushed them against the towering, endless bush. Some of them, after serving a week on Leaves of the Banyan Tree, stopped coming to work altogether even when Malo tried to tempt them with five shillings and sixpence and two free meals a day. The following Sunday, Filipo, who preferred Tauilopepe to Malo because he owed a large debt at Malo's store, preached a sermon on 'God, Money, and Success' and made favourable references to the man who had first used that 'text'. Malo stayed away from church and Filipo's house until Filipo reverted to his usual sermons. At the same time

108

Taifau circulated a new song extolling his patron's virtues. The last verse told of Tauilopepe's ultimate victory in the wage battle:

> Because God's on our side
> we have superior might.
> Because God's on our side
> we will win the fight.

Rumour had it that when Moa accidentally sang this song in front of Malo she got a black eye from him.

By the time the wage battle reached its climax, most of the men were no longer working for Malo or Tauilopepe: they weren't imported Chinese coolies or Solomon Island indentured labourers, they told one another. The few who continued working for Malo at seven shillings a day rested on the slightest pretext and demanded better meals and a longer break at noon. Without hired workers and with his savings seriously depleted, Tauilopepe pitted nearly all his aiga against the defiant bush and the insects and the heat and the feverish sun. At night, after the day's work, he would sit alone, praying and reading the Bible or staring into the shadows lurking at the edge of the light. God's divine intervention would bring victory, Taifau consoled him.

Rumours about Tauilopepe's supposed meanness to his own aiga were spread by the Aiga Malo. In retaliation the Aiga Tauilopepe disseminated stories about Malo's ugliness and Moa's friendliness towards strangers, especially a certain bus-driver. When Niu, who had gone to the pool to fetch water, returned with torn clothes and livid scratches on her face — the result of a fight with a girl of Malo's aiga — Sapepe knew that the rivalry between the two aiga would soon erupt into open feuding.

13 Feud

There it was again — distant screaming. The little bald-headed man dropped the hook into the water. Ah-h! Up. A catch. A basket of newly-cooked octopus! Filipo was reaching out hungrily for the octopus that the little man was holding out to him when he heard the screaming again. Louder this time, right in the core of his head where the little man and the delicious-smelling octopus were. Again the screaming. He scrambled after the octopus as it was dropped back into the sea and tumbled off the bed on to the concrete floor; and excruciating pain, shooting up his elbows and knees into his head, frightened the cooked octopus away for ever. 'Shit!' said Filipo, disappointed that the octopus (and his sleep) had escaped. He stood up and was preparing to go back to bed to continue his midday snooze when Taulua scrambled into the house and shouted:

'Quick, Filipo. They're fighting!'

'What now?' Filipo sighed.

Grabbing his arm, Taulua cried, 'They're clawing and tearing and killing one another!' She steered him out of the house towards the church, weeping about a vicious fight, an 'evil, Satan-inspired brawl'. Filipo was now wide awake and he rehitched his lavalava, the only garment he was wearing. 'There they are, the evil things!' Taulua wailed, releasing his arm and pushing him towards the crowd milling on the road. Filipo hesitated. Taulua pushed him again.

'It's Filipo!' someone called. The crowd parted and left a clear lane for him. At the end of that narrow lane Filipo could see long hair being grasped and pulled by clawing hands, nude sweating breasts and torsos, arms and fists pummelling at faces twisted into obscene masks.

'You fatherless whore!' He heard the words clearly, precisely, above the general roar of spitting obscenities, slaps,

110

and ripping. 'Your father was born in a shit-house!' Filipo stopped. The spectators watched him. 'Here, see this, you pig,' screamed one Amazon, baring her backside, 'it's as fresh as the day *you* were born!' Filipo trembled, gulped. 'Fresh? Touch your arse!' Filipo forced himself down the lane. The crowd closed in behind him, There before him was one of the worst evils of all: brawling, near-naked women — an obscene battalion of them — on the road and in the ditches, tearing out one another's hair, ripping at one another's faces and eyes and skins and clothes, kicking, biting, and — most unforgivable of all — shattering God's peaceful afternoon with foul, very unchristian language.

'Stop!' he shouted. 'Stop, I tell you!' The brawling Amazons took no notice of him.

A massive woman of the Aiga Tauilopepe, right in front of Filipo, hiked up her lavalava, and baring her naked backside in the face of Malo's house shouted, 'There, take that, you motherless, fatherless shit-eaters!' Two of Malo's Amazons jumped on her, toppled her to the road, and clawed and struck at her. Filipo grabbed one of them round the waist and tried to pull her back. She elbowed him in the right eye and pushed him into the ditch. Filipo bounced up, his stinging eye turning blue already, grabbed at his waist, found no lavalava, desperately covered his genitals with his hands, ducked down into the ditch, cursed 'Whore!', hitched on his lavalava again, and sprang out of the ditch and into the midst of the brawlers, slapping out at any Amazon who was near him, shouting:

'That's enough. I'll tell your fathers. I'll tell!' His blows and threats had no effect.

So Filipo wept.

His tears didn't touch the brawlers but they elicited aid from the spectators who converged on the grappling Amazons and pushed and carried them towards their homes. Some of the crowd were disappointed that the most colourful fight in years was over, so they encouraged the brawlers to hurl stones and obscenities at one another.

'I'll see your fathers about this!' threatened Filipo, who was now standing on the no man's land between the separating parties. Stones and swear-words whizzed past him.

'Aue, my beloved!' wailed Taulua.

'I'll see their fathers about this. They're going to pay, I tell you. Look at my eye!' Filipo yelled.

'Those evil women!' sobbed Taulua.

'Has my eye turned black? Has it?' Filipo asked.

That night some of the matai who were not directly involved in the feud visited Toasa and asked him to intervene and restore the peace. Toasa promised he would do something about it but left it at that. He had seen many aiga feuds, all of which had been settled by the aiga themselves. Besides this feud would exhaust Malo and Tauilopepe who would then be easier to control. And if it continued, the matai council would rally behind him against Malo and Tauilopepe.

Six evenings later Taifau and Faitoaga, accompanied by a group of young men of the Aiga Tauilopepe, sat down on the roadside in front of the church, facing Malo's house. The sun was setting, smoke from kitchen fale was drifting up through the bread-fruit trees behind Malo's house, and the children had started to gather on the malae, expecting a good fight. A bus clanked past. Timu, Malo's obese brother, appeared on the store veranda munching taro; he sat down on the veranda railing and observed the group on the roadside. Two youths came out and sat beside him.

'Now there are three!' Taifau said. They laughed.

'Three what?' (The men on the veranda could hear everything.)

'One fat hen and two thin chickens!' Taifau's cohorts laughed again. 'Now there are six. Six what?'

'One fat hen and five thin chickens.' replied Faitoaga.

'No. One fat hen, two thin chickens, and three impotent roosters!' chanted Taifau. The western sky was a deep orange streaked with pink and white. Timu was now alone on the veranda, but on the boulders and grass in front of the store about a dozen men were sitting, and more men were strolling up to join them. Some of the old people watched apprehensively from neighbouring fale.

'The hens are coming closer!' called Taifau when some

112

of the men shifted towards his group. Then he whispered
in Faitoaga's ear. Faitoaga strolled up to the ditch and, facing the store, parted his lavalava and urinated into the
ditch; he shook out the last drops, closed his lavalava, and
stood grinning at the men across the malae. Timu said
something to Mikaele, the bull-like man sitting on the
grass. Mikaele got up and ambled towards Faitoaga, his
head bowed as if he was already sorry about what he was
going to do to the lean youth.

'Goliath cometh!' laughed Taifau, who was now standing
behind his followers.

Mikaele was now standing only a few paces away from
Faitoaga. He was not a blood relative of the Aiga Malo: he
had only married into it and he therefore felt less fanatical
about the feud than the blood relatives did. Faitoaga knew
him quite well but because of the feud their friendship had
had to be put aside.

'Have you no manners, boy?' Mikaele asked. 'Anyway
why parade such a shrivelled and helpless wonder like
yours? It wouldn't even make a woman giggle!'

With the full weight of his spare frame behind the blow
Faitoaga punched at Mikaele's jaw. Mikaele's head jerked
back, only to jerk forward again as he jabbed his right into
Faitoaga's belly. The punch sank in and hurled Faitoaga
back on to the road with a winded UH-H! Immediately
two of Taifau's men struck Mikaele down.

The two sides then rushed at each other with fists and
sticks. Taifau retreated and hid behind the church and
Timu went into the store and watched from a window.

The Tauilopepe faction were soon heavily outnumbered
because the fight was taking place near the homes of the
Aiga Malo. Faitoaga and his group skilfully evaded being
cut off and retreated slowly, now and then leaving behind
a bloody and unconscious comrade, to be cared for, if he
was fortunate, by sympathetic onlookers. Whenever their
pursuers closed in on a cornered comrade, Faitoaga and his
friends drove them off with well-aimed stones. The Malo
faction retaliated in the same way.

Unlike the women, the men did not hurl verbal obscenities as they fought. (A man's courage was not in his

113

mouth, the Sapepeans liked to boast.) So the only sounds were the whistling and thudding of stones, the slap-slap of bare feet on the road, the occasional screams and yells of unlucky men being beaten into unconsciousness, the snapping of sticks breaking over flesh and bone, the heavy panting, and the murmuring of the crowd who, while keeping a safe distance from the fight, shifted along with it as it moved back towards that end of Sapepe which was dominated by the Aiga Tauilopepe. When it reached that area the fight came to a standstill as reinforcements for Faitoaga's group poured out from the Tauilopepe fale and equalised the odds. Stones smashed and gashed heads and limbs; fists and sticks pummelled victims to the ground where they were viciously kicked and trodden into unconsciousness. The women and children of both aiga screamed insults at one another; some women joined the fight, trying to aid husbands and brothers, while the children dashed in and out supplying the men with stones. None of the spectators, not even the matai, dared stop the fight.

Suddenly a bushknife flashed. The crowd scattered. The knife plunged down. A high-pitched scream and Faitoaga collapsed to the ground, his hands desperately trying to block the blood gushing from the jagged wound on his left shoulder. Lupe and Niu and Vao converged on him with sobs and shielded him with their bodies. Another bushknife. Another slash down. Another frantic scream. And one of the Malo men was down. 'My chest. My chest!' he cried.

'Get Toasa. Someone get Toasa!' one of the matai called. Pepe, who had been supplying Faitoaga with stones, ran off to get the old man.

The horizon had swallowed the sun, and at the sky's zenith the cloud mattress was a deep purple. Then Toasa was there in the middle of the fighting men. His walking-stick rose and fell with a heavy thud on the head of the nearest man. The man went down hard. Bruised and bloody and sick of the senseless violence Mikaele turned swiftly, but when he saw who it was he hesitated. No man in Sapepe dared attack Toasa: he was the tuua, the last sacred sanction; if he was destroyed there would be chaos in

114

Sapepe. Toasa's walking-stick caught Mikaele on the side of the head and spun him round; another blow on the shoulder brought him to his knees. His wife rushed blindly at Toasa, claws outstretched, but Mikaele reached out with a vicious slap and pushed her away from the old man.

'Enough!' Toasa shouted. Some of the men separated. Mikaele staggered to his feet. A man sprang at Toasa. Toasa drove the walking-stick into the man's belly, and, as he sagged, gasping, to his knees, Mikaele punched him under the jaw. The man, one of Mikaele's relatives, collapsed with an agonising moan. Mikaele and Toasa advanced into the fight, separating the men. Further away some of the matai started doing the same thing.

'Go home!' Toasa ordered the men when they stopped fighting. 'Both your aiga are going to pay for this. Send me the men who call themselves the heads of your aiga!'

The wounded and unconscious victims of the fight lay under the palms and on the road. Their women and many of the spectators carried them home.

Toasa turned to Mikaele and said, 'Thank you.' Turned and stormed off towards his fale, accompanied by Pepe.

'Was anyone killed?' he asked Pepe.

'No, but Faitoaga and someone else nearly got their heads chopped off.'

'Go and tell your father to come and see me immediately!'

As the gloom of evening settled on Sapepe, invading Toasa's fale like a welcome intruder, the old man continued to beat at the pebble floor with his walking-stick. Most of his aiga stayed in the kitchen fale, safe from his anger. One of his daughters brought a lamp and placed it by the centre post. 'Shall I bring you something to eat?' she asked. He said nothing. She left.

Toasa had been out fishing most of that day and had brought home a large catch of bonito. He had bathed in the pool and was on his way to his fale when Pepe confronted him with the news of the fight, news which had immediately turned the peace he had brought home from the sea into rage.

When Tauilopepe reached Toasa's fale he was still

shaken by what he had seen — wounded and battered men and their women, blaming him with their accusing silence for what had happened. Faitoaga had had to be carried over the eastern range to the next village's medical station. Tauilopepe's fears increased as he peered in at Toasa. He had just returned from the plantations, Lupe had told him about the fight, and he had gone from fale to fale, examining the injured. Pepe had come then and told him that Toasa wanted to see him. Now he was afraid to go in, knowing Toasa wouldn't support him.

In the end he entered and sat down at the opposite side of the fale from Toasa. 'And how are ....' he began. Toasa stabbed his walking-stick into the floor, silencing him. The lamp flickered. Mosquitoes settled on Tauilopepe's body; he ignored them. It was as if everyone had deserted him. In his youth, whenever this feeling had threatened to overwhelm him, he had gone to Toasa, but Toasa was now an unapproachable stranger as his father had been. He was on the verge of pleading with Toasa when Malo broke into the light.

'Sit down!' Toasa commanded Malo. 'You're both children and deserve to be treated as such. You agree, eh?' They didn't reply. They knew that Toasa expected them to keep silent. 'You think I'm a fool? Eh? A fool? You think you own Sapepe?' Malo motioned to speak. 'Shut up!' Toasa said.

'You have no right to speak to me this way!' protested Malo. By now the men of Toasa's aiga were sitting on the paepae, ready to protect him or carry out any orders he might give them.

'Because of what has happened you have no rights in Sapepe whatsoever,' Toasa said. 'None!' The walking-stick rose up threateningly. 'You have both forfeited your rights.'

'Why lay the whole blame on me?' Malo said. 'Your favourite is to blame for the whole affair, for spilling the blood of my aiga.'

'I have no favourites. None. Understand, eh?' Some of the men outside moved closer to the fale posts behind Toasa. 'Both of you want me out of the way so you can

116

battle for power over the lives of *my* people. You may hold the highest titles here but I hold the power. I can break you. Who do you think you are, eh? You are just the arrogant, fatherless descendants of men who drifted here. My aiga found them on the beach and saved them!' Coughing broke his shouting. Stabbing the walking-stick into the floor, he added. 'I can destroy you both. Hear me? One command from me and you're without a village to make your titles mean anything!'

'My father is right in everything. I deliver myself to his judgement and the judgement of the matai council,' said Tauilopepe.

'At least one of you is not a complete fool,' said Toasa. Malo was gazing out into the darkness. 'Well, Malo? Toasa asked.

'I have nothing to say. I've broken no law and therefore see no reason to submit to your judgement,' replied Malo.

'Are you willing to accept any decision of the matai council?' Toasa asked Tauilopepe. He nodded quickly, eagerly.

'So he should!' interjected Malo. 'After all, he is to blame for what happened. And I know the council will support my claim.'

'Get out!' shouted Toasa. The walking-stick came up to his shoulder. Malo scrambled up and ducked the walking-stick that shot spearlike at his head. 'Get out! Appear at the meeting tomorrow, or else....' Malo almost ran out of the fale. 'You too!' Toasa ordered Tauilopepe. 'If your father was alive today he'd be ashamed to call you his son. He was ashamed of you even when he was alive. Go!'

Tauilopepe got up and left. He knew that Malo had committed a fatal mistake by challenging Toasa's authority.

The council waited for Malo, they had been waiting for over an hour. Tauilopepe sat watching Toasa from the corner of his eye. Malo had instructed the matai who owed him money not to attend the meeting but they had all come: if his power was destroyed they would be free of their debts. The people kept well away from the fale, knowing what would happen to them if they disturbed the council in its deliberations. A stiff wind was blowing through Sapepe, ruffling the thatched fale roofs and chasing leaves down the road. Taifau and a large group of men occupied the fale across the road, ready to stop the Aiga Malo if they threatened the meeting. The sun was a blurred shield of light behind a screen of cloud.

Toasa spat into the pebbles. Everyone looked at him. They knew the meeting would be short, especially if Malo didn't attend.

'Well, we can't wait any longer. We'll dispense with ceremony and soft words,' announced Toasa. 'No speeches, they'll waste time. You all know why we are holding this meeting. Two men, who call themselves matai and descendants of the Sacred Aiga who founded this district, have threatened and are still threatening to end the harmonious peace of our community. One of them has submitted to the will of Sapepe, the other looks as if he isn't going to. By not attending this meeting — and we've waited long enough for him — he is deliberately challenging our right to judge him. He arrogantly believes he can do exactly as he wishes in Sapepe. But no man in Sapepe possesses such a right or power. No one.' He paused dramatically and then continued: 'The poison of disorder, caused by these self-seeking men, has spread. It must be stopped now. Stopped before it destroys us all. That is my opinion. Some of you may disagree. Some of you may think this feud will be resolved peacefully by the two aiga themselves. I too believed that, but I know now I was wrong, completely wrong. Each of you, though, has an equal right to voice honest opinions. Just keep this in mind: no one, not even I, can blatantly challenge the authority of this council. Anyone who did so in the past was punished severely. We are nothing without this district, without the history and support of this district which gives meaning to our titles and to who and what we are. This council is the will and voice of all Sapepe and cannot be challenged by anyone. This council cannot be bought and sold, not as long as I am alive, eh. Remember that.'

The matai then spoke in turn. Most of them agreed that both Tauilopepe and Malo should be punished, and

118

because Tauilopepe had submitted willingly to the judgement of his peers he should be treated more leniently than Malo. They decided that the Aiga Tauilopepe should be fined eight pigs, four hundred taro, ten baskets of fish, four barrels of salted beef, and five tins of cabin bread. But they diplomatically refused to commit themselves on how the Aiga Malo should be punished.

Toasa rescued them. 'All right, let me speak again,' he said. 'Malo must be banished. But we must wait and see if he submits to our judgement. If he doesn't do so within the next week his aiga must suffer banishment. All agreed, eh?'

'But surely Malo has shown he won't submit by not attending this meeting,' Tauilopepe protested. The matai looked warily at Toasa.

'You have absolutely no rights in this meeting today,' Toasa said. Tauilopepe gazed sullenly down.

Toasa instructed one of the young matai to convey the council's decision to Malo and dismissed the meeting. Everyone except Tauilopepe left.

'I know now what you want,' Toasa said. 'You want me to sanction Malo's banishment, don't you, eh? But I won't do it. I'll wait and watch you destroy each other. And every time I see your squabble spreading to poison others I'll intervene and help you destroy yourselves further. How's that, eh? Between your aiga and me there will always be love. But between you...between you and me....' Toasa looked away. 'From this moment on there is nothing between us. Go now! Go!'

Tauilopepe left the fale. A few yards out, with the wind tugging at his clothes, he stopped and looked back. Toasa appeared to be weeping. It didn't matter any more, he thought. Toasa was old, soon to die. He would destroy Malo. And God, not Toasa, would help him.

14 Judgement

It was so dark Toasa couldn't see the waves sliding on to the sand only a few yards away. Stench of decaying seaweed and coral and driftwood persisted as did disturbing memories of the youth Tauilopepe had been, the youth his heart had adopted as his own son. Why this had been so he had never quite understood. He had had five children of his own (two had died in the last epidemic) but he hadn't loved them as he had loved the youngest son of his only friend. The swishing of the waves washed through his thoughts. He remembered the woman who had been his children's mother: hair as soft as sand running through your fingers, body as soft as the spring water of the pool where he had first met her and she had offered herself to him. Alofa, that was her name. She had come from Apia to visit relatives in Sapepe, with her teasing laughter and that appealing mysterious quality of Apia which had turned every man's head. Tauilopepe Laau had warned him about her but he had taken her as his wife. Then the five children in quick succession, followed by her many infidelities which he had always forgiven. His forgiveness, he realised later, had been laced with an obsessive need for her to punish him. The more unfaithful she had been the more he had needed her. He had beaten her after every infidelity, and she had enjoyed the punishment. She had even confessed her affairs to him in detail; and after each confession and every beating they had made love violently. Their love had been an affliction, an awful mutual compulsion to destroy each other, he thought now. Then leprosy had eaten bone and flesh and turned her face into a terrifying mockery of what it had been, her limbs into useless stumps, and his love for her first into pity and then into shameful indifference. The day after she was buried he burnt down their fale and everything in it. Their children remained with him, but he left their upbringing to his sis-

120

ters and mother. They would mature into strangers but he wouldn't care because his friend's son was born the evening Alofa died. It was almost as if the boy had been born out of Alofa's death. With the boy his life had begun anew.

Toasa broke the chains of memory and found the dark and the stench of decay and he compared himself to useless driftwood stranded on sand dunes beyond the reach of refreshing tides. He got up and made his slow way over the beach and through the palms on to the road. Only a few lamps were still burning in the village. He stopped in front of Malo's house and watched it for a short while. So many windows yet so little light, he thought. He looked at the church — the blur of whitish darkness and its brooding backdrop of trees. So much concrete. He walked on.

Shadows moving towards him on the road.

In the darkness he couldn't tell who they were but he felt no fear and didn't try to defend himself as the shadows lunged out at him. Their violence was the shattering pain of fists exploding in his face and head, the feel of painful solidity under him as he hit the road and heard the scurrying patter of escaping footsteps, and knew that he wouldn't now be able to stop the council from banishing the Aiga Malo.

The next morning an angry council, after agreeing that Toasa had been assaulted by men of the Aiga Malo, pronounced sentence on Malo. Lafo, who owed Malo a large debt, summed up the discussion: 'From this day on Malo and his aiga will not be allowed to have anything whatsoever to do with Sapepe affairs, and all the people of Sapepe will have nothing whatsoever to do with the Aiga Malo. They will live among us as exiles, as animals without a home and without protection.'

All that morning while the council meeting was on, Tauilopepe and his aiga prepared the fine that he had to submit to the matai. He divided the items making up the fine among the various sub-aiga of the Aiga Tauilopepe, and had only to provide the tins of cabin bread and barrels of salted beef himself. He left the cooking of the pigs and taro under Taifau's supervision and went to buy the tinned food from a store in the neighbour-

121

ing village. When he returned Masina told him about Malo's banishment. He gathered his whole aiga in the main fale for a short service. 'Toasa is very sick,' Pepe whispered to him during the hymn. So when Tauilopepe prayed he pleaded with God to help Toasa recover from wounds inflicted upon him by 'evil and heartless men'. He finished praying and found that Pepe had disappeared.

'The old man may die,' Lupe said.

'Are you blaming me for what has happened?' he asked. Lupe, who was labouring under the weight of advanced pregnancy, staggered up and left the fale. 'I'm not to blame!' he called after her.

'Why haven't you gone to see Toasa?' Masina asked.

'He refuses to see me. I don't know why.'

'Don't worry about it — Toasa doesn't blame you,' she consoled him. 'Time will heal all wounds.'

The sun was a twitching eye in the sky when his aiga assembled the food in front of the main fale for all Sapepe to see. Few other people were about in the heat. Swarms of flies converged on the food; the women drove them off with leafy branches, but the flies continued to regroup and attack again and again. Tauilopepe looked across at Toasa's fale. Two of the old man's daughters were sitting outside Toasa's mosquito net; the rest of his aiga were gathered in the kitchen fale. He knew, like everyone else in Sapepe, that if Toasa died the old man's aiga — the third largest in Sapepe — would openly attack Malo and no one would be able to stop them, not that many Sapepeans would want to. He saw Pepe sitting on the paepae of Toasa's fale. Clutched in his hand was Toasa's bushknife.

He instructed the men to take the food to the council. All the men who carried it wore black lavalava and banana-leaf ula and walked in single file. Tauilopepe and Taifau followed them. Tauilopepe veered off the road and went towards Toasa's fale. Before he reached the paepae Pepe sprang up and ran to join Toasa's aiga in the kitchen fale. Toasa's middle-aged daughters simply glanced up at Tauilopepe and then at the figure lying under the mosquito net swathed in a thick white sleeping sheet. Tauilopepe sat down outside the net. Flies freckled the whiteness of the net. 'How is he?' he asked Toasa's daughters.

Without looking at him, one of them said, 'He's getting better.'

'God has been kind,' said the other.

'I'm glad he is recovering,' Tauilopepe said.

The old man turned over and the sheet slipped off his face. A thick bandage covered the top of his head, livid bruises ridged his face, and his lips were badly swollen. 'Where's Pepe?' he asked. One of his daughters told him that Pepe was waiting outside. Eyes still shut, Toasa said, 'He is loyal. He is my son.' His daughter leant forward and whispered that Tauilopepe was there to see him. Toasa opened his eyes and said, without looking at Tauilopepe, 'Now you have what you wanted. Without knowing it, I have helped you destroy another man and his aiga. I have nothing more to say to you.' He pulled the sheet back over his face.

By this time Pepe was talking to Taifau on the road. When he saw Tauilopepe he ran back to Toasa's fale. 'Children are rash and harsh, sir,' Taifau apologised for Pepe. 'They don't understand.' Tauilopepe walked past him.

'You had better reconsider you decision,' Malo was saying to the council when Tauilopepe entered the fale and took his usual seat. 'Remember, you owe me money, all of you. So you'd better think again.'

It was evident to Tauilopepe that some of the matai were changing their minds. 'Remember what?' he asked Malo.

'We have nothing to say to each other,' replied Malo. 'Absolutely nothing.'

'Think again.'

'About what?' asked Malo. The rest of the council were silent, watching, hoping.

'About the fact, the simple fact, that you no longer belong in Sapepe,' Tauilopepe said.

'Has Toasa sanctioned the council's decision? Has he?' asked Malo. The council looked at Tauilopepe; he had to save them.

123

'This council has pronounced sentence on you and your aiga. By instructing your aiga to brutally beat up Toasa, the tuua of Sapepe, you fashioned your own well-deserved end,' replied Tauilopepe. Most of the council nodded in agreement.

'Instructing my aiga? I did nothing of the kind. God is my witness. I can't be held responsible for the actions of irresponsible men in my aiga!'

'So you admit now that it *was* your aiga who nearly killed Toasa?' asked Tauilopepe.

Malo whipped off his spectacles. 'Yes, I admit that. But I wasn't personally responsible!'

'But who then is responsible for the actions of your aiga?' asked Tauilopepe, knowing that he had trapped Malo. The council looked at Malo, at the little storekeeper fingering his account book, his shirt and face wet with sweat. Malo was no longer one of them, his power was gone, and they would soon be free of their debts to him.

'Apart from that,' stammered Malo, 'apart from that, has Toasa agreed to my — to your decision?' The council looked beseechingly at Tauilopepe.

'Yes, he has,' said Tauilopepe. It was so easy to lie because he knew the council wanted him to lie.

'Yes, Toasa *has* agreed,' echoed Lafo. The other matai nodded promptly.

'You're lying!' shouted Malo, his voice desperately shrill. No one bothered to reply. Tauilopepe gazed out into the heat and sun, the other matai looked at one another; it was as though Malo wasn't there any more. 'You all owe me money,' he said, trying to control his voice. Still nobody spoke. 'You, Tauilo, you still owe me too!'

'How much do these others owe you altogether?' Tauilopepe asked.

'Why? Do you want to pay their debts?'

'How much?'

'You can't pay. They've got to!'

'How much?' Tauilopepe repeated. Malo told him. 'I'll pay the money. Now go. You no longer belong to Sapepe!' Before Malo could say anything more each matai in turn ordered him to leave.

'You haven't heard the last of me. And you haven't won, Tauilo. If I can't destroy you they will!' Malo scrambled up and stumbled out of the fale into the dazzling light and the noonday heat. They watched him as he walked, almost ran, over the malae and into his house. He had forgotten his account book; Lafo threw it out of the fale.

'Bring the food,' Tauilopepe whispered to Taifau who was sitting on the paepae behind him.

'He deserved it,' Lafo said.

'Yes, he deserved it,' some of the other matai said. They found it difficult to look at one another: they all knew that Malo had not been directly responsible for the attack on Toasa.

During the following weeks the matai found themselves working for nothing with the untitled men on Leaves of the Banyan Tree. (Tauilopepe had paid their debts to Malo.) The plantation expanded up the valley floor and was starting to encompass the bottom slopes of the foot-hills; a comfortable fale was built under the banyan tree and Faitoaga went to live in it and watch over the plantation. The Sapepeans started referring to Tauilopepe as 'the man who had succeeded'. Taifau, now Tauilopepe's overseer, composed a song entitled 'How the Battle was Fought and Won', and through the enthusiastic efforts of his children it gained unprecedented popularity. Tauilopepe and Toasa avoided each other. Pepe was the old man's constant companion; they went fishing almost every day, and on Sundays the boy always accompanied Toasa to church. Tauilopepe was too busy with his plantation to notice that Pepe was avoiding him, too busy to realise that Pepe was blaming him for the trouble.

15 Something Cold, Something Dark

Tauilopepe was sitting on a log, smoking and watching the
workers planting lines of banana trees when Vao, feet
bleeding from the sharp rocks of the track, ran up the
clearing to him. They were down at the valley floor, and
the heat, trapped by the sides of the valley, was like thick
liquid around them.

'Lupe is having the baby,' Vao panted, her tattered dress
soaked with sweat. She had run all the way from Sapepe.

'I'll be home this evening,' Tauilopepe said. But Vao
refused to leave. 'Well, what's the matter?

'She wants you there.'

'She's had children before,' he said impatiently. There
was still a whole afternoon of work left and he didn't trust
Taifau to supervise the men honestly.

'But she says she wants you there!'

He got up and said, 'I'll be home soon.' Vao turned
abruptly, ran quickly over the clearing, and disappeared
into the trees in the direction of Sapepe.

The men worked until shadows started growing out of
the valley walls and filling the valley. On the way home
Tauilopepe told them that Lupe was giving birth to another
child. They asked him what he would call his son, for by
then surely Lupe had given birth to a boy. He was to be
named Mosooi after his great-grandfather, Tauilopepe said.
The original Mosooi had eaten a few papalagi and perhaps
the boy would do the same, they joked.

From the road, with the last rays of the sun teetering
precariously on the paepae of his fale, Tauilopepe saw a
number of women hurrying in and out of the side of the
fale where he and Lupe slept. He remembered the worried
look on Vao's face. He started to hurry.

He burst into the midst of weeping women. Masina and
his daughters just looked up and then went on weeping
into their hands. Muffled moaning emerged from behind

the curtain that was stretched across the fale; he rushed to
the curtain and drew it aside. Stopped. Lupe, legs wide
apart, lay writhing in the middle of a group of women. The
village midwife, a toothless and shrivelled woman, was
massaging her stomach. He stepped back out of view. 'Ease
up. Please ease up!' he heard the midwife instructing Lupe.

'Can't. Oh, I can't!' cried Lupe.

'Why wasn't I told about this?' he demanded of Masina.

'You were told. Don't be angry with me,' she said.

'How long has she been like this?'

'All afternoon. The pain is killing her. Our aiga has sinned in the eyes of God!' Masina whimpered. 'Is there anything you've done? Anything that could have angered the
Lord?' Moa and their adultery seared his conscience,
turned his concern for Lupe's safety into fear. He sat
down. 'Pray, pray!' Masina urged him. He prayed. But
God, like Toasa, seemed to have abandoned him. Lupe's
continuing cries drove him deeper into the empty prayer,
and he pledged to God all that he possessed in exchange
for forgiveness and the lives of Lupe and his child. 'Is
there anything?' Masina repeated. Lupe screamed.

'Nothing. There's nothing.' he said.

'She may die!' he heard the midwife say to the other
women behind the curtain. He covered his face with his
hands while Masina prayed.

He didn't see Toasa and Pepe enter. 'Lupe isn't going to
die, is she?' Pepe asked. Tauilopepe looked up at Toasa for
some sign of hope and consolation. Nothing. So he joined
Masina's prayer. Lupe screamed again. Pepe hid in Toasa's
side. The old man put a comforting arm round him.

The curtain was pushed aside and the midwife confronted Tauilopepe. 'We have to take her into Apia Hospital,' she said. Tauilopepe didn't seem to hear. 'We've got to
take her to the hospital,' she repeated.

'How?' Tauilopepe muttered.

'Malo has a truck,' Toasa reminded him. Tauilopepe
shook his head. 'It's either Lupe or your stupid pride. Do
you want her to die, eh?'

'You won't let her die, will you, Tauilo?' pleaded Pepe.

'She'll die, she'll die! It's God's will!' shrieked Masina.

127

'Shut up!' Toasa ordered. 'What's the use of your Bible nonsense now, eh?' Masina wept into her hands. 'Go and get the truck,' Toasa said to Tauilopepe, but Tauilopepe remained kneeling. The pain of Toasa's fierce slap jolted him to his feet. 'Be a man for once!' Toasa said. And, 'Go and get Faitoaga,' he ordered Pepe. Pepe ran out of the fale.

'He'll refuse me,' Tauilopepe said.

'So what? Beg him. Lie to him. Give him your plantation. Do anything, but get that truck! Understand, eh? Get the truck!' When Tauilopepe didn't move Toasa pushed him out of the fale.

Faitoaga steered Tauilopepe along the road through the darkness that was spreading as though it was being born out of the throats of the cicadas crying piercingly. Every time Tauilopepe hesitated as if to go back, Faitoaga held him firmly and edged him on.

He hesitated again in the doorway. Malo was at the far end of the sitting room, huddled in front of a large wireless and barely visible in the gloom. '...*Today two men were lost while fishing off Mulinuu Peninsula*,' the announcer read. '*It is believed that they were attacked by sharks....*' Faitoaga pushed Tauilopepe into the room and followed him in. '...*No traces of the men have yet been found. Fishermen, organised by the police, are still searching....*' Malo was alone in the room. The wireless dial glowed eerily in the gloom. Tauilopepe sat down on the concrete floor and, bowing his head, mumbled, 'My wife... my wife is dying.' Malo turned up the wireless and drowned him out. '...*The Administration today announced political plans to prepare our country for self-government. In a speech to the Legislative Assembly, the Governor....*' 'As a man of God please listen to me. I beg you!' Tauilopepe heard himself pleading. 'Please! She is dying!'

Malo switched off the wireless. For an instant the silence rang in Tauilopepe's head. 'What did you say?' Malo asked.

'She is dying.'

'*Who* is dying?' Malo's voice taunted him from the darkness.

'My wife...we need your truck. I beg you!'

'I thought you didn't need anything. What's it like to know that your wife's life is in my hands? Yes, *my* hands?'

'I'll pay for it. Anything!'

'All your money — and you haven't got much — can't pay for what you've done to me. Can you restore my position in Sapepe? Can you?' Malo emerged out of the darkness into the light streaming in from the store next door. His spectacles shone. 'I want to see you suffer.' He was now standing above Tauilopepe. 'Come on, crawl! I want to see you crawl!'

Tauilopepe would not remember exactly what happened next. Only that someone, a raging replica of himself, sprang up, that choking arms picked up Malo and threw him against the wireless. He wanted to stop the man but discovered too that he suddenly wanted to choke the life out of Malo who was staggering up to his unsteady feet. The violent shadow enveloped Malo again and hurled him against the table, breaking it apart with a shattering clatter, and there was only a dizzy silence in his ears as the man advanced towards Malo again. Faitoaga's fist severed the silence. 'He made me do it. He forced me to do it,' Tauilopepe muttered as Faitoaga pulled him out of the house.

Once safely on the road Faitoaga released him and asked, 'What about the truck?'

'What have I done? What have I done?' Tauilopepe cried. The fale lamps swirled round him in the darkness; the road grew cold under his feet. Faitoaga supported him and led him home.

Tauilopepe refused to enter the fale so Faitoaga went in to tell Toasa what had happened. A few stars, lost in the black wilderness of sky, blinked feebly above Tauilopepe and the chorus of cicadas was a shrill pain in his head. A short while later he felt a soft hand descending on his shoulder. He wept. 'Your baby son is dead,' Toasa said. 'Lupe is well.' He reached up to touch Toasa, to find proof that he had been forgiven; but the old man had already moved off into the darkness.

'I am here,' he heard Faitoaga say. For a long time, while the night grew colder and the dew settled on everything, they sat together on the road. God was still merciful, Tauilopepe thought. God would help him forgive Malo for killing his child, and God would help Lupe forget.

'I didn't do anything wrong, did I?' he asked Faitoaga.

'It's not for me to say,' replied Faitoaga, who had always admired Tauilopepe and hadn't questioned his actions that night even though they had involved his sister's life.

'Malo forced me to do it. He did, didn't he?'

'I suppose he did.'

'I'll crawl to no man. Did I kill him?'

'Don't think so.'

'I should have,' said Tauilopepe. And then, minutes later, 'You're a good youth, Faitoaga. I will never forget that. Wait and see.' Faitoaga didn't reply. He would serve Tauilopepe, the head of his adopted aiga, well, because it was his duty to do so. Some men were born to be matai, others to serve: that was the way it had always been. And Tauilopepe had given him a good home and the responsible job of looking after Leaves of the Banyan Tree. 'Is it wrong to want power and better things for your aiga and people?' Tauilopepe asked, talking more to himself than to Faitoaga.

To Faitoaga, power was something for important men like Tauilopepe who were moved by forces he could never hope to understand. 'I don't know,' he said. 'It is not for me to say. I suppose if a man wants something so badly it's right for him to strive for it.' He paused and then added, 'I've got to go now.'

'Where to?' asked Tauilopepe, wanting to continue their conversation so he wouldn't have to go in and confront Lupe and her sorrow.

'To Leaves of the Banyan Tree,' replied Faitoaga, and before Tauilopepe could stop him he was gone.

Vao and Niu left the fale when Tauilopepe entered. Pepe wasn't there. Masina was smoking under the hurricane-lamp. She said, 'God has been kind.' He sat down a few yards away from her. She brought him some food. As he ate he listened for any sound from Lupe who, he believed, was waiting for him with her accusations. He lengthened his meal and tried formulating the words he would have to say to her. The years would heal the wounds that circumstances (and Malo) had dealt her, he thought.

'Do you want the lamp?' Masina asked when he got up to go to Lupe. He shook his head, pushed open the curtain, and went in.

The blinds were still drawn and he couldn't see her in the darkness. He waited for her to direct him. She didn't do so. A breeze was nudging the blinds, dogs yelped from the direction of the church. He stood not knowing what to do or say to dispel the silence between them. His eyes grew accustomed to the dark and he saw her lying a few paces away from him; he felt her watching him as he groped his way over to her and sat down. She lay completely still. He could barely hear the sound of her breathing above the whispering of the breeze. He pulled the sheet up to cover her neck. 'Are you all right?' he asked. She turned her face away. 'It wasn't my fault.' Masina had placed the lamp near the curtain and they could see each other quite clearly now.

'No, it's never your fault. Do you remember how our baby was conceived? Remember? Not because you wanted him but because you were angry with everybody and everything and used me to forget. . . .'

'This isn't the time to discuss that.'

'What shall we talk about then? Love? The love between us? Even that is gone. Or don't you think it has?'

'I still love you,' he insisted. 'I haven't changed. Everything I've done has been for you and the children.'

She started to whimper into the pillows. 'Look at that over there.' She pointed at the small white bundle. 'That is what our love has become. It's wrapped up in that sheet, and tomorrow it will be buried for good.'

'Don't talk like that. He was my son too.'

'You didn't want him. You didn't care. You were too busy trying to be somebody!'

'I cared, I still care.'

'You didn't, you didn't.' She was sobbing steadily now. He reached for her hand but she drew it back. 'I slaved for you. Brought your children into the world. I never complained, because I loved you. I watched you change though; watched your father's coldness turn you into a husk of anger.' She paused and wiped her eyes. 'There was something between us. There was, wasn't there? Something good, warm, and beautiful. But you took it away, your father took it away, so did your mother and everybody else. They took out the warmth and goodness and left you nothing. Left us nothing. Left me with *that* — my child wrapped up in a shroud. What do I want from a plantation and money? I wanted you. I wanted you and the warmth and the understanding!'

'Nothing has changed,' he said.

'Oh, the cold I feel inside. The strange crying emptiness!' she wailed. He bent forward to embrace her. She pushed him away. 'My child is dead, that's all!'

'I want to help you!'

'There's nothing you can do. Not now. It's too late.'

'It wasn't my fault. I told you that before!'

'Leave me. I'm tired.'

'No one will ever understand me,' he said. 'No one!' He sprang up, kicked open a row of blinds, and left.

She sobbed as she prayed. She had total faith in God; God would accept the soul of her child and heal the emptiness within her. While she was praying Pepe crawled through the blinds and sat down beside her.

As soon as she finished praying he said, 'Tauilo killed my brother, didn't he? Vao and Niu said he did. Why did he do it? Didn't he love my brother?'

She hesitated for a moment, and finally said, 'It was God's will.'

'Why did God want my brother?'

'I'm tired. Ask me some other time, Pepe.'

'But I want to know *now*.'

'No one ... no one questions God's actions,' she said.

'I question His actions.'

She had always been astounded by her son's boldness and proud of it. Throughout her life the Bible had been the main guide of her actions, and it disturbed her to hear her own son challenging the basis of her beliefs. She had to regain Pepe's faith in her, and through her his faith in what she believed in. 'I can't give you an answer, Pepe, because I don't know why,' she said. She reached out and held his hand. 'Some day you will find out for yourself.'

'I'll find out why God took him away, if He did at all. . . . Tauilo did it.'

In an attempt to restore Pepe's faith in his father Lupe said, 'Tauilo loves you and would never do anything to hurt you. You must never stop loving him. He is your father and a good son must love his father no matter how good or bad that father might appear to be.'

'My brother is dead. That is all,' Pepe said sternly.

She told him not to talk any more, and she tried not to cry as she held his hand and the breeze tapped on the blinds. A little later the sound of Taifau's guitar drifted in from the direction of Toasa's fale.

'Some day I'll be able to play like Taifau,' Pepe said.

'Yes,' she murmured, 'you must, so you can play and sing for me.'

They heard Masina shuffling over the mats as she went about tying up the mosquito nets. From a neighbouring fale came the laughter of children. They looked at the white bundle. Lupe began to weep again, and even Pepe's presence could not cure the pain within her. It was like something cold, something dark, lodged there in the core of her being.

16   Who Was He?

A thick forest of gnarled, twisted, tangled trees bearded with moss; a soundless waterfall streaming down a high lava-black cliff into a pool surrounded by wild orchids, ferns, and creepers; and the small child chuckling and splashing at the pool's edge while shadows watched him from the trees. The child started wading into the pool towards the waterfall. He called. The child turned. It had no face, only a brown blank of flesh. He screamed and woke abruptly to a morning sun streaming down on to his face. For a trembling while he sat there convincing himself that he had only been dreaming. Faitoaga was still asleep at the opposite side of the fale. The sun glittered in the dew which covered everything outside; the banyan tree crackled and groaned above the fale.

Tauilopepe and Faitoaga had been living in Leaves of the Banyan Tree for nearly a week, weeding and planting new crops. For Tauilopepe each hour had been a battle against himself, but he had succeeded in forgetting his son's death and Lupe's rejection of him. He had set a relentless pace but Faitoaga had kept up with him. After three such days, when he noticed how Faitoaga doggedly refused to admit defeat, he deliberately increased the pace. But Faitoaga didn't give in and Tauilopepe's admiration for him grew. To allow him a rest Tauilopepe sent him off long before sunset to prepare their evening meals, and in the evenings Faitoaga would put before him a simple meal of taro and bananas. He would eat quickly, stretch out on a rough pandanus mat, and plunge into an aching sleep. Throughout the night swarms of mosquitoes attacked him but he didn't even feel them. Neither he nor Faitoaga visited Sapepe in that time.

Tauilopepe lit a fire and put a pot of taro over it. He smoked while the taro cooked. Down in the valley floor, over the heads of neat rows of young bananas, he could see the high mounds of drying logs and branches, and further up the valley the newly-cut bush turning brown in the sun; in a few more days the dead trees would be ready for burning. When the taro was cooked he took it into the fale and woke Faitoaga.

'We'll rest today,' he said. Faitoaga nodded, waited for Tauilopepe to start eating, and joined him.

The sun crept steadily over the wall of trees to the east, flooding the whole valley with dazzling light. The village and the noise of people seemed far away, something alien to the firm friendship which had evolved between Tauilopepe and the shy youth. 'What day is it?' Tauilopepe asked.

Faitoaga scratched his head. 'Don't know,' he said.

'Doesn't worry you?' asked Tauilopepe. Faitoaga shook his head. 'Why not?'

'Don't need to know, I suppose.'

'Do you know when you were born?'

'Could never work it out. Never went to school. Not past the pastor's school anyway.' Faitoaga pondered for a moment, then added, 'Must be about twenty or something like that.'

'You remember when you first came to us Masina thought you looked like a starving puppy,' Tauilopepe said.

Faitoaga's eyes twinkled. 'She still calls me "the boy who needs a good feed".' Tauilopepe laughed softly.

A few months after Faitoaga was born, his uncle and aunt, who had no children of their own and who lived on the other side of Upolu, had adopted him. He didn't return to Sapepe until that morning when Tauilopepe and Lupe saw a youth get off the bus and walk towards their fale. The youth wore only a dirty lavalava and carried nothing but a bushknife. He entered through the back of the fale, sat down, and said nothing. Tauilopepe got Lupe to bring him something to eat. Tauilopepe then welcomed him. The youth replied in hesitant oratory.

'My parents are dead,' he said. Tauilopepe and Lupe looked at each other, puzzled. 'I have come to you. I bring nothing.'

'And what is the name of your aiga?' Lupe asked. The

135

youth told her. Lupe rushed over and embraced him, suddenly crying and laughing joyfully, while Tauilopepe watched them, still not knowing who the youth was.

They finished eating and Tauilopepe smoked while Faitoaga sharpened their bushknives. The dew had evaporated from the trees and a light mist of steam was drifting up into the sky. Memories of what had happened picked at Tauilopepe's mind. 'Do you want to come to Sapepe with me?' he found himself asking.

'If you want me to,' Faitoaga said. 'I'll go and get some taro and bananas to take with us.' He left the fale and went into the plantation.

Tauilopepe tossed out his cigarette butt and got up to wash his face in the drum of rain water. He saw Faitoaga running back towards the fale. 'They've destroyed the bananas!' he called as he ran. Tauilopepe rushed out and followed him.

He took one sweeping angry look at the senseless destruction and hurried back to the fale. About three acres of newly planted bananas had been uprooted during the night. He picked up his bushknive and started for the village.

When he got home he told Pepe to fetch Taifau. Lupe was ironing clothes in the middle of the fale. He tried not to look at her as he waited for Taifau on the paepae. When Taifau arrived, still rubbing the sleep out of his eyes, Tauilopepe ordered him to assemble all the men of his aiga.

He got a piece of soap from the kitchen fale and hurried to the pool to wash off a week's dirt. Lupe handed him a towel when he got back and stood behind him as he dried himself. They said nothing to each other. She went in and got him a dry lavalava.

'Are you well?' she asked.

He tossed the wet lavalava on to the grass, and said, 'Yes. And you?'

'I'm all right now.' She gave him a comb.

'They've destroyed the new bananas,' he said, running the comb through his hair. 'Pulled them out for no reason at all.'

136

'He...he has been buried,' she said.

'But Malo isn't going to get away with it.'

'Toasa organised his funeral,' she said. (The men of their aiga, all carrying bushknives and yokes, were gathering on the road.)

'Malo has made his last mistake.' He gave her the comb.

'They buried him in the aiga plot near Laau.'

He suddenly noticed that she was pale and shivering and upset about something. 'Are you cold? Here.' He wrapped the towel round her shoulders.

'Pepe called him Faanoanoa,' she said.

'I need a shave, don't I?' he said, more to himself than to Lupe.

'It's a good name, isn't it?'

'What?'

'The name Pepe gave him — Faanoanoa?'

'All the men are here, sir!' Taifau called from the road.

'I'm coming!' he replied. And to Lupe, 'Now you had better go and have a rest. We'll talk about it when I get back.' Lupe turned slowly, mechanically, and walked back into the fale.

Tauilopepe picked up his bushknife and joined the others on the road.

'Malo's aiga have destroyed a lot of bananas,' he told them. 'We've got to guard the plantation.' The men started to move off. As he turned to follow them he thought he heard Lupe crying, so he looked back at the fale. He couldn't see her.

Faanoanoa? Who was he? he asked himself.

17 Just a Matter of Courage

They brought the two intruders into the light ballooning
from the fale. They had caught them in the plantation.
One of them was Mikaele. Faitoaga went into the fale and
woke Tauilopepe who came out and stood on the paepae.
Iosefa, Mikaele's companion, fell to his knees before
Tauilopepe and started weeping, but Mikaele stared
defiantly at him. Behind the two men Taifau and the other
men flashed bushknives and wooden yokes; their threat of
violence was heightened by the still darkness behind them
and the banyan looming above.

'We didn't mean to enter your property,' whimpered
Iosefa. 'Sir, we didn't mean to!'

'Why did you come?' Tauilopepe asked Mikaele. He did
not answer. 'Did Malo send you?' Still no reply.

'We were on our way to our plantation,' pleaded Iosefa.

'Be quiet!' Mikaele ordered. Iosefa whimpered into his
hands.

'I'm going to ask you again. Why did you come?' said
Tauilopepe. When Mikaele still did not answer a yoke
whistled down and snapped across his shoulder; his body
screwed up with the pain but he didn't utter a sound. The
men closed in behind him. 'One more chance. Answer my
question.' No answer. Another yoke snapped across his
back, pushing him down to his left knee, his quivering
head arched back.. He staggered to his feet, his breath
wheezing through his clenched teeth. The other men stepped warily away from him. Iosefa was now wailing mutedly
into the ground where he had prostrated himself before
Tauilopepe. The darkness seemed to have solidified round
them, watching. Tauilopepe stepped up to Mikaele and
said, 'I admire your loyalty to Malo, Mikaele, but you are
not of the Aiga Malo so why suffer on their behalf?'

'Because I owe myself something.'

'What?'

'You wouldn't understand.' Mikaele crumpled to his knees when the yokes shattered across his back and shoulders again, clutching at a useless arm as he swallowed the pain and kept it down inside him. 'You...you wouldn't...understand what courage is!' he muttered. The men fell upon him and he tried to fight them off, away, but the yokes and fists and feet were too many and he broke under the pain and screamed.

Faitoaga, who had moved away from the other men to stand beside Tauilopepe, said, 'He's had enough.' And, without waiting for Tauilopepe to decide, he walked over and pushed some of the men away from Mikaele. 'That's enough!' he said. They moved away.

'Please! Please!' Iosefa cried as the men moved towards him. 'Malo ordered us to do it!'

'Leave him alone,' Tauilopepe ordered. Taifau, who had not participated in the violence, helped Iosefa to his feet.

Faitoaga rolled Mikaele over on to his back. His face was covered with blood which was trickling out of ragged cuts on his forehead and cheeks. Faitoaga got a basin of water, ripped a strip off the end of his lavalava, soaked it in the water, and started cleaning Mikaele's wounds. Tauilopepe and the other men were now in the fale eating; Iosefa had disappeared into the darkness. Mikaele regained consciousness slowly.

'You all right now?' Faitoaga asked. Mikaele nodded, tried to stand up, and crumpled to the ground. Faitoaga wound Mikaele's arm around his neck and lifted him to his feet slowly. His mouth was shut tightly, the pain was almost unbearable, but he wasn't going to cry out and let them know they had hurt him. The men in the fale had stopped talking and were watching Mikaele and Faitoaga. 'Can you walk?' Faitoaga asked. Mikaele nodded, took a step forward, and started to fall again. Faitoaga caught him.

'Don't know what's happened to my left leg. Feels numb and heavy,' Mikaele whispered.

'I'll help you home. Here, put your arm round me,' Faitoaga instructed him. Mikaele obeyed. 'Feel all right?'

139

'Yes, but it's going to be a long walk home. Think you'll be able to hold me up all the way? I'm a big man you know.' He tried to smile.

'We've got all night and I'm tough,' Faitoaga said. Mikaele patted him on the head. 'I'm taking Mikaele home!' Faitoaga called to Tauilopepe.

'Mikaele, don't come back again!' Tauilopepe called. 'Tell Malo not to send you. Tell him to come himself!'

'I'll do that!' replied Mikaele. 'Good night!'

As they hobbled out into the darkness Faitoaga said, 'You shouldn't have come.'

'Why not?'

'Look where it got you.'

'A few cuts and broken ribs, what's that? You would've done the same in my position.'

'I suppose so,' said Faitoaga.

Three nights later, when Tauilopepe had relaxed the patrolling of the plantation, the Aiga Malo destroyed another area of taro and bananas. Tauilopepe, still unsure of the matai council's support, because of Toasa, didn't appeal to the council to punish the Aiga Malo. But, using his position as deacon, he preached a sermon condemning the 'irresponsible and evil actions of a certain godless aiga against the peace and good government of Sapepe.' Filipo repeated Tauilopepe's words during Sunday toonai when all the matai except Toasa were gathered in his house. On the Monday, Malo invited the Mormon Mission into Sapepe. The next Sunday two young American missionaries with crew cuts, white short-sleeved shirts, blue ties and dark trousers conducted services in Malo's house. This only made the Sapepeans more hostile towards the Aiga Malo. 'They have allowed a heretical sect to gain a foothold in the soil which their fathers had meant for only one church, the *true* church,' Filipo argued vehemently. Prompted by Taifau, some of the young men who came to listen to his music threatened the American missionaries verbally and soon afterwards stoned their car as it was driving back to Apia. The council did nothing to pro-

140

tect the Mormon missionaries or the Aiga Malo. The
Aiga Malo, Lafo argued, did not belong to Sapepe any
more; they were aliens. The following night a storm of
stones buffetted Malo's house, shattering all the windows
facing the road.

Toasa had observed the arrival of the Mormon missionaries with concern, knowing that religious division
would lead to further disunity. He had seen this happen in
other districts, and that was why he and Tauilopepe Laau
had kept the Methodists and Catholics out of Sapepe. He
also sensed that the feud was mounting towards another
violent climax; he couldn't let this happen; he knew what
he had to do and, even though it was against everything he
had lived by, he had to do it. He sent for Tauilopepe.

'Why don't you get it over with, eh?' he said. Tauilopepe
didn't reply. It hadn't rained for a long time, the air was
thick with a clinging heat, and the grass beyond the paepae
had turned brown. 'Don't play the innocent angel with me.
Now you've persuaded all other aiga that you represent the forces of God and Malo is Satan's very own,
why don't you move in and defeat the Forces of Darkness,
eh?' Tauilopepe still maintained his silence. Even the
shadows had fled out of the heat and were clinging to the
bases of the trees, fale, and boulders. 'Why the silence?'
Toasa had to ask.

Gazing at Toasa, Tauilopepe said, 'You really want me
to destroy him?'

'So that's it, eh?' guffawed Toasa. 'You want everyone to
know I've agreed. Shrewd move, very shrewd. You're
learning quickly, eh. In a perverted way, if your father was
alive he'd be proud of you even though he would never
have played it this way.'

'Are you sure he wouldn't have?'

'As sure as I'm sure that you're not worthy of the title
you hold.'

'Why do you always talk to me as if I'm a child?'

Toasa clapped his hands and said, 'I have nothing more
to say. If you want my consent to Malo's destruction, you
have it. All right, eh? You have it. Tell everyone I was the
person who told you to destroy Malo. Tell them I forced

you to do it—which is what you were going to tell them anyway, eh!'

Tauilopepe left.

Toasa watched him—watched the limbering menacing shadow trying to evade the heat as it stalked over the brittle grass and rocks. Then he got his pack of cards, shuffled them with trembling hands, and turned over the top card. King of Spades. He screwed up the cards and hurled them out of the fale. They flipped and turned in the air and settled down one by one on the paepae. He wanted so much to go after Tauilopepe and stop him, but he knew that it was too late, years too late.

He saw Pepe running towards him. He straightened up. Some of the cards were flipping over in the breeze that had suddenly started to blow in from the sea as though Pepe had brought it with him. When Pepe reached the paepae he saw the cards and collected each one carefully.

'How did they get here?' he asked.

'Probably flew there on their own, eh,' said Toasa.

Pepe laughed and handed him the pack. 'They're getting old, aren't they?' he said.

'The what?'

'The cards.'

'Yes. Cards, like people, get senile.... What have you been doing?' Pepe sat down beside him and told him he had been playing cricket. 'In this heat?' Toasa asked.

'The heat doesn't bother me,' Pepe replied, 'and I made twelve runs.'

'Am I a sad old fool?' Toasa asked.

'No, you're a young, old king,' laughed Pepe. 'And what's a young, old king?'

'That's a fellow who's bald and covers his head with a sugar crown and when it rains his crown melts and his baldness shows, eh.'

'And does he ever grow old, eh?'

Toasa was staring at the blanket of stinging light on the grass outside. 'Yes, he grows old. And even dies.'

'Dies from sunstroke?'

'Dies from sunstroke because his head is bald,' Toasa said. Pepe laughed.

142

18　Beach Bargain

'Take it,' Tauilopepe ordered. Taifau looked as if he was
ready to bawl; he had already shied away from the letter
twice. The pigs, covered with dry mud, were fighting noisily for the food scraps that Tauilopepe had thrown down to
them from the rock fence where he and Taifau were sitting.

'Has this person ever asked you for anything, sir? No,
he has never complained about anything. Now your obedient servant wants his master to grant him this one *small*
favour. Sir, please don't ask your servant to deliver this
epistle!' And, before Tauilopepe could answer, Taifau's
eyes brimmed with tears. 'The Aiga Malo will surely kill
me if they find me near their home, sir. Unlike you, sir,
Malo is an evil man without mercy. And, as you well
know, this frail person is a *coward*.' He dabbed his eyes
with the end of his lavalava.

Tauilopepe got more food scraps out of the basket and
dropped them down on to the chomping, squealing mass
of pigs. The sun wasn't yet visible through the palms, but
the air was alive with flies and the stench of pig dung and
mud and the stale food.

'Sir, this person knows the very person who'll deliver
your epistle with great speed and secrecy,' Taifau said after
a while.

'Who might that be?'

'One of my sons. He's a boy who can be trusted.'

Tauilopepe tossed some more scraps to the pigs and
asked, 'Will he keep it a secret?'

Nodding furiously, Taifau said, 'My son is a silent one.'
Paused. 'He too would like to work for you, sir.'

'Are you trying to put one across me?' Tauilopepe said,
more out of the desire to reassert his authority than to
refuse Taifau's subtle request.

'No, sir. We have only love and respect for you.'

'All right, he can work for me.'

'The pigs are eating well this morning, aren't they, sir?' Taifau said immediately.

'Go and get him,' said Tauilopepe. Taifau scrambled down from the rock fence and scuttled off to fetch his son.

Tauilopepe had written the letter to Moa the previous night after everyone had gone to sleep. While he was writing it guilt had chipped at his conscience, forcing him three times to screw up the sheets of paper and start over again but, when he finished the letter and reviewed the events which had propelled him that far, a single theme of inevitability (divinely willed, so he believed) emerged to salve his conscience: he hadn't intentionally planned Malo's destruction — events and circumstances and other people had compelled him towards this clash, and because these events had favoured him he believed that God had meant him to destroy Malo.

The pigs, having eaten all the scraps Tauilopepe had thrown down, were now grunting and staring up at him, expecting more. He picked up the basket, turned it over above the pigs, and shook out the remaining scraps. There was a frantic squealing scramble. He heard someone behind him. He turned and found Taifau's son gazing curiously down at the pigs. The youth was perfectly proportioned and so handsome it was difficult to believe he was Taifau's son. Unlike his loquacious father he didn't say much; he was too occupied with admiring the beauty of his own body and its supposed sexual prowess.

'Fat, aren't they?' he said.

'What?'

'Those pigs.'

Tauilopepe gave him the letter. The youth took it, and without looking at it shoved it down between his hip and lavalava. 'You know what to do?' Tauilopepe asked. The youth nodded, jumped down from the rock fence, and started slouching along the path, humming. It was almost as though he hadn't appeared at all.

That evening after the meal Tauilopepe washed in the pool, meticulously. Then he wrapped a clean sleeping sheet round his body and told Lupe he was going to

144

Filipo's house to play cards. Once in the darkness, he made his way to the beach. Nothing would go wrong; he was sure of that.

A half moon hung above the horizon, stirring the sea with its long phosphorescent fingers. The tide was going out, leaving behind it a long curving line of seaweed and driftwood and the smell of drying coral. Moa was sitting on the boulder, outlined against the glowing horizon.

He came up behind her quietly and twined his arms round her. She pushed his arms away and got up. He sat down on the boulder. She turned and faced the sea. 'It's over between you and me,' she said. He didn't speak. 'Why haven't you wanted to see me in all this time?' she asked. Her long hair was a dark stream down her shoulders and back.

'Because of the trouble.'

'It's over between us,' she said. 'You've used me enough.' He started stamping his foot into the pulpy sand. Dogs whined from the direction of the village, and he could hear her breathing above the murmuring of the sea. She folded her arms. 'Because of the feud we're supposed to be enemies,' she added. He continued his rhythmic stamping on the sand. She walked away towards the water across a beach wet with moonlight.

He waited. Watched her at the water's edge rooted in the sparkling wavelets that rolled up to her feet and then away again. She stooped, scooped up some water, and splashed it against her face. Then she came back, and stopped directly in front of him, blocking his view of the moon.

'I'm bad, aren't I?' she said. 'That's what they all told me. My aiga, my pastor. Everyone. That's what everyone in Sapepe thinks. That's what you think too, isn't it?' He said nothing. 'I used to be good once. They all said I was going to make some pastor a good wife. That was before I lost my purity beside a river at night and found I liked losing it all the time. Discovered it was the only real talent I had. Making men happy. And me too of course. I bet you I'm better than your wife. Am I?' She waited for him to reply. He didn't. 'But I had to make a living, so I used my one

145

and only talent. . . . Anyway it's over between us. Besides, you've been using me to make *your* living, haven't you?' She knelt down on the sand and looked into his face. 'You've even made me betray the only aiga I ever had. . . . Do you think God will punish us for what we've done? Do you think He watches people doing it? If it's true He's everywhere He should be in bed too. God's probably got fairy-eyes!' She laughed softly.

'How's your husband?' he asked.

She stopped laughing and said, 'The old fool treats me like a slave!'

'Then why don't you leave him?'

'Think I . . . .' she began. Then stopped and said, 'So that's it; that's what you want me to do!'

He slapped up, his hand catching her under the chin and spinning her round on to the sand. She struggled to get up. He grasped her shoulders and rolled her face upwards to the cold sky.

'No, it's over!' she said. He stood up and his shadow spilt across her. He watched his body descending on her, hands tearing off her lavalava, right hand between her clenched thighs, pushing them apart, left arm and body straddling her waist, pinning her to the sand.

She struggled and whimpered for a while, her clenched fists pounding at his face and chest, but the stunning music of his fingers changed her struggling into an overpowering yearning for the fire that would purge her of that compulsive hatred she felt towards herself and all men. And she moaned and bucked and sheathed him in her desperate hand, all the time cursing him and the father she never knew and her need for him, till the violent fire was within her, raging throughout her flesh, punishing and cleansing her.

He used every trick to tune her into wanting him more and more till she was bucking high, ready to come; then he pulled out. He moved up to her face, knees on her shoulders. 'No, no!' she pleaded. He held the back of her head and pushed her face up to him, and her mouth was around him like the clutching of the sea.

146

'You'll do it, you'll leave him!' he said, pulling her head back. She shook her head. His fingers tore at her hair. 'You'll do it!' She wept and shook her head. She gasped when he turned her over on to her belly, knowing this was to be the final humiliation that she had always feared but wanted. The pain was excruciating when it came and continued to burst up her spine as he stabbed and stabbed at her from behind, his hand over her mouth smothering her cries. She writhed and tore at the sand with her hands. 'You'll leave him?' he asked.

'Yes . . . yes!' she cried.

He pulled out, turned her over on to her back, and descended upon her again, and she was all around him, absorbing every twist and turn of his punishing flesh.

'You'll leave Malo, won't you?' he whispered when he sensed she was near the time of her coming and she murmured 'Yes, yes, yes.' He lunged deep and she came full and strong and gasped into the shadow of his neck, but he continued, and she came again and ripped his back with her nails.

When he came, he spilt his seed within her.

'You'll leave him by the end of this week,' he said.

'But what's going to happen to me?' she pleaded. 'Don't think I'll do it . . . .' He clutched her down there. 'You're hurting me. Please!'

'You'll do it.'

'I'll do it,' she sobbed.

'You've got that bus-driver, run away with him. I'll send you money soon.'

'But I don't want him. I *need* you.'

'Run away and I'll join you later.'

'Where shall I wait for you?'

'In Apia where you used to live,' he said.

'You're not lying to me?' she asked, looking up. He caressed her. She responded immediately. He took her again.

Afterwards he left her before she could say anything more.

He washed in the pool before he went home.

19   To Shape for God

Tauilopepe spent the rest of that week in Leaves of the Banyan Tree. Early Saturday morning Taifau brought him the news that Moa had disappeared from Sapepe. Had she run away with some stranger? Tauilopepe asked, deliberately putting this attractive possibility into Taifau's highly imaginative mind. Maybe it was that bus-driver, Tauilopepe added. It was probably the bus-driver, said Taifau. Tauilopepe asked what his next song was going to be about. Taifau's eyes sparkled immediately.

That afternoon Taifau disappeared from the ranks of the workers.

The next week Taifau's song, aptly called 'The Mormon Woman and the Bus-Driver', spread like a raging fire through Sapepe. Every fine evening groups of youths sang it in front of Malo's house. One night some of Malo's aiga stoned Taifau's house, and the youths, while chanting the song, bombarded Malo's house with stones until all its windows were broken. They also tore down the fale that Malo had built to hold church services with the Mormon missionaries. Malo went to Apia and returned with a squad car of policemen. Every Sapepean who was questioned told the policemen that members of Malo's aiga had stoned their own home.

Bereft of the council's protection Malo became a dispirited and frightened man who rarely left his house; he also became the butt of lewd jokes, a victim of even the children's insults. When he did venture out the young people laughed at him and sang passages from Taifau's song; the favourite verse being:

> Malo hasn't got a wife
> to pass away the night.
> Moa won't come back 'cause
> the driver's got the might.

Except for a few members of his aiga and Toasa no one cared particularly when Malo left Sapepe in his red truck with his brother Timu and the remaining goods from his store. His aiga — secretly angry at him because he had caused their banishment, and unable to pay for the upkeep of the large house — a year or so later would dismantle the house and store and use most of the timber as firewood. Only the concrete foundation would be left to prove that Malo Viliamu had ever lived in Sapepe.

'Now you have the world to shape for God,' Masina said to Tauilopepe the day after Malo left. They had just sat down for their midday meal. Tauilopepe called for something to eat. Lupe brought him some food and then sat down at the back. He glanced at her. She looked away.

'God has been kind and just,' he said.

'Yes, our merciful Father has shown His power toward our aiga,' said Masina. Lupe remained silent.

They ate, waving the flies away with their hands.

'It's strange how Moa disappeared,' Lupe said half-way through the meal. Tauilopepe looked up. Lupe was gazing unwaveringly at him.

'She was a bad woman,' Masina said. 'A woman of the town. And you know what those women are like.'

'Where's Pepe?' Tauilopepe asked. He wasn't hungry any more.

'Probably out fishing with Toasa,' replied Masina.

'Doesn't anyone care where he is?' snapped Tauilopepe. 'Not even his own mother!' Lupe looked away and continued eating. 'For all you care he may be drowning right now!'

'He'll be all right. He's with Toasa,' Lupe said.

Tauilopepe pushed his foodmat away and said, 'Toasa is an old man; he can't look after the boy properly.' Masina got up and said she would look for Pepe at Toasa's fale.

Now there were only the two of them and things to be said for they hadn't really spoken to each other since the baby died, hadn't discussed the things that were wrong between them: her adamant refusal to allow him near her at night, her strange mocking silence whenever he was near her, and now her reference to Moa's disappearance — especially that.

Almost as if he wasn't there Lupe started to pile the food scraps into a basket, preparing to go to the kitchen fale.

'Why that reference to Moa?' he asked. She continued gathering the scraps, without replying. 'Answer me!'

'What reference?' She dropped a dirty plate into the basket and looked at him.

'You know what I'm talking about!'

'I only asked a very simple question. I don't see why it should have got you angry and upset.'

'I'm not upset!'

'You are!' she said, confronting him with a defiance that he had never seen in her before. (He had expected her to withdraw as soon as he became angry; it had always been that way.)

'Be careful,' he warned. 'If you know something, come out with it. If you don't, stop accusing me!'

'Who's accusing you of anything?'

'Careful. You're getting close to being beaten!'

They no longer cared if the neighbours were listening. She gathered the basket and hurled it out of the fale. 'You don't even know his name, do you?'

'Whose name?' He was holding a whole taro in his right hand, ready to throw it at her.

'His name? The baby's name. You don't even know or care!'

'Of course I know!'

'What is it then?'

He bashed the taro on to his foodmat and scattered the food and plates that were on it. 'I can't remember. How do you expect me to remember with all the trouble that was happening? With all — yes, all — the burdens I've had to bear alone. Yes, alone!'

'You didn't care. You don't care now. You'll never care!'

A group of young people had assembled on the road and were watching them.

150

'Keep your voice down!' he said.

'I don't care who hears!'

He was on his feet, ready to rush at her. In Sapepe, quarrels between married couples usually ended with the husband reasserting his authority through the use of his fists, and the people watching Tauilopepe and Lupe were awaiting this. A husband who allowed his wife to dissect him with ridicule without beating her was not considered a good husband by Sapepeans.

'Shut up!' Tauilopepe almost shouted.

'I've got him,' someone said. Tauilopepe wheeled. Masina and Pepe, who were standing behind him, stepped back.

'Where have you been?' he threatened Pepe.

'Fishing,' said Pepe.

'He's all right,' said Masina. 'Nothing happened to him.' She gave Pepe a towel.

'I wasn't speaking to you!' Tauilopepe warned her. Masina kept well away from him as she went to the aiga trunk, got out a lavalava, and tossed it to Pepe. Disappointed that the quarrel had ended, the people on the road started to disperse.

'That's all I get from this aiga — ingratitude. I work my heart out all day and every day, and all I get is ingratitude!' Tauilopepe sat down, picked up his foodmat, and hurled it out of the fale; the plates shattered on the paepae. 'You'd think I was doing it all for my own good. Where would this aiga be without me? Right back there borrowing and living off other people!'

Masina brought Pepe some food and sat beside him while he ate. Lupe brought him a plate of tinned herrings, then she went and sat on the edge of the paepae with her back to Tauilopepe who had lit a cigarette and was sucking violently at it.

'Go away!' Pepe threatened the few children who were still watching from the road. The children fled.

'Did you catch many fish?' Masina asked.

'Twelve, fifteen. Not sure. They were quite big.'

Tauilopepe tossed out his half-finished cigarette and asked, 'Where are they?'

151

'The what?' Pepe replied.

'The fish!'

'We gave them away.'

'You what?' Tauilopepe asked loudly. 'You gave them away after spending all day getting them?'

'Yes, gave them away. Five to Nofo. Some to Filipo. Some to other people we met. Kept the biggest one for Toasa.' He had finished eating and Lupe had brought him a basin of water which he was now washing his hands in.

'What about Masina and me?' Tauilopepe asked.

'Forgot about that.'

'You forgot! The sooner you learn not to give away things you've worked hard to get the better!'

'But everyone in Sapepe does,' insisted Pepe.

'You're not just everyone. You work for something. You keep it. That's the new way. That's the way to get ahead. Why do you think most of the people here are so poor? No money, few clothes, no education, why? Because they share everything with thieves and liars and bludgers and lazy people!'

Pepe shrugged his shoulders and prepared to leave.

'I forbid you to see Toasa again!' Tauilopepe said.

Pepe looked at Masina, then at Lupe, and asked, 'Why?'

'Don't answer your father back,' Masina warned him.

'Because Toasa is the one who's feeding you this non-sense about lions and aitu and sharing everything,' Tauilopepe said. 'I forbid you to see him again. And that's final!' Pepe got up. 'Where are you going?' Pepe didn't answer.

'Answer your father,' Masina urged him.

'To the pastor's school,' Pepe replied finally. He went over and got his slate out of the trunk, glanced angrily at Tauilopepe, and left the fale. Once outside he started running.

'How old is Pepe?' Tauilopepe asked later.

'About eleven. Isn't that right, Lupe?' replied Masina. Lupe didn't reply; she continued to gaze at the gap between the kapok trees through which Pepe had disappeared.

'He's definitely going to that town school,' said Tauilopepe. 'He's got to learn what life is all about.'

'Maybe he'll become a pastor,' Masina said. She began rolling a cheroot.

'Whatever he becomes he won't be like the rest of the good-for-nothing youths we have in Sapepe. A good papalagi education will teach him to work hard and become somebody I'll be proud of.'

Lupe got up and with head bowed followed her shadow into the kitchen fale and Niu and Vao.

'What's the matter?' Vao asked.

'Nothing,' she said, 'nothing.'

Book Two

Flying-Fox in a Freedom Tree

Intro to the Tb Self

There is a buzzing fly in my hospital room. It is hitting against the wire screen all the time, killing the self slowly. Ten o'clock in the morning. A hot sun is coming through the windows on to the foot of my bed. Through the window I see the plain on which this hospital stands dropping down to the ravine, and on the other side the land rises up through taro and banana patches and mango and tamaligi trees to palms at the top of the range. Further up the range Robert Louis Stevenson is buried. (If my novel is as good as Stevenson's *Treasure Island* I will be satisfied.) I had breakfast. A cup of tea, a piece of toast. They tasted like stale horse or something. On the ravine edge stands a shed surrounded by mounds of dry coconut husks. The shed has no walls and I can see, as I have for the last three months, the two old men stoking the fire in the big urn in that shed. Now and then they throw white parcels into the fire. Stink of burning meat, guts, bits and pieces of people from the surgery department. (At least the sun is not ever going to change. It is for ever, I hope.) On the platform outside the shed, which is what the nurses call the crematorium, I think, are kerosene drums full of rubbish and flies and stink. One of the old men, the one with the billiard-bald head and the bad limp, is foraging in a drum. He takes out scraps and puts them in a basket. Food for his pigs, I think. He eats some of the scraps himself. Some nights a pack of dogs hang round the urn and rubbish tins and yelp and howl and fight over the scraps of food and people, and I wake up in a sweat and remember the two old men and the urn and the fire and get scared.

The fly now lies on the windowsill, legs up, still. I could have saved it but what the hell. A fly is a fly. I must not get scared watching the two old bastards stoking their fire with the white bundles. I have no regrets. None.

There is an old woman in the next room. She is dying, so the nurse tells me, from three husbands, eighteen children, and too much money. She groans and moans all night long. She begs God for her life. A pastor comes to see her every afternoon and she weeps and he prays. But she is still going to die. No miracle to save her. Nothing. Just a scared old woman dying in a white disinfected room. I have not seen her. Perhaps like Jesus I can command her to get up, grab her bed, and go home, maggot-proof. But if the pastor cannot perform the miracle I cannot either.

My room is getting hot; the heat is buzzing in my ears. There is a rosary hanging above my head. My wife, Susana, put it there last week. Now and then I get it down and count the beads and look at the silver Jesus on the silver cross, and I think the artist who made the rosary is very good. I do not understand why Susana brought it. I suppose she is still trying to save me because when I die she will not have a steady source of money. You see, like all women, Susana has based her life on safe sources of income. I was her source of money. God, she tells me, is her source of 'moral and spiritual food'. Her poor faafafine — half-man, half-girl — father is her main source of gossip. Her poor nearly-all-male mother is, apart from me, her main source of thrilling punishment. The rest of mankind, so she will tell you, is her source of 'love'. (Love for what? I do not know.) Susana by the way was and is and always will be crazy on the Roman religion. But more of that later. I have to get ready for the doctor's visit.

I am a poet who is three months old. Ever since I got the Tb worm (is it a worm?) I have tried to put pen to paper to make some poetry. Before I got Tb I never had the worm for poetry. Who knows, maybe the two go together. You get Tb and you want to be a verse-maker. I grew old as a poet in three months, and I am now a poet failure. Two days ago I could not finish a three-line masterpiece, one line for every month in hospital, so I decided to become the second Robert Louis Stevenson, a tusitala or teller of tales, but with a big difference. I want to write a novel about me. By the way, here are the two lines of verse I wrote:

> I am a man
> Got a plan.

A novelist, so a palagi tourist once told me, has got to be honest (who with he did not say). So before I continue my novel, let me tell you that I am, as my friends know well, a tall-teller of tales. Or is it a teller of tall-tales? So please read this humble testament with fifteen grains of Epsom salts, and please excuse the very poor grammar. You see, I did not have much formal education. Unlike many of the present generation who went away overseas and returned with degrees in such things as education, drinking, revolutions, themselves, and more themselves etc. And who wave before you the rounded 'r' and the long 'e' and the short 't' in just about everything, especially their own importance. Pepe is local-born, local-bred, local-educated, so please do not expect too much scholarship, grammar, and etc. in this weak novel about his (my) life.

The young palagi doctor came this morning as usual, and as usual I pretended I did not know any English and he pretended I was fit as a ten-ton horse. He smiled as usual, he listened to my cough as usual, and he told the nurse to give me the usual pills as usual. While he did the usual I looked at the juicy nurse by his side. (Me, I am no longer interested in making fire.) I look at her because every time she looks at the doctor she has the clinging octopus eye on him, but he does not know it.

Before he goes out he tells the nurse to tell me I am getting better as usual. He smiles and winks at me as usual. I pinch the nurse's juicy backside and she giggles and runs out after the doctor. 'Get him!' I call after her.

The doctor, who is a freckle-faced, blond-haired, false-teethed, rabbit-eared, woman-scared fellow of my age and who knows the female biology from books only, knows I am a goner but, because he wants to be kind to me, he tells me I am recovering. He thinks like this: let him die without knowing he is a hopeless case and was always a hopeless case from the day he shot out of mamma to the day he shoots back into the six-foot womb. I like this doctor, he is a gentle kid. If the nurse seduces him he will be a better man at biology and everything else. Nothing like a succulent, warm, hot-blooded woman to cure shyness and a

159

nervous condition and stutters, and this doctor is a nervous condition.

I have only a few days to write this novel about the self. I was/am no hero; so if you don't like stories without heroes you better stop reading right here. Sex, violence, plenty-action, love any style, there will be in my novel. God there will not be. No saints either. And no sermons. So straight into it without any pissing around (is that the phrase?), I cannot keep the maggots waiting.

Here we go English-style. Vaipe-style. My style.

The Pink House in Town

My mother Lupe is dead. My father Tauilopepe is alive. He is now one of the richest in these little islands which the big god Tagaloaalagi threw down from the heavens into the Pacific Ocean to be used by him as stepping-stones across the water, but which are now used by people, like my honourable father, as shit-houses, battlefields, altars of sacrifice and so on.

Like all the Tauilopepe men before me I was born in Sapepe, and my aiga is one of the main branches of the Sapepe Family who founded the village and district of Sapepe in long ago times. Sapepe is a long way from Apia, towards the west and, so legend tells, only a short way from the edge of the world. It is one of the biggest villages in Samoa and it is cut off from other districts by low mountains to the east and west and the main mountain range behind it. Because of these mountains Sapepe was separated from the rest of Samoa for hundreds of years, and so Sapepe had its own history and titles and customs, different in many ways from the other districts. Things did not change very much. Life was slow until the papalagi came and changed many things, including, later, people like my father....

I get into the bus in my best clothes and sit beside Tauilopepe (Tauilo for short). I look out the bus window.

160

Lupe, my mother, and my sisters are watching me. I look away from Lupe because I do not want to see her pain. The bus roars, and off we go. I wave. My sisters call goodbye, waving to me. Lupe just stands there. I look back at her till the bus goes round the bend and I do not see her any more. Soon we pass the last fale in Sapepe and we are heading for the range eastwards to the morning sun.

The bus is full of people who laugh and talk like they are going to burn the town with their laughter. I feel hot and uncomfortable in my best clothes. Tauilo is talking with another man who has rotten teeth. Tauilo tells the man that he is going to Apia to take his son to school there. The man says he wishes he had the money to send his son to a town school. Tauilo gives the man an American cigarette. They talk about the Bible and how God is good to men who work hard and all that. It is Tauilo's usual talk. I fall asleep as we come over the range, thinking of my mother.

We get off the bus beside the Apia market, and Tauilo smooths down his clothes and leads me towards my Uncle Tautala's home just behind the picture theatre that looks like a big tin coffin.

'Now, you behave like a man,' Tauilo tells me. 'Tautala is a God-fearing man who does not want any silly nonsense. You understand?' I nod the head. 'You work hard at school. You only going to stay with Tautala until I get enough money to build us a house here. You understand?' I nod the head again.

I have met Tautala many times before. He used to visit Sapepe to see Lupe who is his sister, but it is only an excuse to get from us some loads of free taro and bananas. Tautala is a short man who is nearly as fat as he is tall. Some of my aiga call him 'Piggy' because that is what he looks like. He looks all the time like he is looking for a toilet or bit of bush to shit in. He always talks of palagi like they are his best friends. He works in a government office where he gets twelve pounds a month. Because he is a government worker with the white shirt and shorts and the long socks and shoes, just like a palagi, most of the Sapepe people, including my father, are very impressed

161

with him. Especially when he speaks English, which the Sapepe people do not understand. He is an educated man, Tauilo tells everyone. He is a palagi who does not know how to read, some of my aiga say. A nobody who is small between the fat legs, some of them laugh.

I look at the neighbourhood as we walk to Tautala's house. The fale look like old men who are waiting to die; some of them are made of banana boxes and rusty iron; and the area smells like a dead horse because of the lavatory on the black stream flowing through it. The stream is called the Vaipe, my father tells me. In English that means 'Dead Water'.

We go over the small wooden bridge across the stream and I see some children playing under the bread-fruit trees, and on the steps of a dirty-looking house sit two women who have on the lipstick and coloured dresses. Tauilo sees them and he holds my hand and pulls me quickly through the neighbourhood, and I wonder why. Then we go through a high hibiscus hedge.

And there it is. Tautala's house. The pink house. It has two storeys and many windows of real glass. Next to the house is a fale with a sugar-cane patch behind it. All round the house and fale stands a high hibiscus hedge, just like a wall to protect something from thieves. At the far side, over the hedge and stream, are the police station and prison. Two boys and a girl are playing marbles in front of the house. They come running when they see us. One boy takes my suitcase. He is about my age but smaller. He leads us to the door.

I have never been in a palagi home before, so when I stand on the steps I feel like I am going to enter a temple or something. The smell of the house and the way it is so shiny scares me. Tauilo looks afraid too. Faafetai, Tautala's wife, comes and welcomes us inside. My mother told me once that Faafetai runs Tautala's life. No wonder he looks all the time like he is going to shit his clothes.

'Sit down,' Faafetai says, pointing at two wooden chairs.

'It's all right down here,' says Tauilo, sitting on the shiny floor. I sit down beside him. Faafetai sits on the chair facing us, with a smile.

162

Then Tauilo and her go through the oratory of welcome.
'How is your family?' she asks later.

Tauilo is lost for words. He is a nervous condition.
'They are well, thank you,' he says finally.

'Tautala will be home soon,' she says. She tries to smile
as she looks at me and my suitcase.

'That is good. And how is he?'

'Working hard, very hard. Overtime all the time,' she
says. I wonder what overtime is. 'He is so tired when he
comes home that all he does is sleep.'

'Is he working on important government business?'

'Yes, all the time.'

'Did you hear that, Pepe?' Tauilo asks me. I nod the
head. 'You get a good education and you will be like
Tautala.' I nod again.

While they talk I look around and sigh in wonder. There
are photos of hundreds of people maybe on the walls —
smiling people, sad people, old people, ugly people, and
one dead man covered with ietoga, with Faafetai weeping
beside him. On one wall I see certificates like the ones in
our Sapepe pastor's house. All the certificates belong to
Tautala. I read one. It says that Tautala passed the standard
four examinations.

'. . . I will take good care of Pepe,' I hear Faafetai say.

'Thank you. He is a good boy,' says Tauilo.

At the back of the room stands a table with chairs round
it. I have never eaten on a table before so I look forward
to it. On the other side is the biggest wireless I have ever
seen. It is so shiny I want to go and touch it. Faafetai's
children giggle. The girl pokes her tongue at me. I hit her.
She cries. Faafetai laughs but I know she does not mean it.
Tauilo tells me not to do it again or else.

'I am sorry,' he says to Faafetai.

'It is all right,' she replies.

The boy, the one who took my suitcase, comes over and
sits by me. 'What is your name, boy?' he asks. I do not
answer. 'Have you got a palagi house like ours?' he asks.
'Bet you do not because you are poor.' He is the most
childish kid I have ever met.

'Why do you come to stay here?' his sister asks. 'Cos

163

you are poor, that is why!' She is ugly bad.

My aiga is Sapepe teach me never to let common people insult me so I say to the children, 'Who do you think you are?' They sit up. I repeat what I said but they are too stupid to know what I am talking about.

'You know how to play marbles?' the boy asks.

'That game is for kids,' I reply. 'You know how to spear fish?' I ask. The children get up, poke their tongues at me and leave, and I feel good because I am alone again.

I try to remember Sapepe and how if I was there now I would be out fishing with my friends; but here I am in the pink house with only the self for company.

Then Tautala enters, panting like he is drowning, with the starched palagi clothes and long white socks and brown shoes, with pencils and pens in his shirt pocket.

'Do not get up,' he greets Tauilo. They shake hands. 'Very hot day. And how is our family?' Tauilo makes the usual reply. Tautala sinks into the soft chair next to Faafetai and is wiping his face with a red handkerchief. 'Hot day. Oh!' He gets up and nearly runs out of the room to the back. I have the feeling he is going to the toilet.

'Hot, is it not? Hungry too,' he says when he returns wiping his hands. Faafetai goes out to get the food ready. 'Been working all day adding up government money,' he says. Then he tells Tauilo, who is sitting like a lost boy on the floor, how Dave, his palagi boss, likes him because he can add up difficult sums of money, and how Dave is going to promote him soon. He takes out a silver fountain pen and shows it to Tauilo. 'Dave gave that to me last week!' Tauilo looks at the pen and sighs in envy.

I get bored. I get up and leave the house. I sit on the bank of the stream and look at the jail on the other side. Smoke is rising from the prison umu and two prisoners in striped lavalava are fixing the food. A fat policeman comes and talks with them. They laugh behind the barbed-wired fence.

The stream is narrow at this point, and it has a steel pipe for a bridge across it to the prison. The stream is loaded with rubbish and shit, and it stinks, as I have said before. I pick up a rock and break my face in the water with it. The

164

prisoners and policeman are talking still. I try to hear what they are saying but they are too far way. I bend my head into my hands on my knees and cry. Even when I think of all my friends in Sapepe I am still alone. There is only the black water and the stink.

'Boy!' someone calls. I look up scared. He is a giant prisoner with a bird tattoo on his chest. 'Why you cry?' he asks. 'You got no reason to cry, you not a prisoner!' He laughs. Then he is gone into the prison.

I return to the pink house.

The next morning Tauilo takes me to enrol in the government primary school. (Tautala is a graduate of this school and persuades Tauilo to send me there.) In the afternoon my father gives me two pounds before he leaves on the bus for Sapepe. I stand and hold the money. He waves at me from the bus window. Then the bus is off and I am alone in the market where there are so many people buying and selling. I start to shake. It is the first time I have been alone in the town. But when I see some kids eating ice creams, I run to the shop and buy one.

I whistle and run home past the police station, eating my ice cream.

That night my ice-cream courage leaves me as I lie in the mosquito net. I pray to God, tell Him to look after me. I fall asleep saying I am going to be all right, I am going to fight.

First Day School

There is no one in the classroom. A prayer comes to my mouth. I pray. Giggling behind me. I jump and look round. The two girls look queerly at me. They run away yelling, 'The new boy is a fool!'

I walk into the classroom and stand by the windows and look out at the playground. Many kids are playing out there but they do not look real behind the dirty glass. I turn and survey the classroom.

It is a big box of cement with five windows facing the

playground and rows of desks and a blackboard in front. There are pictures on the walls and diagrams too with English sentences. I try to read a few sentences and get scared because I cannot read them very well. The classroom is so different from the one in Sapepe. There it is an open fale and we sit on the pebble floor and it is not hot like this one.

The slap-slap of sandals. I turn. The afakasi woman looks at me. I at her. Then she comes to her desk at the front and does not look at me any more. She is severe-looking, like Faafetai maybe. About forty years old and going grey in the hair already. She slaps down her satchel, papers spill out on the desk Her finger-nails are long and red with paint.

'You the new boy?' She does not look at me.

'Yes,' I reply.

'You take the empty seat at the back.' She points to the corner desk. She still does not look at me as she puts her papers back into the satchel. I go and put my satchel on the back desk. She is looking at me when I turn. 'I hear you were in standard two?' she says in quick English. I do not understand. 'I ... hear ... you ... were ... in ... standard ... two?' she repeats slowly. I nod the head. 'I am Mrs Brown,' she adds. I nod the head. She picks up a chalk and starts printing on the blackboard.

'My name is Pepe,' I introduce the self. She continues to write like she does not care whether I have a name or not. She is skin and bone in the white shirt and lavalava, not in the group of females that Sapepe people call 'Flesh-meat for the gods!'

I look at the window because I do not know what else to do. I see the other children playing under the tamaligi trees but they are so far away.

Three boys enter, talking all the time, and they do not see Mrs Brown. She turns. 'You know the rule. NO NOISE. Understand?' she says to them. The kids nod. I make up my mind fast that I am never going to offend Mrs Brown. Never. I sit down.

Children come in and go out. They just look at me. I at them. But we do not say anything.

166

Clang-clang-clang! dongs the school bell. All the children leave quickly. I wonder why but I sit there like a fool. She looks at me. I at her.

'Leave. It's assembly time,' she says. I get up fast and out to the playground.

The other children are standing in lines in front of the tamaligi trees which have a platform under them in the shade. I go and join the end of the line of the children who came into my classroom that morning. I stand at ease. Everyone is looking ahead, arms back, chests out. I do the same even though I have never been a soldier before.

'Boy, she in a bad mood today,' someone next to me says. I look round but there is no one. I look down to my left and there he is — the dwarf, the first I have ever seen. He has a shaved head and sores on it and he is only as tall as up to my biceps. Like me he wears no shirt but only a red lavalava with two white stripes on it.

'My name is Pepe,' I introduce the self.

'Mine is Tagata,' he introduces his self. He does not look at me. His eyes are looking up at the roof-tops of the school. 'My father owns the market,' he says. Then he picks his nose.

'She is going to kill someone today,' the boy next to him whispers. The speaker who is not a dwarf is black like midnight. He looks at me and his eyes shine like white coral in all his blackness.

'My name is Pepe,' I say to him.

He nods his head and says, 'Mrs Brown is a...a...a....' But he cannot finish.

'A bitch?' I suggest. Tagata giggles but the black boy looks ahead.

'Simi's father is a pastor, that is why he does not swear,' Tagata tells me. I want to ask if Simi's parents are Solomon Islanders but I do not because it is impolite.

Clang-clang-clang! The bell rings again. Everyone is still like dead soldiers maybe. No talk.

Crunch-crunch-crunch-crunch! The shoes of the teachers march from the building toward the platform in the tamaligi shade. The sun is very hot now, it is hanging over the school like a fat boil. Crunch-crunch! The shoes stop

167

and the teachers get on to the platform. Women in front, men behind. All in white like Sunday. I count six palagi teachers and only two Samoan. Out in front, in long socks nearly to his knees to cover his cowboy legs, is the palagi headmaster.

'That is Mr Croft,' whispers Tagata. Mr Croft has short hair the colour of the sun and white skin like cooked pork. He holds his chest out and his head up.

'Mr Croft,' Simi says. 'He used to be a captain in the army.'

'Ahh . . . ahh . . . ten-shun!' Mr Croft commands.

Bang! Everyone obeys. My English is not good enough to follow his fast prayer. The sun is burning my neck. Tagata is rubbing his bald head.

'NOOWW!' says Mr Croft. Then he is off and his English is too fast for me. All I know is that he is very angry about something.

'What is he saying?' I ask Tagata.

'He is yelling that no one is allowed to go down the road at playtime because some boys stoned his house last night. He says if he catches the culprits he is going to murder them. . . . But he is never going to catch them.'

'Why not?' I ask Tagata.

'Because I am the one who did it,' he says. That dwarf he is not afraid of anyone, not even palagi.

'Why you tell him?' whispers Simi, looking at me. 'He may tell Croft.'

'You going to tell him?' Tagata asks me. I shake the head.

'Why did you do it?' I ask.

'Because he beat me last week for something I did not do,' replies Tagata. I am astounded by his bravery.

'You and Simi be my friends?' I ask. But they do not answer.

Mr Croft finishes. He wipes the mouth with the hanky. Two boys beat drums. 'Left turn!' shouts Mr Croft. We turn. 'Left-right, left-right, left-right!'

We march into the school building.

No one says anything as Mrs Brown takes out her books.

168

'Stand up!' she calls. I do not know she is calling me because she is not looking at me, or at anyone. 'Stand up!' she says again. She looks at me. I jump up. The girls giggle. 'This is the new boy. He is from the *back*,' she tells the others. I look at the floor, at my dirty feet. 'Now he is going to give us a morning talk about his village.' She smiles for the first time. 'What is your name?' she asks.

'Pe...Pepe,' I stutter.

'Louder!'

'Pepe.'

'Very good. Now tell the others about your village.' She speaks slowly. I continue to look at my dirty feet. 'Come to the front!' I do not move. 'Hear me?'

My two dirty feet begin to follow each other to the front of the class. I turn. They are all looking at me.

'Well?' says Mrs Brown. I swallow tears in my throat. 'Well, go on!'

'My...my village....'

'Louder!'

'My village is called Sapepe,' I begin. Everyone laughs at my English, including Mrs Brown. I look at Simi and Tagata at the back; they are not laughing. I stop the tears and look down.

'Please, Mrs Brown,' a boy's voice saves me. I look up. It is Tagata. He has his hand up.

'Yes?' Mrs Brown asks him.

'I want to talk this morning,' says Tagata. He gets up before Mrs Brown says all right and is coming to the front to save me.

'Sit down,' she says to me. I nearly run to my desk.

Tagata stands alone. He looks everyone full in the face. No one laughs at his ugliness.

'This morning I am going to talk about the barracuda my father bought for my mother yesterday at our market,' he begins. His English is the best I have ever heard from any Samoan. I understand what he is saying because he speaks slowly, clearly. 'As we all know, the barracuda is a killer. It looks like a torpedo and it can torpedo through the water faster than any torpedo. And, as we all should know, torpedoes kill people!' Simi's hand is up.

169

'Yes?' asks Tagata.

'What is the torpedo?' Simi asks.

'Well, as we all should know, a torpedo is a bomb fired by a submarine, and when it hits something, like another ship or a whale, it goes BANG and that something is blown to bits,' he explains. But Simi's hand is up again.

'What is the whale?' Simi asks. I realise that they are playing a game like we do in Sapepe. You take a small joke and build it up till you get a deadly joke.

'Well, the whale is a mammal, the biggest mammal on earth, that lives in the sea.'

'What is the mammal?'

'A mammal,' replies Tagata, 'is a big fish with a tail and a nostril and blubber and the fish which swallowed Jonah in the Bible.'

'I understand,' says Simi. I nearly burst with laughter, but no one else is laughing, they are too dumb, including Mrs Brown.

'That is my talk,' Tagata says to Mrs Brown. He comes and sits down and Mrs Brown asks a girl to give a talk.

'Excuse me, Mrs Brown,' Tagata says. 'I want to talk about our horse.'

'What has your horse done now?' she tries to joke.

'Well, Midnight, our horse, had a child horse last night.'

'Go on,' says Mrs Brown.

'Well, Midnight never had children before,' says Tagata. Simi is laughing behind his hand. (I find out at interval from Tagata and Simi that they call Mrs Brown 'Horse' and Mrs Brown has no children either.) 'Not long ago my father gets a stallion....'

'That is enough!' says Mrs Brown. 'Sit down!' Simi's hand is up. 'Yes?' she asks him.

'What is the stallion?' Simi asks her.

'Take out your spelling books, children. Time for spelling,' she orders.

For the rest of that day, she leaves Tagata and Simi and me alone.

That first day at school I also learn ten new English words: HORSE, BROWN, STALLION (Tagata teaches me what this means), BRIGHT, TOWN, SHIT (I see this on

170

the toilet wall and Simi tells me what it means), SUN-
LIGHT, SPEECH, FEMALE, and TOILET.

Lupe is sitting in our fale when I get off the bus. I run to
her, but when I see her sadness my happiness goes. She
embraces me. I tell her about school and my new home
and make my telling sound good and happy so she will not
worry about me.

'Teach us,' she prays, 'to love again as we did, that we
may live always together in peace. Look after Pepe while
he is away in that strange home and school. Teach him to
love....' While she prays I watch her and I feel that the
fire that burnt inside her is gone and with that has gone
part of the good life of my family. She ends her prayer. I
leave to visit Toasa.

Toasa is asleep in the middle of his fale. I go in and sit
down and watch him. I always believed before that Toasa
will never grow older than he is, but he looks older now.
The wrinkles are deeper, the hair is greyer, only the rising
up and down of his chest makes me know that he is alive.
As the afternoon comes and grows old I sit and watch over
him. No one else comes into the fale. It is a rule with
Toasa that no one disturbs him when he is asleep. Some
children call to me to go swimming with them. I tell them
no.

Like a large turtle coming up for breath he snorts and
turns over, and for a while his mouth opens and shuts,
tongue coming out, then in. He holds his lavalava and sits
up coughing. He does not see me for a moment and he
blinks and moves back a bit when he does see me without
recognising who it is.

'Are you well?' I ask. He blinks again and then laughs
and slaps me on the shoulder.

'All right, eh,' he says. 'Are you well?' I nod. 'Still
skinny,' he says. 'Have they been feeding you well?' I nod
again. 'But you had better watch out for Tautala and his
mean wife, eh.' No, Toasa has not changed.

I have the evening meal with him. After it, while he
smokes, he tells me the last story of Sapepe's great hero,
Pepesa, after whom I am called.

The legends about Pepesa do not appear in the stories of other districts. If they do appear they are different to the Sapepe stories in many ways. According to Toasa, Pepesa was born a 'clot of blood' — meaning that he was born too early. He was the illegitimate son of a god and a mortal woman, and because of this his mother abandoned him on the beach. An old woman goes fishing one morning and finds him there and she brings him home and nurses him until he is a youth who is half-god and half-man and who at first is ridiculed by everyone because they find out that he is illegitimate, and he is very cheeky to everyone, but as he grows up and shows his many gifts they become afraid of him. They also learn to respect him when in many of his brave adventures he invents the first fishing-net, cultivates the first taro plantation, grows the first ava plant which people then use for ava ceremonies, and steals the fire from the gods and gives it to them. He catches the sun too and beats it until it promises to go slow across the sky, and that is why we have a much longer day now. He invents the first war-clubs and uses them to conquer all the islands and bring peace and a united form of government. He in fact challenges all the gods and gets away with it, until he is the most famous man alive, a man feared by the gods because of his courage and cunning and humour.

These were the stories which Toasa had told me before I went away to Apia and school. However, he had never told me how Pepesa died. This night, for some reason I can't figure out, he tells me, and tells me slowly as if he does not want me to ever forget it.

This is the summary of the story of Pepesa's death which Toasa told me that night.

Pepesa's father, the god who sired him, is called Tane, father of humankind. But Pepesa does not know that Tane is his father and Tane does not know that Pepesa is his son. Pepesa when he is a man has a daughter called Sina. Because she is his only daughter he comes to love her more than even his own life. When she is a beautiful young woman many suitors come to court her but Pepesa always refuses to let her take a husband. Now Pepesa's home is situated near the sea by a pool called 'Tagi-mai-

Peau', meaning 'the waves are weeping'. Sina goes bathing in the pool every day. One day she finds a small eel there which she keeps and feeds as a pet. Pepesa, her father, does not know of this because she keeps it a secret as he will not let her have any living creature close to her as a friend. She takes food every day and feeds her eel until it becomes quite large. Unknown to her the god Tane has taken the form of the eel. He had heard of her great beauty and wanted her to be his wife. (Tane was notorious for his escapades with women whether mortal or immortal.) One day while Sina is talking to her pet in the pool Tane changes from his eel form into the form of a handsome young man. She is surprised at first, but Tane woos her until she is in love with him, then he takes her virginity. One day she does not return from the pool. Pepesa and his people search for her but cannot find her. They do not know that Tane has taken her to his home in the Ninth Heaven. While Pepesa searches throughout Samoa for her he hears that Tane has taken her as his wife. Enraged by this he plans to trap Tane, kill him, and bring his daughter back to earth. He chooses seven of his bravest friends and, assuming the form of flying-foxes, they journey up into the heavens.

Tane, being a very suspicious god, always has his home well protected by minor gods. No mortal can come close to it without being killed. Pepesa knows this, so when they get there they cling to the bread-fruit tree above Tane's house. Tane's guards believe them to be real flying-foxes. As we all know, flying-foxes are delicious to eat, so Tane's guards try to spear them. Pepesa's friends fly away from the bread-fruit tree and the guards pursue them and leave the house unguarded. Pepesa flies down from the tree, changes into his human form, breaks into the house, and finds Tane asleep. Dominated by his anger Pepesa wakes him up, and when Tane is fully awake and looking into Pepesa's face, Pepesa clubs him to death with his magic war-club. Seven deliberate blows one after the other. Sina enters and tries to stop him. Pepesa pushes her aside. After he kills Tane, Pepesa tries to take Sina back to earth but she refuses, saying that she cannot leave her baby who is sleeping peacefully at the other side of the house. Pepesa goes to the child and with one blow of his club kills it. On seeing this, Sina, his beloved daughter, kills herself.

Pepesa's friends return to find him grieving over Sina's body. They lift him away from her and bring him back to earth.

He was never the same again. One morning a strange old woman, who some say was his mother, visited him. Shortly after his people heard him crying as if he had gone insane with grief. That very night, after the old woman had vanished into the darkness out of which she came, Pepesa disappeared from Sapepe and was never seen again.

One story tells that he killed himself because the old woman had revealed to him that Tane whom he had killed was his father. Another tells that he is still wandering through the heavens in search of Sina and her child whom he had killed out of a blinding jealousy. Yet another story tells that he is not dead and will return to Sapepe one day and reunite the Sapepe Family.

During my two years at primary school I progress until I am nearly top of the class. I master the English quickly and I am always obedient to Mrs Brown, Tautala, and Faafetai. Tagata and Simi and me are like brothers. Every fourth week-end and school holidays I spend at Sapepe. But every time I return to Sapepe it seems like I am returning to something less important, like a step back, and I cannot help feeling this way.

At the end of these two years Tauilo has built a large palagi house for us next to our fale in Sapepe. The house has many glass windows, five bedrooms, a big sitting room with photos on the walls, and a wireless and furniture, a flush toilet which is the first and only flush toilet in Sapepe, and a room which Tauilo calls his 'office' in which he spends most of his time when he is at home, writing and writing. He buys books on bookkeeping and shorthand, and three Bibles, all in English, and a typewriter which he teaches himself to use. Tauilo also buys a safe of iron in which he locks most of his money; the rest he puts in the town bank. My father, the failed theological student who was treated by my family as a disgrace to the family because he had been expelled from Malua Theological College, becomes the most powerful and successful son Sapepe has begotten.

In this time Leaves of the Banyan Tree, my father's plantation, covers most of the valley behind Sapepe village and is reaching out to the foothills and range. Many of the people of Sapepe now work on this plantation for wages. The money has come to stay in Sapepe.

Near the end of these two years I visit Taifau as usual after Sunday toonai. As usual he brightens up on seeing me.

'Your father is a hard man,' he says. 'But he is a good man. Soon he will be the most powerful man here.'

'If he is too hard on you why not leave him?' I ask.

He blinks his half-blind eyes, then says, 'I have a family, Pepe. I have responsibilities now. Not only this, but people respect me now because I am making something of myself. No one respected me before, and respect is what all men want.' He looks away.

'But I respect you. And the young people love your music and songs,' I tell him. He does not reply. I look around at his new fale which Tauilo helped him to build. It is one of the biggest fale in Sapepe. I see the new furniture and photos on the posts, the new clothes on Taifau and Nofo who is feeding her baby, and the desk on which are Taifau's books about the plantation; and I remember Tauilo's promise that he will change Taifau into a hard-working man.

'You got to understand, Pepe,' Taifau says. His voice is shaking.

The young people do not visit Taifau's fale any more because there is less music now and no stories and laughter.

I go and look for Faitoaga, but I cannot find him. They tell me that he does not come often to the village now. He spends nearly all his time in Leaves of the Banyan Tree, where some week-ends I go pigeon-shooting with him up on the mountain slopes where the pigeons now live after Tauilo chased them from the valley. However, even when

I do not find Faitoaga this Sunday evening, I feel that Faitoaga remains unchanged behind everything else that is changing. And I feel safe again.

So I visit Toasa as I do every week-end I spend in Sapepe. The old man does not oppose Tauilo in the matai council now. He hardly attends them. Every night I continue to learn from him the past of Sapepe, a past which he does not seem to be defending against Tauilo any more. He still laughs and tells me about the lions and aitu on the range and how some day I must go up there and see them myself. 'You better hurry and climb the mountains,' he tells me, 'or your father will clear all the bush on the top and the lions and aitu will have to go somewhere else to live, eh!'

Apart from the time I spend with Toasa and Faitoaga I spend most of it with Lupe. I behave like she wants me to behave. I bring all my school-books and I read and study them like she wants me to. She watches me studying and is happy more or less. She grows thin and her eyes are stone most of the time. I count the grey in her hair and they mark every step of her dying for me, and I cannot stop even that. They never talk much now, Tauilo and Lupe. Tauilo talks all the time when he is at home but he is talking to himself and Masina because Lupe and my sisters do not try to listen to him. My sisters live in our big house like they do not belong there. They have a room of their own into which they do not allow anyone else. Lupe too has a bedroom and when Tauilo is not there at night I hear her walking up and down, up and down, and her footsteps are the sound of my own fear for her.

Everyone in Sapepe treats me with respect now because I am Tauilo's son, the most favoured son of Sapepe. I do not want them to do that but even my friends begin to treat me differently like someone important and above them, and my loneliness is deeper.

Before going to high school I go to Sapepe to spend my Christmas holidays there. Christmas time in Sapepe is always a gay time. Cricket playing and dancing and much fiafia. It is also a time for much church-going. Tauilo

176

preaches two short sermons, and parents tell each other that Tauilo is a better preacher than Filipo because Tauilo talks sense about saving your money to send your children to school with and not spending it on worthless things, about cutting out the time the foolish young people spend on cricket so that they can spend more time on the plantations improving them so that the economy (is that the right word?) of Sapepe can be developed, about cutting out many of our customs because they cost too much money, and about adopting many palagi ways so we can make a better standard of living. But even when the older people heed his advice the young people play cricket whenever they get the chance, and they dance and sing on the road at night. After all it is Christmas, Toasa says to me.

The night after Christmas day the trouble in my family breaks out again. It is to do with Vao, who is now a beautiful young lady.

We have been waiting all night for Vao. It is dark and no wind blows and that is why it is very hot. I sit beside Lupe in our sitting room and I am frightened for Vao's sake. Tauilo gets up now and then and goes out to look for Vao. He has also sent out some men of our family to look for her. Masina keeps cursing Vao every few minutes.

The back door opens and Vao comes in. She does not look scared like she ought to be.

'Where have you been?' Tauilo asks her. Vao turns to go upstairs. 'Sit down!' Tauilo's voice is like his belt that is going to lash out at Vao soon. Vao is not scared at all. She sits down in the chair opposite Tauilo. Lupe is ready to weep at any moment now. I put my hand on her hands in her lap.

'You are not sorry about what you have done?' Masina asks Vao.

'What have I done?' says Vao.

'Sinning with Paulo!' Masina accuses her. (Paulo is her boyfriend who Tauilo and Masina do not want because he is from a poor and low-status family.) Lupe's hands are shaking like newly-hatched birds.

'I commit no sin,' Vao says to Masina.

'You lie!' says Tauilo. He takes his thick leather belt

177

from round his waist. 'No daughter of mine is going to disgrace me and this family!' He walks to Vao who looks up at him with no fear. When Tauilo raises his hand and the belt looks like a snake ready to strike Vao I shut my eyes.

The belt whistles through the air. WHACK. It fills me with terror and love for Vao. The tears come to my throat and I hold Lupe's hand tightly. WHACK.

'She's been sinning!' says Masina. WHACK.

'It is not a sin. Not a sin!' cries Vao. WHACK. WHACK. I open my eyes. 'I spit on this family!' cries Vao. And she is my pain and Lupe's pain too. Tauilo drops the belt and hits her with his open hand across the face. She crashes against the chair. But she rises and faces him again. 'I *hate* you!' she says to Tauilo. His hand whips down again and the blood comes from the cut over her eye. But she faces him again. 'I despise you!'

'Did you hear that!' shouts Masina. 'Ungrateful whore!' Tauilo hits Vao again. She crashes down to the floor. She gets on to her hands and knees and tries to stand up. All the time she is weeping.

'Enough!' cries Lupe. But I know Tauilo will not stop unless Vao admits that she is defeated. You see, Vao has stamped on Tauilo's pride and nobody can do that to him and get away with it.

'I hate you!' Vao tries to say. Then I am between them. Tauilo moves to swing down. I push him away, hold Vao, and pull her out the door.

'I'm going to repay him!' Vao cries to me when we are safe outside.

'What will you do?' I ask, to stop her crying. She does not tell me. I rip off the corner of my lavalava and use it to fix her bloody face.

'Look after our mother,' she says to me.

That night Vao eloped with Paulo to another village far way. They never returned to Sapepe ever, and to this day I have not seen her again.

I go to Lupe's room and find her sitting there. 'It is not evil what Vao did, is it?' I ask her. She does not reply. I refuse to cry too.

A Haunted House in the Town

Reader, stop here for a moment for I have to stop because the coughing is killing me. It hurts like hell. I had a short sleep this morning. When I woke up I found the self with an erection, something which surprised me because I have had no such thing for the past few weeks. I think it is because I am nearly dead. I read somewhere that when a man is hanged by the neck until he is dead you find he is hanging up there with his weapon erect like a flag waving goodbye to the hangman. I hope that when I kick the air finally they will come into my room and find my weapon laughing at them. Got to have a rest now. Am finding it hard to write longer than two hours a day.

In my fourth year at high school Tauilo buys us a large house in Apia. The house is opposite the primary school I used to go to; it belonged to a palagi plantation owner from Germany who died at the age of eighty. He had come to Samoa sixty years before. And from what I hear, he died because aitu scared him to death. He did not have a wife or children. He retired from his plantation and settled in this house all by himself. Some people will tell you that he drank himself to the grave and he used to spend his time with faafafine.

The house has many rooms and it is on stilts. It has beautiful gardens round it. Orchids, hydrangeas, boungainvilleas, ferns, hibiscus, frangipani, flamboyant trees, tamaligi, cactuses, flower-of-the-night, puataunofo (I do not know the English for this), lilies, tiger orchids, beautiful creepers and lianas whose names I do not know. In fact it has just about any tropical flower you can think of.

Tauilo is not satisfied with the house. He hires carpenters and they renew it all, change it into a house like our house in Sapepe. He fills it with expensive furniture which he buys cheaply from his business friends, and he has a new toilet built. This toilet is so big you can fit maybe ten people in it. The sitting room, which takes up the whole middle and front of the house facing the road across a veranda, has a blood-coloured wall on which hang all the family photos. There is a big glass cabinet in it too. This is full of crystal glasses and bottles of whisky. (When we were poor my father was against liquor. Now he is rich he loves it despite his deacon's position in our church, and our church preaches against alcohol — called the 'Devil's Water' by the Sapepe people.) Beside the cabinet is a long three-shelf bookcase where Tauilo keeps the books he buys and does not read. Behind the house Tauilo builds a fale in which some of my Sapepe family come and stay to serve us, the people in the house.

Tauilo spends nearly all his week-ends in this house. He puts on parties for his own friends. I never once see a Samoan at these parties. Only palagi and rich afakasi etc. Even my family are not allowed to attend as guests. He is ashamed of his relatives; they are good only as servants to his guests. When I shift into his house away from the Tautala's I am barman at these parties but I am not allowed to touch a drop of the Devil's Water. Lupe, my mother, shifts here too. Tauilo says that the town climate will be good for her failing health.

Lupe is very interested in the old German who owned the house before us. When anybody in Apia visits her she always asks them if they knew the German and how he died, whether he died of aitu or not. Everyone tells her that he died because of loneliness and drink but she does not believe them. When she is alone in the house she goes through it looking into every corner but she does not find any trace of the man who lived there before. Tauilo tried to get members of our family to change the flower-gardens into taro patches but Lupe will not allow it. It is in these gardens that she spends her evenings before the sun sets completely. She wanders through them like a bird looking for a nest which it can never find. If it is dark she never goes near the gardens because she believes that when it is darkness the gardens belong again to the German whose aitu she thinks is wandering the world because he was not accepted into heaven.

It is Saturday. I get out of bed and feel that it is going to be a hot day. When I am dressed I go into the kitchen to eat with Lupe and Niu. I sit down at the head of the table.

180

Niu and Lupe are silent. I feel something is wrong but do not say anything to them. Lupe starts to cry. My hunger goes at once. Niu is looking at her food.

'What is wrong?' I ask. Lupe runs out and up to her room. 'Why?' I ask Niu. She starts to cry too, and I am getting angry. 'What is wrong?' I repeat. She rushes out of the room too.

I call in one of my female relatives who is cooking and ask her. She just looks at the floor. 'Answer me!' I order her.

She tells me quickly and then leaves. I smash the plate on the table. I will wait for him.

I wait in my room all day and I don't feel the heat.

The car roars into the garage. The door opens and slams shut. His footsteps come up the steps and into the sitting room. The whisky cabinet is opened. The tinkle of glass and the sound of pouring whisky. I go into the sitting room.

The light is on. He is sitting on the settee, drinking his whisky. He is getting fat and his hair is turning grey, and in his white clothes he looks like a pastor, a stranger to me. He looks at me. That is all. Drinks his whisky. I stand before him.

'Where is Lupe?' he asks. I shake the head. He drinks again. 'Where is Niu?' I don't answer. 'Where is anybody?' He smiles at me.

'She is not going to marry that man,' I hear the self speak out against him for the first time.

'Who?'

'Niu.' I cannot let him do it.

'He is a good man, a pastor and one of the leaders of our church. She will be happy with him.' Drinks his whisky till it is empty.

'Niu is not going to marry him. She does not want to!'

'You are still a child. You do not understand. Get me another drink.' He holds out his empty glass.

'She is not going to!'

'Do not talk to me like that. I am your father.'

'You have no right to make her marry that old man!' The self is almost shouting.

'I am still your father. I know what is best for Niu. ....
Get me another drink!' It is a command and a challenge.
He holds out his glass. I hit it away and move out of the
room. 'No one listens to me now!' I hear him shout.

A month later Niu is married at Sapepe to the old pastor whose wife is dead. The man is older than Tauilo. Niu
is about twenty. It is Tauilo to blame, and it is me too
because I could not stop the wedding. I cannot forgive
Tauilo for that.

Niu and her husband go away to live in the village in
Savaii where he is the pastor. I hear from my relatives that
Tauilo gave them much money and gifts before they left.
Like Vao: right up to this day I never talked to Niu again.
I avoided her because I still blame myself. Once I saw her
going past in a bus like someone in my dreams that is gone
the next morning when I wake up. But her unhappiness
haunts me because I see it in Lupe every day in the big
lonely house.

Mr Peddle, the headmaster of my high school, sits at his
big desk. On the wall behind him is a sign which says
HARD WORK IS THE KEY TO SUCCESS. I enter and
sit down opposite him. He does not speak for a long time.
He tries his famous stare on me. I look at the floor and
take his stupid stare on my long hair. We call him 'Shark-
bait' because of the way he can smooth-talk you until you
take the bait and believe that what he says is gospel truth,
and then he whacks you and says he is doing it for your
own good. He is tough, a champion tennis player, champion hockey man, champion golf man, champion talker and
con-man. He has three degrees — MA, BSc, and DipEd.
I never found out what the letters stood for but Tagata
used to say, 'MA — Master Arse, BSc — Bachelor Science
Fruit, and DipEd — Dip it in Edgewise.' Peddle used to be
a colonel in the New Zealand Army during the First
World War, so he believes and tells every student that
good soldiers make the best citizens. He is president of
the RSA Club in which Tauilo is a member. Some students
whose fathers are RSA members will tell you that Peddle
has many medals for bravery in combat and two wounds

182

near his navel. Other people say that Peddle was never a colonel, that he was a corporal. Too bad the enemy did not cut out his navel with a blunt bayonet.

I used to be his favourite pupil but now I am opposite him as the enemy.

'Uh-h!' he begins. I do not look at him. 'A bad man is a bad man, Peepee.' (He cannot pronounce Samoan names properly, and does not want to.) 'So are bad pupils. But you are a very good student. ... How is your father?' I say nothing. 'Your father is a good man. Uh-h. One of the best Samoans in this country. A Samoan every Samoan youth should be proud of. You are a very good people, laughing all the time and happy. That is what Polynesians are — happy and easy-go-lucky. Uh-h. And gay. That is why we New Zealanders are here among you.' (I heard from someone that Peddle couldn't get a headmaster's job in New Zealand and that was why he came to Samoa.) 'We are here to help you Samoans find your feet in the modern world. We want to help you. Show you the better ways. Uh-h. Like your father has learnt from us. Why do you think your father is rich and respected by us? Because he is getting to be one of us. He is the new Samoan who is going to help your race achieve a better way of life. Uh-h. Now do not think for a moment that I am saying your beautiful way of life is a bad one. No. Not at all.' Laughs. His false teeth rattle. 'You have beautiful customs and traditions. You respect your old people and things like that. You know how to treat important people. But if you want to stand with the modern people like us you have to work hard like your father. ...'

'Why do you not allow Samoans into the RSA?' I ask suddenly. His teeth nearly fall out.

'But your father is a member, is he not?' Smiles.

'And why not others?'

'Well, because you people have to learn to take your liquor without getting violent. Like knowledge you come to school to get, you have to learn, educate yourselves about drink. ...'

'Why do you think we cannot rule our own country?'

'But we do, Peepee. We do. Uh-h. It is just that you

people are not ready for leadership yet.'

'But we ruled ourselves for hundreds of years before you came.'

'Yes, but look where it got you.' He is growing angry.

'Where?'

He slaps his desk. 'Why did you call that girl prefect a...uh-h...a....'

'A bitch?' I help him.

He slaps his desk again and rises to his feet. 'Now, Peepee. Now, I do not want you talking like that. Hear? You have done wrong to that girl. Now you have to pay!'

'Like my people paid and are still paying?' I smile. 'Like black men and Chinamen are paying all over the world.'

'You are a racist, boy. It is Samoans like you who make our good work here get nowhere. You are like all the other uppity and ungrateful Samoans!' he says. I laugh. 'You...you...you *Samoan*! Get out of my office. Your father is going to hear about this. Hear?'

I move out. Peddle, like Tauilo, is a fake god. I laugh at myself because when I was a hard-working student I used to admire Peddle. Now he has shown his true hollowness and it rattles like his false teeth. Peddle is a corporal with a navel, not a colonel with medals.

At interval I find the girl prefect who caused all the trouble for me. She is alone in the classroom. I walk up and stand behind her. Suddenly I put my arms round her and hold her tits tightly. 'Please, Pepe,' she says but she does not really try hard to get away and I think she likes what I am doing to her. I pull her against me, shove my hand up her dress from behind. She does not make a noise. She is moist down there. I tear off her pants. She turns to face me and does not run away. She is breathing hard the way Taifau told me a woman breathes hard when she wants it. I laugh aloud. When she realises I am not going to do anything more she gets ashamed and runs out the door and screams, 'Pepe, he tried to rape me!'

I laugh and laugh until tears come to my eyes.

That afternoon Peddle sends me a note that I am expelled from school.

The Second World War is ending at this time. Poor

Germans, I think. Hitler is only a corporal like Peddle.

Two days later Tauilo comes to Apia with his wrath. He beats me with his fists, like I expected, and I do not cry. And he makes me pray with him to Jehovah to forgive me for my sin, like I expected. But I only say the words, like I expected, all the time laughing to myself because Tauilo looks so ridiculous sitting there with the pray shooting out of his mouth, like I expected. He orders me never to return to Sapepe without his permission because I am a disgrace. He does not want Sapepe to know from me the real reason why I was expelled. Like I expected, he and Masina told Sapepe that I left school because I was ill. Some of the people believed them because they had expected I would get sick from too much study. Like I expected, Toasa and Taifau and Faitoaga found out the real reason a few days after I was kicked out.

The next day I meet Simi who is still attending the high school and is an ideal student, and he tells me that he is very sorry about what happened. I laugh and shake his hand and say goodbye. (After high school Simi goes to theological college and graduates a pastor.)

Simi came to visit me at the hospital today.

'Hallo, Solomon!' I greet him.

He shakes my hand and says, 'Hallo, Pepesa, Son of the Gods!' He laughs and I join his laughter. It is like old times again when him and Tagata and me were close friends at school.

'You married?' I ask.

He nods. 'Got two children, a boy and a girl.' We laugh about that too.

'You got a wife and kids and religion and I got Tb!' I joke, and we continue to laugh.

'I have been asked by your father and the Sapepe matai to be their pastor,' he tells me. 'Filipo is retiring soon.'

'That is good. You will like Sapepe even though they will treat you like a savage because of your colour.'

'I have not made up my mind yet. Shall I go there, Pepe?'

'Yes, it is a good district. And they will need you to help

them against my father,' I reply.

He doesn't say anything for a while. Then he looks straight at me and asks, 'You are going to die?'

'Yes.'

'Made up your mind?'

I nod the head. 'And you know me, Solomon.'

'You are still the same, Pepe,' he says. 'You make up your mind and you do not change it ever!' And he laughs.

It is just like Simi to ask you straight and expect an honest answer. It is just like him not to talk religion and the after life to me. He accepts me for who I am. And we talk and talk about politics, about Samoa as it is and as it will be, and so on, but we do not talk about the past because he went God's way and I went Hell's way, so some people would say.

When the visiting hour is up he says, 'I have to go now.' I see the sorrow in him as he gets up and kisses me on the forehead and goes to the door. He stops and asks, 'You have no regrets about how you spent your life? About what you chose?' I look away from him. 'I asked a stupid question, didn't I?' he says. 'Goodbye, Pepe!'

'Goodbye!' I call. And he is not there any more, and I hope to myself that his strong honesty will not destroy him in Sapepe, especially with Tauilo there.

I fall asleep, and when I wake with the nurse and my evening medicine I look for Simi in the room because I feel that he is still there. But it is only the night nurse in her white uniform without a smile on her face. From the window comes the smell of the fire and the burning flesh. Through the windows I watch the mountains disappear, like Simi, into the night-time.

'Can I have a piss-pot, nurse?' I ask.

Into the Dead Water

And so I begin my journey into the Vaipe neighbourhood, into what churchgoers call the dark world of sin and all-things, that they believe is against religion and good living.

186

For some years I still live with Lupe and never visit Sapepe because Tauilo does not allow me. And because Sapepe holds little for me now. During this time I do not need to work because Lupe gives me all the money I need. Anyway I only sleep and eat at home, the rest of the time I journey out into Apia and the Vaipe.

Tagata, who left high school three years before me, hears that I have been expelled and he laughs like it is the funniest joke he ever heard. I laugh with him. For months Tagata and me form our own group.

The market, which is owned by Tagata's parents, sprawls over a big area. It smells of rotting food and people and is loud all the time with people's conversation and buying and cheating, but I soon get used to it. Tagata and me go to the movies about every night. The cowboy movies are the best because they have the action and blood and quick justice. Tagata and me wear jeans like the cowboy. We smoke American cigarettes, drink the Yankee Coca-Cola, and talk smooth like the gangsters of Chicago. We can smooth-talk any stranger to make the easy dollar and laughter.

Tagata, because he is his parents' only child, is boss of the market whenever he wants to, which is not often. Because he grew up in the market he knows all the tricks about making easy money, especially off the Yankee tourists. I will never forget one time Tagata showed me how to make the tourist dollar.

A big shiny taxi stops in front of the market. We are waiting in our smooth clothes and shoes and sailor hats. Tagata steps forward and opens the taxi doors. Two Yankee old men get out first, with their crew cuts just like in the movies. After them come their women who are painted as if they are ready for burial. When Tagata bows to them the women giggle: they think Tagata is the funniest sight they have ever seen.

'Howdy frands. Nice day, ain't it?' Tagata greets them in cowboy English. They are astounded. 'Now, today we gonna show ya the real genuine Samoan markit.' The men try not to laugh, but their women do. By this time the kids who sell baskets and vegetables and seafood are all round

187

us, like flies trying to sell their germs. 'Git!' Tagata orders
them. They scatter because Tagata is the boss of the market. 'Youse from Texass?' he asks the tourists.

'No. We are from Chicago,' one man says.

'You know the Al Capone movies?' Tagata asks.

'No!' they say quickly.

'Al was a great guy,' says Tagata. They do not look
happy about that statement.

Now before we arranged to meet these Yanks we
arranged with friends of ours, Lafoga and others, to put a
stall in the market to sell handicrafts and lei and things like
that. It is to this stall that we now take the Yanks. As we
walk there Tagata describes Samoa to the tourists, like it is
Hawaii which he has seen in the Hollywood movies. The
Yanks nod the head. One woman says, 'Gee, it is lovely. I
never believed they are as civilised as this.' Then we are at
our stall.

Lafoga, ex-heavyweight champ and over six feet and two
hundred pounds, is standing in the stall and he is dressed
in rags like a beggar-man we have seen in movies about
India. Lafoga does not look like his usual self; he has
hunched his back and looks only about five feet tall and
full of misery and lice. When Lafoga steps toward the tourists they move away like Lafoga has the leprosy. Lafoga
holds up necklaces and says in Samoan, 'These you do not
find anywhere, sirs. They were given to me by my ancestors. They are hundreds of years old.'

Tagata translates for the tourists and adds that Lafoga is
the last son of a pastor who is dead. Lafoga, says Tagata, is
poor and sick and he is selling these ancient necklaces·so
he and his ten children can have food.

'No, I have changed my mind. I do not want to sell
them,' says Lafoga. (The necklaces are made of tooth-brush
handles, and Lafoga and Tagata bought them for two shillings each from some kids.) 'I cannot sell them because
they belonged to my great-great-great-grandmother, and
they are made of turtle-shell. They are genuine Samoan.
Only two of their kind left.' Tagata translates. The Yankee
women are looking at Lafoga with pity.

'Buy them,' one woman says to her husband, 'poor man

needs the money.' Her husband puts twenty pounds on the counter. Lafoga sighs and does not take the money. The other man puts down twenty pounds. Lafoga is ready to grab the money but Tagata tells him in Samoan not to take it. Lafoga starts to weep.

'Poor man does not want to sell but he needs the money,' one woman says. 'Buy the lot.'

'They are kind palagi people, Lafoga. Take their money,' Tagata tells him in English. There are now eighty pounds on the counter. Lafoga is crying as he wraps up the necklaces in newspaper. The Yankee man reaches out to take the parcel, Lafoga kisses his hand, and the man jumps back. I take the parcel and give it to him. We move off. The Yanks sigh because they are glad to get away from their first sight of misery and poverty. You see, there are no beggars in America, so the movies show you, and it upsets Yanks to see beggars.

By the time we finish taking these Yanks round the market they have spent a lot of money. We are joyful because we will get a cut from all those people who sell the Yanks something. Tagata praises the USA all the while as we go round. He says that the USA is the best goddam country on earth. The Yanks fall for it, because they are hearing what they believe and are willing to pay money to hear a foreigner, a dwarf, saying it.

That afternoon after the tourists go off in a taxi we collect our share of the tourist money from Lafoga and the others. Twenty per cent.

Many tourists, mainly Americans, are now coming to Western Samoa as I write this humble novel. Our government, which is run by New Zealand palagi, wants them to come by the shipload so that Samoa can earn money for what the government calls 'economic development'. My country does not need writers like me; it wants tourists; and I am sure that after I die Samoa is going to be like Hawaii and Tahiti and all the other tourist centres which are tropical paradises in the posters but which are con-men paradises for stripping tourists naked. The tourist trade is going to be the new missionary trade, only this time the

Bible is to be the Yankee dollar, and the priests are to be the tourist owners, and the altar of sacrifice is to be our people, and the choirs are to be 'natives' in 'genuine Samoan dress' from Hollywood, singing 'genuine Samoan songs' from Hawaii, and dancing 'genuine Samoan dances' like the hula. I am glad I am going to kick the bucket before that happens. Even my writer hero Tusitala and his grave on Mt Vaea is going to be a tourist attraction where tourists will go to fuck their women with cameras. My son and all our young people, poor bastards, will inherit that.

'Hey, nurse!' I call.

'Yes, Pepe?'

'Take out my piss-pot. Here is sixpence.'

'What is the sixpence for?'

A tip from a genuine Samoan tourist.'

'Put it up your genuine Samoan....'

'Mouth?'

And we are laughing. At least I will not have to worry about what is going to happen when the tourist barbarian hordes come. I am a dead writer writing a dead novel about dead people mainly.

By the way, like me, Tusitala died of Tb. Perhaps it is a holy disease.

Late Sunday night. Apia is quiet like the graveyard. I suddenly feel we are aitu that are going to haunt Apia for a long time. And I feel invisible and powerful. Tagata and me are in command of the operation, so the movies say. There are twelve of us behind the store. Twelve disciples. In the dark. Just like in the movies, but this is not make-believe, and I shake like the breeze blowing through Apia.

The town clock strikes the midnight hour when Sapepe people believe the aitu come out of their graves to haunt the living. There is nobody in the streets. Only a few street-lights are on. Now!

'Got the kerosene?' I whisper to the boy who is in charge of the fire.

'What building?' he asks.

'Any one on the other side of town,' I reply, without thinking smart enough. 'Start the fire in one half-hour.

190

Make sure it is big.' Five boys move off into the streets.

There are seven of us left. I instruct two to go and hide on the other side of the store and watch out for the police just in case they come too early. There are five left, and Tagata is breathing heavy beside me.

The silence is dead as we wait for the sound of the fire-engine and siren. My throat is dry sand. There are stars in in the sky. Tomorrow will be fine.

The siren wails like madness. One boy runs and tells me that the fire is in full swing. It is the Protestant Church hall that is being eaten away by flames. I do not care.

We smash open the glass doors and rush in with torches. The others fill their baskets with food and clothes and other goods. Tagata and me run upstairs and smash into the office. I break open the drawers and small safe. We fill the bag with money, then move down and out the front door.

The police-car lights hit us for a moment as we dive over the road and then sprint along the waterfront in the shadows.

'Stop!' they shout. We keep running past the wharf. Tagata is too slow, they will catch us. I stop.

'Some bastard told the cops!' he says. I give him the bag of money.

'You go on ahead!' I tell him. He does not want to. I push him forward. He disappears. I rip off my shirt and dive behind the wooden fence.

I hear one coming past fast. I whip behind him, smash down on his neck with the open hand like the detective in the movies, and he goes down without a sound. I turn and run off towards Mulinuu to lead them away from Tagata. The shadows hide me.

I hear them behind me. I dive behind the tree in front of the Crown Estates building. The footsteps come. I step out. He is too slow. I kick up and get him in the balls. He groans and goes down. I kick him again in the gut to make sure he stays down.

They are still coming. The street-light catches me. I break through the hibiscus hedge in front of the Casino Hotel. I duck too late. The night-watchman sees me plain

191

as sunlight. I leave him alone even though he is sure to recognise me.

I look back. The police are in front of the Crown Estates. I run along behind the hedge and into the dark again and cross back over the road and jump on to the beach and into the sea. The cold hits me, gives me back my breath. I swim quietly towards the buoy in the middle of the harbour. Well out, I float and look back at the shore. The police lights go past the Casino, heading for Mulinuu. I am safe.

The buoy rises up and down under me. My teeth chatter. The lights of the town are all on. At one end the Protestant hall is burning quickly to the ground, with a large crowd and helpless firemen watching it. The wind hits me with the cold, and the stars are laughing in the sky. Fear freezes me when I remember the night-watchman.

I wait until the Protestant hall collapses and the flames start to die out. My bones are stiff and hurting. I dive into the sea and start for the market.

Tagata opens the door of his home when I knock. I fall into his arms. He sits me down and gets me a towel. 'They catch no one,' he says. 'But the police will be coming here for sure. They always do.'

He supports me as we hurry home. We keep in the shadows. 'Just like in the movies,' he says to cheer me up. I nod the head.

The next morning I do not leave the house. That afternoon, Tauilo storms into the house. I hear him cursing the people who robbed *his* store. I get dressed and go to him in the sitting room. He is reading his account books. He looks up at me and then back into his accounts.

'What are you grinning at?' he asks. I say nothing, just watch him. He is flabby now and has grey in his hair. We are the same height and I am catching up to him in strength. He has five stores in Sapepe and other villages, twelve buses, also shares in many town businesses. Also two palagi houses, six trucks, about six hundred acres of the best plantation, plenty in the bank, a lawyer, and the whole of Sapepe under his command. I nearly laugh when the thought comes to me that I am his only heir now. Me,

192

the worthless and only son. He looks ridiculous with his spectacles half-way down his nose. He does not need the glasses really. He looks like he is preparing a sermon.

Lupe enters and sits down. I look at her from across the room where I am sitting and notice that life seems to be returning to her as she watches Tauilo, knowing he has been robbed. And I believe then that she hates him in some ways.

'About a thousand pounds in damage and goods and money!' he says, and stands up.

'What happened?' Lupe asks as if she does not know already.

'Get me a whisky,' he says. She does not move. I get one for him.

Lupe leaves and goes into the garden. I watch her from the window. She starts planting flowers. It is the first time I have seen her doing this.

I get Tauilo another whisky and then leave for the market.

Three policemen are talking with Tauilo when I return home in the evening. I feel no fear. I sit down. I know all the policemen. One of them is Galo, the sergeant I know from the time I stayed with Tautala. Tauilo is very angry about something with the police. I wait for it. The police do not look at me.

'You do it, boy?' Tauilo asks me. I look puzzled. 'Did you rob *our* store?' I shake the head. 'See, my son says he did not do it,' Tauilo says to the police. 'And my son does not tell me lies!' The police look at each other; they are afraid of Tauilo.

'The night-watchman at the Casino tells us that it was your son who did it, sir,' Galo says softly to Tauilo.

'You believe him or me?' Tauilo warns. Galo looks at the floor. 'Pepe is not a liar. He is my flesh and blood!'

'They have to do their job,' I tell Tauilo. 'Ask me any question,' I tell Galo.

'Go on,' Tauilo says. 'Ask him anything. He will tell you he did not do it.'

Galo clears his throat and asks me, 'Where were you last night?'

193

'Sleeping in my room,' I say.

'You prove that?'

I look at Tauilo and suddenly want him to lie for me. 'Ask my father,' I tell Galo. There is silence.

'Yes, he was sleeping here,' Tauilo says.

'Did you see him, sir?' Galo asks.

'Of course I saw him. You do not take my word for it?'

And immediately the police are lost. Tauilo tries not to look at me. I burst out laughing and the police are puzzled.

'I did it,' I tell them. They looked scared. Tauilo has his back to me. 'I did it alone.'

'You sure?' Galo asks.

'I am sure,' I reply. I stand up. 'We go now?' I walk to the door.

'He tells you a lie!' Tauilo shouts to the police.

I stop and face him. 'My father is the liar,' I say to them and walk out.

The police follow me.

Tauilo slams the door behind us.

Trial of the Native Son

Galo brings to my cell a breakfast of butter and jam and bread and tea. He sits down opposite me while I eat.

'You know something?' he says.

'What?' The bread and tea tastes good for I have not eaten for a day.

He looks away from me and says, 'You can be free.'

'Can I have some more tea?' I ask. He pours me another cup.

'They are calling it "The Big Robbery" already'.

'Who?'

'Everyone, even my sons. You are a hero. They are going to make songs about you. But me, I am going to be the villain in them. I do not mind though because I am doing my job.'

'How long you been a police?' I ask.

'Twenty years.'

'Long time. Good job?'

'It is a job someone has to do,' he says.

We do not say anything for a while.

'You can be free,' he says.

'How?' I extend the empty cup. He fills it.

'The night-watchman has no proof you are guilty. It is only his word.'

'But he tells the truth.'

'It is his word against yours,' he says. I hand him the empty cup and plate.

'Who you afraid of?' I ask. 'Is it my father?'

He gives me a cigarette. 'Pepe, I have known you a long time. You got everything. Money, brains, a future. Me, I got nine children and a big family. I struggled to get where I am.'

'Galo, I am not changing my mind.'

'You sure?' he asks. I nod the head. 'Anything else you need?' I shake the head. 'Do not blame me, Pepe.'

'For what?'

'For what I will have to do to you.'

'It is your job,' I reply.

'Yes, it is my job,' he says. Then he leaves.

After noontime, when my cell is hot, they come and take me to the office for questioning. 'Who you taking the blame for? Who else did it with you?' they keep asking. But I stick to my story. They keep on for hours until they are sweating and their uniforms are soaked. Galo leads the questions; he does his job well.

'I also hit those police and I burnt the hall down,' I add. I notice they are not writing anything down for evidence.

'If we charge you with robbery, arson, and assault,' says Galo, 'the Judge is going to send you to prison for a long time.'

But I do not budge.

The palagi Commissioner enters and sits down beside Galo. He smokes and watches me, the others continue their questioning. The Commissioner, so the Vaipe people have told me, is a cruel man. There are stories of Mr Towers (that is his name), about how he likes to watch

195

people suffer. His wife, after one year in Samoa leaves him and returns to New Zealand. Towers goes with many women, especially after he watches somebody suffering. A few years before, three men escape from Tafaigata Prison and one of them puts a rifle bullet in Towers' lung. They say the bullet is still there and is poisoning him slowly.

'Why you telling all these lies, boy?' Towers suddenly asks me in English. 'You never did it alone.' Galo starts to interpret into Samoan.

'You scared of my father too?' I ask him in English. Towers jumps up.

'Boy, your father is a good man. I do not know how he comes to have so bad a son like you,' he says. I do not reply; I stare back at him. 'You believe in religion, boy?'

'It does not interest me,' I say.

'You love your mother, boy?' He is smiling now. I am suspicious about his questions because they have nothing to do with my crimes. 'You love her?' he repeats.

'Yes,' I say.

'You lie, you are never home, you do not look after her. You are destroying her slowly. Am I right?' I do not reply. I notice Galo is now writing down everything. I am puzzled by this.

'If you are a Christian why you burn down the Protestant Church hall?' Towers asks next.

'Because God does not live in it, and I do not want to burn places in which people live,' I reply.

'You an atheist?' Towers is like the preacher on the pulpit, like Tauilo.

'What is atheist?' I ask.

'He is an atheist,' Towers say to Galo. 'Put that down.' Galo writes it in the book. The other police look at me in a strange way as if I have a aitu inside me. 'Bring the Bible,' Towers instructs them.

When the Black Book comes Towers holds it out to me and says, 'Take it.' I smile and take it. 'You ready to swear you alone committed the robbery, arson, and assault, boy?' I nod the head. It is all ridiculous. The other police look afraid; perhaps they are waiting for their God to strike me dead if I lie on the Black Book.

196

'Say it!' Towers says.

'I swear by your almighty God and your almighty Book that I robbed your store and bashed your police. All right?' I say. While I say it Galo is looking up like he is expecting the holy thunderbolt to burn me to cinders like the church hall.

'And you burnt God's hall,' Towers adds.

'And I burnt your hall to ashes,' I say.

'Put that down. Every word of it,' Towers instructs Galo.

'What does all that prove?' I ask. Towers smiles.

'You will find out. Wait till you appear before *him*.'

'Him?'

'The Judge. He is going to put you away for a very long time of hard labour!' He laughs for the first time. Some of the police join him as if the joke is on me now. It has something to do with the Judge, but I do not understand as yet.

That evening before the sun is fully set Galo brings Lupe to my cell. I turn away from her who is no longer the Lupe I knew. She stands and cries.

'Stop crying,' I tell her.

'Pepe, you tell them you did not do it, please!' she pleads. I sit her down on the cell bed. I stand looking out the window at the blood-red west where Sapepe is and always will be, at where the alive Lupe I loved is buried. And I can never forgive Tauilo for that. 'Pepe, please tell them what they want. You're the only thing I have left!'

'It is too late,' I tell her. I do not know what else to say.

'It is not. They told me if you confess they will set you free!'

'You do not understand,' I say. 'Not any more.'

'But I do, Pepe!'

'We are both different people now.'

'Tell them everything, Pepe. I understand you just do not want to tell on your friends. That is what Tauilo told me!'

And I know then that they and Tauilo are using her again. 'So it is for Tauilo you are doing this?' I turn to face her.

'No, Pepe. It is for me, your mother!'

197

'You do not remember any more what he did to you and what he is doing to you now! He destroyed you — and I hate him for that.'

'He loves me, Pepe. He loves you too still,' she cries. And I have to look away from the suffering and death I see in the woman who gave me birth and life.

'You better leave. It is late, too late,' I tell her. She is weeping again and I want to shut my ears and heart to her, to the beautiful memory of her back there in Sapepe in the years of my childhood before Tauilo destroyed it all. 'Galo!' I call.

He enters and looks at her and then at me and I see the dislike in his eyes for me. 'Take her out,' I tell him. I turn to the windows. The sun has drowned in Sapepe at the edge of the world.

Her footsteps fade away from my life.

The court-room is like the inside of the Sapepe church. On my left is the high pulpit in which the Judge will sit in his throne. On the wall behind Him is a picture of the New Zealand and Samoan flags. I am sitting in front of the pulpit with my back to the windows that look out on to the main street and harbour. Opposite me at a desk sits the prosecutor in his police uniform. To his right is a wooden cage with a bench inside it. This is where the accused usually sits but seeing I am defending myself I do not have to sit in it. The congregation has been coming in all the time and sitting on the rows of benches that extend right to the back, all facing the pulpit. Soon the court is full and the congregation are looking at me. The Judge is late. Two reporters come in and sit near the prosecutor. They look at me, their eyes say nothing, all they want is news. Some of the congregation are talking, and I know they are talking about me, making up stories they will return to the villages and tell the others. Most of my Vaipe friends are in the congregation.

'Stand!' commands the policeman who enters and stands in front of the pulpit. The police behind me tell me to stand. Silence. No one moves.

The door behind the pulpit to the right opens. The

Judge enters. He looks like a priest in his black silk dress and white wig and shiny black shoes and steel spectacles. My Judge, my priest, my confessor. He looks at no one. The sound of his shoes taps across my heart and up into the pulpit and throne.

The congregation bow their heads. The Black-Dress, my Judge is praying. I begin to understand with fear why the Commissioner and police asked me about religion and God.

They tell me to stand up again.

One police in a loud voice reads out the crimes I committed. The congregation sighs in wonder.

'You plead guilty or not?' the police asks.

'Guilty,' I reply. The congregation talks in surprise because I am not fighting. The reporters are writing.

The Black-Dress wants to speak. It wants to know. 'Bring him forward,' It orders. The police take me up to stand in front of the pulpit.

My fear begins but I want to know who the Black-Dress is. I look up at the face. It is pale behind glass and the mouth is thin; the eyes are deep under the forehead and they show nothing, like the eyes of the owl that was the Tauilopepe Family god in the ancient times. The head is with a wig. The rest is black like wet river stone. It is a face you can see everywhere but you do not take much notice of it because it is the face of everybody you do not really remember. It is not important whether the face is white or black or brown or yellow.

The Black-Dress is going to speak.

'What is your name?' It asks in English of me. The interpreter starts to interpret. I silence him. The eyes of the Black-Dress burn for a moment, then go dead. I will play my joke.

'My name is Pepesa, son of Sapepe and the gods of Sapepe,' I declare in Samoan. The congregation talk in surprise. They know I am fighting at last, putting on a good show like in the movies.

'Pepesa? Why Pepesa?' It asks in Samoan.

'After the Sapepe hero who challenged all the gods and won,' I reply. But It does not smile nor is It amused.

'Good. But why "son of the gods"?' It asks.

'Because it is my genealogy!' I am feeling relaxed and want to tell It everything because It is taking my joke seriously.

'To the gods?' It asks.

'Yes, to the gods.'

'In our century as well?'

'Yes, in our century,' I extend the joke. It thinks for a moment.

'This is the twentieth century. There is one God.' It looks at me dead-on down. This is not a joke to It and It does not know who I am yet. 'You know who the missionaries were?'

'Yes, I know.'

'Who?'

'They break through the skies of our world and bring guns and the new religion and the new God and drive my gods into the bush and mountains where they live today,' I declare, nearly laughing. Some of the congregation talk loudly. The Black-Dress raps the hammer down.

'The missionaries brought the Light!' The voice is hard like the steel of Its spectacles. I hear the silence round me and in me.

'It is not for me to say whether the missionary brought the Light as you call it,' I reply. The right arm of the Black-Dress rises up like the wing of a black bird. It starts to recognise who I am.

'Why not?' It demands.

'Because they are dead and gone and I am still here. We are still here,' I say. Some of the congregation talk again. The hammer goes bang-bang-bang! Silence again. It coughs, picks up the glass, and drinks the medicine.

'I cannot believe you,' It says after It wipes the mouth. 'Are you a Christian?' And now I understand why the police asked me all those questions, and my courage to joke begins to go. 'Are you a Christian?' It repeats.

I remember a trial scene in one American gangster movie, and reply, 'I do not want to answer that in case I will incriminate myself!' Some of the people laugh. It silences them with the hammer.

200

'Now, boy, if you are not serious I will punish you severely. Understand?' It says. The Black-Dress has no sense of humour like all other preachers and gods, the modern type. But I cannot go back on my challenge, I am committed to Pepesa. 'I repeat, boy, ARE YOU A CHRISTIAN?' Everyone waits for my answer.

'I do not know because I do not know what a Christian is,' I hear the self saying aloud.

'You go to church?'

'One time I did,' I reply. It says nothing to that.

'Why you burn down the Hall of God?' It asks me slowly.

'To take the police away from the store I was robbing.'

'Do not lie, boy. You have said already you are a pagan, a heathen!' It stops, then says, 'I ask you again: do you believe in Jehovah?' I shake the head. 'Speak up!'

'No!' I reply. The congregation is in an uproar; most of them are against me now. The Black-Dress makes them quiet.

'Why you not believe in *our* God?' It asks next.

'You will not understand,' I say.

'Answer now!' It commands. Suddenly I get the feeling It is afraid of me.

'Because I know there is none.'

'How?' It says quickly.

'Because of who and what I am.'

'And what is that?' It looks amused.

'You were the one who told me who I am,' I reply, looking straight into the steel spectacles.

'A pagan?' It is smiling. I bow the head. 'Then you live in darkness and have nothing.'

I look up and say, 'I have the darkness and myself.'

It sighs for me and what It is going to do to me. 'No wonder you took to crime. You are evil. You are sick.' It stops for a moment. 'Do you think there is something or someone like God?' It asks. It is still not satisfied.

I nod the head slowly. I know what the next question will be and I feel I no longer have the courage to answer it honestly because they will not understand and never will.

'What is it then?' It leans forward. I hear It breathing.

'Go on.'

'I have only my darkness and my self living in my world, therefore . . . .' I stop.

'Therefore what?'

I look straight into Its face. 'Therefore I am my God.' It blinks. The congregation is stunned. The criminal is mad, they now think. A few people laugh.

'Now I know why you committed all those evil things. You are a victim of your own madness. The Devil has led you astray.' It stops. 'That is why I am going to be lenient — yes, lenient — on you. Your father is a good man. Perhaps you will become like him after we train you in jail to join us again. You were the ideal son who fell by the wayside, a prodigal son. No human being can be God, boy. There is only one God. . . .'

As It talks on and on I think I am listening again to my father Tauilo, to all preachers in their wooden thrones who do not listen to their own message because their hearts are stone. 'We will pray for your repentance, for the healing of your madness by our Loving Father,' It ends Its sermon. 'You got anything to say, Pepe?' It asks. This is the first time It calls me by my name.

What is the use? The world now is their world and they will not understand anything I say. So I shake the head. I turn and face the congregation. Except for my friends they all look at me with their silence as if I am the aitu the missionaries banished. There is a world between us I feel. A sky of stone, a river of stone, a silence as deep as the grave door, between them and me and people like me. I can do nothing to change that. Nothing.

The police make me take my seat.

The Black-Dress stands up. We stand and wait for It to leave the throne. Down the steps It comes. It suddenly stumbles to Its knees, the wig falls off Its head. Black human hair. The Black-Dress is human after all, naked without his wig of power. He looks at me, grabs his wig, puts it on, and hurries out the door with my smile chasing him.

I get four years hard labour.

202

Death of the Sacred Warrior

The first few months outside jail I spend with Tagata at my home. We go out to the movies and the billiard saloon, but that is all. The first time Tauilo meets me again he says, 'You have to be thankful I stopped them from sending you away for the time you really deserved.' I say nothing. I look repentant. He gives me some money. 'When you change your ways, come to Sapepe. You are still my son.' But I know it is only words. He is ashamed of me.

I think more and more of Sapepe and Toasa. My relatives tell me everything about Toasa. Ever since I went to prison, they tell me, Toasa hardly leaves his fale. He spends the time playing cards or plaiting sinnet or just looking at the road like he is waiting for someone, for me. They say that his mind is going away slowly because he is old, and he gets sick quite often. Every week-end I send a relative to him with food and money, but I tell the relative not to tell Toasa who these things are from. Toasa is the only strong tie I have left to Sapepe. Taifau is a different man now. I sometimes think of Faitoaga but I know he is all right because Tauilo can never change or harm him.

The high wailing like a nightmare wakes me from my bed. I rush out. It is Lupe beating her face with her hands. A messenger from Sapepe is opposite her.

'What is the matter?' I ask him. He tells me slowly. The heat presses in on my head. I sit down. Lupe's wailing is the sound of my pain. *Toasa is dead*. Dead. Father of my life to ashes has fallen. The Sacred Warrior who taught me the ways of the sea and bush and men, who talked of our world as old as Sapepe memory, as old as the love I feel for him. He is dead, the Banyan Tree, and I am the shell that will walk the earth like the shadowless noon.

All the way to Sapepe in the truck I try to recapture my childhood with Toasa, but the memories evade me like mosquitoes that bite you and then are gone before you can catch them. Everything outside the truck is like the old useless photos that hang on the walls of Tauilo's house. They have no meaning. The journey is like going back to where I never came from, a world where only Pepe, the boy, belongs.

The truck stops in front of our Sapepe house. I realise my clothes are of the town so I go into the house and put on one of Tauilo's lavalava and take off my shirt. As I come out there are many of my childhood friends on our store veranda. They look at me and I at them. There is a world between us now. I bow the head and walk towards Toasa's fale.

I stop under the palms. The fale is full of people and surrounded with people. Under the trees and in nearby houses more people. I see the mounds of food behind the fale and guilt hits me. I have not brought anything to my father's funeral. I go to the kitchen fale and sit on the paepae. They all watch me, as they will watch a stranger. Some children come and surround me. Toasa's family chase them away. 'It is Pepe,' I hear some people tell others. The people in the front fale turn and look at me too. The prodigal son has returned, I see that in their eyes. A hand falls on my shoulder. I look up. It is Faitoaga.

'Have you come?' he greets me. I nod the head. 'He waited but you never came.'

'Now it is too late,' I hear my mouth say.

'He will be glad you came for his last day. Before he died he told me to tell you to please forgive him,' Faitoaga says. I look at him. 'He said that it was his fault you became what you are. It was his fault, he said.'

'It was not his fault,' I reply. We say nothing for a while. More and more people arrive.

'Do you want to go in and see him?' Faitoaga asks.

They all watch us as we walk up to the fale. The people on the paepae make way and we go up into the fale with my body burning inside like the stones under my feet.

He is surrounded by his daughters in black who are weeping quietly. He is covered with ietoga and white silk. Only his face is not covered. I do not look at anyone else. I force my body to go forward to him, to his face going black with death already. I kiss his coldness as is the custom. I sit down by his head.

The women stop their weeping. 'Pepe is here, Toasa,' one of his daughters says to his body.

'What are you doing here?' Tauilo's voice cuts into me. But I keep my back to him and the other Sapepe matai who are now all his lackeys. I bow my head and compose the words of sorrow, as Toasa taught me to compose them, the lament of death, and then I begin my song, the final song of parting, something which most Sapepe people now think is unchristian, pagan.

> The Sacred Warrior is gone,
> he has fled to the mountains
> and the sea breaks in blood.
> Aue, my father is lost in the storm's eye.
> His flight is broken. . . .

The song he taught me carries me into my pain to free me of it.

> Search for him in the mountains,
> Aue, look for him in the sea's depths,
> search for him in the black river
> and in the dark clouds.
> Perhaps he is in the House of Sorrow
> banished to the cold dark
> where I will not find him. . . .

'Your father wants you to leave, Pepe,' Faitoaga whispers to me. I turn. Tauilo now occupies the most high ranking post which rightfully belongs to Toasa and me because Toasa promised it to me. 'Please, Pepe, it is Toasa's last day!' Faitoaga begs me. I push up and out and Tauilo shifts aside to let me out the front way.

I stand on the paepae to face the road and Sapepe and every stranger there. 'Sapepe!' I shout my challenge. 'It is me, Pepesa. What is mine, bequeathed to me by Toasa, my father, I now bequeath to the dogs!"

'Please, Pepe!' Faitoaga tries to stop me.

'The man who calls himself my father sits like a dog in *my* place, and you are all afraid of him! Sapepe, do you hear me, I bequeath you all to him because he is a dog, and you deserve each other!'

No one dares to stop me and my insults. And they get out of my way as I rush to Tauilo's house, take down Toasa's photograph, and rip it to pieces.

'Are you satisfied now?' Masina shouts at me. 'You are Satan's disciple!' She comes at me with her claws. I push her aside. She curses me. I pick up the Bible which has been in my family since the missionaries came to Sapepe and rip it to bits and spit on it.

The fist explodes in my face. It is Faitoaga. He holds me. I cry into his understanding.

He puts me on the truck and tells the driver to take me back to Apia.

All night I sit in my room in the darkness. Toasa is with me. His death has taken away my freedom. The dark is like my new prison and I want so much for morning to arrive.

The first cock crows. The breeze comes softly into my room through the windows and my courage begins to return. The second cock crows. I stretch my body. Toasa starts to disappear from my fear. The third cock crows. It is light. I find the courage to believe, without hate or regret, that I have nothing, nothing, now that Toasa is dead.

The dawn brings me sleep.

He drags me from my bed. I push him away. He punches me. I move away. He swings again, and again. I move away. Nothing is said. His breath comes out sharply. 'You must never hit your father, that is the sacred way; no matter if he is wrong he is still your father and you cannot change that', I hear Toasa remind me. The blow catches my face, and I fall against the bed. I stand up and face him again. His fists catch me over and over again on the face until I bleed. But I keep to my feet. I feel my strength going as the pain of his blows blinds my head and body. I fall to my knees. I rise slowly and stare at him, at the other self which I despise so much in my own self.

'Stop! Stop it, please!' Lupe cries.

'I am going to teach him a lesson he will never forget!'

206

he pants. He beats me to my knees. I hold on to the bed
and push up.

'Please!' Lupe cries.

'You...you had enough?' he shouts to me. I stand and
face him, and the darkness is filling my head.

'He has had enough!' says Lupe. 'Tell him, Pepe!' I
refuse. I steady myself for the last blows that will bring me
down to defeat. But he turns. I hear the door slam. My
other self is gone from me for ever. I collapse to the bed.

That afternoon I leave our house for good. I shift to live
with Tagata behind the market.

Lupe died a few months later. I did not go to her funeral. Tauilo buried her with great style and expense and
pretence in the Apia cemetery. A year after Lupe is under
expensive concrete and the statue of an angel Tauilo mar-
ries Teuila, one of pastor Filipo's daughters who is about
my age.

Lava

'...This world that people believe they want so much is
only true in the movies because people make the movies.
You get me?' says Tagata. I shake the head. 'Okay, well let
me explain it this way,' he says. 'Have you seen the lava
fields in Savaii?' I shake the head again. 'Two years ago I
went there with some friends. You travel for miles through
forest and so many villages where the people have ruined
the beauty. And then.... And then it is there. You feel
you are right in it at last. Get me? Like you are there
where the peace lies, where all the dirty little places and
lies and monuments we make to ourselves mean nothing
because lava can be nothing else but lava. You get me?'
He stops for a while and looks at me. 'The lava spreads for
miles right into the sea. Nothing else. Just black silence,
like the moon maybe. You remember that movie us guys
saw years ago? Well, it looks like that, like the moon's surface in that movie. A flood of lava everywhere. But in
some places you see small plants growing through the

cracks in the lava, like funny stories breaking through your stony mind. Get me? I felt like I have been searching for that all my miserable life. Boy, it made me see things so clear for once. That being a dwarf or a giant or a saint does not mean a thing.' Tagata's eyes glow brightly. 'That we are all equal in silence, in the nothing, in lava. I did not want to leave the lava fields, but...but then you cannot stay there for ever because you will die of thirst and hunger if you stay. There is no water, no food, just lava. All is lava.'

Wife and Son

As I am drinking faamafu with Tagata and other friends in the fale on the other side of the picture theatre Susana enters. She is the daughter of the man who owns the fale and the faamafu that costs two shillings a bottle. She is younger than me but she is the best-looker I have ever seen. She has graduated from the Sisters' school and is a typist for the government. As she goes behind the curtains on the opposite side of the fale she stops and looks quickly at me before she disappears. All my friends are after her but her parents make sure no one gets near her.

We drink some more. Some of the men start talking sexy about Susana. I am getting angry about that. 'Bet you she be terrific in bed!' laughs someone. 'She virgin for sure!' They laugh again.

All around the lights of the other fale and shacks are on, and people are moving about preparing the food and bathing and getting ready for sleep. Susana comes out of the curtains. The other men stop talking and look at her. She is frightened and walks quickly out to the back fale where her family are having their evening meal.

I drink until the head turns round and round and I cannot sit properly. Tagata and others hold me up and take me home and put me to bed. All the time I am mumbling to Tagata that I sure want to be with Susana. He says he will fix it for me. Before this, after I leave our home for good, I am never attracted like this to any female. For me there is no shortage of women at the market. They come from everywhere. Village women, nurses, wives, half-virgins, fun women, unsatisfied women, women who go willing for money, plain women, pretty women, cat women, old women, cold women, ugly women, tourist women who look for the Polynesian noble savage with the mighty club, but no one like Susana.

The next night Tagata disappears from our home. He returns laughing and tells me what happened.

He walks right into the fale and sees Susana's father who is a man greedy for money and the Roman religion. Tagata sits on the floor and faces him. Tagata buys some faamafu and they drink and talk about religion and everything. Now Tagata, as you know, is a professional gun-fighter at conversation. He can talk on the Bible and dazzle anyone, which is what he did to Susana's father. In the middle of their talk Susana enters and irons clothes not far from Tagata who knows she is listening to everything he is saying. Before Tagata ends his talk he asks the man (and Susana), because they are devout Christians, to pray to Jehovah to forgive him because he has been a sinner all his life. The man, who wants favours from Tagata because he owns the market, prays for Tagata who bows his head, but from the corner of his eye he sees Susana praying too. After the long prayer Tagata asks Susana questions about her religion. He tells her he is interested because he wants to join the 'true church'. Susana, with her father's permission, at once goes into a long talk about her faith. Her father starts to fall asleep. Tagata tells him politely to go to bed. Because he still does not trust Tagata the man goes to sleep behind the curtains. From there he can hear if Tagata tries anything with Susana. Tagata soon hears him snoring, so he tells Susana that he has a best friend who is keen on joining her faith too. Susana asks who it is. He tells her that it is Pepe who told the Judge that there is no God. She falls for that. 'When you going to talk to Pepe?' he asks her. 'It has to be soon because he is low in sin and there is nobody to help him see the Light.' She says, 'Very soon.' 'But what about your father?' he asks. 'I will fix that,' she says.

Tagata ends his story and we are laughing. As I said before, Tagata is a great story-teller and I do not know whether the story is all true or not but I believe him.

The next night I dress up respectable and go to the fale. They sit me down. Susana's mother is there too. I get the feeling they do not only want me to be a Roman follower but also a husband for Susana. (They know Tauilo is a rich man and I am his only son.) They talk all the time about religion. Susana's parents, I mean. Susana looks everywhere but at me. I get bored with their talk but I look interested in it.

Near midnight I leave.

For four nights or so the same thing happens when I visit them. I get angry because the plan is not working. It is soon Vaipe talk that I am after Susana as my permanent wife. Susana's father spreads this rumour. Her mother, who is more man than woman, starts to visit the market, which I am helping Tagata's parents run, and acts there like she owns me already. My friends laugh at me. I want to give up this stupid courting but every time I try to I remember Susana more alive than before. It is like the attraction of some people to religion, the sinner to his confessor and forgiver, the miser to his money. She is like the Hollywood dream. It is a new madness for me.

On the seventh night I run through the rain to her home and am surprised because she is by herself. Her parents are ready for sleep behind the curtains and the rest of their family are in the back fale. She does not look at me. She watches the rain.

She starts talking the usual about religion but her voice is unsure. I watch her closely. I let her talk on. I find myself moving over slowly till my knee is against her knee. She jumps away a bit, but she remains next to me. Her lips quiver, and even though it is chilly she looks hot.

Now, as you know, fale are open on all sides and everyone can see inside when the light is on. People run by in the rain. It is impossible for me to win her right there where every shadow can see us. As she talks my right hand falls to lie on her knee. She pretends my hand

210

is not there. 'Now, Pepe, God is good to all men,' she is saying. My hand slides down to her thigh. She talks faster. Her parents will not hear because of the rain. 'He will be good to you if you repent....' My hand slides down her lap. She is shivering a bit. 'God is everyone's Father, and He loves you and me....' The hand caresses down there and discovers soft hair, and the fingers are alive and they play slowly. 'Now if you are a sinner and you want to be with God you got to be good and repent now....' Her legs move apart a little bit and her lavalava opens more and I see the black down which is a small forest where the fingers are searching for the stream, and my heart beats in my ears and eyes and head. Her voice chatters like she is cold but she keeps talking. I find the stream. The fingers caress. The stream flows. 'Pepe...God...God is love...God, ohhh!' Her eyes are shut tight.

'Susana!' her mother calls. Susana pushes my hand away and jumps to her feet. 'Go to bed!' her mother says. She moves to leave. I whisper to her that I will come and see her when the light is out. She says nothing. She goes over and switches out the light and I hear her running down the back steps into the rain and then into the back fale which has no light on now. I creep after her.

I stand outside and can see little into the back fale. My eyes get used to the darkness. I am nearly soaking wet. I now see figures of people sleeping, but not Susana. Soon, however, I see someone waving to me from the far side. It is her. I enter. All the people are asleep, some are snoring. One step, two steps. Someone in front of me moves. I stop dead. If they catch me they will kill me alive. The person is still again. I step over him. One step, two steps, and over the next person. It is the longest walk I ever made. I step over the fourth person. And then Susana is there lying under the sheet.

I lie down beside her. She lies still and does nothing. I move closer to her till I am against her warm side. All the while my ears are wide open. They will kill me for sure. I caress her hair and slowly pull down the sheet off her. My hand falls to her breasts, she draws the deep breath. I pull up her shirt till it is round her shoulders and my fingers play tunes on her breasts and belly. Her skin is smooth like sleep.

'No, Pepe. It is a sin!' she whispers. But she does not stop my cheeky fingers that have reached the top of her lavalava and are undoing it. 'Please, Pepe. It is a sin!' The lavalava is now down by her sides, the fingers are caressing her thighs and soon find the forest again. She does not move at all and she has her arm across her face. I kiss her face and body and then I am lying on her and she moves her legs apart. 'It is a sin, sin!' she whispers. I kneel between her legs. I shed my human clothes.

And then kneel down on she. The barrier is there in her sea. She starts to cry. Her virgin-ness is strong. I try slow. No show. All the while her sound is complaining it is a sin.

Hard. Success at last. She folds up in pain. I embrace her and move slowly in her sea, and she is responding as a woman should. Every trick I try to make her come but I find the self too eager and I am giving her the seed and the fire explodes in my eyes.

She flings her arms around me. 'Pepe, I love you,' she says. That hits me in the gut. I am not in love with her, and I know she does not feel that about me. 'It is a sin what we did,' she says. 'But it is not a sin if we get married in the church. That is what my mother said.'

I put on my clothes and creep out of the fale. I am never going to see her again. The whole dream is a fake, hollow. They planned it all.

For a few months Tagata's parents go to American Samoa for holidays, and Tagata and me are left to manage the market. I slowly notice that something is happening to Tagata: he looks sick but he never tells me the trouble, he does not do his job properly so I do all the work and the market makes more money than before. I introduce new methods and keep account books. Some people tell that my success is because I am Tauilo's son and because business runs in my family's blood.

Tagata starts to stay in his room most of the time and he

212

grows his hair long. Sometimes he does weight-lifting and goes for long runs to get fit. To cheer him up I join his exercises. He is escaping I think, and it is like a new madness. He is like the flying-fox, which is his nickname, that has no nest with the other birds because they laugh at him and treat him different because he is not what a bird should be. Now he, my brother, is trying to grow and be like other men, that is my understanding of his problem. Why he suddenly starts to do this I never found out.

Because of the hard work at the market and my worries about Tagata I forget Susana.

Tagata takes up the LMS religion. I am really worried because it is against what he believed before. Every Sunday he puts on his white clothes and goes to church. But when he returns and I see he is happy my worry goes away. It is at this time that Susana comes into my life again.

In the small market office I am working on the books. There is a knock on the door. I open it. It is Susana's father.

'Have you come?' I greet him.

He stands looking at the floor and says, 'Yes, sir.' When he calls me sir I get suspicious at once. Most people in the market when they want something for free start to flatter you.

'Sit down.' I give him a chair.

'No thank you, sir.' He stands there. I know him very well; he has the reputation for taking the last penny off his starving mother.

'What do you want?' I ask him straight.

Then his wife fills the doorway. Susana does not look like both of them put together. The mother is like the cow and the father is like a sick pig.

She sits in the chair without asking me and says, 'Hot day, is it not?' I stare straight at her. 'How is the business, Pepe?' Then she laughs. I do not reply. She scratches the armpits. Her husband is still looking at the floor. 'You not been for a long time to see us,' she says. 'We still have the best faamafu. For you it is free!' She roars with laughter again.

'I have much work to do,' I say.

'You go ahead,' she says, winking at me. 'Boy, you really educated and brainy as your father. Look at all those figures and books you are adding up. You wrote all those?' I do not answer. She picks up one book and looks at it. 'Pepe is bright,' she says to her husband. 'Look at all this English and figures. He is as bright as any palagi. You making much money these days?' she asks. 'Business is bad for us. We find it hard to feed all our big family.'

'What you want?' I ask. She looks at her husband, he is still looking at the floor. She coughs but he still not do anything. 'What is it?' I ask him.

He blinks and whispers, 'It's our Susana, sir.'

'Louder!' she commands him.

'It is about our Susana, sir,' he repeats. She nods.

'What about her?' I ask. She is looking at me like I am the fly and she is the spider.

'She is with child, sir,' he says, and he looks at me for the first time that day.

'What has that got to do with me?' I demand. He does not say anything.

'Tell him!' she orders.

He blinks again and says, 'Susana says . . . .' And stops. Blinks and says, 'She says you are the father, sir.'

'Now we not saying that you are the father, Pepe. Susana is saying it,' she says.

'You trying to blackmail me?' I ask.

'No, but Susana said . . . .' she says.

'Said what?' I demand.

'Tell him!' she orders. He shakes the head. 'Tell him what your daughter said. Go on!'

'She may be lying,' I say.

'Oh, Pepe, she does not lie to me. Oh, no. She is a religious girl,' she says.

Yes, Susana is a good girl,' he says. 'She is not like other girls in the Vaipe.'

'If she is so good,' I say, 'why she got the fat belly now?' I have them. She sits and he stands, they are both looking at the floor.

I sit and look out at people passing by and I remember

Sapepe and my mother Lupe and my anger goes. The desire for someone of my own flesh to care for and give meaning to me fills me as I watch the market people. My own child growing in Susana's womb, the meaning perhaps to all the gone years. A son or a daughter.

Tagata bursts into the room. 'It is all a lie!' he laughs. 'I am sick of religion!' It is the same Tagata again and I am full of joy. He stops his dancing when he sees Susana's parents. He looks at them and then at me. 'What is the matter?' he asks me.

'Susana is going to have my child,' I tell him. He jumps up and down, then he runs out into the market. I hear him telling our friends that he is going to be an uncle.

'I will take her as my wife but I do not want you to come near me and my family. Understand?' I threaten Susana's parents.

'Yes, sir,' he says.

She gets up angrily and leaves.

So it passes that Susana, who I do not love really, comes to stay with me in Tagata's home which is now my home too. She insists we get married in church. I refuse absolutely.

Because I have a family to support now — Tagata and his old parents and Susana and my child who is to be born soon — I work harder at the market. Most of the time I am away from Susana but that does not worry me because Tagata spends all his time helping her and dreaming and talking of the nephew he is going to have soon. Most nights I go home to find nearly all my Vaipe friends there, such as Lafoga. Tagata tells them that the baby is going to be a boy and his name is going to be Lalolagi which means the world.

'Why Lalolagi?' Lafoga asks him.

'Because Pepesa was the father of mankind,' Tagata replies.

'But that is not the right legend,' someone else says.

Tagata gets angry and says to them, 'That is the trouble with you, you do not know your own history and legends. You are uneducated. Anyway, even if it is not the right

215

legend, his name is going to be Lalolagi!'

Susana has never liked my friends. She tells me they are the worst sinners and criminals in Samoa, so when she hears about our child's name, she says we are not going to call him that.

'Why not?' I ask.

'Because my mother says that the baby's name should not be chosen by criminals!'

Bang! her head spins with my slap. 'You call my friends that again and I will send you back to your mother who sold you to me!' This is the first big quarrel of many to follow. She does not leave. Her mother does not want her back because Susana, so Tagata tells me, is supplying her family with much free money and food.

I try to get close to Susana. I really try. But she wants me to be the husband she wants me to be — the man who works hard, brings home the loot, a non-drinker and a staunch Roman follower who will marry her in her church. I want her to accept me as I am but it is too late as she is a Roman permanently. Bitterness forces me to try to drive out her coldness with my flesh but the cold of her upbringing is the coffin of her self.

The child is born. It is a male child as Tagata said it would be. He lies in my arms. Flesh of my flesh. Proof that life who made me still has faith in me. I hold him as the preciousness of my childhood years in Sapepe, as Lupe held me for the first time, and as Toasa did. I hold him as the true meaning of my years and the years to come, as Tauilo held me. I hold him as I hold the memory of Niu and Vao. And weep with joy.

When Susana and my son return home from the hospital my friends gather. Tagata holds up my son and to everyone tells that his name is Lalolagi.

'Lalolagi who?' Lafoga asks him. Susana is looking at me. I say nothing because it is the custom that a child takes the first name of his father as its surname but not the family name as is the palagi custom.

'Lalolagi *Tauilopepe*,' Susana tells them. Everyone looks at me. 'That is what my mother says his surname should be,' Susana says.

216

'That is not the custom,' Tagata tells her. My friends agree with him. 'His name is Lalolagi Pepesa.'

'Let us have a party!' Lafoga suggests. Our youngest friends go into the shack behind our home and bring back dozens of faamafu. And there is singing and dancing and laughter and food. Tagata's parents come down from upstairs and give Susana presents for the baby, kiss him, and then leave for somewhere else. Susana is forgotten in the corner. The party continues. As he drinks, Tagata holds Lalolagi.

Everybody is quiet suddenly. A woman about my age and dressed in a blue dress and white lavalava is standing in the front doorway. 'Please,' she says, 'does Pepe live here?' No one answers. A man appears beside her. I look at him and recognise him as a relative of mine. He holds a large basket with a cooked pig in it. I go to them. 'We brought these for your wife and the new-born child,' she says. It is the custom. The man, whose name I have forgotten, brings in the pig and puts it down in the middle of the room. Two women, both my relatives, follow him in and place baby mats and sleeping mats by the pig and then leave. But I am puzzled still as to who the woman is. The party behind me is alive again. She turns to leave.

'Thank you,' I say.

'They are from your father,' she says. Now I know who she is. It is Teuila, Tauilo's new wife. 'Here is something from me.' She gives me a small parcel. 'It is for your child.'

'Come in,' I invite her.

'I have to go somewhere else,' she says. 'Is it a boy?' I nod. 'Your father wanted to know. He will be happy when he hears. I must go now.' I walk with her out to the veranda. Tauilo's car is parked out front.

'Is he here?' I ask. She shakes the head. 'We are strangers now, my . . . .'

'Yes?' she encourages me.

And I say it at last after all these years, 'We are strangers, my father and me. I do not hate him any more.'

'Can you forgive him?' she asks. 'He is not a bad man. He is hard. He is a lonely man too. He wants everyone to be like him. . . . I have to go now.' She goes down the steps. She stops and asks, 'He wants to see him, the child I mean. What shall I tell him?'

'Yes, tell him yes.' And I know that if it was not because of her I would not have agreed.

'Thank you,' she replies. 'What is the boy's name?'

'Lalolagi.'

'That is a good name. I will tell him.'

'Come and see him whenever you want to!' I call as she gets into the car.

During the party, when nearly everyone is drunk, Susana suddenly runs to Tagata and tries to take Lalolagi from him. Tagata laughs and dances away with Lalolagi. 'Stop them!' Susana calls to me. 'They are going to hurt him.' She rushes to Tagata again and before I can stop her she slaps his face. 'Let go *my* son!' she yells. 'You are going to make him evil!' Everyone is quiet. Tagata does nothing to her because of me. He gives her the baby and runs out of the house.

'Do not ever do that again!' I warn her.

'You are all the same!' she tells me. My hand whips up but stops because Lalolagi is in her arms. She runs away and up the stairs.

'Bitch!' I call. Everyone is still.

'Drink up, there is more faamafu to see the stars together with!' laughs Lafoga, and the tension eases again.

For four years I watch my son grow and find the gift of speech. Tagata is his bodyguard and napkin changer and big brother who takes him everywhere he goes. Most of my friends, especially Lafoga, buy him anything he wants. Tagata starts to teach him how to read, and when Lalolagi does not want to learn he says to him, 'You want to be like me? Ugly and uneducated?' And Lalolagi takes the lessons. In the afternoons when Susana is not around, Lafoga comes and starts to show Lalolagi how to box. Lalolagi cries at times but Lafoga does not give up; he bribes him with sweets and tells Tagata to feed the boy with steak and taro all the time so that Lalolagi can grow up big and be a boxing champion. Susana wants him baptised in church. I allow it because it is up to Lalolagi to find out himself whether religion is true for him or not.

I continue to run the market, enlarge it, and paint it up, and it makes more money than ever. Tagata talks me into buying a car and he uses it to take Lalolagi every second week-end to Sapepe to stay with Teuila and Tauilo. Someone else has to drive because Tagata is too short. Then on Monday he goes back to get Lalolagi. I want Lalolagi to learn about Sapepe and the past of our people. At first Susana objects to him going because she says that she does not want him to grow up and be 'an ignorant villager from the back'. But she thinks again and realises that Tauilo is a very wealthy man and, because I have refused to be his heir, Lalolagi will probably inherit Tauilo's money. So she encourages him to go all the time.

When he is able to talk, Lalolagi returns from Sapepe and tells everyone that his grandfather is very good to him and gives him everything he asks for and he wants to be like his grandfather when he grows up. This scares me but I want him to find out for himself. He goes to church every Sunday with Tauilo and Teuila, and he comes back on Monday and asks me, 'Why do you not go to church? Susana goes and so do Teuila and Tauilo. Church is for good people. Why do you and Tagata not go?' Tagata laughs but I do not say anything. How do you explain your life to a child?

All Is Vanity

As I have said before, Lafoga, who I consider a brother like Tagata, completes what we call our 'three-man family'. He used to be heavyweight champion of Western Samoa. Like me he was not born in the Vaipe but came from a far-away village. Years ago his village encouraged him in boxing because he was strong like a bull. They bring him to town every Friday night to fight in the boxing contests and he cleans up every opponent in one year and gets the chance to fight for the heavyweight title. He knocks out the champion in two rounds with a left-right combination to the jaw and belly and becomes the most popular champ in the country. People who saw him fight will tell you that Lafoga had little style, science I mean. He went in like a stone wall and the punches just bounced off him, then he went one-two-three and his opponents saw stars.

When he has the title he shifts to live in Apia. For six years he is champ and most boxers are afraid to fight him. Then all this glory goes to his head and he stops training hard. He gets to love the drink and the women and large quantities of food, and gets flabby and slow. He boasts all the while of his strength and speed but these slip away from him. A young policeman, a really scientific and fit heavyweight, comes up the championship ladder and wins the people's cheers. Lafoga tries to train for the title fight but is not honest about his training. In the twelve-round bout the policeman just moves in one-two-three and away, and Lafoga is left hitting the empty air. The policeman does this for eight rounds until Lafoga is standing in the middle of the ring like a defeated bull with no strength left. In the ninth round the policeman nails him like a machine-gun stitching up a gangster. Left-right-left. Head and body. And Lafoga is crucified by the crowd's booing because he can no longer fight back. He goes down. He gets up. He paws at the light. The policeman moves in with the rapid fire. The crowd is booing Lafoga. The ref stops the fight.

From this defeat on, Lafoga's head goes funny at times. Whenever he thinks of that defeat he is not himself, and everyone must get out of his way. He wanted to return to his village but he could not face the disgrace, so he stayed in Apia, in the Vaipe. When I run the market I employ him to do odd jobs but mainly to keep order by stopping any quarrels or fights. And we become firm friends.

On Lalolagi's fifth birthday Lafoga appears at our house with a woman we had never seen before. He tells us that she is from his village and he met her at the market and she is now living with him as his wife. Her name is Fanua and she is nearly as big as Lafoga. She is very shy, saying very little, but you can always feel her presence in any gathering. She is about Lafoga's age and had obviously married before and had given birth to children. But we do not ask her because we sense that Lafoga is satisfied that he does not know very much about her past. Lafoga, we notice straightaway, is a different person. He is more quiet and happy and loves Fanua very much. He does everything she wants, and works more hard and regular at his job with me. He even drinks less and no longer takes part in the crimes that him and his friends did before. We do not resent Fanua for changing him because we are all glad that Lafoga has found some calm, peace, and joy in his life. Somehow she heals the feeling of defeat that he has always suffered from.

As we come to know Fanua we too come to accept her completely as one of us, as someone we cannot do without. She has the gift of peace, of healing people's fears, Tagata tells me. When she is around we feel whole again. Only Susana does not accept her. Every time Fanua is in our house Susana makes up an excuse to leave. It is like she is afraid of Fanua, scared that Fanua will win her affection and turn her into a different person.

One day at the market I see Fanua talking to a man I have never seen before. I think nothing of it. I go into my office and when I come out a few minutes later the man is gone. Fanua comes over and I buy her some ice cream at one of the stalls. As we eat our ice creams I suddenly notice that she is upset about something. I ask her but she just shakes her head and laughs softly. Lafoga appears and I buy him an ice cream too. He tells us he has just settled an argument between two women vendors.

'How did you do it?' Fanua asks him.

'I bang their heads together!' he laughs. We laugh too.

As they walk away from me I notice how large both of them are. Like giant puppies, I think. Or dolphins. Just before I turn to go back into my office I see Fanua looking back at me. There is a look of fright on her face, I think, like she is trying to tell me something, ask me for help.

Two weeks or so later I see her and the other man again. This time they look as if they are arguing but not

221

wanting to look as if they are. I go up to them but the man turns and goes away before I can see what his face looks like. Fanua starts talking quickly to me and I know she is trying to distract me and also to hide how she is feeling. I do not mention anything about it. She is wary of me now, I sense. As she talks I suddenly see something about her that I have never noticed before. A colour in her eyes, a movement in her body, a feeling about her that suddenly makes me want to hurt her, the same thing I had seen in Lupe in her last years and the thing which forces many people to punish themselves or get others to punish them. The man she had been talking to is a threat to her, and her very fear is bringing this out in her, I tell myself after she leaves me. But I do not mention this to anyone. I even forget it as the weeks go by and I notice everything is well between Fanua and Lafoga.

The door of my office opens quietly. I am busy writing and I don't look up. I only notice a man's shadow extending from the open doorway to my desk. 'Yes?' I ask. Only silence. I look up and recognise him at once.

'Sir,' he says, 'does a man called Lafoga work here?' I nod the head. He says nothing. He steps into my office. I do not invite him to sit down. I do not like him but do not know why I feel this way about him. Then I remember Fanua and how I had felt about her after he had talked to her. As I challenge his unblinking stare I think that he is the force that people always invite to punish them — like my father. He is only a fragile-looking man, someone you never notice in a crowd, but his very appearance of weakness is his strength, the power like a hypnotist I once saw in a movie that draws you in, sucks out your resistance, and you welcome the pain. 'Can you tell me where I can find him?' he asks. I shake the head. His face reminds me of the joker in a pack of playing-cards, the face smiling, the eyes a dead emptiness. 'Do you know of a woman named Fanua?' he asks. I nod the head. Nothing will stop him, I think, except death. He is committed to what he is going to do.

'Why are you looking for them?' I ask.

He continues to look at me but I sense he is looking into himself. 'Because there is something I have to do,' he says.

'What?' I ask, feeling fear in my breath.

'Only Fanua must know,' he says. 'She is my wife.'

Before I can say anything else he thanks me and leaves, taking his shadow with him.

I send for Tagata and tell him what may happen. He does not believe me. Who would ever think of harming her, he asks. I try again to convince him but he refuses to believe me. Fanua will heal her husband's jealousy, if he is her husband, he tells me. He goes and brings in Lafoga and tells me to explain to Lafoga. I try again. But Lafoga just laughs. She was not married before, he says. How does he know? I ask. Because Fanua has told me so, he says. I get them to agree to go and look for her. That afternoon they return laughing and tell me she is at home and she is all right. Lafoga brings her to our house that night. Fanua never drank before, but this night Tagata offers her some faamafu and she drinks it. Lafoga is glad of this, he says. Now she can keep him and Tagata company. We all drink late into the night and Fanua is very drunk and talkative and dancing when Lafoga takes her home. We are all glad that nothing is wrong. I push the man out of my mind.

The next evening as Tagata and me are sitting on the veranda Lafoga is suddenly standing there and we see the madness gripping him. Then he bellows like a wounded bull, 'She is dead!' Tagata holds him. Lafoga flings him away. 'She is dead!' Lafoga repeats and he falls to his knees like the whole air of the world is forcing him down. Then he forces himself up. I jump at him. Too late. He is gone to chase the night and avenge Fanua who was the living part of him.

Tagata tries to follow him. 'I will go and get that man with Lafoga!' he cries. I hold him but he struggles out of my grip. I punch him hard and he is unconscious, and I carry him into the bedroom. Then I leave to look for Lafoga.

My search is like looking for the end of the night-time.

The night holds me, and Fanua is inside me haunting me. And I understand fully now why Lafoga and Tagata loved her. Like Toasa was the heart of Sapepe, Fanua has become in that short time the heart of the Vaipe, the woman who gave birth to us in the beginning. She is gone like Toasa, and the night is real and forever.

I return home and sit by Tagata and wait. For what? Inside us we carry the seed of our own end, and I remember Toasa's words: 'The vanity in each of us makes us beasts of prey upon each other and all other living creatures. We must heal ourselves, destroy our self-love. If we do not we will continue to excrete our own self-destruction. We are capable of so much beauty.' I sit in the darkness and all I see is the face of Fanua's executioner, the joker in the cards grinning at me. It is like I am again looking at that other side of my self that I have tried all my life to drive out, like a priest in ancient times would try to exorcise an evil aitu.

Near dawn four of our friends bring back Lafoga. We force him on to a bed and tie him down. He screams and screams. I send for one of my doctor friends who comes and injects him and he goes to sleep finally.

Tagata wakes. 'It is all my fault!' he weeps. 'I did not believe you, Pepe, when you told me!' There is no need for me to speak of my own guilt too.

Dawn breaks the grip of the darkness. I wake up Susana and Lalolagi and tell them to go and stay with Teuila. I go with Tagata to the hospital and bring Fanua's body home.

The grave lies open under the frangipani trees. Lafoga and Tagata stand at the head. The grave is the deep mouth that swallows her when we lower the coffin down. We stand like turning to salt. Birds fly above us, to the sea perhaps. We step forward to the spades but Lafoga commands no. So alone he picks up a spade. We watch. The spade looks like a toy in his hands. The sweat comes forth as he works furiously to bury his self. Every time he hurls down the earth he shuts his eyes. The earth mounts up like the rising sea-tide till we see her no more for the earth has reached the forever level.

224

Lafoga throws down the spade and runs for home.

I do not try to stop Lafoga. He hunts even into the depths of the village of his birth for the man who killed Fanua. Tagata returns to tell me, 'It is over. He has given himself up to the police. He is a coward, he says, because he wants the police and the Judge to take his life. He cannot end it himself. He says to tell you thank you.'

The next week Lafoga goes on trial. We do not attend it. The Judge rules to hang him. The Judge says he will pray for Lafoga's soul. Who will pray for the Judge's soul, I ask myself.

Last Will and Testament of the Flying-Fox

...One morning I wake to find Tagata gone. I send friends to look for him. They cannot find him anywhere. Even the police and the hospital do not know where he is.

I wait for him for six days. On the seventh day he returns. His hair and beard are long and uncombed and his clothes are torn and dirty and his eyes glow like those of the prophets in the desert.

'I went back, Pepe. Back to the lava, and it has brought me up from hell again. Lava is the only true thing left. It cannot change. The rock from whom we came, and it is with us at the back of our souls. You get me?' he says. 'It is where I found the self again. And the courage to accept all that has happened!' He laughs then and he seems his usual self again and I believe he is going to be okay. So I leave for work in the market.

That evening when the sun sets over the sea and the birds fly back to the mountains and the forests and the market is empty and shut down I return home.

I find him hanging down from the mango tree behind the house.

I cut him down and take him into the house.

I bath him.

I dress him.

225

I find this letter in English on my table:

To His Excellency,
Pepesa Tauilopepe,
Illegitimate Son of the Gods.

My Beloved Brother Condemned,
I know you will understand because you understand this dwarf and brother condemned really well. As I before said to you, I am the free man who got the right to dispose of his self. This life is the only life, and it is a good life because it is the only one we have. I was born a small man with a big man inside, the flying-fox with an eagle in the gut. All my life I tried for to free this eagle so he can fly high and dazzle the world. Anyway, on this my last day and hour, you will find the eagle flying on the mango tree with his one wing of rope. Life, as I said and always wanted to preach to you, is good. It is good because it is ridiculous like a dwarf is ridiculous, an accident caused when parents make fire too much. Because life is ridiculous it has to end the most ridiculous way, in suicide like Christ. Laugh, Pepesa, because I am right there inside the death-goddess which no one believes in any more, and her sacred channel is all lava. Laugh, Pepesa, because her lava machine is grinding me, the Flying-Fox, to dust. Laugh, Pepesa, because there is nothing else to do.

The papalagi and his world has turned us and people like your rich but unhappy father and all the modern Samoans into cartoons of themselves, funny crying ridiculous shadows on the picture screen. Nevermind, we tried to be true to our selves. That is all I think any man with a club can do.

To you, your godly Excellency, I apologise because the Flying-Fox has nothing to leave in this my will, but 1001 laughs, as the movies say, which I desire you, your Excellency, to laugh one laugh every night from now on until you die. One laugh laughed loud will keep away sorrow and your father and the Romans and the LMS and the modern aitu and the police and the Judge and bad breath. One laugh will turn everything to lava and joy and forgiveness.

226

For all this wealth I am leaving you, your most intelligent Excellency, I ask one last tiny favour. It is this. Dig a small hole on the bank of the Vaipe and into this hole dump this dwarf carcass of mine. Then fill it fast with Vaipe mud before it stinks our most excellent Vaipe neighbourhood. Plant on it taro and I swear on the lava that the taro will grow like nobody's business because I am excellent manure. When the taro is ready, give it to the market people. I am sure, as I am sure I am dead, that they will all die from greedy diarrhoea.

So long, Pepesa, I am moving down and out, as the cowboy says.

All is well in Lava. Tell your son and my nephew that, but do not tell Susana who, as your Excellency knows, is a bitch.

> *I remain forever dead,*
> *Your humble self,*
> *Tagata, the Flying-Fox in the Mango.*

I bury him on the banks of the Vaipe.

Exit

It is hot in my hospital room, so hot it is hard to breathe, especially when I have rotten lungs. This morning, the nurse tells me, my father came again to try to see me; he comes every day but I refuse to see him. I look out the window; the two old men are stoking their fire as usual. The pain is getting too hard to bear. As usual the nurses are fixing the beds in the next ward. The old woman patient next door is dead, she died last night, her family collected her corpse this morning, there was much weeping and wailing. But hospital life goes on as usual.

I got out of bed this morning after the nurse bathed me and I carried my skeleton to the mirror. When I looked at the man in the glass I found him a stranger, and an ugly one at that. The skin hangs off his bones like old clothes.

The eyes have no laughter in the hollow sockets. The skull is rising to the surface of his face; soon the skull will have no skin-face. Only white bone. I staggered back to bed and coughed out the blood. I lay there as usual and waited for the doctor's visit.

They enter, the nurse and the red-haired doctor. I hide my pain and am the usual gay self. The doctor smiles and examines the patient on the bed. I watch his hands as they go over the body, the skin and bone, and pronounce it living still. He tells the nurse in English to give me the usual medicine. The nurse writes it down.

'Is it alive?' I ask him in English. He is surprised because it is the first time I have spoken English to him. I laugh and repeat the question.

'Is what alive?' he asks.

'This body,' I reply.

He laughs and says, 'Yes, it will rise and go home soon.'

'That is what you think,' I joke.

'You will be all right.' He does not joke now. The nurse leaves.

'Have you made fire with her yet?' I ask. He does not know what I am referring to. 'With the nurse? She is mad on you.'

He stands up and his face is red like his hair. 'I am married,' he says.

'That does not matter,' I reply.

'My wife would not understand.'

'A pity. That nurse can teach you much,' I laugh. He is smiling this palagi who has become my first palagi friend.

I have forgotten my novel on the table near my bed. He sees it and says, 'What are you writing?'

'A letter.'

'A long letter, is it not? Who is it to?'

'To my self,' I say. There is an amazed stare on his face.

'It is in English?' he asks. I nod the head. 'Well, happy writing!' He walks to the door.

'I am going to die, am I not?' I call. He stops but does not turn to face me. 'Am I not? I want you to admit it to me.'

'Yes,' he says. He turns to look at me.

'Think of the nurse,' I tell him.
He leaves the room.
I continue to write this for the last time.

From the world of Sapepe, which my father destroyed by changing it, I came. From the world of Lupe and Toasa and Taifau and Faitoaga and my family to the world of the Vaipe and Tagata and Lafoga and Fanua and all my other friends, only to find them steps toward my self and my end. From the dark of Lupe's womb to the other dark of the death-goddess, I, Pepesa, have travelled and have seen what there is to be seen and felt and done what there is to do, and I found laughter.

Last night as I lay in my bed after the pain left me and sleep came I dreamt I saw the lava field black like the night sea flow in to cover Sapepe, the Vaipe, Apia, the market-place and all the mistakes and monuments we make to our selves. And I found myself above the lava sea as it flowed in deep and forever. And like the sun in the sky I saw Tagata laughing as he hung from the freedom tree.

A few more sentences and I am done with this novel about my life. A few more and I am done. Outside the hospital window the bald-headed men are feeding their fire.

The maggots are impatient. Soon they will break out from my flesh like bubbles as beautiful as diamonds.

All is well in Lava, so spake the Flying-Fox.

Book Three
Funerals and Heirs

1 Funeral Fit for a King

Tauilopepe returned from the hospital and went into the sitting room of his Apia house. Two chromium-topped tables glittered in the centre of the room; on one of them stood a vase filled with plastic flowers; gaudy-coloured armchairs lined the far wall which was covered with framed photographs of his aiga; the floor was a shimmering expanse of red and yellow linoleum; a door led off to the dining room on the left; near the door stood a large glass cabinet filled with expensive glassware and bottles of whisky; on the right, two large French windows opened on to a wide veranda; louvre windows lined the other two walls.

Tauilopepe sighed heavily and sat down in an armchair under the louvre windows. The breeze from the windows cooled his neck and back. Across the room near the liquor cabinet was a long three-shelved bookcase nearly filled with leather-bound encyclopaedias which he hadn't read because of his very limited English. (Whenever he had the time he browsed through the volumes, reading aloud the words he recognised.)

He heard someone in the kitchen. 'Get me a drink,' he called. Teuila, his wife, entered with a jug of ice. 'He refused to see me,' Tauilopepe said. Teuila opened the liquor cabinet, took out a half-empty bottle of whisky and a glass, put some ice in the glass, half-filled it with whisky and then poured water into it. 'Didn't you hear me?' Tauilopepe said. She nodded and handed him his drink. 'Well?' She sat down and faced him from across the room. He drained his whisky. She got him another. This time she put the bottle and jug of ice on the table in front of him. He sipped his second whisky and stared at the bookcase.

'Are the aiga at Sapepe well?' she asked. (He had spent the week in Sapepe.) He didn't answer. They remained silent, with her gazing softly at him for a long time.

233

Teuila's marriage to Tauilopepe had been arranged by Taulua, her mother, and Masina a year after she graduated from Vaiuta College, a residential school owned by the LMS, where girls were trained to be suitable wives for pastors. Filipo, her father, who was ready to retire from his position as pastor of Sapepe, had happily agreed to Taulua's plans.

The first night Tauilopepe came to court Teuila they didn't speak to each other. Her parents and Tauilopepe talked while she just sat, as was expected of her, and studied him from the corner of her eye. She couldn't believe it — Tauilopepe had always been for her a man to be admired as one would admire a great hero in the Bible, a man you never dreamt you would really know, let alone marry. However, as she watched him, and felt him watching her, her feeling of wondering disbelief diminished. But they did not speak to each other until the day they were married in the Sapepe church. That day Teuila immediately felt an inexplicable yet compellingly attractive fear. Before their marriage she had never been allowed to get close to any man; she had been chaperoned almost everywhere. Even when she had learnt from some of her friends that their relationships with men were not confined to innocent wooing she had never once felt an urge to do likewise. To her, no moral issues were involved in preserving her purity until her marriage night, and if fulfilment had come outside marriage she would have accepted it without feelings of guilt.

Teuila's first night with Tauilopepe was not terrifying as her mother had predicted. She accepted and enjoyed the pain, thus transforming the experience into the beginnings of love for the man who that night ceased to be legend and became, for her, human flesh with all its sorrows and joys and hopes. As time passed she accepted Tauilopepe as he was; and thus he could not destroy her by being who and what he was. She came to realise that what he called love was not a giving of himself but a taking and shaping in his own image of everything within his reach. This was the main reason, she came to believe, why an honest and admirable son like Pepe had devoted his whole short life to rebelling against Tauilopepe and what he represented.

Now, as she watched Tauilopepe, the father of the man who was dying in the hospital, she realised that the two men were so alike yet so very far apart.

She would tell Tauilopepe now. . . . 'Pepe said to me yesterday that he is going to . . . to be dead by tomorrow night.'

'Only God possesses the power to end human life,' Tauilopepe said. 'It is just another one of Pepe's *jokes*.' He held out his empty glass. She refilled it. 'He is bad, isn't he?' She said nothing. 'There was . . . is . . . no love in him.' He looked at her. 'You have taken his side like all the others, haven't you? His mother and his sisters and Toasa — they all took his side.'

'You want him to ask for your forgiveness. But you know he won't do that. Like you, he is too proud,' she said. He shook his head. 'Have you ever told him you loved him?'

'It's too late. He was evil. That's it — he was *evil*!'

'You always speak of evil and goodness as if you alone are the judge of such things!' she said. It was the first time she had ever criticised him openly. Before he could refute her, Pepe's son, Lalolagi, ran into the room and hurled himself into his arms.

'I've come, Papa!' the boy said, burying his face in Tauilopepe's chest.

'Perhaps he has come back,' Teuila said, as she got up and went to the dining room.

'Yes,' Tauilopepe whispered into the boy's hair. 'Yes, my son's come back.' Lalolagi couldn't understand why his grandfather was crying.

Tauilopepe returned to Sapepe in the afternoon. That night passed without sleep, and the next day dragged by in an emptiness of neat account books. The second night passed in prayer for a miracle to stop Pepe's fearful prediction of his own death from coming true.

No miracle.

Taifau brought Tauilopepe the news. He locked himself

in his study and wept, cursing Pepe for having turned against him. Drank himself to sleep finally. He woke early in the morning, summoned his whole aiga, and instructed them not to spare any expense for Pepe's funeral.

Tauilopepe hurried into the hospital corridor. The red-haired papalagi doctor and three Samoan doctors greeted him respectfully. He only nodded.

'I am very sorry. ...' the papalagi doctor started to say.

'Where are he?' Tauilopepe asked in English.

The papalagi doctor pointed to the door at the end of the corridor.

Tauilopepe walked slowly towards it. The doctors followed him, and one of them pushed the door open. Tauilopepe stepped into the room, startling a young nurse who was sitting next to a black coffin lying on a bed in the middle of the room. On the other bed lay Susana, asleep. She stirred, jumped to her feet when she saw Tauilopepe, and started to weep. Tauilopepe told one of the doctors to take her out of the room.

'We took the liberty of providing your son with this,' one of the Samoan doctors said in Samoan, placing a hand on the coffin.

'Where my son's things?' Tauilopepe asked in English. The Samoan doctors looked at their papalagi colleague who in turn looked at the frightened nurse.

'He come with nothing,' the nurse said in English.

'It seems, sir, your son came here with very little,' one of the Samoan doctors said in English.

'Where are the clothes he came in with?' Tauilopepe asked in Samoan. The Samoan doctors looked at their papalagi colleague who in turn looked puzzled for he didn't understand Samoan.

'We burn them,' the nurse replied in English.

'Thanking to you,' Tauilopepe said in English.

'Do you want to take him home now?' one of the Samoan doctors asked in Samoan.

'No, leave us,' Tauilopepe replied in Samoan.

The doctors and nurse started to leave the room. 'Tell my son's wife to go home. I don't want to see her when I

236

come out!' Tauilopepe called to the nurse in Samoan.

Alone in the room which smelt faintly of decaying frangipani and disinfectant, Tauilopepe couldn't take his eyes
off the coffin, as if his own body was locked within that
black box, the focus of all superstitions surrounding death.
Maggots squirming, burrowing into his flesh. He dug his
finger-nails into his arm. He had never been able fully to
accept the truth that everyone had to die.

He had to do it. He shut his eyes tightly and shuffled up
to the coffin. His sweat tasted bitter in his mouth as his
hand touched the black velvet covering. Nothing happened. God was his invincible armour. Opened his eyes
but refused to look down. Something glittered on the low
cupboard across the room. He went to it. It was a rosary.
His fingers caressed the crucifix which hung from it, then
he dropped it into his pocket. He opened the cupboard. It
was completely bare. He slammed it shut. Pepe was dead.
Now he would never know what his son had really been
like.

He turned to the coffin. Advanced. Stopped. Looked
down through the small glass window at Pepe's face.
Jumped back. Stifled a scream. He would never know anything about Pepe. Nothing. The black face with the mocking smile, preserved especially for him, told him so.
Another death-mask clogged his head — Toasa, the same
mocking grin. He took out the rosary and flung it at the
coffin. It broke, the beads scattering across the floor. He
fled from the room.

No, they weren't going to win.

They were dead.

He sat in his car which was parked in the shade of a
tamaligi tree in front of the hospital dispensary, smoking
cigarette after cigarette. His clothes were drenched with
sweat. A group of people were weeping in front of the
surgery only a short distance away. An old man, legs thick
with filariasis, watched them from the office veranda. A
white dog ambled up and sniffed at the old man's legs. The
old man whacked it across the back. Yelping loudly the dog
disappeared under the office building while the old man

scratched his balloon-like legs. Nothing that Tauilopepe knew about Pepe seemed real now; only the death-mask, the mockery, were left to haunt him.

The truck, with Faitoaga and other men of his aiga, arrived from Sapepe. From the car Tauilopepe ordered them to go into the hospital and bring out the coffin. A few minutes later the men emerged carrying it on their shoulders. The group in front of the surgery made way for them. The old man on the veranda stood up and watched. As the men were lifting the coffin on to the truck which was decorated with black cloth and flowers, the old man shuffled down from the veranda and stood behind them. Tauilopepe saw that Faitoaga was weeping freely. He could not understand why Faitoaga and most other Sapepe people had had so much affection for Pepe even after he rejected everything they believed in. He, Tauilopepe, had given Sapepe wealth, a better way of life, yet they were afraid of him and loved this worthless son.

As he drove behind the truck towards the hospital gates he glanced back. The old man was still standing there, his swollen legs anchoring him to the ground, gazing after them, hands shielding his eyes from the sun's glare. The dog lay near his feet. Just as he turned into the main road he saw the old man kick the dog viciously.

Tauilopepe's house and Taifau's house and all the fale of his aiga were crowded with mourners when they arrived in Sapepe. It was well past noon. In the main fale, the one which Pepe had been raised in and which now looked conspicuously old beside the double-storeyed green and yellow house, Masina was sitting by the pile of mats on which the coffin was to be placed. Filipo occupied the post next to her. The highest-ranking matai were at the other posts. The oldest women of the Aiga Tauilopepe occupied the back of the fale; they started to wail mutedly when they saw the truck.

Taifau and Faitoaga and the majority of the matai of the Aiga Tauilopepe had insisted that Pepe should be accorded a traditional funeral, although soon after Toasa's funeral Tauilopepe and the council had banned traditional funerals, arguing that they were a burden, a waste of money and time, and unsuitable for children to watch. Funerals, they had said, were for the souls of departed ones, not for the benefit of the greedy living who attended them in order to get ietoga and a share of the food.

Under the trees near the fale and on the veranda of Tauilopepe's store stood other groups of mourners. Many cars, belonging to Tauilopepe's Apia friends, lined the roadside, and children were swarming round them like moths drawn to a dazzling light. No one would work that day; even the school was closed. On the paepae were stacks of food for the taking. The tulafale, who had arrived early, were already eyeing them.

A large crowd immediately gathered round the truck when it stopped in front of the fale. As the men approached the fale with the coffin, Masina began to wail at the top of her voice, the other women in the fale joined her, and the whole area was soon resounding with the high-pitched sound. When the coffin was placed on the pile of mats in front of Masina she lunged forward and lay on top of it, wailing, 'My son, my son!' Most of the Aiga Tauilopepe, especially the women and children, crowded round her and the coffin. Tauilopepe stopped outside and watched them. Some of the men unscrewed the coffin lid. There were frantic shrieks as it came off. Through a gap in the crowd Tauilopepe glimpsed Masina embracing the corpse. He turned and hurried to his house.

Taifau, who was in charge of the funeral arrangements, had seated all the Apia mourners in the house. It was the proper thing to do, he had informed the Aiga Tauilopepe. These important people were used to chairs; to seat them on the floor of a fale would be an insult to them. Everyone had agreed with him.

Tauilopepe went round shaking hands with the town mourners. Most of them were afakasi who owned stores and businesses in Apia; two of them were Chinese who relied on Tauilopepe to supply their restaurants with taro and beef. The five papalagi occupied the most comfortable chairs, with Mr Ashton, Tauilopepe's lawyer, sitting in the softest and biggest one. All the town mourners were dress-

239

ed in suits, black shoes, and black ties. (It was taking four youths all their strength to stop the Sapepe children from crowding to the windows to stare at these strange men from Apia, especially the papalagi and the Chinese with their pork-white skins and unintelligible languages.)

Mr Ashton — everyone who knew him called him *Mister* Ashton — shook Tauilopepe's hand gravely. Tauilopepe sat down beside him. Everyone fell silent. Placing his pudgy hands firmly on the arms of his chair, Mr Ashton pushed himself up to his feet, cleared his throat, straightened his tie, pursed his lips, and coughed. 'We are gathered here today on this sorrowful occasion,' he began slowly, knowing that Tauilopepe didn't understand much English, 'with great sorrow in our hearts, sir. One of *our* sons, one we all knew well and who was dear to us all, has passed away. ...'

He orated for fifteen minutes or so. The other town mourners began to sneak furtive glances at their watches. Time was money. Mr Ashton, after living in Samoa for nearly twenty years, had become vaguely familiar with Samoan funeral customs, so he ended his speech by saying, 'I know that these gifts' — and he pointed at the stacked cartons of tinned meat and fish and the barrels of salted beef at the back of the room — 'are only meagre ones but they are a small token to show the respect and the love, yes love, which exists between you and me. Ahh, between you and *us*.' He motioned to sit down, remembered and added, 'Oh, and the respect which existed between your departed son and us. Thank you.'

Tauilopepe got up. He spoke softly in Samoan. His speech, unlike Mr Ashton's, said little about Pepe. The verbal creation of saints out of corpses couldn't be carried out successfully on this occasion because Tauilopepe knew that everyone else knew that Pepe had been a thief, an arsonist, and an atheist. '... Now I go join my Samoan people,' he said in English to end his speech. He shook hands with the Apia mourners and left the house.

As soon as Tauilopepe was out of sight the Apia mourners disbanded. The afakasi went in a separate group to their cars, the Chinese went in a separate group to their cars, the papalagi went in a separate group to their cars, and they separately chased away the children who were dirtying their cars, got into their cars separately, and headed for Apia separately. Business was business, time was money. On their separate ways to Apia one of the afakasi discovered to his angry disgust that some Samoan child had smeared Samoan excrement over the separate steering-wheel of his car, one of the Chinese discovered to his swearing anger that some Samoan child had urinated Samoan urine on the separate back seat of his car, and Mr Ashton discovered, and thought angrily of informing the police, that some criminal Samoan child had got his Samoan dog (or was it pig?) to shit Samoan dog (or was it pig?) shit on the separate floor of his car. And, as one, in their separate cars, they all cursed, in their separate and unintelligible languages, those bloody upstart, uncivilised Samoan village people!

In the fale Tauilopepe was greeted formally by the other matai who then, one after the other, offered their condolences in long ornate speeches. Masina and the other old women looked exhausted from weeping. Filipo had his head bowed and appeared to be praying. Tauilopepe did not look at the corpse in the open coffin — he would avoid doing so the whole day. The church choir entered and filled the fale, from the coffin to the back posts. They started to sing a hymn. The organist was one of Filipo's sons, who — looking stern in his father's spare pair of spectacles — played the organ with exaggerated hand gestures. Hymn followed hymn. More and more mourners from all over Samoa arrived and presented gifts of ietoga, money, and food. (Taifau had paid for the news of Pepe's funeral to be broadcast over the national radio station.) Tauilopepe's tulafale welcomed them with customary oratory.

Later Filipo told Tauilopepe that Pepe had been a truly good son but that the town had destroyed him. Apia was the Devil's domain, he said; and he consoled Tauilopepe by adding that if Toasa was alive the old man would have agreed that Apia had ruined Pepe. But Toasa was to blame for Pepe's evil growth, Tauilopepe told himself, for it was

241

Toasa who had nourished his worshipping son on that ridiculous nonsense about aitu and lions and, above all else, on that pagan drivel about Pepesa, that irresponsible, deranged hero of Sapepe's pre-Christian and cannibalistic past. Toasa had deliberately turned Pepe against him, Tauilopepe concluded. But he had defeated the old fool in the end.

When Pepe didn't return home after he had been expelled from school, Toasa stopped combating Tauilopepe's rising power in Sapepe; he even stopped attending council meetings. But Tauilopepe never once under-estimated the old man's influence, and as his wealth increased he tried to regain Toasa's support with expensive gifts and unlimited credit in his store. However, Toasa always returned the gifts, saying that he had no further use for such trifles. Tell Tauilopepe to send him a coffin, he would say. (Tauilopepe did just that when Toasa died.) Meanwhile, whenever they met, Toasa behaved as if Tauilopepe didn't exist. Tauilopepe preached often and Toasa either snored or got up and left the church. And yet, Tauilopepe now told himself, the final victory had been his. By bringing prosperity to Sapepe he had isolated Toasa, turned him into a quaint reminder of things past.

After Pepe's trial Toasa had withdrawn into a tragic silence. Some nights Tauilopepe would see him shuffling past his house, barely visible in the darkness. Almost a ghost, Tauilopepe would think, wanting to tell Toasa to come out of the cold and be reconciled with him. While Pepe was still in prison Toasa fell ill, and the night before he died he sent for Tauilopepe. Tauilopepe went, expecting Toasa to ask for his forgiveness. But Toasa didn't apologise, didn't ask for forgiveness. He simply gazed up at him and said: 'I will win in the end — Pepe will see to that.' And Tauilopepe saw the grin, the defiant mockery, that he was later to see on Pepe's dead face.

'Where are you going to bury him?' Filipo asked. 'You must put him beside Toasa. The old man would like that.'

'No!' Tauilopepe heard his mouth utter. 'He will be housed with his mother in Apia.' Keep them apart. Apart.

The funeral and the wake lasted the rest of that day and

the whole night. Tauilopepe, Masina, and Teuila, who had come from Apia that afternoon, hardly left the fale. The corpse, already black with death, lay in the open coffin, gazing up into the rafters, grinning.

The long line of cars and buses and trucks followed the truck bearing the coffin, which was surrounded by many of the young people of the Aiga Tauilopepe. The line moved slowly, solemnly. It took nearly two hours to reach Apia. On the outskirts of the town Masina ordered Taifau to direct the line of cars to turn down Taufusi Road and up the main street so that everyone could see how plushly dignified her grandson's funeral was. More cars joined the cortège as it moved along Beach Road and people came out of the shops and businesses to watch the longest funeral cortège they had seen for years. (Besides the ten trucks and two cars belonging to Tauilopepe there were twenty taxis and ten buses which Taifau had hired.)

As the blazing afternoon sun clung to them, Tauilopepe, Masina, Teuila, and Filipo stood at the head of the open grave while the other mourners crowded all the available space down to the gates of Magiagi Cemetery. Children from all round the neighbourhood squatted, stood, sat, and lay on the concrete walls. In their ragged, dirty clothes they looked like scavenging birds. Faitoaga, who had organised the digging of the grave, stood behind Tauilopepe, leaning on a crowbar that was rooted into the ground.

Filipo leant on Tauilopepe's shoulder and started to recite the prayer for the dead. Tauilopepe gazed down at the glass window exposing Pepe's face. The rocks and earth would soon hide that mocking face, he thought, and tonight he would be able to sleep. He almost slipped into the grave when something clicked near his ear. He straightened up. It was a photographer. Taifau had hired him to take photographs of the funeral. As the photographer moved round the edge of the grave, photographing the coffin and the mourners, Tauilopepe took out his handkerchief and started to weep silently into it.

Masina shrieked when the first spadeful of earth was

thrown on to the coffin. Teuila held her tightly, restraining her from jumping into the grave as she cried: 'My son, my son!' Tauilopepe turned his back to the grave, but the thudding sound of each spadeful of earth thundered in his ears.

'Get away!' he heard Faitoaga ordering someone. He turned. The ragged mob of children were scurrying through the gaps between the mourners towards the grave. 'Get away!' Faitoaga repeated.

'Let them be!' Filipo said. And some of the children perched themselves on the surrounding tombstones; others climbed up into the frangipani trees and watched from there, the few really brave ones crawled right up to the grave and sat at the edge.

Filipo put his arm round Tauilopepe's shoulders and said: 'He is gone to God. He is fortunate. He has escaped the sorrows and tribulations of this sinful life. Be glad.'

'I now have no heir,' murmured Tauilopepe.

'God, through Teuila, will give you another son,' Filipo consoled him.

Tauilopepe jerked away from Filipo and stumbled through the crowd of mourners. Only Teuila and a doctor at Apia Hospital knew, and his shameful secret was safe with them. Pepe's death mask jumped into his mind. Pepe knew, he knew, that Tauilopepe's seed could no longer produce children, that it had been cursed by God.

When they reached Sapepe that evening he went into his study, locked the door, closed the curtains, opened a bottle of whisky. Drank long and deep for two days.

'Open the door, Papa!' his grandson called.

'Go away!' he replied. But Lalolagi went on knocking and calling to him to come out and have someting to eat.

In the end he opened the door. Lalolagi gazed up at him. He looked away. Lalolagi took his hand and started to lead him towards the dining room, but Tauilopepe said that he wanted to go upstairs.

As they thumped up the stairs Lalolagi stopped and said, 'It was a big funeral, wasn't it, Papa? Pepe would have enjoyed it.'

244

'Yes, your father would have liked it,' Tauilopepe said.

'Are you going to have a big funeral too when you die, Papa?'

2　A New Heir

After a breakfast which he only picked at, Tauilopepe asked Teuila to send someone to get Taifau. Then he went to his study. There was no trace left there of his two-day drinking bout. Teuila and some of the girls had spent the night cleaning the room. He stood at the window. Across the road Taifau's wife, Nofo, was sitting on the veranda, combing her hair; her baby was rolling round on a mat at her feet. He watched them.

Someone coughed behind him. It was Masina. 'You know you shouldn't drink so much,' she said. 'It's bad for your health, and you're a deacon.' He just looked at her. 'Perhaps *he* has gone to God,' she added. He looked away. 'Will you ever forgive him?' she asked.

'Will you?' he accused her. She gasped and shuffled back down the corridor.

When Masina was told that Pepe had been expelled from school because he had tried to rape a girl she condemned him in front of their aiga as an 'evil son'. 'Wait and see,' she warned Tauilopepe. 'The Devil will claim him.' Tauilopepe knew that she had tried everything to win Pepe's affection during his childhood but that in the end he had rejected her. This was why she had turned against him. 'He is no longer part of my blood!' she had screamed when she heard that Pepe had burgled a store, burnt down a church hall, and beaten up some policemen, and she collected all his possessions from the Sapepe house and burnt them. She became as terrified of him as she was terrified of the midnight darkness—the time, she believed, when the world was in spiritual chaos and aitu rose out of the graves and played havoc with the souls of the living. When Pepe came to Toasa's funeral and in a rage spat on their aiga's Bible and ripped it apart he became for her one with the Devil, completely beyond redemption. Of course she had hidden her true feelings about him from the people of

Sapepe. 'Perhaps her grief at Pepe's funeral was genuine?' Tauilopepe now asked himself. He dared not answer his question. Masina was his mother and he would continue to respect her and care for her as was expected of a dutiful son.

When Taifau came into the room, Tauilopepe pointed to a chair. Taifau sat down, put on his thick spectacles, opened a thick notebook, and started to read out the list of funeral expenses. 'In all, three hundred and two ietoga were received and two thousand five hundred pounds and ten shillings was spent,' he concluded a few minutes later, having recited each item precisely, concisely. 'It was a funeral worthy of an alii,' he added. Tauilopepe was looking at the photographs of his aiga on the far wall. . . . 'I too was responsible,' Taifau said after a time. Tauilopepe looked at him. 'I too was responsible for the way he turned out,' repeated Taifau.

'No one was responsible. Every person is vested by God with free choice. Pepe chose the *other* path.'

'We didn't give him much of a choice, did we?'

'Forget him!'

Ignoring Tauilopepe's remark, Taifau said, 'We allowed Pepe no choice but to become what he became.'

'What *did* he become?' Tauilopepe asked.

'Well . . .' Taifau said, 'he became . . . a lost youth.'

Tauilopepe laughed. 'A lost youth!' And laughed again.

'What was he then?'

'Certainly not a lost youth. He chose. Got that? He *chose* the other way.'

'What way?'

'He was a weakling, and a weakling always chooses the easy way, Satan's way,' Tauiliopepe replied. 'He wasn't born to lead. That's all.'

'All right. But would a weakling have had the courage to destroy himself, especially the slow painful way he did?'

'Yes. It doesn't take courage to end your life. But it takes courage to live it.'

'Straight out of a cowboy film,' said Taifau.

'Anyway the Lord forbids suicide.' The Bible was the final word.

Taifau thumped his hands on to the arms of his chair and, admitting defeat, said, 'We always take refuge in the Book, don't we. But tell me this. If he didn't believe in the Book what then? Didn't he therefore have the right to act even if it was contrary to the Book?'

'He is still answerable to God's laws,' Tauilopepe said. 'When Pepe denied God he sinned — and he paid for it.'

The argument was over. To argue against or beyond God's laws, beyond the Book, would be heresy. So they didn't talk but watched the sunlight flooding into the room and destroying the cool of the morning.

The door burst open and Lalolagi ran in. 'It's time to go, Taifau,' he said. Taifau got up. 'Taifau's taking me pigeon-shooting,' Lalolagi told Tauilopepe who had his back turned to him. 'Come on, Taifau.' And he pulled Taifau out of the room.

'Look after him!' called Tauilopepe.

The jeep was on the road leading through the plantations. The road's construction had been a communal project, the Sapepe men providing the labour and Tauilopepe a bull-dozer which he had hired from the Public Works Department. Tauilopepe had argued in the council that a road would facilitate the transport of produce from the planta-tions to the village. The other matai had agreed, forgetting that only Tauilopepe owned trucks. When the road was opened they found themselves paying for the use of Tauilopepe's trucks whenever they wanted to bring pro-duce to the village. Most of them reverted to using horses and yokes.

Taifau, who was a nervous driver, overcame each pot-hole and bump with meticulous care and fought the bends and curves with a mumbled fury, right hand poised over the handbrake. Beside him Lalolagi played with the sleek rifle, pointing it at the trees and pressing the trigger. Each sharp click of the trigger made Taifau shudder.

'Stop that!' he eventually ordered.

'May I fire it today? Please, may I?' Lalolagi begged. (On their previous trips Taifau had rested in the fale in the centre of the plantation and Faitoaga had taken Lalolagi up

248

into the foothills but he had not been allowed to fire the rifle.)

'It's up to Faitaoga. If he says yes then it will be all right.'

'Are you as good as Faitoaga?' Lalolagi asked.

'At what?'

'Shooting. Faitoaga's as good as a cowboy.'

Taifau wrestled the jeep away from the ditch and said, 'Don't talk to me. See where you nearly got us!'

Soon they were entering Leaves of the Banyan Tree. The palms which Pepe had planted years before to mark the entrance to the plantation were now full-grown trees, their leaves ragged and half-eaten away by rhinoceros beetles. The road shot straight ahead. Taifau sighed and wiped his forehead. No more pot-holes, bumps, bends, rocks, traps. The Banyan — and every Sapepean now called the tree that — towered above the cacao trees at the road's end. Roots twisting up and up; then, poised in the sky's belly, spread out in strangling branch and foliage.

'Put on the speed!' Lalolagi urged. Taifau pushed down on the accelerator and the jeep shot forward. 'Ahhh! Ahhh!' shouted Lalolagi. Taifau chuckled nervously.

To their right the long lines of palms with cattle grazing under them tumbled down into the bottom of the valley and up the other side. On the opposite side the lush barrier of cacao, taro, tapioca, and banana flashed by. No trace of bush left. Just the sun hovering in the sky; and the Banyan growing in size as the jeep rushed towards it: the Banyan with arms outstretched ready to embrace the machine and the boy who was now standing and gripping the high front window of the jeep, his hair rippling, his right arm beating at the wind, yelling 'Ahhh! Ahhh!'; and the man gripping the steering-wheel, sweating, stubbornly refusing to slow down because he didn't want the boy to suspect he had once been known as the most chicken-hearted man in Samoa. And the dust rising furiously behind the machine.

'Slow down!' yelled Lalolagi.

Screeching brakes. Machine jerking in spasms, crunching tyres gripping the quick road. The road held. The machine dug in. Stopped. Taifau bowed his head and sighed into the steering-wheel.

'You nearly didn't make it that time,' Lalolagi said. 'Look where we are.' Taifau looked up. They were under the cacao trees at the end of the road. 'Not bad driving, Taifau,' added Lalolagi. 'But not as good as Papa.' Taifau rested his forehead against the steering-wheel. 'What's the matter?' Lalolagi asked.

'Nothing,' murmured Taifau, getting out of the jeep slowly. 'Run on ahead and go hunting with Faitoaga.' Lalolagi whooped, jumped down from the jeep, and ran off up the track to the fale under the Banyan.

Taifau peeled off his sweat-soaked shirt and spread it out to dry in the sun. He lay in the shade of the nearby cacao trees and was soon asleep. . . .

The rifle shot exploded in his head. On to his feet, ready to take cover. Remembered Lalolagi and Faitoaga and sighed. The sun had rolled past noon and he was thirsty and hungry. His shirt was dry so he put it on and went up towards the fale.

Brown butterflies, ants, and lizards teemed in the cool shade under the roots of the Banyan. Broad-leafed lianas, he noticed, were again starting to throttle many of the Banyan's roots and he decided that he would get some of the workers to clear them away. The men always grumbled when he made them weed and clear away the lianas and creepers from the Banyan. 'Anyone would think we ate banyan trees,' he had once heard one of his overseer sons saying to the workers. But not even his son dared disobey his orders. All of them knew that Tauilopepe was also attached to the Banyan.

The fale was cluttered with a wooden bed and chairs made out of banana boxes, and a collection of axes and bushknives hung down from the rafters. Otherwise it was clean, tidy. A cool breeze smelling of sun wafted in from the open side overlooking the deepest part of the valley. No one was about so Taifau went into the extension of the fale that nestled against the massive roots of the Banyan. Faitoaga's wife sat with her back to him, plucking a chicken and shoving the feathers into a basket, while her baby

250

grappled with one of her breasts.

'Is there any water?' he asked. When she turned, the child lost the breast and started to cry.

'It's over there,' she said. She gave the child her breast again. Taifau went to the bucket on the shelf, scooped up some water in an enamel cup, and drank it. 'It's very hot, isn't it,' she said. He nodded and drank a second cup of water. 'I'm sorry but I haven't cooked anything yet,' she added.

'I can wait,' he said. He dropped the empty cup into the bucket and went back into the main part of the fale.

He took off his shirt again and sat in a chair and gazed down at the deepest part of the valley. The cool fingers of the breeze started to caress his chest, arms, and face. The rifle fired again from higher up on the foothills. He thought of the past years: of the sweat and the burning, the bush retreating steadily, the rich virgin earth yielding her fruit in a day — or so it seemed now. His eyes followed the dirt road meandering up the valley to the sea of cacao creeping over the foothills, and beyond that the brown dry expanse of recently cut bush that was like a reef keeping back the tide of wild bush which clung to the range and the edge of the sky. He smelt the aroma of chicken roasting on charcoal. Sucked it in, held it with eyes shut. When he opened his eyes again he saw a small framed photograph hanging from the top of the front middle post of the fale. It was a photograph of Pepe — a gangly twelve-year-old in his Sunday best standing on the steps of the Sapepe church, face frozen in an awkward almost frightened smile, right hand clutching a Bible to his hip. Taifau had seen the photograph at Tauilopepe's house.

'Faitoaga didn't mean to take it without asking Tauilopepe,' Faitoaga's wife apologised. Taifau turned to reprimand her. She repeated her apology.

'It's all right,' he said. She left.

He sat thinking of Pepe and Toasa, but when such memories threatened to make him reach certain disturbing conclusions about what he had become he forced himself to stop. He looked at his watch — an hour had passed. He gazed down and saw Faitoaga and Lalolagi moving down

251

from the foothills over the track through the palms. Now and then the rifle on Faitoaga's shoulder flashed in the sun.

'The food is ready,' Faitoaga's wife said. He turned and saw the chicken and some taro and luau on a foodmat in the middle of the fale. 'It is not much,' she added. He told her that Faitoaga and Lalolagi were returning and that he would wait for them.

'Look what we got, Taifau!' Lalolagi called as he entered the fale, and he dangled a bloody string of dead pigeons in front of Taifau. Taifau's appetite decreased rapidly. 'I shot this one. See?' Lalolagi held up one bird and stabbed his fingers into the gaping hole where its entrails had been. 'I really got it, didn't I, Faitoaga?'

'He's not a bad shot,' Faitoaga said, sitting down opposite Taifau. His wife put a foodmat before him.

'I shot fifteen bullets and only missed ten of them. That's good, isn't it, Taifau?' Lalolagi said.

Taifau told him to sit down and eat. Lalolagi was soon lost in his food. As Taifau ate he tried not to look at the string of pigeons that Lalolagi had draped across the arm of one of the chairs. A steady trickle of blood was dripping on to the floor and spreading across it.

'How long will you take to finish clearing the rest of the foothills?' Taifau asked Faitoaga.

'Two weeks, three weeks. Not sure.'

'Can't you do it in two?'

Faitoaga shrugged his shoulders, his mouth round with taro, and mumbled, 'Don't see why not.'

'But what's going to happen?' Lalolagi asked.

'Happen to what?' asked Taifau.

'To the pigeons? Pigeons need trees.'

Taifau caught Faitoaga looking over at him, and he sensed that his answer to the boy's question was important to Faitoaga. 'Never thought about that...' he said, paused, made up his mind he wasn't going to assume any responsibility for the pigeons, and added, 'You'd better ask Tauilopepe.'

'I'll do that,' said Lalolagi. 'But I suppose the pigeons can live on the mountains, can't they?'

'Yes, there are better trees on the mountains,' replied

Taifau, not looking at Faitoaga.

'There are aitu on the mountains, aren't there, Taifau? And lions too?' said Lalolagi.

'Who told you that?' asked Taifau, trying not to laugh.

'Faitoaga did. Do you think I can trap an aitu and a lion?'

Gazing at Faitoaga, who looked as if he was totally pre-occupied with his food, Taifau said, 'No one in Sapepe has done so yet because there aren't any aitu or lions up there.'

'But Toasa did,' insisted Lalolagi.

Taifau chuckled and asked, 'And *who* told you that?'

'Faitoaga. Faitoaga said that when Toasa was a boy he disappeared into the mountains and returned days later with an aitu in a small magic basket. But when people asked to see it Toasa opened the basket and let the aitu escape back to the mountains. Faitoaga said Toasa said he didn't want *his* aitu to belong to other people because they would hurt it. Toasa must have been a magician. Was he?'

Taifau coughed to try to attract Faitoaga's attention but Faitoaga wouldn't look at him, so he said, 'Toasa was a great man.'

'As great as Papa?'

'Yes,' Faitoaga replied before Taifau could answer.

'If Toasa had been as great as Papa he would have told me. Papa never talks about Toasa. No one is as great and as rich and as good as Papa. Not even Pepe.' Lalolagi paused, and then said, 'Pepe was a criminal, wasn't he?'

Taifau and Faitoaga looked at each other, each wanting the other to reply.

'Who told you that?' Taifau asked finally.

'Some people in Sapepe. And Masina.'

'Don't ever believe them. Pepe, your father, was a good and kind man,' Faitoaga said.

'But he went to prison, didn't he? And only criminals go to prison. Anyway I don't care. Papa is *my* father.' Lalolagi picked up the rifle and left the fale.

Neither man knew what to do. 'He must be told what his father and Toasa were really like,' said Faitoaga. 'Before it's too late.'

'You haven't made a good start, have you? Telling him about aitu and lions.'

'But they were true for Pepe and Toasa,' insisted Faitoaga. His wife was clearing away the foodmats and scraps.

'They were only stories the old man made up.'

'If I'm going about it the wrong way you talk to Lalolagi then. *You* tell him about his father. Tauilo and Masina are already telling him the wrong things. *You* tell him!'

'You don't need to get angry. I'll tell him,' Taifau said cautiously. Faitoaga was feared in Sapepe; he seldom visited the village, and when he did it was often to avenge an insult against the Aiga Tauilopepe or to beat up someone who had bullied his children. Tauilopepe and, more recently, Teuila were the only people who could stop him from assaulting people. Taifau (and most other Sapepeans) knew that the memory of Pepe and Toasa was sacred to Faitoaga. Except for Tauilopepe, anyone who slighted that memory had to be fast with his fists, and no one in Sapepe was as fast or as fit and fanatically determined as Faitoaga. Faitoaga hadn't set foot in church since Toasa died but Filipo never reprimanded him for it from the pulpit. Faitoaga was also the only adult person in Sapepe who didn't contribute anything to church and village projects. No matai in the council asked that he should be fined because of it.

'Would you like a cigarette?' Taifau asked. Faitoaga uncurled to his feet, pulled a bushknife out of the rafters, and went out to weed the banana trees opposite the fale. 'Fool!' Taifau whispered. Like the rest of the Sapepeans he was afraid of Faitoaga. And yet, except for Tauilopepe, Faitoaga was his only friend in the district.

A short time later Taifau went out to Lalolagi who was sitting under the Banyan. A flying-fox, which seemed to have come out of nowhere, flew up to the top of the Banyan and hung down from one of the topmost branches. Taifau couldn't stop the boy. The shell was snug in the rifle and Lalolagi was on his feet, rifle to his shoulder. As Taifau moved towards him he saw Faitoaga running out of the banana trees. The rifle fired. The flying-fox unclutched from the branch, spread its wings, caught the air, and flapped off towards the range. Faitoaga wrenched the rifle out of Lalolagi's hands, his right arm raised to strike the frightened boy.

'Don't!' Taifau ordered him.

Faitoaga pushed the boy away. 'Don't you ever do that again. Understand? Never again!'

'What's so important about a flying-fox?' cried Lalolagi. Faitoaga threw down the rifle and marched off into the banana trees. 'I was only shooting at a flying-fox!' Lalolagi said to Taifau. 'What's the matter with Faitoaga?'

'It wasn't the flying-fox,' Taifau replied.

'Well, what then?' asked Lalolagi, starting to cry.

'It was the Banyan.'

'That's not true. It's an old useless tree!'

'It's important to Faitoaga,' Taifau tried to explain.

'They were bad people!' said Lalolagi. 'I'm going to tell Papa on Faitoaga. Faitoaga shouldn't have hit me like that!'

'But he didn't hit you.'

'He did. He did!' Lalolagi grabbed the rifle and ran off down the track.

3   Choice of a Parent

They were in the spacious sitting room that opened into the night in a series of louvre windows. It was extremely humid. The heat clung to them. (They had just had their evening meal.) Tauilopepe and Taifau, both without shirts, were on the settee facing the windows and Teuila and Susana, Lalolagi's mother, who had come to visit them six days before. Moths fluttered noiselessly around the six lights spaced on the blue ceiling. They could hear Masina reading the Bible to Lalolagi upstairs; the sound of her voice was heightened by the muffled murmuring of the surf. Tauilopepe was on his sixth whisky, and Taifau, now a teetotaller, was sipping a glass of chilled orange cordial. The two women were talking softly between themselves.

When Tauilopepe finished his whisky one of the girls who served in the house came and refilled his glass. 'And when are you returning to Apia?' Tauilopepe asked Susana.

'I think we'll be leaving tomorrow if that's all right with you, sir,' replied Susana.

'We?'

'Yes. Lalolagi and I.'

'Does he want to go?' asked Tauilopepe.

'I haven't asked him yet, sir. But, being my son, he'll want to come with me,' Susana said.

'And where is he going to live?'

'With my parents.'

'What will they be able to give him? A job selling faamafu? No education?'

Susana bowed her head and said, 'I'll try my best to give him what he's used to here.'

'I won't allow him to be brought up in that neighbourhood. The part of Apia you live in is evil and will destroy him like it destroyed his....' Tauilopepe couldn't say it.

Teuila had never succeeded in forging a close friendship with Susana but now she said, 'How long is this going on

for? How long are you going to use Pepe as an excuse?'
She expected Tauilopepe to rebuke her but he didn't.
'Give her Lalolagi. He is her son.'
'Never!' said Tauilopepe. 'What kind of mother is she,
eh? All she wants is money, my money. Use my son's son
to get money off me!' He looked at Susana and asked,
'Isn't that right? Answer me!'
Susana started to weep. 'I only want my son. He's all
I've got now,' she said.
'Eight dollars a week,' said Tauilopepe. 'How's that? I'll
give you eight dollars a week until you find yourself
another husband.' Susana was one of the reasons why Pepe
had turned against him, he had often thought; she was a
cunning, heartless harlot after his money. 'Or do you want
more?'
Susana wiped her nose with the back of her hand. 'I only
want my son!' she said.
Tauilopepe called for another whisky. The girl rushed
into the room and refilled his glass.
'Why don't you let Lalolagi choose?' suggested Taifau,
convinced that the boy would choose his grandfather
because where else would he get everything he demanded.
Also Taifau had never liked Susana. When Pepe had first
introduced her to him in Apia he had discerned quickly
that under her physical beauty lay a frightening emptiness.
Teuila left the room and went upstairs. Tauilopepe got
up and refilled his glass while Susana sobbed quietly.
Taifau started to regret his suggestion. Tauilopepe would
never forgive him if Lalolagi chose Susana. They waited.
The door opened. Lalolagi stopped in the doorway.
Teuila nudged him into the room. 'Come here,' Taifau
said. The boy looked at Susana, then at Tauilopepe. Teuila
nudged him again. Lalolagi came in and stopped in front of
Taifau. 'Go to your mother,' Taifau said. Lalolagi moved
closer to him. 'Go on,' Taifau encouraged him.
'Teuila's my mother,' said Lalolagi.
'But you're my son!' cried Susana. Lalolagi ran to stand
by Tauilopepe's chair. Tauilopepe put an arm round him.
'You've turned him against me!' Susana accused Teuila.
'How can you be so cruel!' Teuila left the room.

'Tell her to leave,' Lalolagi whispered to Tauilopepe.

Susana heard him and looked up. 'Hypocrite!' she shouted at Tauilopepe. 'You know why your own son hated you? He hated everything about you because you're a hypocrite! You're filth just like your filthy son who filled me with sin. Sin which begot that brat!'

Tauilopepe sprang to his feet. 'Go! My son has chosen!' Susana clawed at her hair and face and continued hurling obscenities at him. Taifau held her and struggled to get her out of the room. She beat him off with kicking feet and ripping nails.

'She never loved me, Papa,' Lalolagi said. 'She beat me all the time!' Tauilopepe's open hand cut through the brilliant light and spun Susana to the floor.

'Filth! You filthy shit!' she screamed.

Tauilopepe advanced towards her. Taifau clutched the collar of her blouse and jerked her to her feet. She lashed out with her claws, but he ducked under them, lifted her, and carried her kicking and screaming to the door.

'He'll destroy you like his father destroyed me!' she cursed Tauilopepe. 'His evil father lives in him!' Tauilopepe slammed the door behind them. Heard the heavy thud as Taifau dumped her on the floor outside the door.

Tauilopepe struggled to control his anger as he listened to Susana fighting Taifau and members of his aiga who were trying to take her out to the car and out of Sapepe for ever. Then silence. Lalolagi rushed over and buried his head in Tauilopepe's belly. The car roared and backed out of the garage on to the road. Tauilopepe picked Lalolagi up and carried him to the settee. The car revved and roared off towards Apia. She'd never see Lalolagi again; he'd make sure of that. Such Roman Catholic filth! But, as he gazed at Lalolagi, her last words echoed in his head. No, it wasn't so. Lalolagi wasn't Pepe. Pepe was dead and Lalolagi was his only heir, his name.

Teuila came down and took Lalolagi up to bed. Tauilopepe switched off the lights and drank whisky after whisky until his head was a trembling daze surrounding a fearful picture. He had watched Susana the evening before.

258

She had not known that the shower door was open. Susana, shimmering in her nakedness as the water rippled down her body. Silver snakes of water caressing her high upthrusting breasts and her belly and the black triangle between her legs. Her hands, his hands, as they soaped the burning skin, his skin burning from the pit of his loins to his aching finger-tips. The exhilarating truth that she had been Pepe's woman heightening his desire.

'Shall I put the light out?' Teuila asked when he stumbled into their bedroom in the early hours of the morning. He went over and stood above the bed. 'You shouldn't have treated her that way,' Teuila said, reaching out and holding his trembling hands. He sat down on the edge of the bed. She sat up, unbuttoned his shirt, and took it off. 'You shouldn't drink so much.' She unbuckled his belt and pulled it off. 'What's the matter? Are you feeling ill?' He reached out and embraced her. She murmured softly as he caressed her. 'Wait, I'll take my dress off.' He lay on the bed while she undressed.

Susana in the shower — Pepe's woman moaning and stirring on the bed as his hands rippled like water over her body. 'Come on!' the woman whispered, and he was inside her. 'Ah, ah, you're bigger than him!' She moaned all round him. 'Faster, faster! That's it...that's it! Ahhh. .... Come! I'm coming. Coming! You're the best!'

'Am I better than *him*?'

'Yes, yes, yes!'

He woke and found Teuila slapping gently at his face. 'What's the matter? Were you having a nightmare?'

'Yes, a nightmare,' he murmured.

He had fallen asleep while Teuila was undressing.

4   Failure of a Guardian

Taifau's house, the second largest in Sapepe, was the only house beside Tauilopepe's that had electric power. Tauilopepe's generator supplied it. Like Tauilopepe's house it was furnished with gaudy, expensive furniture, shiny linoleum in all the rooms, two radios (one in the sitting room and one upstairs), and a large wood-stove in the enormous kitchen. Photographs of Taifau's aiga covered one sitting-room wall and one wall of his office — a smaller version of his employer's study — in which he stored all the account books and papers relating to Leaves of the Banyan Tree and Tauilopepe's other businesses. Over the years Taifau had acquired an insatiable taste for novels about the Wild West. He bought three or four every time he visited Apia, and rows of them now filled the only bookcase in his office. Taifau's house also possessed the only other flush toilet in Sapepe, and only Taifau, Nofo, and important visitors used this toilet. The rest of his aiga had to go to the draughty outhouse. Taifau's most precious possession was his bedroom: its ceiling was navy blue, its walls pink, its floor blood-red; louvre windows with yellow curtains opened out on to the road; and a four-poster bed, with brass posts almost reaching the ceiling, occupied the centre of the room. Taifau had bought the bed from a pastor who had inherited it from his pastor grandfather who in turn had inherited it from a papalagi missionary who for a decade had watched his wife dying in it. The shiny monstrosity, which Taifau's young daughters had to polish once a week, supported a heavy tasselled mosquito net. A huge kapok mattress, birthplace of most of Taifau's business schemes but none of his children, because Nofo had her own bedroom, anchored the bed to the floor. A varnished cupboard stood near the louvre windows; no one was allowed to open it.

Taifau's children now rivalled Filipo's brood in number:

seven sons—three married and working as overseers and storekeepers for Tauilopepe, one a pastor in Savaii, one a pupil at Samoa College in Apia; six daughters—three married and living with their husbands and children in the fale behind the house. All his children were sane, hardworking, godly, obedient, and thrifty. None resembled in character the cowardly, lazy, godless, spendthrift Taifau of the past, not even the eldest children who had known and suffered *that* Taifau. Some of the Sapepe elders still talked about the chicken-hearted, half-blind musician and his hilarious exploits, but not when Taifau and Tauilopepe were about. When Taifau's younger children heard these stories they refused to believe that their father, who was to them a conscientious provider, had been a lazy fool and the cause of goodness knows how many illegitimate children, bawdy jokes, and songs. The youthful Taifau, his children discovered from what the elders said, had possessed only one admirable trait—he had been the best musician in Sapepe (and Samoa). The existence of the now legendary guitar, which his children knew was locked up in the cupboard in their father's bedroom, was proof of this. Taifau never talked to them about his past. His stories concerned mainly three people: Toasa and Pepe, now both dead, and Tauilopepe. Combine the best of these three men and you would become a man second only to Jesus Christ, he told his children.

So it was for the children an unexpected but marvellous occurrence when, soon after Pepe's funeral, they heard the sound of the guitar coming from their father's bedroom one night. The chords were harsh, unmusical—the clumsy efforts of a learner. But, as the nights passed and the periods of practice lengthened, they gradually became music. One night the children caught their mother listening intently to the music, a wonderful glow suffusing her face. The music ended abruptly and they heard Taifau slapping and swearing at the guitar. 'He has lost the gift,' Nofo said sadly. Then a week or so later they heard their father singing, a deep baritone, searching to couple with the lilting roll of the guitar. 'God has been kind, perhaps He will restore the gift fully,' Nofo said. Her

261

youngest son asked if it was true that Taifau had been the best musician in Samoa. Nofo said, 'Yes. And,' she added, 'Pepe's death will restore the sight your father once possessed.'

'But Taifau was half-blind then,' one of her daughters insisted. Nofo didn't reply so the girl asked her what Pepe had to do with it.

'Pepesa, Tauilopepe's only son,' their mother told them, 'loved Taifau's music, but Pepesa has gone away.'

'"Pepesa?"' her Samoa College son asked.

Nofo told him that Pepesa was Pepe's full name, and that it meant Sacred Child. 'He went away and left Taifau alone,' she said sadly. The children looked at one another puzzled.

A few days after the quarrel between Tauilopepe and the woman who, the children heard, was Lalolagi's mother, Taifau disappeared up into his bedroom straight after his evening meal. The children cleared the table and went into the kitchen to eat, extremely puzzled by their father's behaviour because he usually listened to the radio or read a cowboy book in the evening. They ate quickly, washed the dishes, and showered; then, wrapping their sleeping sheets round their bodies, they went into the sitting room, pretending that they were going to listen to the radio. The Samoa College son casually asked Nofo if anyone was going to visit them that night. She said she didn't know. Samoa College son, the only child that Taifau allowed to touch the radio, switched it on, and the others gathered round it. Nofo asked if anything was the matter. When they assured her that nothing was wrong she told them to do their homework. They got out their books and pretended to work.

The door behind Nofo, who was now combing her long black hair, opened. The children gasped in wondering surprise when Taifau entered, holding the legendary guitar. 'What are you staring at?' he asked.

'Nothing,' replied Samoa College son, who was Taifau's favourite because he was the brightest of his sons and the only one who had succeeded in getting into Samoa College, *the* high school. Taifau placed the guitar gingerly on the table in the middle of the room. The children gathered round it, wide-eyed, slightly wary of it. Taifau sat down behind it. He warned them not to touch it. A moment later one of the girls asked him how much the guitar had cost.

'A million,' Taifau replied. Nofo laughed. (She knew without anyone telling her what he had brought downstairs.)

'That's a lot of money,' said College son.

'What is a million?' the youngest boy asked College son.

'It's one plus six noughts,' was College son's learned reply.

'That's right,' Taifau assured his youngest son.

'Where did you get all that money from? Even the palagi and Tauilopepe don't have that much,' his youngest son insisted.

'I didn't mean a million dollars,' Taifau explained, 'but a million laughs.' College son started to laugh but stopped when he noticed that his father wasn't joking. One of Taifau's daughters, whose head had been shaven clean the week before because of lice, asked him if someone had given him the guitar. College son sniggered, called her a bald-headed fool, and insisted that their father had bought the guitar in a store in Apia.

'No!' said Taifau. The other children, especially the bald-headed girl, laughed at College son. 'Pepe, yes, Pepe gave it to me,' Taifau told them.

'But....' began Nofo.

'But what? Pepe gave it to me for a million laughs,' Taifau said.

'That's not....'

'That's not what? It's not the same guitar,' he said quickly. She knew he was lying; later on he would explain his reasons for lying to her.

So she said, 'That's right. I forgot.'

The children asked Taifau to play the guitar but he told them that he was expecting a visitor. They started grumbling. He told them to go and sit on the road and when his visitor left he would play for them. They went out reluctantly but instead of going well away from the house, they sat under the front windows of the sitting room. College son told the others to be quiet.

'Pepesa didn't give you the guitar, did he?' they heard Nofo ask.

There was a pause. Then their father said, 'No.'

'But why lie to the children?'

'It was important.'

'Why?'

'You ask too many questions.'

Another lengthy pause.

'Why was it important?'

'Because of Pepe. I want them to treasure Pepe's memory. ... Why do I always have to explain everything I do or say?' Taifau said. Nofo didn't reply. 'I lied because I don't want our children to know what kind of man I was. Would you like them to know what I was?' She remained silent. 'You're tying me up in knots. You're so dead blind but you can see right into me, can't you?'

'Why did you take me as your wife then?'

'Don't start that again,' he said.

'Was it because I was pregnant? Was it pity?'

'Because of your gift of blindness,' he tried to joke.

She chuckled and said, 'And I grabbed you because no one else would tolerate my blindness.'

'Wrong. You fell in love with my guitar and my one-string bass guitar!' he said. They both laughed. Outside, College son ordered the other children not to listen any more.

'Yes, your two guitars *used* to sing quite ably,' Nofo said.

'"*Used* to"?' he said. 'Both of them are still fit and able, as you well know. Which one would you prefer now?'

'Right this minute?'

'Yes, right now.'

'The black one.'

'With the one string or six?'

'The six.' And they laughed as their children had never heard them laugh before.

The youngest boy asked College son what their parents were laughing about. It was none of his business, College son replied sternly. Why didn't Taifau stop talking and

264

start playing, one of the girls said. They were getting cold because a chilly breeze was shuffling through the trees and flowers.

Taifau and Nofo stopped laughing and the children heard the clinking of glasses. College son stood up and peeped through the window. Taifau was placing three empty glasses on the table beside the guitar. He then went into the kitchen and returned with a jug of iced orange cordial. He filled two glasses and handed one to Nofo. College son ducked down out of sight.

'Who's coming tonight?' they heard Nofo ask.

'Lalolagi. I hope he comes.'

'Why do you want him to come?'

'You don't like him?'

'He's very cheeky and arrogant. Not like Pepe when he was a boy. Remember how he used to treat me? Take my hand and lead me to church and bring me food. He was always polite to me even when we were so poor and everyone treated us so cruelly. Remember?'

'Yes, I remember. Let's not talk about it any more.'

'Remember the joke he used to make whenever Toasa was angry with him? "I am Pepesa, rear-end of the gods but front-end of Sapepe." And Toasa would laugh and forget his anger.'

'Let's not talk about him.'

'What did he become, Taifau? I mean after he went away to Apia? You met him when he became a man, what was he like? Had people cut out his heart?' As she talked the children sensed that their mother was nearly crying.

'I don't know what he became. Stop crying. I honestly don't know. Everything would be so easy if I knew the answer. Stop crying!' But Nofo continued weeping softly.

Then in the still silence the children heard the first delicate chords, and they saw in their minds' eyes the deft fingers plucking the waking strings. And the marvellous guitar sang for the first time in their house, and even the trees and the stars were listening, they imagined. Such a guitar could even wake the dead — the mythical Toasa and Pepe and the musical magician their father had been.

Across the road the front door of Tauilopepe's house

opened. The children saw Lalolagi outlined in the blazing doorway. Then the door shut behind him, cutting off the light. 'Why does he have to come here!' one girl exclaimed.

'Spoilt brat!' hissed College son. (Most of them had suffered Lalolagi's arrogance at one time or another.) 'One day I'm going to hit him.'

'You're scared of him. You're bigger and older than him but you're scared of him,' one of his sisters said. He quietened her by threatening to slap her.

Lalolagi stepped into the light outside the front door of their house. The youngest boy's arm whipped back to throw a stone. College son hit it out of his hand. 'I'm not scared of him,' declared the youngest boy. Lalolagi went into their house. The children peered over the windowsill into the room. Taifau had stopped playing. Lalolagi stood in front of him. Taifau pointed to the chair opposite him. Lalolagi sat down.

'Never knew you could play,' Lalolagi said. 'May I have a drink?' Taifau pointed at the empty glass, and Lalolagi had to pour his own drink.

'What did you do today?' Taifau asked.

'Went to Apia with Papa. Came back this afternoon. That's all. Oh, saw a cowboy picture in Apia.' Lalolagi paused. 'Whose guitar is that?' he asked.

'Mine,' replied Taifau. Even since that day just over a year before when Faitoaga had nearly beaten Lalolagi for shooting at the Banyan he had treated Taifau and Faitoaga with mounting indifference.

'What did you want to see me about? Something important? I was playing cards with Masina,' said Lalolagi.

'Thought you might like to hear me play,' Taifau replied.

'Your father used to come to listen to Taifau. He always said that Taifau was the best,' said Nofo.

'Best at what?' asked Lalolagi.

Before Nofo could reply Taifau started to play. The children suddenly felt that something important was missing from the music, the quality which had made them believe that the guitar could wake even the dead. And

266

their animosity towards Lalolagi deepened. Lalolagi sat rapping his knuckles on the arm-rests of his chair.

'Toasa and Pepe used to play a game,' Taifau said as he played.

'What game?' Lalolagi asked with a loud yawn.

'Toasa used to ask: "Who are you?" and Pepe would reply, "I am Pepesa Tauilopepe, descendant of the great heroes of Sapepe, son of the gods, heir to...."'

'Oh, that!' said Lalolagi. 'Masina told me about that. She thinks it was a stupid game. And so do I. Adults shouldn't play such games, should they? Papa thinks the game is stupid too.'

Taifau stopped playing. Lalolagi yawned again. Taifau put the guitar on the table, face upwards to the blaring lights like a helpless turtle. 'It wasn't a stupid game,' he said. Lalolagi sat up. 'It contains the whole history and future of your aiga and Sapepe. Some day you may be given the Tauilopepe title, and there are....'

'Papa has already said I am to be the next Tauilopepe,' Lalolagi interrupted.

'There are certain responsibilities and duties that go with the title. These responsibilities are emphasised in the game Toasa and your father used to play. Now does the game still seem stupid to you?'

'But Masina said....' insisted Lalolagi.

'Said what?'

'You shouldn't get angry. I don't think the game is... stupid. It's just that Papa wants me to go to boarding-school first and then to university in New Zealand or America like the sons of other rich Samoans. Papa says I can learn our ways later.'

'It's late. You'd better go home,' Taifau said. 'It's no use.'

'What's no use?' asked Lalolagi.

'Nothing. Go home to bed.'

'Good night,' said Lalolagi. He got up and left.

The children crept round to the back door and went upstairs to their bedrooms, extremely disappointed that their father hadn't thrashed Lalolagi for being rude.

267

Taifau picked up the guitar. 'What are you staring at?' he almost shouted at Nofo. She shook her head. He stamped out of the room, taking the guitar with him.

'I'm sorry!' she called.

5 Of Ancient Wisdom

And it came to pass that Masina died on the morning of Monday, 15 March 1959, two weeks and a day after her seventy-ninth birthday and four years, five months, and two days after Pepe's memorable funeral. Cause of death: old age and her worthy desire to accept admission into the Heavenly Kingdom.

Because she was Tauilopepe's mother Masina had wielded almost unlimited power in Sapepe. The Sapepe Women's Committee, over which she reigned with an autocratic hand, was terrified of her. In donations to Sapepe charities and communal projects no one could compete with her — not that anyone dared to. She became the most loquacious exponent of a literal interpretation of the Bible and of what she called 'the everlasting doctrines of the LMS church, the only true church', and the most original authority on the religious interpretation of dreams, nightmares, visions, and the varied ways of gaining admission to Paradise. At Women's Committee meetings she always spent the first hour or so relating in her inimitable basso voice the dreams sleep had blessed her with during the week. After this narration, which even the most bored listener was afraid to interrupt, she unravelled with her own quaint logic the religious symbolism of these dreams for the benefit of the other women, whom she called, when angry, 'ignorant products of commoners' or, when pleased, 'my daughters with Christ'. Heaven, she claimed, was a 'city paved with gold and flowing with milk and honey', a city where the Blessed — whom she was sure she would join one day — sat at God's golden-sandalled feet (God had feet even though she described Him as a 'Ball of Fire'), singing hymns with the choir of angels, all eternity long. So, if in her dreams she saw anything that glittered like gold she interpreted it as a holy sign that she was getting ever so close to Heaven and free admission to that utopian colony. Hell, on the other hand, was an unfathomable chasm stormy with liquid fire in which the Damned screamed all eternity long, while the Devil, a debauched papalagi with fiery eyes and frothing mouth and tail, prodded them with a three-pronged spear. When she glimpsed Pepe among the drowning Damned screaming out to her for water she wept and said that he was there because she had not tried diligently enough to save him for the Lord. Anyway Pepe had been given free will by his Maker, so it wasn't exactly her fault he had chosen Darkness and Sin.

Seven days before she died she got her aiga to shift her to the fale. She had been born in a fale, and like all true full-blooded Samoans she wanted to die in one. She summoned the Aiga Tauilopepe so that she could make her last mavaega, thus reviving a custom which had fallen into disuse in Sapepe. Snug in an expensive blanket she lay in the middle of the quiet throng, gazing up into the fale dome and holding Tauilopepe's hand.

She was born, she began her mavaega, the humble daughter of a humble pastor. Had qualified as a pastor's wife — one of the first in Samoa — from Vaiuta College, but had married for love an ignorant but aristocratic Sapepe matai against the wishes of her parents whom, everyone knew, she had loved; had brought four sons into this sinful world, as was her duty to God; had watched, without sorrow because they were going to the Land of Happiness, three of her sons, all religious youths worthy of Jesus, die during the influenza epidemics, leaving only Tauilopepe, who had cared for her as no other son could and had proved a most God-fearing man. To this her most worthy son she verbally willed the Aiga Tauilopepe and all the lands and other property pertaining to that aiga. To him the Aiga Tauilopepe must remain utterly loyal, rendering to him their complete obedience, love, and service, and through him and her church they must devote their souls to God. She had nothing to bequeath to them all but her chaste memory as a faithful lover of Jesus Christ. In conclusion she said tearfully: 'I have lived, I have loved, I have obeyed the Lord's Commandments, and I have found the Light of Truth. Now I am ready, pure in heart and soul, to

270

meet my Maker. Do not weep for me.' (Most of them at once started to weep.) 'Weep for yourselves for you still have to live in this sinful world which God is freeing me of so I may live in Paradise with Him. Amen.' She sighed and closed her eyes, expecting the Angel of the Lord to take her away that very minute.

By the end of her mavaega all her aiga except Tauilopepe were weeping profusely. They sang hymns, read the Bible, and prayed to Jehovah to please accept their beloved mother who was sick and frail into the Holy City.

Tauilopepe remained beside her after the others had gone, clutching her hand. The women had pulled down the fale blinds against which a strong wind was now blowing. As he gazed at her wrinkled face the cheek-bones looked as if they were rising up through the flesh. The blinds flapped unexpectedly. Tauilopepe turned swiftly. Sighed. Her fingers tightened round his hand. He jerked his hand away. Her eyelids opened slowly.

'I am here,' she said. 'I have arrived.'

'No, it's just the light,' he whispered, relieved that she hadn't died gripping his hand.

She looked at him, 'I am not dead then?' He shook his head. 'Where is Lalolagi?' she asked, eyes shut again.

'In Apia with Teuila,' he replied.

'Send for him.'

'As you wish.'

'Send a car tonight.'

'But it's . . . .'

'*Now*.'

'All right,' Tauilopepe said. The tense silence that had existed between them ever since Pepe died was setting in again. He wanted to make her talk about the causes of that silence but he didn't know how to start.

'Are you still here?' she asked.

'Yes, I am still here.' Paused. 'Masina?' She nodded her head. 'One person was missing tonight,' he said, watching every movement on her face.

'Lalolagi?'

'No.' Paused again. 'Pepe.' She gasped. 'You all right?' he asked, holding her hand again. He sighed when he discovered she was still alive. Remembered he had already ordered a very expensive coffin for her. Dismissed the thought.

'Please...don't...talk...to me...about him,' she said, and groaned as if it was her last breath.

'Why not?'

'Don't want...to.'

'But why? You can't go away feeling like that about him!'

'Like what?' Normal speech tinged with anger.

'You despised him and still do.'

'No!'

'You do.'

'No, no!' New tactic — tears. 'Please don't ruin my last day!'

'You can't go to God hating Pepe.'

'No, no!' she said.

'You feared him then?' he asked.

'No!' She was weeping steadily.

'I feared him, Masina,' he said. A tactic to counter her tears. It worked.

'Yes, I was afraid of him,' she whispered. No more tears. Eyes still shut.

'Why?'

'Because ...because....'

'Because what?'

'Because he was just like....'

'Like who?' He felt her hands trembling. He took his hand away.

'Like....I can't. Please don't make me. I can't betray him!' Turned her face away.

'Betray? Betray who?'

The face turned round slowly until it was staring straight up at him, eyes closed, the bones emphasised by the piercing light; then the blue-veined mouth opened and the words tumbled out, *'Your father!'*

'My father?' he asked, thinking she was trying to evade the issue.

'Yes, your father. Pepe was just like your father!' The face turned away again.

272

'But how like him? I don't believe you.'

'Don't you?'

'No!'

The head moved up and down, as if laughing. 'Why don't you believe me?'

'Because...because he was a *good* man.'

'"A good man"?' The head was still.

'And you loved him!' he insisted, convinced now that she was telling the truth.

'Loved him?'

'Yes, you *must* have loved him!'

'Didn't.'

'Didn't love him?'

'No!'

'But why?' he asked.

The face turned towards him. The bottomless eyes, pits in the skull, gazed into his eyes. 'Why didn't you love *your* son? Why were *you* afraid of Pepe?' she said.

He sprang up and broke through the blinds into the oppressive darkness and the roar of the incoming tide.

Nothing else was said between them.

She died six days later.

In accordance with her last wishes Filipo, who had retired and was living in Tauilopepe's house, conducted her funeral service, his last such service before he too died a few months later and gave Simi, the new pastor, the opportunity to conduct his first funeral service in Sapepe.

Like Masina, Filipo died mainly from old age. He had retired two years after Pepe died and shifted with Taulua and their youngest son to live with Teuila and Tauilopepe. He would have enjoyed Tauilopepe's generous hospitality for a few years longer if he hadn't succumbed to his host's generous supply of whisky.

Throughout his lengthy pastorship — at least up to the day he discovered that Tauilopepe wasn't a teetotaller — he had led a fiery anti-liquor campaign, using the invulnerable pulpit as his campaigning platform and the matai council as his police force. During the afternoon service on the last Sunday of every month, after which the congregation were to donate money towards his upkeep, Filipo usually spoke verbosely against the evils of the 'Devil's Water'. This monthly sermon had led Toasa to spread the attractive rumour that Filipo sermonised so because he was scared his congregation might take to drink, spend all their money, and have nothing to contribute to his upkeep. Filipo himself argued from the pulpit that the Devil's Water was conducive to high spending and rebellion against the godly habit of giving generously to the church.

Inspired by its spiritual mentor the matai council ruthlessly suppressed all faamafu-brewing. While Toasa was alive only a few of 'Satan's disciples' (Filipo's term) foolishly brewed faamafu in the plantations; they were usually caught — betrayed by someone who had not been given a free drink — and fined. One man was caught a second time and banished from Sapepe with nothing but his wife and the clothes on their backs. Total prohibition was enforced until the day Filipo discovered a half-empty bottle of whisky on Tauilopepe's sitting-room table. He politely exacted a promise from Tauilopepe not to drink in public, and from then until his retirement his sermons on liquor changed subtly: those people who needed alcohol for health reasons would be allowed to drink it but only in small doses. This category didn't include males under forty-five or females of any age. Tauilopepe was male and over forty-five.

In the doddering years of Filipo's spiritual reign, with more and more Sapepeans drifting to Apia and after a few years returning fully conversant with the art of drinking and brewing the Devil's Water, faamafu-brewing took to the bush. Now that Sapepe was enjoying a high standard of living a few madly courageous men saw rich profits in the enterprise and built faamafu-brewing fale deep in their plantations. The men who thirsted after the Devil, and their number increased over the years, crept to these dens at night and spent their two-shilling pieces on what they called 'Filipo's Spiritual Stuff'. Some matai took to the night-bush also. However, after Filipo and Tauilopepe, supported by the council, banished two of them, the rest of the matai who thirsted after happy forgetfulness stayed clear of the bush dens, took furtive trips to the Apia faamafu dens where they drank until the stars toppled in their heads, sobered up, and returned to Sapepe to champion the cause of prohibition.

Just before Filipo retired the bush dens were raided by a band of vigilantes organised by the council. The culprits were fined heavily and then, to their angry surprise, banished for two years apiece. Filipo claimed this to be his last glorious victory against the faamafu-brewing vanguards of the Devil, a victory he described enthusiastically to anyone who would listen. (There weren't many.) When he shifted to Tauilopepe's house the victory story ended with a definite moral: Filipo told the Aiga Tauilopepe that he had pursued his campaign with such unrelenting tenacity because the Devil's Water had caused Pepe's downfall. Once Taifau interrupted Filipo's narrative and asked why God hadn't punished Tauilopepe who drank whisky. As if stung by an oversized mosquito Filipo blinked, coughed, and replied that Tauilopepe was Tauilopepe and, besides, Tauilopepe only drank for medical reasons. There!

Living with the Aiga Tauilopepe was not easy for Filipo at first. He had been used to running his own household like a general commanding troops. For him to relinquish this enjoyable role was like being demoted to private and an invalid private at that. Teuila, his favourite daughter, was responsible for this, he believed. She didn't even allow Taulua to give orders to the children of the Aiga Tauilopepe, let alone suggest what he should eat because of his delicate stomach. For the Tauilopepe household functioned along papalagi lines when it came to meals. Instead of the two meals a day — a custom which Filipo cherished — there were three main meals and two minor snacks (called morning and afternoon tea) every day except Sunday when tradition was adhered to. Filipo didn't object openly, however; he tolerated his diarrhoea stoically — the Tauilopepe toilet was luxurious and efficient and he was being cared for with best things money could buy. Even Taulua was thriving on a life of no work and no worries; she grew fatter while Filipo grew thinner.

Filipo discovered a religious and intellectual companion

in Masina. Before she died they had long discussions about the geographical, social, and political structure of Heaven and Hell and the entrance qualifications for each. They also had endless discussions about the nature of man and concluded that mortals were 'sin-ridden through and through'. It was, they agreed, an apple that Adam had eaten so foolishly and not the 'unmentionable something' that modern Devil's disciples were suggesting in those irreligious books being sold in Apia. Filipo also agreed with Masina's versions of Sapepean history and genealogies which claimed that the Aiga Tauilopepe were the true rulers of Sapepe. In short they agreed about everything, including the nature of the papalagi: only missionaries and doctors were *good* papalagi, the rest were godless, uncivilised foreigners.

Filipo found Tauilopepe an enlightened host. At night whenever he was at home they had pleasant discussions in his study. They usually discussed politics first. Tauilopepe had been a member of the Legislative Council but had resigned because he refused to support the Independence Movement. Independence, he told Filipo, would ruin their country: Samoans were incapable of running the country properly, justly; the leaders of the Independence Movement were usurpers of paramount titles and were using the ignorant Samoans to get high office and money and power; one of them was even secretly betraying their movement to the Chief of Police. If Independence came, and he doubted whether it would because his friend the Governor had promised it wasn't going to, he would sell everything and get out of Samoa. Filipo agreed.

Then they usually discussed agriculture, God, and religion, in that order. Lastly, after comparing modern young people to their own generation, they agreed that the present generation, excluding Lalolagi, was composed of 'irresponsible, ungrateful fools who were only interested in drinking and gambling and pursuing the unmentionable'. They discussed Lalolagi's future with boundless optimism. Filipo was sure that he would be the 'Great Child of Light'. Tauilopepe agreed.

They never discussed Pepe. Or Toasa.

These discussions were usually accompanied by the velvety tune of whisky being poured into Tauilopepe's glass and down his throat. As the nights passed and Filipo watched Tauilopepe drinking, curiosity chipped at the will-power of the retired champion of prohibition, and Tauilopepe discovered that every time he poured and drank his whisky Filipo's mouth dribbled. One night, while Filipo was in the hectic middle of a drawn out analysis of Genesis, Tauilopepe filled a second glass and pushed it across the table. Still talking, Filipo picked it up and emptied it down his gullet. Tauilopepe forced himself not to laugh when Filipo jumped out of his chair, his hands clutching a stinging throat and chest. They joked about it afterwards, and Tauilopepe never poured his father-in-law another whisky. Nevertheless, when he got home in the evening he usually found that someone had been drinking his whisky. He didn't mention it to anyone, including Filipo, who now sang in the late afternoons as he showered. Everyone else thought Filipo's strange behaviour was due to advancing senility.

One person whom Filipo had always detested, though he never revealed it publicly, was Taifau. He classed Taifau with Toasa as an uncouth bully who humiliated him publicly, deliberately, and at the drop of a cruel joke, which was very often. And it was Taifau, the once 'blind, stench-oozing coward' (Filipo's words), who first discovered the secret of those loud, unintelligible shower songs. Early one afternoon, a month after Masina had been laid to rest with Filipo's prayers, Taifau came into Tauilopepe's study just as Filipo was gulping down his fourth furtive whisky. Filipo dropped the glass, his eyes wide with fear, his hands poised in mid-air, like a child caught playing with his unmentionable. Taifau laughed and laughed. And laughed. Filipo hurled the jug of water at him. Missed. Filipo burst into tears as Taifau left the room.

During the next few days Filipo never touched a drop. But he couldn't forget Taifau's laughter. It haunted him even while he was praying at the evening lotu. Prayers, in short, were useless charms in his attempt to exorcise Taifau's laughing aitu. So he tried fasting, but hunger only served to increase the size of the laughing aitu. And he tried sleeping, but dreams only increased the size of the aitu. And he tried cold showers at dawn, but they only gave him influenza which nearly killed him. And he tried fondling Taulua, hoping that physical passion for the unmentionable would burn out the unmentionable aitu, but Taulua, whose unmentionable it was, boxed his ears and ordered him to act his age and think of his fragile heart condition. So he tried physical passion with his own unmentionable, but that unmentionable was too old to stand up like a champion and fight the laughing aitu.

When all these home-made remedies had failed, having reduced their old inventor to a cringing, shaking, thin old man with an older heart condition, Filipo sought refuge again in Tauilopepe's whisky cabinet and the happiness glass. After his seventh whisky (or thereabouts) he forgot the laughing aitu but he also forgot that he was a cringing, shaking, thin old man with an older heart condition.

That night before lotu Tauilopepe found him sprawled across the table, clutching the empty happiness glass. The room stank of whisky. So did Filipo's mouth. It also stank of the scandal that would erupt in Sapepe if the people found out that Filipo had died of a heart attack brought on by too much alcohol. So Tauilopepe cleaned the room, hid the whisky, washed out his father-in-law's mouth with toothpaste, and emerged from his study to announce that their great and beloved father in Christ had passed away.

Two months after Filipo's memorable funeral the Aiga Tauilopepe celebrated Lalolagi's twelfth birthday and his graduation from primary school. He was to go to boarding-school in New Zealand at the beginning of the new year, 1961.

6   Farewell

All the furniture had been removed from the sitting room and the elders sat around on the floor. Lalolagi sat between his grandfather and Simi, the new pastor, feeling itchy in his new white shirt and blue tie, his first pair of long trousers, and his expensive shoes; but he bore the discomfort proudly because the farewell was for him, the first Sapepean to go to a New Zealand boarding-school with his own aiga paying for it. Already there were other Samoan youths in New Zealand boarding-schools but they were on government scholarships.

Among the children who were at the windows peering into the room were some of his close friends but he couldn't invite them in because such farewells were for the elders. He heard his aiga in the kitchen fale preparing the feast and he wished the rest of the elders would come because the church service wouldn't start until they did, and the feast wouldn't start until after the service.

While he was waiting he observed the new pastor. Simi was the blackest man he had ever met. All Solomon Islanders had kettle-black skins, one relative said. Being black, Simi would also speak the black islanders' language, which was similar to ape-talk in the Tarzan movies, someone else had added. So Lalolagi was disappointed when he attended the pastor's school and discovered that Simi couldn't speak a word of ape-talk. Having been told too that all black people were champion boxers and athletes, he was even more disappointed when Simi didn't look fit, fast, and savage. He was, so Lalolagi discovered, simply a black pastor who spoke better Samoan than most Samoans and was kinder than all the other pastors he had known. After a few weeks Lalolagi realised that he respected Simi, but he didn't admit this to his friends who were still waiting for Simi to reveal his athletic ability and to talk ape-talk. When his grandfather had invited Simi to be their

279

new pastor, other Sapepeans, Lalolagi knew, had resented it and claimed that having a black savage as their pastor would make them the laughing-stock of Samoa.

Taifau and Nofo were the last elders to arrive.

'We'd better start,' Tauilopepe said. Formally he welcomed the elders and then said that his son Lalolagi had been chosen by God to represent Sapepe in youth's competition to gain knowledge from overseas. Samoa, founded on God and chosen by God to achieve great things, needed citizens who had the new knowledge. Looking at Lalolagi, who was gazing at his shoes, he declared that his son wouldn't fail God and Samoa and Sapepe and him. Lalolagi was carrying with him all the hopes of Sapepe, and if Satan-inspired temptations threatened to undermine his resolve he was to pray and their Loving Father would protect him. The world of the papalagi was a sinful world of pleasure, sin, and sudden death; he must therefore be on his guard always. Lalolagi sensed that Simi, who was gazing intently at Tauilopepe, didn't agree with this opinion. His face showed something else — bafflement? amusement? 'Never trust a black man' an aunt had told him. They were all proud of Lalolagi, Tauilopepe was saying, and if Pepesa, his father, was alive he too would feel proud. Simi blinked as if Tauilopepe had hurt him, and Lalolagi remembered that, according to Teuila, Simi and Pepe had been close friends. Then he remembered this was the first time that Tauilopepe had praised Pepe publicly and realised that Simi had caught out Tauilopepe's lie. With that simple blink Simi had turned his grandfather's speech into hollow words. Tauilopepe ended his speech and the elders applauded with traditional phrases of praise.

'Be patient a little longer,' Tauilopepe whispered to Lalolagi, 'there's a lot of food.'

Simi announced the hymn. Except for Lalolagi, who was picking at the heel of his right shoe, everyone sang. After the hymn Simi addressed himself directly to Lalolagi. He didn't want to listen but Simi's commanding voice gradually destroyed his suspicions. 'I know little of papalagi,' Simi said, 'but, because they are human beings, you needn't fear them. All you have to do is to try to understand them, for with understanding will come love, and with love, trust.' Lalolagi noticed that most of the elders were studying Tauilopepe's reaction to Simi's speech.

Their people who had been to New Zealand, Simi continued, claimed that it was a land of people who lived in small rooms and did not want to know their neighbours, a godless land of lonely old people, a land where the Maoris, the original settlers, had been dispossessed, their culture and pride destroyed. But he couldn't tell Lalolagi if these claims were true. Only Lalolagi who was going there could find out. It was his future that was at stake. No one, not even the people he loved, had the right to choose his future career. Tauilopepe was staring at Simi; Lalolagi put his hand on Tauilopepe's knee; Tauilopepe looked at the floor again, and Lalolagi knew everything would be all right. Many of the elders looked uncomfortable knowing this was the first time anyone had contradicted Tauilopepe's opinions publicly.

'Your father was my friend,' Simi continued. 'He was a good man, and you would have admired him as I did. He loved other people deeply. ...' As Lalolagi listened he began to regret not having known his father whom his grandfather despised so much. But it was years too late: Pepe was dead, and he, Lalolagi, was going to a land of pagan white savages. When he felt Tauilopepe's hand on his knee he again chose his grandfather's hopes and dreams as his own. He would never let grandfather down — he mustn't, because Pepe, his own father, had turned against grandfather. Simi ended, 'Live up to the memory of your. father. Don't be afraid of other men. Choose to love all people whether brown, white, yellow, or *black*.' Some of the elders chuckled but Simi didn't seem to notice. He announced the last hymn.

Tauilopepe didn't sing, Lalolagi noticed. Served the black pastor right. He shouldn't have angered grandfather, and all because of a dead and worthless Pepe.

After the short concluding prayer enough food to feed three times the number of guests was brought in. But it took them, Lalolagi calculated on the gold wrist-watch which Tauilopepe had bought for his last birthday, only a noisy teeth-chopping, mouth-slopping, bone-sucking half hour to reduce it to scraps. Much food went to the crowd outside. Immediately afterwards Simi thanked Tauilopepe, who avoided looking at him, said good night to the elders, who avoided looking at him, and went home. As was the custom pastors were not expected to participate in the other festivities.

Teuila, who had supervised the feast, came and sat with Lalolagi and Tauilopepe and the three of them joked and laughed freely. While the guests smoked and picked their teeth most of them listened. No other child in Sapepe joked like this with his parents; and no one ever dared joke like this with Tauilopepe; it was a pity the Aiga Tauilopepe were developing these traits.

All the children outside and the people who had served up the feast came in and formed a choir.

'Let's see if you can still conduct and dance!' Tauilopepe challenged Taifau.

The other elders challenged him also.

'Go on, sing!' Taifau ordered the choir. He jumped up high and landed in a crouch in front of the choir. Everyone laughed. With Taifau conducting, the choir started to sing. His whole body served as a baton. Quickly he mesmerised everyone into loud, abandoned singing and clapping. 'See this?' he yelled, pounding his chest. 'See this muscle? Nothing like it!' Coughed and wheezed like a Tb patient. Everyone laughed again. 'Come on, palagi boy!' Taifau called to Lalolagi in English. 'See dis Samoan boy, he a tough and good dancing boy. He going dance like da moon and da Russian sputnika!' And, extending his arms into aeroplane wings, he dipped and dived round the room spluttering like an aeroplane engine, all in time to the singing and clapping.

A wizened old man whooped up to his unsteady feet, bared his toothless gums at the audience, ape-walked out, and, stopping in front of the choir, took off his shirt, hitched up one side of his lavalava to reveal part of his tatau, extended his almost fleshless arms, and danced, his feet planted firmly on the floor, his hands and arms curv-

282

ing and twirling like swooping, diving birds. Everyone clapped, and the elders told one another that this *was* the siva, as timeless and beautiful as the sea, like paddles dipping and turning in the murmuring stillness of water, like the wind swirling lazily over sand. The song mounted steadily to a crescendo. The old man kept up to it — hands, arms, legs, and body, dipping, buckling, turning, fingers tracing intricate patterns in the air — till his body and tatau glistened with sweat and he was panting raggedly. Extended his arms. Bowed. The song ended. Everyone clapped as he shuffled back to his seat, chuckling to himself.

After nearly all the guests and many of the choir had danced, and after more hilarious clowning and dancing by Taifau, Teuila danced with three old women who whooped and growled and danced around her. When she finished she dragged Lalolagi up. Some of his friends danced round him. 'Malo! Malo!' the elders encouraged them.

'You have a lot to learn about the siva!' Tauilopepe joked when Lalolagi and his friends finished dancing. The boys giggled.

'You show us then,' Lalolagi said. Tauilopepe shook his head. 'Papa, you show us!'

'Taifau!' Tauilopepe called. Taifau, who was resting behind the choir, jumped up. 'Sing that song!'

'What song, man of Apia?' Taifau replied.

'The one that made the women fall asleep, man from Russia!'

'Ha, *that* song! The song I composed which got me all my wives?'

'Yes, ugly man!'

Only the elders and Lalolagi laughed; the rest of the audience remained silent: it was impolite to laugh at jokes between your elders, especially elders of Tauilopepe's stature.

Tauilopepe took off his tie and shirt, hitched up his lavalava, slapped his chest and stomach with his hands, whooped, and uncurled his huge frame towards the light. Taifau kicked up his right leg and the choir burst into song, using the traditional singing voices of old men. No clapping this time, just the thudding beat of two sticks on a mat drum.

Only the few oldest men and women had seen Tauilopepe dance as a youth, so when he started the siva most people were surprised. Supple, agile, graceful, limbs and body glistening in the light. 'Malo! Malo!' the elders cried.

'Well, Russian? How's that?' Tauilopepe called.

'Not bad, not bad!' laughed Taifau.

'Watch this!' And he was away — turning, whirling, slapping his arms, heels, and chest in time to the beat of the mat drum, never missing a beat. Stamped his feet. Laughed. Then he danced the graceful style of the manaia better than anyone they had seen before. Even better than Toasa, the elders would tell their children.

Suddenly Taifau joined Tauilopepe and imitated his actions with exaggerated gestures; the laughter erupted again. Shaking with laughter, Tauilopepe picked up his shirt and left. Taifau slumped down beside Nofo who started to fan him with a folded sheet of newspaper. Soon after almost everyone dispersed. Teuila went into the kitchen while Lalolagi and his friends talked.

Lalolagi promised that he would write to them every week; they were, he emphasised, his best friends. One boy said papalagi kids were weaklings, and because Lalolagi was a good boxer he would outfight them. Another friend, the fattest one, claimed that papalagi were poor and ate horsemeat and dogmeat sometimes and the women wore false teeth and false hair. And so they went on. Teuila came in and told them it was late but Lalolagi pleaded with her and she said good night and went upstairs to bed.

Lalolagi said he was going to study law after high school. 'What's that?' Taifau's youngest son asked. The others laughed at his ignorance. Law, explained Lalolagi, was to do with the courts. 'Like what?' Taifau's son persisted.

Trying not to get angry Lalolagi said, 'Law is something which if you break it you go to jail, like when Fono stole one of Papa's cows and went to jail for it. And a person who's studied law is a lawyer.'

284

'Like that fat palagi who often comes to see Tauilopepe?' Taifau's son asked.

Lalolagi nodded. Papa's lawyer, he said, was called Mister Ashton, and Papa wanted him to be a lawyer like Mister Ashton so he could protect all Papa's property.

'What if you don't return?' Taifau's astute son asked. The other boys glared at him.

'Why shouldn't I return?' asked Lalolagi.

'You could die in an accident.'

'Boy, you're stupid!' reprimanded Lalolagi's closest friend.

'Yes, stupid!' chorused the others.

'If I die I die!' Lalolagi joked. 'And if I turn into a palagi I turn into a palagi.' The others laughed at Taifau's son.

The boys asked Lalolagi whether they could all come to the airport to see him off. 'Yes,' he said.

'What about him?' Lalolagi's closest friend said, pointing at Taifau's son who had been pushed to the back of the group.

'No!' chorused the others. 'He's too small and stupid!'

'I didn't mean it, Lalolagi,' the boy pleaded.

'No, there won't be enough room for you,' said Lalolagi.

Almost in tears Taifau's son sprang up, ran to the front door, stopped, and called, 'I hope you die there. I hope you become a stupid fat palagi like Tauilopepe's fat palagi lawyer!' Then he vanished into the darkness before they could catch him.

The four trucks and two cars and a jeep carrying nearly all the Aiga Tauilopepe and Aiga Taifau, Simi, the important elders, and a large group of Lalolagi's friends arrived at Faleolo Airport on the Sunday morning, an hour before the plane was to leave. All of them except Tauilopepe, Teuila, and Lalolagi rushed into the hangar-like terminal building or scattered to gaze through the mesh-wire fence at the plane only a few unbelievable yards away. Lalolagi, unable to control the wild butterflies in his stomach, left the car, which Tauilopepe had parked just above the beach opposite the terminal building, and stood gazing at the sea shimmering away over dark patches of coral.

Tauilopepe followed him. 'Are you afraid?' he asked.

'Yes, Papa.'

'I was afraid like you once.'

'When, Papa?'

'When my father took me to Apia for the first time.'

'But Apia is a safe place.'

'And so will New Zealand be once you get used to it.' Tauilopepe placed a reassuring hand on Lalolagi's shoulder.

'It's nearly time!' Teuila called from the car.

'Be brave,' Tauilopepe said as they walked towards the terminal building, followed by three men carrying Lalolagi's suitcases.

Teuila clutched Lalolagi's hand and they stopped in the middle of the noisy, brilliantine-smelling crowd. A long line of passengers extended from the airline's counter. Tauilopepe pushed his way up to the counter, and Lalolagi watched him talking to three men in uniform. One of them was a papalagi with a thick beard. Tauilopepe turned and called them over. Teuila pushed Lalolagi to the head of the queue. No one objected. Tauilopepe took out Lalolagi's tickets and passport and gave them to the papalagi official who examined and stamped them and returned them to Tauilopepe.

'My son going to be a lawyer,' Tauilopepe said.

'He's a lucky lad,' the papalagi said. Some of the other passengers behind them were starting to complain.

'Here my son's suitcases,' said Tauilopepe. The papalagi pointed to the two Samoan officials. They picked up the suitcases and put them on the scales.

'Who do they think they are!' Lalolagi heard a woman remark.

'That's the trouble with this country. It's not *what* you know, it's *who* you know that's important!' someone else added.

'Thanking to you,' Tauilopepe said when the suitcases had been weighed and the papalagi did not demand payment for excess weight. 'Thank Mr Pool too for me.' Mr Pool was the airline's manager.

'It's not what you know, it's who you know' Lalolagi remembered as they left the building, followed by waves of Sapepe people. Self-importance, conjured up by his grandfather's importance to the officials, had stilled the butterflies inside him.

They stopped at the mesh-wire fence. Workers were loading suitcases and bags of mail into the plane. A short squat man on the nearest wing was feeding fuel into it through a long hose connected to a strange-looking machine on the ground. Lalolagi watched. Simi came and stood beside him and he started feeling the butterflies again and wished Simi would leave him alone.

'How long will it take for the flight?' Simi asked.

'About six hours.'

'So you're not angry any more? You were angry with me last night, weren't you?' Simi asked. Lalolagi shook his head. 'That's good. I thought you were.'

Sparkling like a knife-blade, the plane seemed incongruous against its backdrop of palms, hills, and blue sky. And it would soon be carrying him away from those he loved.

'There is no need to be afraid, Lalolagi.' Simi handed him a small envelope. 'This is for you.'

'Thank you,' Lalolagi said, sheathing the gift in his breast pocket.

'I'll say goodbye now,' Simi said, and he shook Lalolagi's hand and gazed sadly into his face. 'You look just like your father the day I first met him,' he whispered. 'God bless you.' He turned and walked away. Lalolagi would forget Simi's gift until, cold and homesick in his school dormitory, he would open it to find a soiled pound note and a small photograph of a boy who looked like him, a bald-headed dwarf, and a black boy: his father and Uncle Tagata and Simi laughing in front of the Apia market. And he would cry.

Teuila came and put her arm round his shoulders. He sensed that she was nearly crying and realised he was ready to cry too, but he didn't want to in front of all those people who moved up and encircled him separating him from her. He couldn't see Tauilopepe. Most of the women were sniffing tears into their hands and handkerchiefs. Behind him the plane spluttered and kicked the butterflies inside him to life again. One by one the elders embraced and kissed him and said goodbye. He was a man and men didn't cry in public. Then the weeping women surrounded him, twining ula round his neck, kissing him, and telling him to be brave. And he did cry. Then the other men, without tears, embracing him with their precarious bravery, stuffing money into his pockets, then retreating to hide behind the sobbing women. Then the children around him sniffing, sobbing, shaking hands.

'Time to go!' someone called. Teuila broke through the circle of children and steered him through the crowd.

Weeping people packed the terminal building. Some old women were wailing. Tauilopepe and Taifau were standing at the door leading out to the plane. Sobbing into Lalolagi's hair, Teuila crushed him against her, pushed him towards Tauilopepe, turned, and stumbled back into the crowd.

Only the passengers were allowed out to the plane, but Tauilopepe and Taifau held Lalolagi's hands and walked through without the police objecting. 'Goodbye, Lalolagi!' the Sapepeans called from the fence. He waved and saw through his tears Faitoaga jumping over the fence and running towards him, past the policemen. He ran to Faitoaga who embraced him tightly and lifted him up.

'Be strong. Strong like your father!' said Faitoaga, putting him down. Two policemen came, held Faitoaga's arms, and pulled him away. 'Remember your father wasn't scared of anyone!'

'Hurry please!' the air hostess called from the top of the gangway. All the other passengers were seated.

Lalolagi reached out and embraced Taifau. 'Faitoaga is right,' said Taifau. 'Be brave like Pepe.'

Tauilopepe steered him up the gangway. Half-way up Lalolagi stopped.

'We're late already!' the air hostess called.

'You must be brave. Be brave like Pepe, your father!' Tauilopepe said

'Yes, Papa.'

Lalolagi ran past the hostess into the plane without looking back.

Tauilopepe turned back down. Workers pulled away the gangway. Immediately the purring changed into a furious roar; the wind from the propellers kicked up the dust and whipped at Tauilopepe's clothes; but he stood and watched the plane moving forward.

The plane turned on to the runway, wheeled, and faced the east. Tauilopepe waved. The plane surged forward, lifted, lifted, its body flashing in the sun as it cleared the palms at the end of the runway and escaped towards the high mountains and the mist.

Escaped with his only heir.

7 Correspondence between Worlds

In his first letter home, written in Samoan and dated 10 February 1961, Lalolagi told them that although it was summer he was cold, he was also homesick and not used to palagi food. He described his plane trip and how other Samoan passengers had looked after him and how big Auckland Airport was. Mr Stubbs, one of his teachers, he said, met him at the airport. Mr Stubbs was a famous Rugby player. It was a school rule to play Rugby. After a meal in his first New Zealand restaurant, and he didn't eat much because he felt every palagi watching him and he didn't know how to use a knife and fork, they took all night in a train to get to New Plymouth. He couldn't sleep: the train was noisy and hot and smelly and he was afraid and so homesick.

He slept in a dormitory with twenty other boys, and despite his poor English got on well with them. He was in 3 General, the second highest form, but Mr Stubbs had told him that when his English improved he would go up to 3 Professional. There were over six hundred boys in the school; a few of them were Maoris. One of the Maoris, Hawley Kuru, was his friend already and had invited him to spend the holidays with his aiga. Hawley's father was a lawyer. 'Should I go?' he asked Tauilopepe.

Every student wore a blue uniform—blue shirt, blue shorts, blue socks with a gold stripe, black shoes, and a blue cap. They all had numbers. His was 134 and it was on all his clothes. The palagi had a strange custom: they called everyone by his last name, so they had started calling him Tauilopepe but they couldn't pronounce it properly so he'd told them to call him Pepe.

He was missing them all and said he got only two shillings weekly to spend. Other boys' parents sent them extra so would Papa please do the same.

'There is no LMS church,' he said, 'so I'm going to the Methodist one. Is that all right Papa? By the way,' he ended, 'there is no snow in New Plymouth except on Mount Egmont. Don't forget the money. I love you all very, very much.'

In his reply Tauilopepe first praised God for looking after Lalolagi and then asked if he had received the ten pounds he had sent, and emphasised how important it was to learn the value of money early in one's life. Because Hawley's father was a lawyer, he said, Lalolagi could go there for his holidays. 'I am extremely disturbed,' he added, 'that everyone is calling you Pepe. You should be proud of your own name. Mr Ashton is writing to the principal to make this clear. Calling you Lagi would be all right.'

Lalolagi was to send a photograph of himself, Tauilopepe said, wearing his uniform. He was to work hard at improving his English and be promoted to 3 Professional. He should also learn to write all his letters in English which was the only language worth knowing well. Samoan got nobody anywhere, especially in business.

Rugby was a dangerous game and Lalolagi wasn't to play it, despite the school rule. It was good there was no snow because snow caused pneumonia.

In a letter dated 20 May 1961 Lalolagi described his hoilday with the Kuru family in Hawera, thirty miles outside New Plymouth. They had a large beautiful house and two cars. Mr Kuru was half-Maori and his wife was a Pakeha, which was the Maori word for papalagi. They treated him like their own son. Pakehas and Maoris had a funny custom: Hawley could say anything to his parents and even tell them off if he was angry. But Hawley didn't do this again after he, Lalolagi, had told him it was impolite. There were more cows than people in Hawera and every man was a milk farmer. He had visited Mr Kuru's brother's farm. It was about two hundred acres, much smaller than Leaves of the Banyan Tree. Compared to Samoa the Pakehas and Maoris treated animals much better.

It was growing very cold but he was getting used to it. He was playing Rugby. (In a previous letter he had persuaded Tauilopepe to let him.) Mr Stubbs was impressed with his ability. All Samoans made excellent Rugby players, Mr Stubbs had told him. 'Please send money for my Rugby gear,' he said. 'And, Papa, there's no need to worry about me being hurt.'

Was it true that Western Samoa, their beloved country, was getting Independence soon? he ended.

Tauilopepe replied, 'I am opening an account for you at a New Plymouth bank so you can draw money whenever you need it. Yes, our country is to be self-governing early in 1962. With Independence will end the prosperous times. The papalagi, all highly educated men, have ruled justly and fairly. But our own leaders, all uneducated and ignorant men, will ruin our country. I am buying a house in Auckland in case our country collapses after Independence.'

He and the council, Tauilopepe said, had decided that Sapepe needed a new church. They were the most prosperous district in Samoa and could well afford such a church to glorify God. Fund-raising would start the next week.

About this time Teuila began to correspond with Lalolagi. Simi was against the church project, she wrote. Not even Papa knew all his reasons but Simi believed their present church was big enough. After Lalolagi left, Papa invited Simi to talk with him in the evenings. At first they joked and laughed and Papa did not drink at all. Then things suddenly went wrong and just before Simi stopped coming altogether she had heard them shouting at each other. Papa refused to tell her anything about it. However, there was nothing for Lalolagi to worry about.

For the first time Lalolagi's replies were written in English. He proudly pointed this out to his grandfather. How much was their new church going to cost? Unlike Samoans papalagi didn't give much to the church. And that was a sin, wasn't it? Concerning Independence he wrote: 'It is bad our country is to be Independence. We got no leaders who is as good as the European who ruled us. It is good

292

you are buying a house for us in Auckland just in case the new government of ours goes flop.'

He ended his letter: 'I tell everyone not to call me Pepe. They call me Lagi now. It is Lagi, number 134. It is easier for the European to say that.'

He boasted to Teuila about his English too and then attacked Simi for his stand against the new church: 'Simi is a stranger to Sapepe but he is opposing Papa who give everything to Sapepe. Simi is jealous of Papa. Simi is like Pepe. They think they know everything. It is probably to do with Pepe the cause of the trouble between Simi and Papa. Papa will win. Our church will be built because it God's church and Papa wants a church built.' He reminded Teuila to remind Papa to get Mr Ashton to send more money to his bank account.

'Dear Mummy and Daddy' he started his next letter, dated 15 June 1961. He apologised for not replying sooner to their earlier letters. It took him all his spare time to do his school work. For a blooming week it had rained cats and dogs. Hawley was still his best cobber but he now had lots of other mates. None of them were as good as him in the Rugby game. He was brassed off because they had school rules about everything and the food was terrible — they got rice pudding all the time and blooming hash every morning. He wished he had some Samoan food. How was the church coming along?

In a lengthy reply Tauilopepe congratulated him on his 'beautiful English'. (Taifau had translated Lalolagi's letter for him.) The papalagi had a very colourful and precise language. Did it really rain animals during winter? He warned Lalolagi to keep away from his girl-friends (his 'mates', as Lalolagi had called them) and to concentrate on his studies. The time for mates was when he had gradu- ated. 'Please obey the school rules,' he said, 'they are made for people's good. Where would the world be without rules? Pepe destroyed himself by not living by the rules.'

They had collected eight thousand pounds already for the church, he ended, and should have sixteen thousand pounds by the end of the year. Teuila was sending him some taro.

Teuila's letter, sent without Tauilopepe's knowledge, told of the trouble between Tauilopepe and Simi. In his sermons Simi was advocating reform of the LMS church: it had become too worldly, too preoccupied with money and building churches and pastors' houses and was neglecting its spiritual role and its quest for social and political justice. Simi was working his own plantation and refusing his congregation's monthly monetary contributions. Pastors and the church had become a burden on the people, he declared. Teuila said that there was much truth in this statement. Simi was very much like Pepe, she added. As yet, even though some Sapepeans were siding with Simi, none of the matai had deserted Papa. The council was still collecting a hundred and fifty pounds from each aiga and Simi had not publicly opposed the collections. She hoped he wouldn't as it would cause a serious clash between him and Papa.

She asked him not to mention what she had said to Papa as it would upset him.

In his reply Lalolagi said he would not write to them any more in Samoan. Simi had no blooming right upsetting Papa; he was the kind of joker that was not a good pastor. Their New Plymouth minister did not meddle in town affairs, and Simi should be like that. Papa would be dead right if he got the council to boot Simi out of Sapepe. Their church was a great church, the best in Samoa. All Simi was doing was ruining it. Simi was as stupid as Pepe had been and Pepe ended up a fair dinkum drunk, poor and all, with nobody loving him. He was never ever going to be like Pepe.

In the middle of September Tauilopepe wrote that the church building would start in February 1962, a month after Independence. He was happy that Lalolagi was coming near the top of his class, and scoring ninety points during the Rugby season was a great feat. He was gratified to hear that Lalolagi's school had a military training programme. Many of his Apia friends had been soldiers in the Second World War and they had told him that military training produced the best citizens. In a previous letter Lalolagi had asked him to stop drinking, so Tauilopepe ended: 'I have carried out your wish. I don't know why I ever started drinking.'

After a month of not hearing from Lalolagi Teuila wrote to ask if she had hurt him in any way. He was her only child, she said, and she was feeling so alone because Papa was drinking heavily again. It was to do with Simi and the new church. A few aiga were no longer attending church, ordered by their matai not to do so until Simi stopped opposing the church project. Papa had not done the same with their aiga but he would be forced to sooner or later. She spent her weekdays in their Apia house looking after their aiga's children who attended school there. The previous week-end in Sapepe she had tried to stop Papa from drinking too much. He took no notice of her. Papa admired Simi but he was not going to give in to him. 'If men admire each other why do they have to quarrel?' she asked.

For the first time she admitted to Lalolagi that Pepe had been good, kind, and gentle. Simi knew this and had tried to make Papa believe it but Papa was stubbornly refusing to do so.

She begged Lalolagi to write to her because she felt so alone, knowing what would happen and being unable to prevent it.

Lalolagi replied promptly. He said that he had been too blooming busy with his swot to write. She had nothing to worry about because Papa had written to say that everything was jake, the church would be built because it was God's wish. Simi, even though he was a bad pastor, would realise this soon. God would open his eyes.

Pepe was dead and hadn't done Papa a scrap of good; leaving him nothing but a bad name. Like a good son, he Lagi, loved his father, Papa, and he would love Papa and her forever because they had chosen him as their only son. 'Now please don't worry, Mum. I'm jake and Papa will make sure everything will turn out fine. Can I have some more money?'

In a November letter Tauilopepe apologised for not having written for three weeks. He had been too busy as chairman and treasurer of the church project. He had picked other matai to collect the levies but they had helped themselves to the money. No wonder the papalagi didn't trust Samoans. Lazy, irresponsible, wanting something for nothing, Samoans could not be trusted. In Sapepe he could trust only Taifau and Faitoaga, and even Taifau kept asking if he thought the new church was a good idea. Taifau was one of the people who had suggested it in the first place.

He had little time to rest in their Apia house now. He had struggled all his life for their ungrateful aiga and Sapepe, yet everyone was turning against him. All he wanted now in his old age was to relax and see the people he had helped carry on with what he had created. But all he saw were good-for-nothing relatives who were still expecting him to slave for them. 'People can disappoint you, hurt you,' he wrote. 'Trust only your own ability. You are the one I rely on totally. When you return, with honour and education, I will be able to stop working and enjoy the last years of my life. Life is a fierce struggle with everyone trying to destroy you. Samoans are noted for this. When they see another Samoan achieving something worthwhile they dig pits to try and bury him in.'

Two days after Tauilopepe's letter, Teuila told Lalolagi that Papa was spending a few weeks in Apia; he was ill; he said little, drank a lot, and got angry with everyone. Lalolagi was to write to Papa and cheer him up. Papa would be sixty-one in two weeks and they were preparing a big birthday party. It was to be in Apia because Papa didn't want to return to Sapepe as yet.

Lalolagi wrote to Tauilopepe immediately, offering very strong advice. Their relatives owed Papa everything, he said, so if any of them got out of line Pape should boot them out. If Taifau, who owed Papa even the shirt on his back, questioned the project any further Papa should sack him too. Banish those matai who pinched the church funds. He was ashamed of being a Samoan because of those thieving matai. 'Wait until I get home,' he ended, 'I'll help you straighten out everyone, Papa. I will never betray you, and you'll be able to retire and let me run everything. Get tough, Papa.'

Teuila replied that his letter had done wonders for Papa. When it had been translated and read to him Papa had laughed and returned to Sapepe. Before leaving he told her he was going to have his birthday party in Sapepe after all and everyone had better watch out. He also swore off drinking.

In her next letter she described the birthday party and said they had missed him. Everyone in Sapepe except Simi had turned up and had danced and sung all night. Everything was back to normal. Simi had stopped preaching against the new church. He had, she sensed, resigned himself to the fact that it was going to be built. Papa had hired the builders. While everyone else in Samoa was busy rehearsing dances and songs for the Independence celebrations Sapepe was rightfully preoccupied with building something really worthwhile. The church would be completed by the end of 1962, ready for Lalolagi's first vacation at home.

But because of the delays in completing the church and because of the power struggle that was to occur in Sapepe over the next five years, Tauilopepe was to keep postponing this vacation.

8   A Memorial

Western Samoa was now an independent nation 'founded on God' so the national motto proclaimed. The national celebrations at Mulinuu Peninsula had been a dazzling, thrilling, sanctimonious, spectacular, spendthrift, pious, sometimes drunken, and verbose week, to which Tauilopepe, even though invited to most of the official functions, had not been a witness, but of which most of the mobile Sapepe population had been wonder-struck, laughing, awed, wide-eyed spectators who had spent their money as fast as the Independence flag had sped up the Independence flagpole, while the New Zealanders, who had come to realise that colonies were a thankless luxury, had sighed deep sighs of relief.

It was Monday evening, two weeks after Independence and two days before workers were to start marking and digging the foundations of the new church. A chill wind, weaving in from the mountains, had silenced the cicadas and chased the dogs to shelter under the houses and fale. Tauilopepe had spent all day inspecting his plantation; he had even climbed with Faitoaga to the recently cleared area near the summit of the range, and he was now feeling tired as he ate his evening meal — thick, well-cooked steaks, fried eggs, and a hefty pile of taro. When he finished eating he reread a translation of Lalolagi's latest letter. One of the girls who had served him his meal came in, squatted down by his chair, and told him that the pastor was at the door. He told her to ask him in and to bring them some coffee, folded Lalolagi's letter, and took off his spectacles and waited. For about a month he had deliberately avoided Simi.

Simi entered with bowed head and sat down in the armchair opposite Tauilopepe, who greeted him formally, as was the custom, but who was then lost for anything else to say.

298

'Are you well?' Simi asked.

'Yes, I am well. And you?'

'I am well, thank you.'

Awkward silence again.

'I think you know why I have come,' Simi said finally. 'It is a shame, sir, that we have to disagree on so many things.' Tauilopepe poured himself another cup of coffee. A woman was singing in the kitchen, an Independence song about self-sacrifice, martyrs, and sorrow. 'I have never asked you directly, sir, but I feel I must ask now: Why does this church *have* to be built?'

Tauilopepe steadied his cup in the saucer and said, 'Because our people want it built!' The woman was singing of the New Zealand guns that had created eleven martyrs, of the period of political repression when a tamaaiga had died from machine-gun wounds. The governor was to blame, she sang, the governor pulled the trigger. 'I too want the church built,' added Tauilopepe.

'But why do you want it built?'

'Because our present church is too small,' replied Tauilopepe. Simi reminded him that this wasn't true, so Tauilopepe shifted his ground. 'It is an old church,' he said, 'a church unworthy of God and of Sapepe's high standard of living.'

'That is your main reason?'

'Yes, that is the only reason.'

'The other matai have agreed?' Simi asked. Tauilopepe nodded. 'What would they do if you changed your mind?'

'I cannot change their decision. It is their church, their money, their decision.'

'Is it their decision that the church is to be a memorial?'

'Memorial? Memorial to what? To whom?' Tauilopepe replied.

'Memorial to your son? I have heard some people talk of it.'

'Most of our people have agreed that it should be so!' Tauilopepe said defensively.

'I came to discuss, not to argue.'

'I am not angry,' said Tauilopepe.

'The church is to be a memorial to Pepe then?'

Tauilopepe nodded emphatically. 'I hope, sir, you won't be angry at what I am going to remind you of,' Simi said.

'You may speak freely. . . .'

'And honestly?' asked Simi. Tauilopepe nodded and refilled Simi's cup. 'This memorial, will it not be a Christian memorial to a non-believer? You yourself know Pepe did not believe.'

'But he did,' said Tauilopepe, smiling. 'Pepe *did* believe.'

'In what?'

'In what all men must believe in.'

'God? The church?'

'Yes.'

Simi was silent for a moment, then he said, 'Are you going to ask me what I think?'

'There is no need to.'

'Why?'

'Because it was you who by your obvious admiration for Pepe forced me to reconsider my views about him. Remember?'

Simi shook his head slowly. 'If I did anything it was to try to make you love Pepe again. Not to make you believe that he believed in God.'

'But if you, a man of God, respected him you must have done so because he believed; a man of God would sin if he trusted and loved a non-believer, an enemy of the church. Well, wouldn't he?'

'I respected your son knowing he did not believe. Your son, Tauilopepe, was an atheist.'

'You admit that? You respected an atheist? You, a pastor, a servant of God?' said Tauilopepe. Simi nodded. 'I cannot believe that. You people preach belief in Christ, belief in converting non-believers. If, like you, all men of God preach acceptance of atheists what are we, your congregation, to believe? That the church is for atheists and the godless as well as for believers?'

Looking at the floor, Simi said, 'I respected Pepe for what he was. . . .'

'An atheist?'

'No, a man with pride and courage.'

'And the plain fact that he did not believe, that he was a

300

godless man, did not matter?'

Simi looked up. 'With Pepe it did not matter. ....'

'Why not? Tell me, why not?'

'Because he had the gift of Christ.'

'The gift of Christ?'

'Yes. He tried, the best way he knew how, to love other people in the here-and-now. He did his best not to harm anyone.'

'What do *you* know about him harming others? Tell me, what do you know about it?' Tauilopepe was breathing heavily. 'You talk about love, pastor, but do you know what he did to me, my own son who I nursed and devoted my life to?' Paused. The light seemed to chain him to his chair. 'He took my love, took my heart, and tore them to shreds. Tramped on them like a dog would tramp in its own filth. He may have loved others but he denied me. He treated me like I was nothing, just a dog to spit on!'

'I am deeply sorry,' Simi said.

'When he went out of my life—and he did so deliberately—he took my hopes and dreams and love with him. You know what he did with them? He sold them at that dirty filthy market for the belief in nothing. Nothing! Am I worth nothing, Simi? Because that is what he sold me for.' He stopped and gazed out into the darkness. 'You tell me he believed in people,' he continued after a moment, 'but he didn't believe in me. To him I was worth going to jail for. Is that what I am worth?' He looked at Simi but the pastor looked away and remained silent. 'Listen to the wind, look at the darkness, just like on the night he was born. I held him in my arms and my world was full with hopes and plans. Was I so bad, so heartless a father?' Paused again. 'But he went away. He cursed me. I don't care whether he believed in God or not! Hear me. I didn't care then and I don't care now. All I wanted was for him to love me, respect me. I didn't ask for much. I gave him so much and had so much more to give him. ... But ... he .... He is ... dead and he haunts me. My own son!' He bowed his head, hands cupped to his face.

Wind moaning through the darkness, humming wistfully through the louvre windows and ruffling the table-cloth and the account books, bringing with it the feel of heavy rain the next day and the day after that when Sapepe would lay the foundations of a memorial to many things: Independence for some people, God for most; but, for Tauilopepe, a memorial to his son; to his conscience, Simi thought.

'You do not think it wrong then to erect a religious memorial to a son who did not believe?' Simi asked after a time.

'Do you?' replied Tauilopepe.

'I am not sure any more. Perhaps it is not important.'

'You are a strange man, Simi,' said Tauilopepe. 'You believe, yet you doubt. You say there is room in our church for men like Pepe. You talk more about men than about the God you serve.... No, let me finish. You feel more fervently about men than about your God. Your opposition to the new church is based on this: a new church will mean a great financial and physical burden on the people. I admit it is a burden but it is a burden worth carrying because it is for God.... Please let me finish. If Pepe was alive today would he oppose the project? Simi, I am asking you now as a friend. Tell me, would Pepe deny such a church?' The pastor was gazing out at the darkness moving beyond the edge of the light.

'I do not know any more,' he said. 'I only knew Pepe when we were both very young, when, I think, we had not confronted the world as it really is. Those were joyful, happy days free from the dust that blurs our vision as we get older and more afraid. You too, sir, must have known those days, those years when the heart was a dove, free in the shifting wind. Free to soar to the limits of the world, free to fly into the arms of God. But I grew old and afraid and chose the solidity of the known world. Pepe and I went our separate ways. He remained young I think, brash, foolishly brave, confronting the tarnished image of the people and things he once believed in and respected, refusing to accept that things and people change. We changed, we compromised, and became deadly human, partly human and partly dead. Signed away for "peace and mind" — call it what you like — our ideals and courage, the very qual-

302

ities that would have kept us free and human. For a self-destructive peace confined our lives—or is it deaths—to meaningless possessions, money, friends, aiga, stale prejudices, ridiculously meaningless attitudes, fears. To the very deadly dust we grovel in....'

'To God?' interrupted Tauilopepe.

'But Pepe clung on to what we once believed in but are now too afraid to believe in any more.' Stopped and, looking directly at Tauilopepe, continued: 'And he paid the price we are not willing to pay—a life alone, a life without God if you like. Lonely yet not lonely. Raging against the fearful darkness yet embracing it without fear. Laughing at us and our ridiculous rituals in our gilded cells yet loving us. Rejecting our little cruel hypocritical efforts yet understanding why we make them. Wanting to change us, to reform us in the image of the beauty we are capable of growing toward, yet knowing that the living dead cannot be resurrected. He could not lead us out of our self-imposed bondage, out of our Egypt, because he was not Moses. Moses believed in a Promised Land, believed, like all our modern Caesars and tyrants, that some of the Israelites had to be sacrificed in the wilderness in order to achieve the Promised Land. Pepe refused to believe that people should be sacrificed in order to bring about Canaan.' His voice had faded almost to a whisper.

'You—you do not believe?' Tauilopepe asked, more as an assertion than a question.

'Believe?'

'Yes, believe in God?'

'I think...I think so,' Simi said.

'You think so!'

'That is all I can do.'

'All? But you are a pastor, a man who has dedicated his life to serving God. You *must* believe.'

'I was firm in my belief. I think I still am. Until....'

'Until what? Tell me. I must know.'

'Until I went to see him in the hospital.'

'But why?'

'Because he was not afraid.'

'Afraid of what?'

'Not afraid of dying believing there is no God, no after life.'

Tauilopepe shook his head furiously. 'I cannot believe that. He must have been afraid!'

'Why?'

'Because every man is afraid. He must have pretended he was not afraid. That's it. He was lying to you!'

Simi stared at Tauilopepe for a moment, then, emphasising every word, he asked, 'Do you believe Pepe was capable of such a lie?'

'Yes!' Tauilopepe almost shouted. 'Yes, he was capable of anything. Hear me — anything!'

Simi sighed. 'I thought you understood him. Earlier tonight, when your love for him swept away the dust, I thought you did understand him.'

'But I do. I do understand,' insisted Tauilopepe.

'We suffer from the same fatal disease, Tauilopepe. We suffer from the same vanity. And the new church will be a memorial to that, not to Pepe nor to God.'

'Remember, servant of God, if it is a memorial to my vanity it is a memorial to your dwindling faith in the God you serve.'

Simi stood up. 'It is late. I must go.' And without waiting for Tauilopepe to say any more he walked towards the door.

'Does this mean you will support the church project now?' Tauilopepe called. Simi stopped but didn't turn round. 'Do I have your support now?'

'Yes.'

'And you will conduct the service commemorating the start of the work?'

'Yes, yes, yes,' said Simi as he hurried into the darkness.

Tauilopepe went into his study, poured himself a double whisky, and drank it quickly. He was sure of two things: he no longer feared the pastor, and the church would be built. It had to be built. His motives? His reasons for building it? They were irrelevant.

9   The Cost

The church was built. It cost two years of their lives, twenty thousand pounds, two men killed, five maimed, and Tauilopepe's first heart attack.

It cost two years because a church of such extravagant size and vanity demanded that time: two long, arduous years of compulsory communal labour. For the first three months or so all the Sapepe men worked on the project. They dug the deep foundations, carried the rocks and boulders on their shoulders and backs, sang, joked, laughed, and sometimes argued as they worked. When the foundations had been laid and the massive concrete walls began to rise all the aiga in Sapepe took it in turn to provide the builders with workers, food, and cigarettes for a week.

It cost twenty thousand pounds, five thousand pounds more than they had expected, because the church plan, which Tauilopepe had approved, and the delays and mistakes demanded that extra cost. The congregation, through levies imposed on each aiga by the council, raised fifteen thousand pounds. Tauilopepe donated an extra thousand pounds. To raise the money some aiga pledged their cacao and copra to Tauilopepe months before the harvest; other aiga borrowed from various sources, but chiefly from Taifau and Tauilopepe; and many aiga were sent money by their relatives in New Zealand. The fifteen thousand pounds ran out months before the church was completed. A further levy of fifty pounds an aiga was decided upon. Some aiga, already heavily in debt, were reluctant to pay the new levy. Tauilopepe contributed another five hundred pounds in an attempt to encourage them, and Simi preached forceful sermons on the virtues of giving to the church, which surprised everyone and encouraged them to give generously. Simi also gave the council the money he had saved over the years for his children's education.

305

It cost two men killed and five maimed in various ways. The first man to die did so spectacularly in mid-1963 when the towering walls had been constructed and the hefty roof-beams were being hoisted by a crane borrowed from the Public Works Department. His name was Uaita. He was one of Taifau's sons-in-law, with six children, a large debt at Tauilopepe's Sapepe store, and a passable Christian record. He died, so everyone later agreed, through no fault of his own. He was one of the daring men on the walls, trying to swing the roof-beams into place. Swung out too far, too daringly, grasped at the afternoon, and screamed as he plunged down to the floor. They stopped the work for two days while they mourned and buried Uaita, the shrouded bundle of smashed bone and flesh. The council agreed that the new pulpit would be built as a memorial to him.

The second man to die did so undramatically six months later, after the roof-beams were in place and the roofing iron was being nailed on. His name was Sione; he was nobody's son-in-law, without children, without debts to Tauilopepe, but with a poor Christian record. He died, so everyone later agreed, through his own stupid fault. He was one of the lazy young men at the foot of the walls, picking up timber ends, the carpenters' cigarette ends, and any other useless ends that happened to come down or by. At least that was what he should have been doing, but he wasn't. He was at the foot of the walls in the middle of the night, picking his eager girl-friend's end, as it were, when out of the darkness descended a sheet of roofing iron which neatly cut off his head-end and thus ended his life, permanently. His girl-friend, not wanting anyone to know she had been enjoying Sione's end, fled home and told no one. They found Sione the following morning. He was as cold and as stiff as the bloody sheet of roofing iron lying beside him. In keeping with his lack of status they stopped the work for half a day. There would be no memorials to Sione.

The first maimed victim was Meti, a cross-eyed, ring-wormed sage whose only claim to sagehood was his definition of ringworms. Ringworms, according to Meti, were 'reefs in the sky'. He lost his right foot when he used it to try to stop two of the unstoppable boulders used to fill the foundations from clashing against each other. A foot, no matter how hard-working its owner might be — and Meti was noted for his dogged diligence — did not rate a memorial or a burial service. When the church was opened Meti would find it very difficult to climb one-footed up its forty massive front steps.

Solofanua, a fifteen-year-old with a fifteen-year-old record of obedience and exemplary behaviour at the pastor's school, decided, one hot afternoon when no adult was looking, to walk the length of the northern church wall. No harm, the carpenters argued later, would have come to Solofanua if he had walked the wall at ground level. But Solofanua, disobedient for the first time in his short life because Olofa, Simi's youngest and most vivacious daughter, was watching, decided to scale the literal heights of bravery — a dazzling sixty feet or so above the ground. Half-way along the wall he stopped to see if Olofa was still watching (and admiring) him. She wasn't. He missed the next step and fell to the unforgiving ground, and to a shattered hip, six months in hospital, and a lifetime of obedient cripplehood without Olofa, who never looked at him again.

The number 3 is a lucky number, most Sapepe people believed. Taking this logic to its logical conclusion, they argued that Eletise was lucky: he broke only one arm, one leg, and four ribs, when he should have lost his life. (How lucky can a person be!) Eletise was in his early twenties. He had returned to Sapepe a lucky scholastic failure after five expensive lucky years at Samoa College, where he had learnt bad English and passable papalagi manners and attitudes; where he had acquired a junior certificate in arithmetic, social studies, science, and book-keeping and an unquenchable yearning to be a clerk in the government which had no clerk's position for him. After three months of almost unbearable manual work constructing a monument to some supernatural being that Samoa College (and his atheist science teacher) had trained him to be sceptical of he drowned his scepticism in six bottles of faamafu one evening, decided he was the most fluent English speaker in Sapepe (and Samoa), climbed up the scaffolding on the wall facing the malae, and, inspired by the peaceful scene before him and the crowd that had gathered to listen to his English oratory, shouted in the inspired Shakespearean tradition — he had studied Shakespeare at Samoa College — 'Sapepeans, countryman, loan me your ear!' The crowd roared their approval, but the scaffolding, obviously disapproving, collapsed from under him with a loud disapproving roar.

Faifeau, the fourth man to be maimed, was a slow-witted and never-been-to-school middle-aged lay preacher. He lost all his hair (and eyebrows) for ever. He was burning rubbish in the yet unroofed church, fell asleep because of the heat and a hearty meal, and toppled head-first into the blazing fire and screaming wakefulness. When he came out of hospital he resigned as a lay preacher. What was the use of preaching about a beautiful God when the preacher was a hairlessly ugly thing?

The fifth victim (and only female to be seriously injured) was the aggressive, loud-mouthed, more-than-female Leagafaia, wife of an aggressive, loud-mouthed, more-than-male man who had disappeared with someone else's wife from Sapepe years before. Flirting aggressively with the head carpenter, Leagafaia insisted on helping to paint the walls. While she was giggling lewdly at one of the carpenter's lewd jokes she reached over to fondle the carpenter's carpentry, as it were, and incurred the wrath of the carpenter's wife who considered her man's carpentry her personal possession. A vicious more-than-female brawl erupted. When the carpenter's wife, fragile daughter of a fragile pastor (and the carpenter's fourth wife), was knocked unconscious the carpenter suppressed his yearning to have his carpentry carpentered by Leagafaia and carpentered Leagafalia's face with his expert fists. Tauilopepe forced Leagafaia's aiga to exile her to Savaii until the church was finished and the carpenter had left Sapepe for good.

Before its completion the church also cost its most dedicated creator a minor heart attack, the first in his life.

Leaving the running of his plantation and business to Taifau and his capable sons, Tauilopepe worked six days a week on the church. Only the years when he had started hacking Leaves of the Banyan Tree out of the bush equalled these two years in sweat and frayed nerves, in frustration and worry, in exhausted muscles, will-power, and determination. As he confined his attention to a vision of a glittering church, his church, he shed the flabbiness that had accumulated over the comfortable years. He stopped drinking, forgot Teuila and his aiga, forgot also that he wasn't the youth he had once been, forgot that Faitoaga, who worked each day by his side, was still as tough as the trees being cleared on the mountain slopes. Watched Faitoaga, one morning three months before the church was ready for its final coat of paint, hugging a massive boulder and, inch by agonising inch, lifting it off the ground; watched Faitoaga's face and body a quivering, rippling structure of blood-veins, muscles taut, like the envy Tauilopepe was feeling, lifting the boulder up to thigh height; watched Faitoaga laughing and rolling the boulder away from the church steps while the other workers applauded. On his way to the church the next morning Tauilopepe saw that boulder. Only a few men were about. The boulder seemed to pull him towards it. He had to prove it to himself. Found his arms round the boulder, gripping it hard. Sucked in his breath. Lifted. No effect. Gripped again. Lifted. Up. Up. Heart, head, eyes, vibrant with blood, ready to burst. Now! Up to rest on his thighs. One step forward. One more. Now. Boulder dropping out of his arms! The stabbing pain broke through the numb throbbing in his ears, caught his breath, and twisted and twisted at his side.

He spent nearly four weeks in Apia Hospital, recovered quickly, and against the doctor's orders returned to Sapepe, where Teuila and Simi persuaded him not to do any more physical work at the church.

After the church was painted and the scaffolding was dismantled, Tauilopepe and Simi inspected it one morning. They stopped in the centre of the building and Tauilopepe gazed up at the ceiling — a shimmering expanse of varnished timber that sucked up his breath in a sigh. Then he gazed down the length of the church at the pulpit, which was twice the size of the old church's pulpit, at the three huge stained-glass windows behind the pulpit, at the rays of the morning sun dancing through the figure of a fearsome papalagi Moses holding up the slab of rock on which the Commandments were written, at the snow-white angels blowing trumpets of fire.... And Tauilopepe bowed his head.

'Are you satisfied now?' Simi asked.

'Are *you* satisfied?'

'Whether I am or not doesn't matter now, does it?' Simi looked away.

'*Our* church is complete,' said Tauilopepe. The Moses was a blazing figure of yellow and gold and white, and the angels round him a whirl of almost blinding white. Tauilopepe put his hand on Simi's shoulder as they turned and walked to the front door.

'What's going to happen to the old church?' Simi asked.

'We'll start pulling it down next week. The council has agreed. The old must make way for the new,' Tauilopepe said, patted Simi's shoulder, and laughed. 'Our church will be envied by every other district. While they wasted their time, money, and energy on a worthless Independence we worked to glorify God....' He stopped as he suddenly noticed the beginning of tears in Simi's eyes.

It took them four weeks to demolish the church that Tauilopepe's grandfather had taken five years to build; they left only the concrete floor and the twenty steps, which now led up to a sky of memories, like a tomb which had been plundered by efficient thieves.

10   The Second Coming

It was a hot afternoon. Wisps of cloud floated lazily in the sky; the tide was out and from the beach to the reef outcrops of coral protruded through the water; a few sea-birds, barely distinguishable from the brown rocks and coral, were strutting across the reef, searching for food. Most people were sleeping fitfully in the heat of their fale and houses; only two small boys were out in the heat, playing an almost noiseless game of hopscotch in the ruins of the old church.

The boys looked up from their play to watch the red, dust-coated bus as it stopped opposite the new church. There were few passengers. The boys waved but no one waved back as the bus coughed and moved off, leaving behind it on the roadside a tall man dressed in a blue shirt, a white lavalava, and a hat, and holding the biggest suitcase the boys had ever seen. The heat swimming up from the road made him look unreal, almost like an aitu which had been exorcised from the bus. He just stood there wiping his face with a small hand-towel and staring at the new church. The boys walked cautiously towards him. As they neared him they saw that the stranger was as tall as Tauilopepe, the tallest man in Sapepe, and that he was smiling at the new church. The boys stopped a few yards away from him. The stranger didn't seem to notice them as he took off his hat and wiped the sweat from his forehead and the back of his neck. He was going bald, the boys noticed, amazed that this disaster was happening to so young a man. (The stranger looked as young as their uncle, and he was only twenty-something years old.) The stranger had a thin nose, a thin mouth, and hollow cheeks, like the joker in the playing-cards or a papalagi. But when he smiled at them the boys grew less wary of him.

'Could you direct me to the home of the Aiga Malo?' the stranger asked.

'There is no matai of that name here,' the older boy replied politely.

'I know that,' said the stranger, smiling. 'But his aiga are still here, aren't they?' The boys looked at each other. 'Well?' said the man.

'Well, what?' replied the younger boy who was not known for politeness.

'Well, where do they live?' the man asked. The boys looked at each other again and shrugged their shoulders. 'I was told they lived opposite the church,' the man added.

'Which church? The old one or the new one?'

The man looked at the new church, then at the ruins, and said, 'Must be the old church.'

'Oh, *those* people!' said the younger boy, pointing to the two small fale under the bread-fruit trees behind the creeper-covered site of the house in which the last Malo had lived years before. 'They're very poor and they're not people of our village. Are you sure they're the people you're looking for?'

The man turned without answering and started to walk towards the fale.

'You've forgotten your suitcase!' called the older boy. The man turned round. The boys tried to lift the suitcase but couldn't. 'It's too heavy!' they called. The man came and lifted it up as if it didn't weigh anything at all.

'He's tough,' the older boy remarked, as they watched the man walk across the malae.

'Bet you he's not as tough as Faitoaga,' said the younger boy. 'No one's as tough as Faitoaga.'

'Tauilopepe used to be stronger than Faitoaga,' the older boy said as they walked back to the ruins.

'Who told you that?'

'My father. And I bet you Tauilopepe's still tougher than that stranger.'

'Bet you he's not. Tauilopepe's an old man and old men aren't tough!'

Over the years after their banishment most of the young men and women of the Aiga Malo had disappeared from Sapepe to other villages or to Apia where their disgrace was not known. The small group who remained lived as strangers in the district their forefathers had helped to establish. At first they were ridiculed by the other aiga; then, as time passed, they were ignored, forgotten, as though the Aiga Malo had never been part of Sapepe. They even had to attend the Mormon church in the next village, and were the only aiga which had not benefited from the new prosperity. Into this poor but staunchly united aiga walked the stranger; no one knew where he came from, but everyone in Sapepe knew by the following morning that a tall funny-looking man with a big suitcase was visiting those poverty-stricken Mormon people under the bread-fruit trees.

His first week there the stranger rarely left the fale, but everyone, excluding Tauilopepe who was in Apia, was surprised when they heard the Mormon people having evening lotu no different from theirs. On Sunday morning many of the elders watched to see if the Mormons would go to the next village to their Mormon church. They didn't. The stranger emerged from the fale in a shiny white suit and lavalava and black sandals, with an LMS Bible in one hand and an LMS hymn-book in the other, crossed the malae and, as casually as the breeze breezing in from the dancing sea, nodded to everyone as he climbed the forty steps of their church, floated in through the massive doors of their church and up their church aisle, head held high, and settled into the second row of their church pews reserved especially for their matai — and just behind Tauilopepe's empty pew in the front row. But no one said anything to him, not even Taifau who came and sat beside him. The man sang their hymns without looking at the hymnal and uttered their prayers exactly like they uttered them but they refused to believe he was LMS like them. They knew that he knew they were scrutinising him disapprovingly, but he didn't seem to care. He was acting as if he wasn't a stranger, as if he had been attending their church all his life; and they didn't want him to do that, because how do you get to know a stranger if he doesn't act like a stranger and let you come up to him and say 'Welcome to our church'? He'd probably sit in

Tauilopepe's pew next time; then he'd be made to know his rightful place as a stranger who was stranger still because he was a Mormon. Or was he a Mormon? He had to be a Mormon; all those people under the bread-fruit trees were Mormons and he was one of them. Or was he? They noticed after the service that Simi laughed and talked with him on the church steps. Perhaps Simi knew him well—after all Simi was a stranger and the stranger was a stranger, and you never know what one stranger knows about another stranger.

He didn't attend Simi's toonai, as they had expected and wanted, but he came to the afternoon service and sat beside Taifau (who, they noticed, didn't once talk to him), laughed and talked with Simi again after the service, and then, nodding and smiling at everyone, retreated back over the road and into his little fale. Some of the matai asked Taifau if he knew who the man was. Taifau didn't. Why didn't they ask the Aiga Malo, he suggested. Everyone wanted to but nobody did.

Tauilopepe returned from Apia on the Monday, and while he was having his evening meal with Taifau a group of matai visited him on the pretext of wanting to play cards. Just before they went home late that night one of them casually asked Tauilopepe if he knew there was a stranger living with the Aiga Malo. Tauilopepe looked questioningly at Taifau, who usually knew everything that was occurring in Sapepe but Taifau looked questioningly at the others and they looked questioningly at Tauilopepe. Simi seemed to know who the man was, one matai told Tauilopepe. Simi knew a lot about him, echoed another. Tauilopepe asked them why they were so concerned about the man. Many people visited Sapepe; they usually left after a few days; and if they decided to stay longer there was nothing criminal about that. 'But, with the Aiga Malo?' said one of the oldest matai who had witnessed the feud between Tauilopepe and Malo years before. 'I'm sure the man will leave soon,' Tauilopepe said. Concern about the stranger was contagious. Even Tauilopepe was worried now, more so than the other matai.

On the following Tuesday, as the sun was licking the

dew off the malae, a truck loaded with timber, bags of cement, axes, bushknives, and four men turned off the main road and parked under the bread-fruit trees beside the small fale. A gaggle of children surrounded it as it was being unloaded, and most of the adult population watched from the safety of their homes. The truck and the four men didn't leave that evening as everyone had expected. The next day, after the morning meal, the four men and all the other men of the Aiga Malo started to build a large fale on the site of Malo's old house. Periodically the Sapepeans glimpsed the stranger supervising the work. They refused to believe that he had come to stay but they also refused to ask the Aiga Malo about him.

That Sunday they saw not only the stranger approaching their church but, to their horrified amazement, the whole Aiga Malo as well. Up their church steps, the stranger smiling as usual, his companions nervously afraid, they entered the church through the main doors. A bewildered, hostile silence descended as they entered. Everyone stared at them. The stranger pointed at the three empty rows of pews near the back, and his companions sat down. He then turned, walked up the aisle, and, finding all the pews except the one next to Tauilopepe occupied, said 'Excuse me', bowed as he passed in front of Tauilopepe, and took the vacant pew which was reserved for Teuila. Everybody was amazed, offended, surprised when Tauilopepe didn't tell him to leave.

Simi started his sermon by welcoming the Aiga Malo. The silence became more silent, as it were. Most of the congregation looked at Tauilopepe. When Simi talked about forgiveness they realised he was addressing himself directly to Tauilopepe and they asked themselves why. Only the oldest Sapepeans knew why: Tauilopepe had been responsible for Malo's banishment, and Simi was trying to persuade him to readmit the Aiga Malo into Sapepe. Simi related the whole history of Sapepe and pleaded that all Sapepeans were descendants of one Aiga, one fountain-head. His voice sounded unreal in the silence. Not many of the congregation were listening to him: in their minds the stranger was of greater importance now.

315

How was Tauilopepe going to react to Simi's plea? It was obvious to them that the Solomon Islander whom Tauilopepe had foisted on them as their pastor wasn't going to give in as easily on this issue as he had done on the question of the new church. But then again Tauilopepe might support Simi; they knew he was deeply attached to the pastor. Simi ended his sermon by frankly asking that the Aiga Malo should be readmitted.

Just before the last hymn ended the stranger stood up and, with thudding breath, they realised that he was going to address them. They glanced at Tauilopepe, expecting some negative reaction from him, but he looked as if he was half asleep.

The stranger asked Simi if he might speak. Simi nodded. The elders murmured in protest but Tauilopepe, the only person who could reverse the pastor's decision, did nothing.

The stranger walked up the aisle, stopped beneath the pulpit, and faced the congregation. They waited for him to make a fool of himself. But when he spoke they had to admit to themselves that his Samoan was almost perfect, as good as Simi's, the type of language acquired at the theological college. And he wasn't afraid of them either. There was a feeling about him at once threatening and compellingly attractive, like a guilty memory you want to forget but whose accusing details you pick at until they all confront you. The stranger's knowledge of Sapepe's history was vividly accurate, his style of oratory extremely mature for one so young. They tried not to listen to him but his voice eased past their resistance.

'My mother,' he said, 'was a daughter of Malo Tavita and sister of Malo Viliamu who disgraced our aiga and was rightfully banished from Sapepe. You, the Dignity of Sapepe, banished him because of his misdeeds, his lies, his arrogance, his double-dealing. If I had been born then I would have helped you banish him.' He bowed his head. Most of the congregation were sure he was telling the truth. You could feel it in his words. He was speaking from the heart and the heart never lies, they thought. When he looked up at them they thought they could see

316

tears in his eyes. 'My aiga was a partner in Malo Viliamu's crimes but what aiga will not support their matai? For isn't utter loyalty to our matai the basis of our way of life?' He paused. Some of the matai nodded. 'My family has been without a leader for over twenty-five years. Most of us fled Sapepe to forget our disgrace. We have suffered a long period of ridicule and poverty. We have even been forced to adhere to a faith we do not believe in.' His voice broke. 'Sapepe, what more do you demand of us? More suffering? Another twenty-five years of life without God and the community our forefathers died for? I beg for your forgiveness. I promise if you admit my aiga into Sapepe we shall serve it with utter loyalty.

'My aiga has not contributed to the construction of the new church,' he ended his speech, 'so I now give five hundred pounds to it.' And, with his head bowed to hide what they thought were tears, he hurried out through the side door near the pulpit.

The next day, while they were driving into Leaves of the Banyan Tree, Taifau asked Tauilopepe what he was going to do about the stranger's request. Tauilopepe said he hadn't even thought about it. But didn't the man remind Taifau of someone they had known, he asked. Taifau shook his head. A moment later Tauilopepe gasped audibly and whispered, 'Pepe! At least the Pepe we thought we knew, not the Pepe Simi admired so much.' Taifau told him that he was imagining things. 'The stranger is about the age Pepe was when he died,' Tauilopepe said.

While they were having lunch with Faitoaga he told them that the stranger and his aiga were starting to replant the old Malo plantation. Tauilopepe said nothing.

The Aiga Malo completed their main fale and built two more behind it while Sapepe watched and waited impatiently for Tauilopepe to decide whether or not to readmit them. Many members of the Aiga Malo who had been living elsewhere began to return to these fale, bringing with them their children who had been born in exile. Within a month the new fale and the old ones were full. The stranger lived alone in the main fale which was furnished

317

with a high double bed, wooden chairs, and his huge suit-case. A week after he moved into the fale all Sapepe knew about his collection of English books—thick books, thin books, all sorts of books—which they saw him reading every night in the blazing light of a hurricane lamp. They concluded from this that he was a highly educated man; he must have attended high school because only high-schoolers and the few scholarship students who had been educated in New Zealand read such books. But where had he been to school? No one knew and no one asked the Aiga Malo. They also assumed that he was good with guns because he was always polishing an expensive-looking shotgun that he kept under his bed. He was devoutly LMS as well for he never missed a church service. But why didn't he ever talk to anybody but Simi and his own aiga? He showed no interest in the Sapepean women either. Perhaps he was married? But where was his wife? They were puzzled that he never left Sapepe, not even to go into Apia. Why? Surely he was from Apia? (He was dress-ed like a towner—trousers and shoes or boots.) Oh, why didn't someone tell them something definite about him?

While they worried about the man he hired workers from the neighbouring district to help his aiga expand the old Malo plantation. After a month or so of Tauilopepe's doing nothing about him nearly all the Sapepeans were convinced that Tauilopepe *must* do something—if not ban-ish the man to wherever he was from then make him divulge who and what he was. This nerve-racking game of waiting was just too much! But then who was going to per-suade Tauilopepe to act? Who was brave enough (or fool-ish enough) to say to Tauilopepe: 'Sir, you either banish him or tell us who and what he is.' (After all you couldn't banish someone you knew nothing about and especially someone whose aiga had been banished already.) One Sunday during toonai the council chose Simi to be that foolishly brave man. Simi protested but they told him they were the council and they had decided unanimously that he, Simi, their Man of Peace, was to *consult* Tauilopepe. Simi saw Tauilopepe that evening. Tauilopepe said he would call a council meeting the next morning. But ...?

said Simi. 'But what?' asked Tauilopepe. Simi left without telling him his errand.

For many years Tauilopepe had maintained the fale in which he was born for council meetings and welcoming malaga. But thatch had given way to corrugated iron, poumuli posts to concrete pillars, the stone paepae to a three-tiered concrete floor; and the fale now lay like a gigantic metal-roofed beehive between the store and the house. All the matai were on time for the meeting. They sat talking about the stranger while they waited for Tauilopepe and Taifau. The three main posts, reserved for the holders of the Tauilopepe, Toasa, and Malo titles, were vacant. Taifau entered and occupied the Malo post. He had refused over the years to hold any matai title, but after Toasa's death Tauilopepe had installed him at Malo's post. None of the matai had objected openly though they felt annoyed and insulted, because the three main Sapepean titles branched from the same fountain-head and all three branches traditionally had a strong say in who received any title which fell vacant. No one occupied the Toasa title — Tauilopepe had stopped Toasa's children from conferring it on their eldest brother. Many people believed that Tauilopepe wanted to assume the Toasa title but he had not done so. When Toasa died his aiga had turned against Tauilopepe at first, but after he had given them money and whatever else they needed for many years he won their support and became in practice the head matai of the Aiga Toasa. Consequently at council meetings he occupied whichever of the two posts he preferred. No one dared to occupy the vacant one.

Everyone fell silent when Tauilopepe entered and sat down. He immediately announced that they knew why he had called the meeting. They nodded. (Over the years council meetings had assumed a papalagi form in many ways: all ceremonial trimmings had been discarded and long and verbosely ornate speeches were frowned upon because, according to Tauilopepe and the younger matai, they were a waste of valuable time, as were ava ceremonies. Tauilopepe acted as chairman. Taifau as secretary kept detailed records of each meeting. And, although the

319

traditional principle of unanimous agreement for all decisions was still adhered to, whenever discussion threatened to take up too much time Tauilopepe put the issue to a vote.)

'You don't know who the stranger is or where he comes from, or do you?' Tauilopepe asked. The others shook their heads. 'Therefore I for one,' Tauilopepe continued, 'don't want to decide either for or against admission until I know more about him.'

Only Taifau nodded his agreement with this statement. The other matai were unwilling to commit themselves yet. 'Before you decide,' Tauilopepe said, 'I want to tell you the truth about why the Aiga Malo was banished. Toasa and the council ordered the Aiga Malo to refrain from attacking my aiga. But two men of Malo's aiga viciously beat up Toasa, the tuua of Sapepe at the time, and nearly killed him. That was why the Aiga Malo was banished. Whether they have repented of their crimes I don't know.

At this point Tauilopepe looked at Taifau who said, 'We can't risk readmitting the Aiga Malo and then regretting it can we?'

The other matai immediately agreed with Taifau because they knew that this was what Tauilopepe wanted, hence they found themselves back where they were before: pregnant with nervous curiosity about the stranger and yet not knowing who would undertake the responsibility of obtaining detailed information about him, information that would either dispel or confirm their fears. They were too afraid to ask Tauilopepe to do it, so it was up to Tauilopepe to pick someone — Taifau, for instance; after all he was *not* a matai and he was the only one there who was *employed* by Tauilopepe. But, if Tauilopepe didn't pick Taifau, who would? During their generous breakfast of buttered cabin bread and cocoa (provided by Tauilopepe as usual) he rescued them from their predicament by asking Taifau to visit the Aiga Malo and talk with the stranger.

'What about Simi?' Taifau asked.

'What about him?'

'He wants the Aiga Malo readmitted without delay.'

320

'We are not answerable to our loving, very forgiving pastor,' said Tauilopepe. 'He's answerable to us, and to God.' The other matai laughed.

'Our black pastor is so gullible. ...' someone else encouraged the laughter. But Tauilopepe and Taifau didn't laugh so the others stopped abruptly.

'Let us hope Simi doesn't cause trouble if we decide not to readmit the Aiga Malo,' said Tauilopepe. 'Foolish and naive though he is, he is a very good man.' He looked at the others. They all nodded in agreement. 'He believes in justice, peace, and love like we all do,' Tauilopepe emphasised. Grave nods again, and Tauilopepe knew that the matai would never again dare to criticise *his* pastor publicly. Simi has more courage than all the other matai put together, he thought as he left the fale. Perhaps the stranger was a man of courage also.

11   A Most Expensive Gift

It was on a night like this, Taifau remembered as he strolled towards the fale of the Aiga Malo, with stars sprinkled across the sky and a gentle wind nudging him like a playful puppy, that Mr Thorn had found him unconscious in a ditch. It seemed so long ago. Before that he had wandered from village to village, living off relatives (and others) who sooner or later had ceased to be amused by his jokes and songs and stories and had reverted to treating him as the bludging coward everyone believed he was. Then he would move on, occasionally finding warmth between a woman's thighs — a woman who through loneliness or curiosity could tolerate his ugliness and reputation. He had lived by his wits, his ridiculous songs, by the skin of his teeth, as he called it; had transformed through the versatility of his imagination the dingy loneliness of his youth into something worth believing in. Some children murmured good night as he passed them in the darkness. Most aiga, he noticed, were getting ready for bed. He walked slowly, unbuttoning his shirt so the wind could cool his body. To survive he had quickly learnt, through trial and error, when to expect people's cruelties, their grudging favours; to protect himself by acting as a coward. His gift, for he came to believe it was a gift, was his ability to change colour like a lizard to suit the people he happened to be living off at any particular moment. He had fooled them all, becoming for all of them their lovable coward, their pet fool, who, with false praise, they could get to spin yarns and dance to his own bawdy songs. Until the night they caught him on top of that matai's wife and nearly killed him. Fighting for his life, he had forgotten he was supposed to be a coward and had knocked the matai's eldest son unconscious with a guitar blow on the head, kicked someone else between the legs, and bitten a finger off another attacker. After this the villages became hostile territory for him. So he had drifted to Apia where, one lonely year later while working as a labourer on the wharf, he had gone to a faamafu den, got drunk, and been beaten up viciously, for fun, by the three companions he had gone with. Mr Thorn found him in the ditch the next morning. (He noticed that he had wandered to the edge of the malae. The church was a black hill outlined against the starlit sky, and through the mango trees beside it he could see the pastor's house, with its blazing hurricane lamps and the girls hanging up mosquito nets.) Mr Thorn took him to the hospital and after a doctor had treated his wounds brought him to his home and installed him as gardener, guitarist, and, later, chauffeur.

Mr Thorn was a widower: his wife had been killed in New Zealand in a motor accident. He was also a very important official, something to do with administration. (Taifau never found out what exactly.) But Mr Thorn, a chubby little man who spoke with a stutter, was the first human being to treat him as an equal. Mr Thorn wasn't even ashamed of having him around when other important papalagi officials visited the house, and he helped the servants serve the drinks and food. Mr Thorn would deliberately introduce him to all the guests and watch their often frightened reaction to his appearance. It was Mr Thorn who taught him to read and write in English; who encouraged him to compose more songs and play the black guitar that he bought for him; who, late into the night, described to him what life was like in other countries, and then spoke always of death, of his wife's death and of how he had killed her because he had been drunk when he drove their car. Taifau listened intently; he did not understand much of what was said. But, he realised, it was as if Mr Thorn had chosen him to be his special confessor, a confessor who could neither condemn him nor forgive him. Mr Thorn never once treated him unkindly, and Mr Thorn wasn't a kind man — he wasn't, to Taifau's knowledge, kind to anyone else. He treated his servants harshly, abused anyone who annoyed him, instantly fired any worker who did anything wrong, and talked constantly of Samoans as lazy, ignorant thieves. He also told Taifau never to trust

323

other papalagi because all of them, especially those in Samoa, were uncouth, uncivilised beachcombers and fucking racists. Why Mr Thorn had chosen him to be generous to Taifau would never fathom. Only that it had something to do with what Mr Thorn called 'Taifau's talent for being human.'

A year before Mr Thorn returned to New Zealand he hired Nofo as a house-girl. The other servants and his papalagi friends thought he had gone mad: Nofo was completely blind. Like Taifau, Nofo was highly paid, for washing and ironing the clothes and for just being there in the house, with her blindness confronting Mr Thorn's guests and unnerving them. Shortly after Nofo started working for Mr Thorn he told Taifau that he should get himself a wife. 'Who?' Taifau asked. 'Nofo of course,' replied Mr. Thorn. Mr Thorn didn't believe in churches or marriage ceremonies, so Nofo and Taifau simply shifted into the main servants' quarters as man and wife. Mr Thorn provided them with everything they needed. A few weeks before Mr Thorn left for New Zealand, Nofo gave birth to a son. They called him Feleti (Mr Thorn's Christian name was Fred), and Mr Thorn, though not a believer, acted as the boy's godfather and had him baptised because, he said, babies liked holy water being sprinkled on their heads. Mr Thorn wept like a child the night before he left for New Zealand; it was the first time they had seen him weep. They wept too. At the airport he gave them some money and got them to promise that they would return to Sapepe to live. Apia would destroy his godson, he told them. They returned to Sapepe and, in order to survive, Taifau had once again become the lovable coward. No one in Sapepe knew about those years with Mr Thorn. Taifau told no one because Mr Thorn's memory had become a sacred part of his inner and secret self; to divulge that memory would be a betrayal of who he really was, a betrayal of his talent for being human.

As he stopped at the edge of the light blossoming from the stranger's fale Taifau asked himself why he had suddenly thought of those years. Was it because he had become afraid? Afraid of what? He looked into the fale.

324

The stranger was sitting in a chair under the hurricane lamp, reading. Afraid of the implications of that man's presence in Sapepe?

'Come in!' called the man. Taifau spat into the darkness and entered the fale. The man indicated the chair opposite him and Taifau sat down. He didn't want to look at the stranger because he sensed, with a hollow beating in his belly, that the stranger was observing his every move. He realised, however, that if he didn't look up at him the man would interpret it as a sign of weakness, and then he might as well not have come, so he looked up and relaxed slightly when he saw that the man was smiling.

The man welcomed him, as was the custom. Feeling there was no need to be formal Taifau said that he was honoured to be there and was sorry he hadn't visited the man sooner. 'Beautiful night,' the man said. Taifau nodded and remarked that the fine weather should last for a few weeks longer.

'Yes, it should,' said the man, 'but I suppose nothing good can last for ever.'

'No, I don't suppose so,' replied Taifau.

After a pause the man said, 'I have always wanted to meet you, sir. For years I have heard so much about Tauilopepe's "right arm", and of course a lot about the musician of your youth. But now that I am actually talking to you, I don't know what to say.' He laughed softly, the light dancing across his face, softening his sharp features. 'You don't need to look surprised, sir. I know a bit about Sapepe. I may appear a stranger but I don't feel like one. I think I even know why you have come.'

'So I may as well tell you!' chuckled Taifau. 'May I?' The man nodded. 'Well, why are you here?'

Shrugging his shoulders, the man said, 'It's where I belong, I think.'

'That's a good enough reason.'

'I know it's impolite to introduce oneself, but as we are friends now I might as well do so. I am Galupo.' Taifau asked who his father was. The man told him, and then added casually that his father was dead. His mother had always wanted him to return to Sapepe, and had taught

325

him the little he knew about it—its history, genealogies, legends. He paused and then said, 'You've got to belong somewhere, haven't you, Taifau?' Taifau nodded quickly. 'You ought to know, Taifau. You wandered these islands for years and then chose to return and settle down where you were born. Love for a place must be in the blood.'

Feeling uncomfortable because he now suspected that Galupo knew a lot about him, Taifau asked how the work on his aiga's plantation was progressing. 'Well enough considering I've never done plantation work before,' Galupo replied. 'I've spent my working life in an office, writing meaningless letters and reports to noboby. Sometimes I've even written letters to myself.'

'Are you going to stay here for good?' Taifau asked, slowly, deliberately.

Galupo hesitated and then said, 'I don't know. The heavy work may defeat me; then I'd have to take another soft office job. I'm not tough like you, Taifau.' He looked directly at Taifau and asked, 'Who was this Toasa I've heard so much about?'

At once Taifau grew warier. 'He was our tuua a long time ago,' he replied.

'He must have been a great man,' Galupo said. 'It's a tragedy so many of our wise old people are dying. I mean, when they're all gone so much of our unrecorded history and traditions will go with them. Nowadays all our children are getting a completely papalagi education and nothing about our own culture. That's one of the main reasons I've come to live here. I want to learn more about our way of life.'

Taifau couldn't understand how a man could be *that* interested in learning about his own culture, but then, from the stacks of books behind Galupo, he must be highly educated and one never knew what these modern, educated young men chose to be interested in. 'You will learn the true faa-Samoa here in Sapepe,' he found himself saying. 'Sapepe has retained it better than all the other districts.' (He actually believed this.) He held out his packet of cigarettes to Galupo who shook his head. Taifau lit himself a cigarette. 'I smoke only two a day,' he said.

326

'I've heard about that,' said Galupo.

'What else do you know about me?'

'Not much else. You want me to tell you?'

'We might as well discuss me, since it looks as if we're going to discuss everything else.'

Galupo nodded and said, 'You are over sixty years old; you were born a year before Tauilopepe. You married Nofo ... now let me think. ... Yes, you married her when you were about twenty-six. Is that correct?' Taifau nodded. 'You married her while you were working for a palagi. I think his name was Thorn. Is that correct?' Taifau nodded again; his hand trembled as he raised his cigarette to his mouth. 'Before that you spent about six years moving from village to village, and — I hope you don't mind me boasting for you — sired about ten, or was it twelve, children?' They both laughed momentarily. 'You worked for Mr Thorn — and I think I'm the only person in Sapepe who knows about Thorn — for nearly, let me see, four years?' Taifau nodded. 'That makes you about thirty when you returned to live in Sapepe.'

'Go on, young man,' said Taifau, now wanting to find out how much Galupo knew of the life he had kept hidden from everyone.

'I'm not being impolite? A man's life is his own business.'

'No, go on. It's very interesting.'

'Well, from the little that I know about your youth, everyone believed you were. ... You don't mind me saying it, sir?'

'Go ahead.'

'Well, they thought you were the most cowardly man in Samoa.' He paused and looked at Taifau; then, emphasising each word, said: 'But that wasn't true, was it, sir?'

'What is true and what people choose to believe is true are sometimes worlds apart!'

'I mean they believed that because you wanted them to believe it. I may be wrong. But I've always admired you because — well, because you weren't a coward.'

Taifau threw his cigarette butt out of the fale. 'What was I then?' he asked.

'A person trying to live the best way he knew how. You know, sir, after all these years of studying palagi books and films I'm convinced you would have become a great stage actor if you'd lived in Europe.'

'Stage actor?'

'Someone who acts out someone else's life on a stage.'

'Stage?'

'Well, like actors who act as heroes or villains in cowboy films.'

'Do you really think I would have been a great cowboy actor?' Taifau asked. Galupo smiled and nodded his head. Taifau suddenly found himself laughing uproariously because it was good to know, after all these years, that someone understood him. 'What do you think I am now, Galupo?' he asked.

'You want me to be honest?'

'You've been very honest so far; I don't see why you should stop now.'

'All right. For one thing, you're no longer acting.'

'Why not?'

'Because you aren't scared of *them* any more.'

'Them?'

'The people who treated you so badly.'

'Oh, them. Why not?'

'Because the actor is now a star. Successful. Rich. Powerful. You don't need to act any more.'

'Perhaps I have forgotten how to,' Taifau said.

'Have you?'

Shaking his head, Taifau said, 'Who knows. I don't for one.'

'I read a book once, Taifau. It was about a great English actor who reached the top of his profession after years of struggling only to find he had lost the gift.'

'Gift?'

'Yes, the gift of being anyone at any given time, of being able to live out, at least on the stage, many lives, to be many other people. But, according to one famous French writer, a man has to pay a heavy price for the gift.'

Taifau hesitated, not daring to ask, but said finally, 'And what is the price?'

328

'The loss of one's true self.'

'But why?' Taifau asked.

'Because only God who gives us this gift can play creator. And that is what an actor plays at: being a creator of other selves, other people, even if it's only on a stage. Sooner or later, if he's gifted, the actor wants to play the ultimate role.'

'And what is that?'

'He wants to play God.'

Taifau guffawed loudly. 'I hope you don't mind me laughing, but I think that's very funny.' He suppressed his laughter when he saw that Galupo wasn't amused.

'Anyway,' said Galupo, 'it was just an idea of a writer who was probably insane.'

'But it's a very interesting idea.'

'Do you want to hear what else he said?' Taifau nodded. '"Once an actor, or any human being for that matter, wants to play God, he becomes a tyrant."' There was a still, accusing pause, while Galupo gazed intently at Taifau.

'Are you referring to anyone in particular?' asked Taifau. 'Me, for instance? Or Tauilopepe?'

'There is no need to get angry, *old man*. It was just an interesting idea from a book by a Tb-ridden French writer who had grown old in the head.'

'I am not an old man who is old in the head!'

'No one said you were, Taifau. I was merely citing the ideas of an *old* Frenchman. You needn't get angry.'

This upstart young man was needling him deliberately, Taifau decided. 'But why were you referring to Tauilopepe and me?'

'I was not referring to anyone in particular. Least of all to your *employer*.'

Taifau lit another cigarette, and dropped the box of matches. Galupo picked it up and handed it back to him.

'What is the real reason for your coming to Sapepe?' Taifau asked eventually.

'To claim what rightfully belongs to my aiga. Honour, pride. And the place we paid for with over twenty-five years of suffering.'

'And if the council refuses?'

329

'You mean, if you and your employer refuse.'

'All right, if Tauilopepe refuses, what then?'

'If he refuses there are other ways, other means of getting what I want.'

'For instance?'

'As the French writer said: "Take the stage and audience away from him." Everyone in Sapepe, including you, old man, owes Tauilopepe large debts and many people have deep-seated grievances against him. What would you do if someone offered to free you of those debts or to satisfy those grievances? Think back, old man. Think. Back to the days when Malo Viliamu was banished by your employer. To be free of their debts to Malo who did the council support?' Taifau got up. 'This, I hope, Taifau, will not destroy our friendship. Out of all the people here I admire you most of all. Like you when you were young I have nothing to lose and everything to gain. And like you I am a capable actor — perhaps a brilliant one.'

Turning towards Galupo, Taifau said, 'Bold words, young man. I don't know why I'm going to tell you this. Maybe it's because you remind me so much of another young man I loved and respected. ...'

'Who?'

'Pepe.'

'Your employer's son?'

'Because you remind me of him let me warn you now: Tauilopepe may be old but *we* have our unique ways of dealing with trouble-makers!'

'Like you succeeded in destroying Pepe? ... You don't need to look so stunned, Taifau. You know as well as I do that Tauilopepe destroyed his own son. And you, old man, did absolutely nothing to stop him.'

Taifau almost ran out of the fale.

Hollow-eyed, his head aching from worry and lack of sleep, Taifau ate a meagre breakfast without speaking to any of his aiga, and then strolled towards Tauilopepe's house. Even the mellow morning light hurt his eyes, and the pain aggravated his feelings of helplessness, his acute

330

awareness that he *was* old. A bus went past, creaking painfully as though it was going to break apart. He watched the
unsmiling passengers, then crossed the road which was
still slippery with dew. The sitting room curtains in
Tauilopepe's house were still drawn but he could see
Tauilopepe in one of the upstairs bedrooms, combing his
hair. Smoke was rising like a long white banner from the
kitchen chimney. As he walked past the rows of garages he
noticed that the trucks had already left for the plantations. The strong smell of exhaust fumes, grease, and
diesel stung his lungs; he coughed and spat out the
phlegm. Instead of going into the house he sat down on
the front steps and stared at the road glistening with sun.
His deepest loyalty was still to Tauilopepe, the only friend
he now had in Sapepe, the man who had rescued him from
his humiliating poverty and steadily stripped off his mask
of the coward, the man to whom he owed everything.
Nearly all his Sapepe generation were dead, most of them
from stomach ailments caused by over-eating and lack of
exercise. When he was younger he had boasted that being
a *matai* was an invitation to obesity, ulcers, strokes, and
heart attacks. His youngest daughter, dressed in a red and
white school uniform, came out of their house and started
hurrying towards her school. She waved to him. He waved
back and was suddenly afraid for her safety. Another bus
went by. He heard Tauilopepe come downstairs and go
into the dining room. Perhaps he should take his aiga away
and make a fresh start. And leave all this — the house,
comfort, Sapepe? Realised, with increasing depression, that
he couldn't do it, not now. He was too old, and for his
aiga's sake he could no longer afford to be poor.

Getting up slowly, he went round to the back of the
house and sat down on the rocks overlooking the pool, the
beach, and the sea. He was afraid of Galupo because he had
spoken the truth about Pepe's death and about the youth
he, Taifau, had been and the man that youth had become.
A lone canoe was bobbing up and down near the reef. Not
many people went fishing now, he thought. It was easier to
buy tinned fish from the stores. Beyond the reef the sea

was an ink-blue plain holding up an almost cloudless sky. Waves were pancaking on to the beach which curved to the west and disappeared behind stands of mangroves; as the waves rolled in they flattened out on the sand and, surging up between the boulders surrounding the pool, pushed the discarded rubbish into the mouth of the cave out of which bubbled the fresh spring water. Only the children swam in the pool now and often defecated in it, but none of the elders cared. He gazed up at the sun whirling and spinning above the eastern range in a sky flaked with fingers of cloud, and he thought of Pepe and of how Pepe had warned him of the perils of the comfortable life which Tauilopepe had promised and given him. Galupo was so right — he had done nothing, absolutely nothing, to save Pepe, and in betraying Pepe he had betrayed Mr Thorn and betrayed his 'talent for being human'.

Teuila called to him from the kitchen window to come in and have breakfast with Tauilopepe. He brushed the dirt off the back of his lavalava and went into the house.

Tauilopepe had finished eating and was smoking at the table. Taifau greeted him, accepted a cup of tea, and sat down at the table. Tauilopepe talked about the new acreage of coffee and cacao up near the summit of the range. Taifau grunted yes now and then. Flies were crawling over the egg-stained plates. He could hear someone singing in the shower.

'I visited him last night,' he said. Tauilopepe looked at him. 'That young man.'

'And?' asked Tauilopepe.

'I can say one thing for him, he's very honest.'

'One of our young educated trouble-makers, eh? Is he genuinely related to the Aiga Malo?'

Taifau nodded. 'As far as I could find out from him. But whether he's Malo's nephew I'm not sure. He's very educated.'

'Where is he from?'

'I don't know. He said he had worked in an office so I suppose he's spent most of his life in Apia.' Taifau paused as if he didn't really want to tell Tauilopepe, pondered for a moment, then said, 'His name is Galupo. As he said in

332

church his mother was Malo Tavita's sister.'

'Yes Malo Tavita had a sister. She left Sapepe even before I returned from theological college. She never came back. He could be telling the truth. Do you think he is?'

'Not sure yet,' replied Taifau.

Tauilopepe examined Taifau's face closely and asked, 'Are you well?'

'Must be getting the flu,' Taifau lied.

'He told you something else, didn't he, Taifau? I know you too well.'

Taifau nodded his head and, looking away from Tauilopepe, said, 'Yes, he told me what he had come for.'

'And?'

'He wants his aiga readmitted.'

'But he has said as much already.'

'He is not going to take no for an answer.'

'Quite a remarkable young fellow, eh!'

'He is deadly serious about it, Tauilo,' said Taifau. Everything would be so easy if Tauilopepe freely readmitted the Aiga Malo. If he didn't? Taifau stopped himself from thinking beyond this; he had thought about it all night. With Galupo's determination it could mean another feud, blood, perhaps the loss of everything he possessed — his wealth, status, influence, comfort. Conversely it could mean the destruction of Galupo, a young man so like Pepe, a repetition of Pepe's death and of his own guilt, for he would do nothing to save Galupo.

'Why the sad looks, old friend?' Tauilopepe asked. 'Have you in one night grown fond of this fellow Galupo?'

'As you said, he is remarkable — in many ways.'

A dog barked loudly from under the windows. They looked out and saw it chasing a rat towards the pool. Over by the fale two women were sweeping up the fallen leaves, their long coconut-frond brooms scraping rhythmically across the grass.

'Did he tell you what he would do if the council refuses?' Tauilopepe asked.

'No,' Taifau lied.

'Anyway we can't do anything about him yet.'

'Why not?'

333

'We still don't know enough about him. He's waiting for us to make a move, so let us wait him out. I don't think he is all that dangerous.'

Taifau remained silent. The women were now piling the leaves into large baskets. A boy in a dirty lavalava appeared, picked up the baskets, and started walking towards the pool. Taifau remembered that the pool was now used as a rubbish dump, and said, 'The pool is full of rubbish.'

'What did you say?' asked Tauilopepe. Taifau shook his head slowly.

12 Veterans, Novices, Heart Attacks

Tauilopepe had been drinking since lunch-time. He had
gone to the Samoa Club for 'one beer', had run into John
Weber, and the one beer had turned into hours of the best
whisky, with Tauilopepe paying for it, which he didn't
mind because he was known to be one of the wealthiest
members of the club. The businesses and offices were
closed now and the club was filling quickly. John Weber,
nicknamed 'Johnso-Boy' by everyone, had talked almost
non-stop since noon in a colourful mixture of English and
Samoan, but Tauilopepe had stopped listening after his
fourth (or was it his sixth?) whisky.

Johnso-Boy was a failed planter who had become a failed
independent trader and who was at that moment failing as
a commercial fisherman. When he inherited his German
father's cacao and copra plantation, a substantial bank
account, a herd of cattle, a Samoan stepmother and six
half-brothers, a seaside bungalow, and a fatal thirst for
enjoying the fruit of his father's frugality, he had been the
most devoutly generous member of the Samoa Club. Eight
spendthrift years later the plantation and herd were gone
and he sent his stepmother and half-brothers back to their
village. In his mother's village he set up a small store and
tried to confine his thirst to whisky (usually someone
else's), gullible girls, and tinned corned beef. Four years
later he lost the store, was accused by the village of stealing a thousand pounds of their money, and was driven out.
After two whiskys Johnso-Boy would tell you he had been
unjustly treated.

A cool breeze was now blowing in from the harbour.
From the patio where they were sitting Tauilopepe could
see a large group of men round the pool tables. At this
time he usually joined them, but he suddenly didn't want
to lose any more money, and Johnso-Boy was annoying
him so much that he wanted to tell him to shut up and go

away. The billiard-balls clicked in his head but he wasn't drunk; his sight was as clear as the ice in his glass, he thought. He knew most of the members who were coming out to the patio but they avoided his table because (so he thought) he was one of the club's most respected members. Every time a group was seated he ordered bottles of beer and sent the waitress to take them to the group. They would call thanks but not shout him back — because he was rich and poor men didn't shout the big men, Johnso-Boy would say. To all the members Tauilopepe was a generous man; to the confidence men he was an easy touch, always good for free drinks as long as you flattered him; to other rich members he was an uncouth show-off who gave away free drinks to prove he was as rich as they were, and they were waiting for him to go bankrupt or get violently drunk (like all Samoans) and break up the club furniture. In fact he always out-drank them, and he had continued to make more and more money. To aggravate the insult the bastard couldn't even speak proper English.

'Get some cigarettes,' Tauilopepe said in Samoan, handing Johnso-Boy a pound note. Johnso-Boy, who didn't like Samoans ordering him about, looked at the note. Tauilopepe smiled. Johnso-Boy waddled off to the bar. Tauilopepe called the waitress and told her to take Johnso-Boy's glass away.

'Keep the change,' he said to Johnso-Boy when he returned.

'Thanks a lot,' Johnso-Boy replied, looking to see that no one was watching him as he shoved it into his pocket.

'Now go drink somewhere else,' Tauilopepe said in Samoan. The pale light of the setting sun deepened Johnso-Boy's pallor to the colour of dead fish. 'Bugger off!' Tauilopepe repeated in English. And Johnso-Boy was off, to look for someone who disliked Tauilopepe and who, providing him with whisky, would listen attentively to his tale of woe. 'Afakasi shit,' Tauilopepe murmured, and ordered another double.

As Tauilopepe drank, his fears about Galupo bubbled up through the liquor haze to confront him again. During the past months, while he had delayed doing anything about

336

him, Galupo had enlarged his plantation and built a small store in Sapepe, a store to which Tauilopepe was now losing customers who owed him substantial debts, and who, if they were cleverly manipulated by Galupo, would become his political enemies. He had done this to Malo; and Galupo was now doing it to him. 'Clever bastard!' he mumbled to himself in English. He had to give it to Galupo, he thought: he *was* clever; as clever and as ruthless as he, Tauilopepe, had been. If only he had a son like Galupo! If only! 'Whisky!' he called to the bar. The people near by stared at him, but he didn't care. Afakasi and palagi arse-licking bastards! he felt like telling them. Now Galupo wasn't an arse-licker, not a smiling, cringing, fast-talking leech who wanted something for nothing. Galupo was a courageous enemy, and he admired that. He caught sight of Ashton at the bar. Ashton, *his* lawyer, *his* friend. 'Ashton!' he called. The other members tried not to look at him, so did Ashton. 'Ashton!' he called again. Ashton's face rounded into a fat smile of recognition and he waved to Tauilopepe who beckoned him over.

'How are you?' Ashton laughed, patting Tauilopepe on the back.

'Take seat,' Tauilopepe said in English.

'Any time, friend,' Ashton said.

'Have drink,' Tauilopepe ordered. Laughing still, Ashton protested that he had friends at the bar he had to drink with, but Tauilopepe got the waitress to bring him a drink.

'Okay, just one then,' said Ashton. 'How have you been keeping?' Tauilopepe pointed at his head. 'Had one too many, have you?'

'How is money?' Tauilopepe asked.

'Money? Oh, you mean *your* money. Oh, it's fine. Safe and snug in the bank and plenty of it.' Ashton wasn't drinking his whisky so Tauilopepe handed it to him. Ashton laughed again and, raising it to his lips, said, 'Cheers, friend!'

'Drink all,' said Tauilopepe. Ashton drank until his glass was empty. Tauilopepe got him another one.

'No, friend. Gotta go!' said Ashton.

'Drink!' Tauilopepe said. Ashton was *his* lawyer who was

337

costing him a lot of money and who therefore couldn't do
without him, but someone he would do without once
Lalolagi, his grandson, returned as a lawyer from New Zealand. 'Drink!' he repeated.

'Okey-doke, friend,' said Ashton. 'But this one must be
the last!' He drank.

'Need advice,' Tauilopepe said.

'Okay, fire ahead. That's what you pay me for.'

'I pay you enough?'

'Sure. More than enough!'

Tauilopepe nodded and said, 'If you got enemy who is
trying to take what you got what you do?'

'Depends, depends.'

'On what it depends?'

'On what you think you've gotta do. Follow me, eh?'

'He is causing much trouble in mine village.'

'Oh, one of those educated Samoans who break the
peace and good government of a village?' asked Ashton.
Tauilopepe nodded, eyes half-closed. 'Well, get tough with
him. Get tough. Show him that if he doesn't behave he
gets axed!'

'Axe?'

'You know — knocked on the head hard a few times.
Nothing like force to meet force, teach any trouble-maker
to mend his ways!'

'Okay,' replied Tauilopepe, convinced his problems were
over. He had been too lenient with Galupo. Ashton got up
to leave. 'A bottle!' Tauilopepe called to the bar. The waitress brought a bottle of whisky. She opened it and
Tauilopepe told her to fill Ashton's glass.

'I really must go!' Ashton protested in a whisper.

'Sit down, friend,' Tauilopepe ordered. Ashton sat down
again. 'Cheers!'

'Cheers!' replied Ashton, trying to smile because
everyone was watching. 'Don't you think you've had
enough, Tooilopeepee?' (Ashton could never pronounce
Samoan names correctly, not that he had ever wanted to.)

'No, friend. Got money enough for to buy this whole
place!'

338

'That is correct,' said Ashton, looking warily at the bar. He caught sight of Paul Heely, General Manager of the Government Plantations and one of Tauilopepe's favourite drinking companions. 'There's Paul,' he said. 'I'll call him over. Okay?' Tauilopepe nodded.

Ashton and Heely were New Zealanders who had lived in Samoa for over twenty years; they were both separated from their New Zealand wives who had returned home years before, thereby allowing their husbands to live openly with their Samoan mistresses. Heely had come to Samoa as a clerk in the New Zealand Administration, had befriended the then Manager of the Government Plantations, and had been hired as Assistant Manager. When the manager died suddenly of a stroke, brought on by too many whiskys and over-fit mistresses, Heely, through his many political friends in the Administration, had been appointed General Manager. Like Tauilopepe, Ashton and Heely belonged to the Samoa Club elite.

'Had a few too many, eh, mate!' Heely said, slapping Tauilopepe on the back. Heely wasn't as tall or as fat as Ashton (but then no other club member was). He was a well-groomed ball, a 'mini-hippopotamus with the eyes of a barracuda', as Johnso-Boy described him behind his back.

'Our mate here has a problem, Paul,' Ashton said.

'Is that so?' replied Heely, drinking a glass of Tauilopepe's whisky. (Heely never bought a round for anyone; well, not anyone who didn't possess anything that Heely wanted — as, for instance, political pull, money, a nubile daughter, original ideas about running plantations, breeding cattle and so on.)

'Yes, but it's an easy one,' said Ashton.

'Okay, mate, tell me!' laughed Heely, 'I mean I've been in this country long enough to know a little about it!'

'Shall I tell Paul?' Ashton asked Tauilopepe. He nodded. 'Well, there's an educated native who's causing our friend here some trouble. You know, the usual native with education gone to his head trying to take over our friend's village.'

'Yeah, he want for to take what is mine,' mumbled Tauilopepe.

339

'You know what I used to do with my plantation workers when they tried to ruin my plantations by not working hard enough? I used to tie them up to a tree and whip the shit out of them. That's what you should do to this character who's so up-himself. Correct, Ash?' Heely said. Ashton nodded his head repeatedly.

'I get tough with him,' said Tauilopepe, no longer able to clear his head of the ringing dizziness, his vision blurring.

'You've just got to keep these educated Samoans in their place,' said Heely. 'Cheers!' They drank until their glasses were empty. Unexpectedly Tauilopepe hurled his glass over the patio fence and laughed loudly when it shattered.

'Another glass!' Ashton ordered the waitress.

'You okay, mate?' Heely asked, reaching across the table and patting Tauilopepe's shoulder. Tauilopepe had always out-drunk Heely, and now he, Heely, had the opportunity to show Tauilopepe (who was a Samoan) and the whole club (who were mainly afakasi) that he could out-drink anyone. 'Cheers!' he encouraged Tauilopepe, who grabbed his glass and raised it unsteadily to his mouth. 'Bottoms up now.' And Tauilopepe drained the whisky in one gulp. Heely half-emptied his; Ashton took a sip.

'Going for to get tough with Galupo,' mumbled Tauilopepe, trying to keep his heavy eyelids from closing.

'That's the way!' said Ashton.

'Cheers, mate!' said Heely, refilling Tauilopepe's glass. Tauilopepe drained his glass while they watched him.

'Has the bastard been drinking long?' Heely whispered to Ashton.

'Looks like it,' replied Ashton.

'He's only faking it. Here, have another one, mate,' and he filled Tauilopepe's glass again, whispering to Ashton as he did so, 'Pretty groggy, isn't he? Look at his bloody eyes.'

'I'd better ring the bastard a taxi,' suggested Ashton.

'No, he's okay,' said Heely, refilling Tauilopepe's glass. 'It's his bloody whisky anyway.' The glass dropped and shattered on the floor when Tauilopepe tried to raise it to his mouth. Everyone looked at them, and the waitress rushed over and began to pick up the bits of glass in a cloth.

'Give me that rag,' Heely said. And making sure that every important club member was watching, he dabbed Tauilopepe's face with the wet cloth.

'You shouldn't do that,' Ashton whispered.

'Who says so, mate. He needs a cool face-wipe.'

Tauilopepe put his head on his arms on the table and went to sleep.

'What are we going to do now?' Ashton asked.

'Leave him to get home on his bloody own.'

'But we can't do that!'

'Who says so, mate!' Heely waved to his friends at the bar, glanced mockingly at Tauilopepe, and went off to drink with his friends. Ashton got up hurriedly and followed him.

After having failed to shake Tauilopepe awake the waitress went to ring his wife. 'Serves him right for trying to act like a palagi!' she muttered to herself.

A week later Tauilopepe heard that the Aiga Malo were going to bestow the Malo title on Galupo. He at once called a council meeting and instructed all the matai that no one, absolutely no one, was to attend Galupo's saofai. (Acting on Ashton's and Heely's advice, he was getting tough.) He even sent Taifau to tell the Aiga Malo that the saofai was not to take place. 'Tell your employer,' Galupo said, 'to take his objection to the Lands and Titles Court.' And, with the united support of his aiga, he went ahead with the saofai, knowing full well that if it came to a court case the Court would rule in favour of Tauilopepe because he had the support of the Aiga Toasa and all the other aiga connected with the Malo title.

That Christmas was a tense time for the people of Sapepe because Tauilopepe's conflict with Galupo was now out in the open. If it was permitted to grow it would destroy the peace and prosperity which Sapepe had enjoyed for over a quarter of a century. Most of the matai remained loyal to Tauilopepe but the few who owed

341

heavy debts (and held grievances) continued to cultivate Galupo's friendship secretly. The new year, 1965, began with a week of almost constant rain which turned the tracks and paths into precarious mud and confined the people to their homes. There they discussed in hushed tones the trouble between Tauilopepe and Galupo. One Monday night an announcement came over the national radio station of a court case between the Aiga Tauilopepe, supported by the Aiga Toasa, and the Aiga Malo. It was to be heard at the Lands and Titles Court, Mulinuu, on 12 February.

Tauilopepe had not returned to Sapepe since Christmas, so Simi went into Apia to plead with him to drop the case. 'For the sake of Sapepe, Tauilopepe, leave it as it is. After all, the Aiga Malo is still not part of Sapepe,' Simi pleaded.

'Don't you want the Aiga Malo readmitted any longer?' Tauilopepe asked.

'Yes, I do,' Simi insisted, 'and Galupo has promised to relinquish the Malo title if they are.'

'There's no guarantee that he'll do that,' replied Tauilopepe.

'Isn't it enough that he's given me his word?' Simi said emphatically.

Over the years Tauilopepe had learnt one effective way of controlling *his* pastor: tell him what appeared to be the truth, reveal to him what sounded like your innermost secrets, and you immediately won his sympathy. So he now told Simi that he admired and trusted him and looked upon him as his own son, but that he was naive to put his faith in Galupo who was a cunning, unscrupulously ambitious youth who would stop at nothing to gain power.

After Simi left, Tauilopepe sat drinking and thinking about some remarks Ashton and Heely had made to him several times: there were no sinners, they had said, only misunderstood people and criminals; laws were made to be used by the powerful; everyone wanted something for nothing, that was the basis of all human transactions; men like them had the right to manipulate the weak in the interests of building a wealthy, God-fearing nation — if it wasn't for them Samoa would be back with the cannibals.

342

Then he remembered the only time he had got blind drunk at the club and he hoped that Ashton and Heely and his other palagi friends had forgiven him for it. He had behaved like any other stupid, ignorant Samoan.

A week before the court case Galupo collapsed with what everyone heard was a 'severe illness'. A doctor visited Sapepe and gave him a medical certificate which stated that he could not appear before the Court. Consequently the case was postponed until such time as the leader of the defendant party, one Galupo Malo, was medically fit to appear. Galupo's recovery took two months. By that time his plantation had expanded further; some of Tauilopepe's matai debtors were openly increasing their debts at Galupo's store and addressing Galupo as Malo; the Aiga Tauilopepe and the Aiga Toasa were threatening to drive the Aiga Malo out of Sapepe once and for ever; and Tauilopepe had suffered sixty-two nights with little sleep, which led to frequent outbursts of almost uncontrollable anger, quenched usually by lengthy drinking bouts.

As soon as Tauilopepe heard that Galupo was sitting up in bed and eating great quantities of corned beef he sent Taifau to Mulinuu to petition the Court to set a new unpostponable date for the case. The Court was fully booked for at least three months, but the Registrar, who was one of Tauilopepe's Samoa Club friends, postponed two other cases and set the Tauilopepe-Malo case down for 20 April. When Galupo was issued with a court order he was overcome by another fit (which everyone in Sapepe, except the Aiga Tauilopepe and the Aiga Toasa, started referring to as 'his epilepsy'). Tauilopepe personally met the Registrar at the club over two bottles of whisky, which he paid for, and got the Registrar, the only other Samoan included in the club's elite, to send a doctor appointed by the Court to examine Galupo. This doctor declared that Galupo was medically unfit to appear before the Court for at least four months.

Galupo's fale was stoned that night. But the Aiga Malo didn't retaliate in kind because Galupo, acting the winning role of peace-lover, ordered them not to. However, through the women of his aiga, he spread the rumour that Tauilopepe was deliberately trying to provoke his aiga into a violent feud but that he, Galupo, refused to be provoked. When Tauilopepe heard this he summoned the council and ordered them not to believe Galupo's lies. Most of the council agreed to follow this order; those who didn't keep quiet, but after the meeting they continued to foster their friendship with Galupo and to increase their debts at his store. Taifau paid each of them a visit and in polite aristocratic language demanded that they should cease their disloyal activities! They appeared to obey, but secretly promised Galupo their support when the feud erupted. Simi preached respect for God, law, and order, but his sermons went unheeded.

In a letter dated 27 September 1965 Teuila told Lalolagi that Papa was in hospital suffering from pneumonia but there was nothing to worry about because the doctors were sure he would recover quickly. Papa wanted to see him, but it would be better for him not to come home for the Christmas holidays as they had planned. Papa had told her to congratulate him on having done so well in his examinations. She would send him plenty of money for Christmas, she said. What she didn't say was that Tauilopepe had suffered another attack while drinking heavily two weeks earlier. And, as in all her letters since Galupo had appeared in Sapepe, she did not mention him or say what was really happening there.

Tauilopepe had collapsed in his Apia home and had been rushed to hospital. Taifau came from Sapepe, saw his condition, and guessed at once what Galupo would do if he heard. So he returned immediately to Sapepe and told the council that Tauilopepe was only suffering from a minor ailment and would be all right in time for the case in November. But Galupo at once left his bed for the first time in a month and sent a man into the hospital to check. When he was told that Tauilopepe was in a critical condition after a heart attack and would take months to recover fully he relayed this information to the matai who opposed Tauilopepe, who in turn told the rest of Sapepe. The case was postponed until some time in 1966. Faitoaga came in from Leaves of the Banyan Tree to live in the village and, with Taifau, to make sure that the council and the Aiga Malo did not rebel against Tauilopepe while he was in hospital. The Aiga Malo kept the peace but used Tauilopepe's absence to further consolidate their position in church affairs, to expand . their plantation and the number of customers at their store, and — through subtle innuendoes and rumours, and promises of a more prosperous future without Tauilopepe — gradually to undermine his influence and decrease the Sapepeans' fear of him. Now that they weren't sure whether Tauilopepe would ever successfully challenge Galupo's right to hold the Malo title, more of them began referring to him publicly as Malo — but none of them ever called him Malo within the hearing of the Aiga Toasa or the Aiga Tauilopepe.

Tauilopepe, to everyone's amazement, recovered faster than Galupo had hoped. After just over two months in hospital, where he had been given the best possible private room and medical care — the latter from a heart specialist flown in from New Zealand at Taifau's insistence and expense — Tauilopepe was back in Sapepe, hiding his paralysed left arm in long-sleeved shirts and the pain in his eyes behind thick sun-glasses. He was more dictatorial in manner, abruptly impatient, and easily roused to a fearful anger. The sun-glasses, his hair now heavily streaked with grey, his gaunt frame, his brooding silence in public, his deliberately slow walk, all combined to make his presence more ominously real and feared. As soon as he came home, 31 January 1966 was set as the new date for the case. No more postponements; the Registrar personally told Galupo: if he could not appear in court he must send someone in his place. Simi tried to intervene again. Tauilopepe refused to see him. When Simi tried to persuade Taifau to persuade Tauilopepe, Taifau explained that Galupo had lied about being ill. Prove it, Simi challenged him. So Taifau told Simi that Galupo had bribed the doctors who had examined him into signing those medical certificates.

13   Into the Storm

The rain woke him. He lifted his paralysed left arm with his right hand and went to the windows. The rain was swirling across the road, cutting off his view of the range and butting the windows as if it wanted to touch him. His body ached, the result of three weeks of late nights preparing his court petition opposing Galupo's claim to the Malo title; he had worked on it with the oldest matai in his aiga. Now ten typed copies were snug in the safe in his study. The case was only a day away. He gazed at the rain, convinced he would win but when he remembered how ruthless Galupo was, apprehension jabbed at his confidence. The house creaked, the windows were now wincing surfaces of water, a door slammed downstairs. He turned and looked at Teuila, at the round face relaxed with sleep, the sensuous lips parted slightly, the long black hair covering her pillow like a soft web, the supple fingers clutching the sheet to her breasts. One more attack — the pain flashing up from his chest to explode in his eyes — and he would be finished. He glanced at his useless arm as he turned to the windows again.

Teuila coughed and he heard her sit up.

'Had that dream again,' he said. The wind was rising, sweeping in from the north-west and hurling the rain against the house. She brought a light blanket and draped it over his shoulders.

Shrugging it off, he said, 'I'm ... I'm not ... an in-invalid!'

His stutter was nearly gone: he spent an hour each evening locked in his study, talking and reading aloud to himself; but the stutter returned whenever he was agitated.

'The same dream?' she asked.

'Dreamt of the same place,' he began slowly. 'Of bare lava traversed by deep chasms. And the silence, the awful silence ringing in my head. And a cool wind caressing my eyes, picking at my flesh, stripping it till I was a skeleton.

A skeleton, Teuila. Alive but not minding being a skeleton.' He paused. 'Last night it was slightly different. I saw my father and Toasa emerge out of the lava and approach me. Young again they were, and smiling as they approached. Then that wind came again and my bones rose up through my flesh. Toasa and my father were reaching out to save me but the lava opened up and swallowed them.' He bowed his head. 'I awoke again to what I have become—a cripple, a useless cripple!' She reached out to embrace him. 'No! Please.' She obeyed and went downstairs.

Then he was suddenly gazing at his reflection in the window, at the hollow-eyed, grey-haired figure pulsating in glass, an aitu brought to him by the storm. He stepped back and this caricature of the man he had once been disappeared. God had withdrawn His blessings, he thought bitterly. Galupo was a further curse God had sent to punish him. After the court case, what else?

When he had finished his breakfast he glanced at his watch. It was 10 a.m. The twenty-ninth. He shuffled to the windows overlooking the harbour. The palms near the beach flapped wildly as the wind attacked them; huge waves hurled themselves on to the sand. He couldn't see the horizon through the rain and low ponderous clouds. As long as the wind didn't change direction they were safe. Hurricanes usually blew in from the south-west. He went into his study, reread his petition, and asked himself questions he thought the judge and panel of assessors would ask. An hour or so later he sensed that fear had edged into the house, into the very walls around him, and he knew the wind was swinging towards the south-west. He rushed out. Teuila and some of the women were staring out at the raging sea and whirling heavens. He pretended nothing was wrong.

'What's the matter?' he asked Teuila. She shook her head. He told the other women to go back to their work.

Teuila sat down beside him on the settee. 'When was the last hurricane?'

'If you must know'—he tried to calm her fears—'the last one was in 1899. Three American and three German warships were wrecked in Apia Harbour.' He paused and then said, 'Why don't you do some sewing?'

On the table beside her was a radio. She switched it on. A country and western number immediately filled the room. 'Lagi is doing well at school, isn't he?' she asked. 'Pity he didn't come for Christmas.'

'You know I don't want him here while Galupo is causing all this trouble!'

'...*We interrupt this programme to bring you a special weather report.*' They looked at the radio. '*A hurricane, which formed north-east of Samoa and which was heading towards the Fiji Group yesterday, is now approaching Samoa.*' Teuila gasped. '*Fresh gale-force winds are being recorded at Mulinuu Observatory. They are expected to increase to strong gale-force winds by late this evening, perhaps reaching 82 knots or 94 miles per hour....*'

His plantation, his stores, his houses, his church. Everything he had worked for. Everything! 'Get Taifau!' he ordered Teuila.

'Where are you going?' she asked when she returned from sending a boy to fetch Taifau.

'To make sure the plantation is safe.'

'But you're not well!' she insisted.

Shaking her by the shoulders gently, he asked her to get his boots. When she didn't move he pushed her towards the stairs. 'Quickly!' he called, trying not to shout.

As they drove into the plantations everything around them was a shaking, steaming, flapping cacophony of shrieking wind and rain. 'Faster!' Tauilopepe ordered Taifau. 'Put your foot down!' As yet no trees had fallen across the road.

'This is foolish!' yelled Taifau. 'We can't save the plantation!'

'We've got to save what we can!'

Before the jeep had stopped completely Tauilopepe jumped out and started to hobble towards the cocoa dryer. As he followed Tauilopepe, Taifau cursed the storm and the cold clinging tenaciously to his bones, making him feel old and useless. He glimpsed the Banyan. It was shaking

348

furiously, limbs creaking and groaning, leaves scattering skywards. He veered away from the dryer, where Tauilopepe and the workers were scrambling about with nails and hammers, and hurried up through the clattering cacao trees to Faitoaga's fale. Mud flowed away from under his feet and he slipped repeatedly.

While the storm screamed he helped Faitoaga board up the fale with banana boxing and sheets of corrugated iron. As they were finishing, Tauilopepe appeared out of the storm, his hair and clothes plastered to his body, a frantic look in his eyes. 'Get some men and take them to Apia to board up the house,' he ordered Faitoaga. Faitoaga hesitated but Taifau assured him that he would look after his aiga, and he ran off down the track. 'The Banyan will fall,' Tauilopepe said.

'It'll weather the storm. It's strong enough!'

'We've got to save it!'

'How?' asked Taifau. Tauilopepe blinked, realising his stupidity, and limped to the side of the fale overlooking the valley. Taifau gathered Faitoaga's frightened wife and children and sent them down to the waiting trucks.

'Why me? Why is He doing this to me?' Tauilopepe muttered, flapping his useless arm.

'Who?' asked Taifau. Tauilopepe stamped out of the fale without replying. Taifau gazed down. The wind, pushing the rain before it, was funnelling up the valley floor, hitting the foothills and screaming skywards, and he knew that the new plots of coffee and cacao on the foothills and the bananas on the valley floor would be destroyed.

When Tauilopepe refused to get into the jeep Taifau grabbed his arm and pulled him in. On their way back Taifau could hardly see the trucks in front of him. The jeep skidded often. Fallen trees blocked the road; they chopped through them with axes. The dark sky dropped closer to the land, and the earth trembled as the wind stripped away its cover of trees and the rain turned its flesh to pulpy mud.

After boarding up Tauilopepe's house and stores the workers sprinted towards the church. Most of the fale and houses were now lashed down with ropes and timber.

Some children were bathing merrily in the overflowing ditches. Taifau chased them home. Sapepe seemed a deserted village of closed cells, with the storm, God's fearful flail, as its warden.

The church, completely closed to the wind, was an echo chamber of whispering sound. 'I've sent word to everyone that we're having a service this evening,' Simi told Tauilopepe.

'Anything you need?' Taifau asked. Simi shook his head. Galupo was by the pulpit folding up the altar linen.

'What's he doing here?' Tauilopepe asked.

'Helping.'

Tauilopepe turned away and left the church.

Tauilopepe changed and joined his whole aiga who had assembled in the sitting room, dining room, and kitchen. Teuila sat in their midst, singing a baby to sleep. Everyone looked up at him as if he alone could save them. He went to the windows. Most of the bread-fruit trees were down, and through the swirling curtain of rain he glimpsed the sea lashing the beach, and the darkness beyond that.

'We have sinned!' wailed one of the old women.

'That's enough!' he ordered. 'The storm will die away soon. You are all to sleep in the house. Your fale may collapse in the wind.'

Shadows had crept in, chased there by the storm; they were huddling together to form a steadily thickening darkness; the house was shuddering almost continuously, contracting around them, with the rising stench of mud and sweat and fear.

'Let us say Psalm 23,' Tauilopepe said. '"The Lord is my Shepherd, I shall not want. He...."' Soon, even the children were reciting the psalm, and their voices rose in unison until the storm was a mere droning at the edge of their fear. God would be appeased, He would withdraw His anger, His fearful wrath.

Hurricane-lamps hanging down from the rafters of the church cast an eerie, swimming light over the congregation. Magnificent in his blackness Simi gazed down at them. He was their most intimate connection with God, the intermediary who would calm the storm as the ancient priests had appeased the gods in pre-Christian times. In their dread they had forgotten that Simi was a black man whom they had never fully accepted as one of their own.

'We are afraid,' Simi said, 'because we believe that the storm is an expression of God's wrath. This is not so. Our God is a God of love and such a God will not punish us this way. God is with us in our despair. Many men will argue that our God has no forgiveness. It is not so.' (This was not what they had come to hear; they wanted to be consoled, to confirm their innermost fear that God *was* a God of wrath.) 'Perhaps I can ease your fears if I tell you what a hurricane is. A storm becomes a hurricane when its speed exceeds sixty-three knots or seventy-two miles per hour. The usual diameter of a hurricane is from three to four hundred miles. A hurricane is a huge whirlpool of air circling a small still centre known as the "eye". And hurricane winds are accompanied by massive clouds and torrential rain . . . .'

'We have sinned! God we have sinned!' a woman cried, hands clutched to her face.

'. . . No one knows how hurricanes start but scientists know how hurricanes, once they are born, maintain their ferocious strength. Once a hurricane starts, it sucks up air at sea-level and whirls it to great heights in the circling air currents. As the air rises the water in it condenses and falls as rain. This condensation releases heat which causes the air to rise even faster . . . .'

'Listen to me!' Galupo called from the back. Everyone looked round. Simi motioned as if to resume his sermon, but Galupo hurried up the aisle, stopped under the pulpit, and confronted them with a wild look in his eyes. 'Our pastor is a very learned man but he is doing nothing to allay the storm that is wrecking everything we own!' he said. 'We all know why the hurricane is here. God has sent it to punish us for our sins.' Paused and then asked, 'But is He not punishing us because of the sins of our fathers and of certain men in Sapepe?'

'That's enough!' ordered Simi. 'I won't let you use God's

351

house to create hatred between our people!'

'Let Galupo speak!' a matai who owed Tauilopepe a lot of money called out.

'Does not the Book say that the children pay for the sins of their fathers?' Galupo continued.

Tauilopepe got up slowly. 'That is enough!' he ordered.

'See this man, people of Sapepe,' Galupo said, pointing at Tauilopepe. 'It is this man's sins that have caused God to punish us!' Some men of the Aiga Tauilopepe sprang up and advanced towards Galupo.

'No!' Tauilopepe stopped them. 'Let him speak!' The men sat down again.

'See this haunted, grey-haired cripple,' Galupo said. 'Why are you all afraid of him? Why? Because you and your pastor have made him your god. We should not be afraid of the hurricane but of men like this cripple!' Gazing at Tauilopepe, he asked, 'Do you know who I *really* am?' No one moved — the howling wind, the rain, the violent crashing of the sea, the shivering earth, all seemed to await his revelation.

'No, and I don't care. All I see in you is evil,' Tauilopepe replied.

A strange smile spread across Galupo's face. 'The evil in me, people of Sapepe, is the evil in this cripple. When he looks into a mirror he is staring at me. Yes, me. Why?' He paused. 'Because, people of Sapepe, I am his son, a son he begot in sin.' A hushed silence, with everyone staring at Tauilopepe. . . .

'Go home to your aiga!' Simi said, and the people dispersed quickly.

'He was lying!' Tauilopepe called. 'Taifau, tell them he was lying!' Taifau swung round but the church was now bare rows of pews, an emptiness of waving light.

'I am deeply sorry I defended Galupo to you,' Simi said, as Tauilopepe started to shuffle towards the front doors.

He went to his bedroom and stayed there. Downstairs the children slept in their parents' laps; many of the elders were asleep on the floor in mosquito nets; Teuila sat with those who were awake; beyond the light's edge the storm was a black beast trampling through the trees. A tree crashed down, a child woke and started to cry. Soon all the children were awake and crying. Their parents hushed them into silence. Shortly afterwards the lights went out; the wind had broken the lines from the generator. The children began to cry again. Lamps were lit and placed round the room and they stopped crying. Teuila got her transistor radio and, sitting with it in her lap, debated whether to switch it on as many women gathered round her. About an hour later she switched it on. For a time there was a hymn. Then it came: '*According to our Observatory the worst is nearly over. Record winds of 82 knots were recorded an hour ago, but the wind's speed is decreasing. We repeat, the wind is dying. God has been merciful ....*'

Some of the women wept. Teuila rushed upstairs.

'Tauilo, it's over!' she said into the darkness of their bedroom. 'Tauilo?'

'Yes?' his voice came out of the darkness. She groped her way over to where he was sitting facing the windows and sat beside him. 'You don't believe him, do you?' he asked after a while.

'Who?'

'Galupo.'

'No, I don't believe him.'

'But if it was true that he is my son would it matter?'

'No,' she murmured. 'No, it wouldn't matter to me.'

They listened to the storm for a long time. Eventually she fell asleep in her chair. He covered her with a sheet.

Galupo must be destroyed, he thought, but first I must make sure he isn't my son; I must postpone the case until I find out.

He woke to a weak light filtering into the room. The rain had stopped. He didn't wake his aiga as he went through the sitting room to the garage. As he got into the jeep he remembered his paralysed arm, got out, and started for Taifau's house. Nearly all the bread-fruit trees had been uprooted, houses were without roofing iron, people were picking their possessions out of the wreckage, trees were stripped bare of leaves. So much had to be done, yet he wasn't as worried as he had been during the night. The smell of fear had vanished. A new beginning.

353

He sucked the cool morning air into his lungs and held it there for a moment. A new challenge to keep him alive. But did he have the time?

One of Taifau's grandsons opened the door when he thumped on it. 'Taifau isn't going to like this mess,' the boy said, surveying the damage.

'Why don't you wake Taifau for me?' Tauilopepe asked.

'Don't think he's feeling well,' the boy replied, starting to urinate into the grass. 'He had a sore stomach last night.' Patiently Tauilopepe waited for him to finish and go in and get his grandfather.

'Is your stomach better?' Tauilopepe asked Taifau when he came out, his eyes red from lack of sleep, his clothes rumpled and smelling heavily of sweat. When Taifau looked bewildered Tauilopepe laughed and said, 'You've got another Taifau for a grandson!'

Some matai awaited them outside the garage. The oldest of them, a wizened and almost toothless sage, well-known for his tall stories, said, 'Lot of damage. Whole of Upolu, Savaii, and American Samoa have been hit, flattened. What are we going to to?'

'Build again, that is all we can do,' Tauilopepe said.

'Years of work, years. Gone. Just like that,' the old man said, clapping his hands. Tauilopepe started to explain how they could organise to repair the damage. 'Sir?' coughed the old sage. 'Sir, we know it is not our concern. Every man, and especially you, sir, has the right to enjoy as many women as he wants to. Take me, for instance, I've got, well—one, two, three, four children by other women.' Everyone laughed.

'If you are referring to Galupo,' said Tauilopepe, 'I don't know if he is my son.'

'But if he was your son would you like that?' the old man asked.

'Would *you* mind?'

The old man raised his eyebrows and said, 'I might. But he's a devil, isn't he? Who ever would be brave enough or foolish enough to use the hurricane and the church to do what he did? Otherwise he's a hard-working boy, isn't he?

354

And he can read all those foreign books. And you haven't got a son left, have you, sir?' Tauilopepe patted the old man on the back and told the other men to go to his house where Teuila would give them a meal.

It took over three arduous hours to clear the road to Leaves of the Banyan Tree. Against Taifau's advice Tauilopepe worked and joked with the men, swinging a bushknife with his good arm. Taifau was puzzled by Tauilopepe's high spirits, considering he had lost almost everything in the storm. But Tauilopepe, he reminded himself, always thrived best when he was confronted by new challenges and always had sound reasons for everything he did. So, when they stopped in front of the cocoa dryer, now a skeletal structure standing alone among uprooted cacao trees and bananas, Taifau asked, 'What if Galupo is your son?'

'If he is then he's in for something he didn't bargain for,' said Tauilopepe, and Taifau was more puzzled than ever.

They used a ladder to climb to the top of the dryer from where they surveyed the devastation. Only a few cacao trees and bananas were standing in the area surrounding the dryer. Beyond that was a landscape of broken trees and overturned taro crops striped by rows of undamaged palms. The wind sang mournfully over the fields and down into the valley, taking with it up to the range the stench of dying vegetation. The sky was a light-grey ceiling, bare of clouds, tired, spent of its fury.

'Trust it to survive,' Tauilopepe said, pointing to the Banyan.

'Yes, but just look at it. Not many leaves left. Hands and limbs broken, twisted, shaved off. That will teach it not to be so arrogant,' said Taifau.

'Yes,' whispered Tauilopepe, looking away.

'We just have to rebuild,' Taifau said when they got back to the garage that afternoon. They went in and had something to eat. Afterwards Tauilopepe said he was going to take some men into Apia to repair any damage to the house there. Taifau accompanied him to the truck.

'Ask Galupo to see me tonight,' Tauilopepe said. 'Persuade him to come. I'll be back this evening.'

'But why?'

Tauilopepe winked at him. 'We have to make time, don't we?' he said.

'One day I'm going to have a house like yours,' Galupo said, sipping his coffee noisily. He had arrived just as Tauilopepe was starting his evening meal, had accepted his invitation to eat and as he did so had talked about everything but the scene in church the previous night. 'I've got it all worked out — hard work, love other people and God, and I won't be poor.'

'I don't see why you can't have a house like this. You work hard enough. I admire people who work hard,' Tauilopepe said.

'If I may say so, sir, you work twice as hard as anyone else I've known,' Galupo said. Tauilopepe offered him a cigarette. 'No, thank you. I don't smoke.'

'A drink then?'

'I don't drink either.'

Tauilopepe said, 'You surprise me, *Malo*. ... You don't mind me addressing you by your title?'

'No, sir. I think a man should always be addressed by his title, that's if he has a title.'

'Well, Malo, you surprise me. You are obviously of the town, yet you don't smoke or drink and you aren't married.'

'I could never afford those luxuries, especially a wife!' laughed Galupo.

They continued in this manner until Teuila came from the kitchen, wished them good night, and went upstairs. Then Tauilopepe invited Galupo into his study.

Not long after they were seated in chairs facing each other across Tauilopepe's desk, Tauilopepe asked, 'Why did you choose last night to attack me publicly?'

'I thought it was a good move at the time.'

'You couldn't have chosen a better time. I would have picked a similar time, at your age.'

356

'Thinking about it afterwards I regretted having done so. Will you forgive me?' Galupo bowed his head. Tauilopepe laughed immediately. 'You don't miss a trick, do you, sir!' laughed Galupo.

Shaking his head, Tauilopepe said, 'I know you too well.' 'Because you were like me?' asked Galupo. Tauilopepe nodded. 'Did you like the bit about the mirror?'

'Yes, but I did not like the bit about me being your father.'

'That? Well, that *is* the truth,' said Galupo. And in that instant when Tauilopepe gazed into Galupo's face he knew that this unscrupulous young man whom he sensed he could never learn to trust was indeed his son, begotten in sin. 'I can't say I'll ever be proud of having you as a father,' continued Galupo. 'I feel nothing for you and I sense you feel the same way about me.'

'Yes, I feel nothing for you.'

'I suppose you've guessed by now who my mother was?' Galupo asked. Tauilopepe nodded. 'She's dead. Died when I was about ten. But I don't suppose you cared then, or now. No one did.'

'You don't have to talk about it if it is too painful.'

'But I do. I do. You see, before you have that final attack that'll burn your brains out for good I want you to know what you did and to accept full responsibility for it.' There was no anger or hatred in his voice. 'At the end of my tale of woe, if you want to feel sorry for me and my mother, feel free to do so.' Looking directly at Tauilopepe, he said, 'Do you want to hear about me — an accident in time? Or shall I say, an accident on the beach nearly thirty years ago?'

Tauilopepe nodded. He had to learn more about Galupo, who was the time, the hands, the mind and cunning he needed to rebuild Leaves of the Banyan Tree, the man he could use to continue his line until Lalolagi, his only legal heir, came of age and the debt he owed Pepe was paid.

14 The Mythology of Night-Wave

Galupo's mother had gone to Apia to live with her parents and wait for Tauilopepe. When she realised that he had betrayed her she tried to abort her child. She failed. Seven months after leaving Sapepe she gave premature birth to Galupo and decided to save him — her son would avenge her betrayal. Her aiga helped her begrudgingly so she sold her flesh whenever she needed money.

Galupo was a strange child, with brooding eyes too old for a child's body, and he was soon the butt of cruel jokes. His mother was always there to protect him. 'You have a father who hates you!' she reminded him constantly. 'He's rich and it all belongs to you!' She beat him when he didn't pay attention to her remarks about his father, crying, 'We are what we are because of him.' And Galupo, silent tears in his eyes, would nod his head.

At first he didn't mind the men she brought home at night. They gave him money and called him 'the young devil', which made him feel grown up. Sometimes when he was in his grandparents' fale, listening to them discussing the biblical heroes, especially Jesus Christ who was crucified by people called the Jews, he imagined he was Christ up there on the cross saying 'I forgive you.' But his mother always rescued him, so he came to believe, from this fantasy of martyrdom by reminding him that everybody was against them.

When he was nine she expelled him from the warm security of her bed. He was now a little man and men didn't sleep with their mothers; it was a sin, she explained. And the terror associated with sin entered his world: sin had something to do with sleeping with mamma, and sleeping with mamma had something to do with what she did in the dark with those men. He asked her about it and why she didn't do it with him; after all he was a man too — she had told him so. He was too young and anyway it was a sin to do it with mamma because mamma had given birth to him, she said. He was, he gradually realised, the unwanted result of this sinful act, and as he matured he could never dissociate his birth from sin. And sinful people, his grandfather explained, ended up in Hell where they boiled for ever. Out of no fault of his own he had been conceived in sin and would therefore go to Hell, he thought. He must destroy the cause of that sin, his father. Mamma was innocent: she had been sinned against, violated. So he came to fear his mother's male visitors: they were trying to destroy the only person he loved, the goddess who had breathed life into him.

His mother got pregnant again. He didn't know until she was taken to hospital and he heard an aunt saying that his mother had tried to kill the child inside her. His relatives took him to the hospital. He stood by her bed, fists clenched, swallowing his pain. Come closer, she motioned. She embraced and kissed him and he tasted the stunning emptiness that was to be. She died the next day.

In the following months he was shifted from one relative to another because no one wanted him. He tolerated their jokes about his mother, the heavy work they made him do, and the beatings the other children inflicted on him. He trained himself to ignore the pain.

Late one afternoon his grandfather summoned him. 'This is Falesa, your mother's older brother,' his grandfather said. Galupo looked warily at the man sitting opposite his grandfather.

'I'm taking you with me,' the man said.

He's a useful boy,' his grandfather replied. The man tossed over a roll of money. Galupo's grandfather caught it and stuffed it under his legs before his aiga could see it. 'Go to Falesa,' his grandfather ordered him.

'He's a bit underfed, isn't he?' the driver said to Falesa when they got into the taxi.

'Nothing a good home won't cure, eh? Falesa said, ruffling Galupo's hair. For the first time Galupo smiled, meaning it.

As a young man Falesa had deliberately severed all his ties with his aiga and the faa-Samoa, condemning such a life as unproductive, spiritually sterile, and humiliating. He worked as a clerk until he could buy his first taxi, which over the years turned into seven taxis, a modern bungalow at Vaiala beach, a wife and two daughters, a healthy savings account, a respected niche in the business community and the English-speaking Protestant church, and now a son.

Malama, Falesa's attractive wife, immediately accepted Galupo. At first his daughters, Moli and Tasi, who were about the same age as Galupo, were slightly afraid of him. But, as time passed and they discovered that he was in most ways like other boys, they too accepted him. Their almost perpetual laughter, generosity, and gaiety seeped into his heart in unguarded moments and threatened to turn him against the sacred memory of his mother. And he never forgave them for this. Anyway they were only pretending they loved him, he thought.

Under Malama's generous care his body flowered. He attended school for the first time and, hating it, secretly blamed Falesa and Malama. He obeyed his teachers but made sure that they and the other students avoided him: he was safe enough; they would never venture into the circle of ominous silence he put round himself. He was of average ability, his teacher told his adopted parents. Yes, he *was* average because he wanted them to believe that. If he showed that he was brilliant he would be vulnerable and they would attack him. He tried especially hard to hide his passion for books.

Books became his obsession: the ideas and dreams and power in them made him quiver with the desire for more books, more visions, more flights, even into the dark recesses of people's fears and madness. As he progressed through high school he hoarded all the books and magazines he could find or buy or steal in the hut which Falesa helped him build behind the bungalow. Novels in particular were his world. He lived in them as if he was swimming through a coral reef which changed shape and colour and mood continuously, watching the fabulous fish dancing in the wonderful silence, and then the predators

360

darting out, killing. Novelists were gods: they created worlds, fashioned and then destroyed their own creations.

No one, not even his adopted parents, was allowed into his hut. He cleaned it himself, meticulously searching for and killing all the insects which invaded it; he dusted his books carefully once a fortnight. He thought of his hut as a vibrant mind in which he read and dreamt, safe from the world, until he was called to the bungalow where he was the well-mannered son. The hut was his world, as distinct from what he started calling the 'Other-World', which was inhabited by 'Other-Worlders'.

In his last year at high school he helped Falesa run the taxi business and drove a taxi at week-ends. Once behind the wheel in his peaked cap he out-smiled, out-talked, out-mannered, and out-drove the other drivers, and brought in more money. Class, style, brains — he was unbeatable, he congratulated himself. He used his pay to buy more books and to entertain the girls he sometimes enticed into his taxi.

He was allowed to do whatever he liked with his spare time. Most of it he spent reading in his hut. Some nights, when he had done his homework, he would take the car and see a film or pick up a girl, drive to Mulinuu Point, *use her* efficiently (that was his description), and never see her again. On Sunday nights he always accompanied his aiga to church. Publicly he was devout and his parents were proud of him, and when he finished high school he became a Sunday School teacher. Only Other-Worlders believed in Holy Ghosts, he thought, and he knew more about the Other-World religion than Other-Worlders because he had studied it in his books: he was convinced that destructive illusions (or was it delusions) had been spread through the centuries on behalf of a ridiculous Holy Ghost. Other-Worlders believed these lies because they were weaklings.

When he graduated from high school his parents wanted him to work in a government office but he persuaded them to let him help in their taxi business. Through stricter supervision and modern book-keeping he reduced the losses from dishonest drivers, and by the time of his twenty-first birthday three more taxis had been added to the fleet.

361

His parents hired a large hall and a band, prepared a sumptuous meal, and gave him his first birthday party. He invited all the drivers and their wives, the minister and other officials of their church, and some of their neighbours, and Falesa invited all his business friends. Not one of them could he call a real friend — he had no friends and that was good, he thought. He enjoyed his party immensely, danced with all the stern church wives and their daughters, encouraged the minister and his flock to drink and peel off their Sunday skins and reveal petty lusts and jealousies, and laughed secretly at the drivers who got viciously drunk and disappeared outside periodically to commit sly adulteries with one another's wives. In this *exhilarating display of immorality* (his description) only his adopted aiga remained sober, happy, innocent.

The party reinforced his belief that there was no genuine love in the Other-World, only pretence and vanity. Other-Worlders' so-called love was a mask for their true feelings towards him — he was their object of charity, the child of a wayward woman. The Aiga Falesa had given him a home but they had done it because of what Other-Worlders called 'conscience', a moral clock ticking inside them, telling them what was right and wrong.

Moli started to worry him intensely at this time. He couldn't fit her into his Other-World concept. She was seemingly without feeling for anything, and he couldn't discern any weaknesses in her. Even when he became the idol of their aiga she remained indifferent to him, waiting behind a beautiful mask, he thought, to strike at him.

And finally he brought Siaki a new driver, home for dinner. The others had eaten and Moli served him and Siaki and then sat down and talked to them. As they were leaving the house Siaki remarked that Moli was very attractive. 'You'd better not...,' Galupo warned him.

'I didn't mean it that way,' Siaki said.

During the next few days he thought about Siaki's remark and avoided Siaki and Moli. He was getting sentimental, he told himself, allowing weak sentiment to undermine his beliefs about Other-Worlders. He couldn't

let this happen or he would become like them. He retreated into his hut every night after dinner.

'...You know what went through my head those nights?'
Galupo continued, ' "Siaki wants to *use* her," I thought,
"and it may do her a lot of good. No. But why not? You
want to use her yourself. It wouldn't be incest, you're not
her brother." ' He paused, smiled at Tauilopepe, and then
continued, 'I've always been honest with myself, honest in
my own unique way. And I was being honest about Moli. I
wanted to do her, violate her innocence, and through her
the innocence of her aiga. Do you know why I hated
them? Because they were not yet Other-Worlders: they
were innocents and I wasn't. Not that I wanted to be like
them. No. I wanted them to be like the rest of the
Other-Worlders — corrupt, petty, unclean, miserable, so I
could pity them. I wanted them to see themselves honestly, without lies.' He paused again. 'I was born un-
innocent, a creature of the Fall. Even in the womb I was a
product of your sin. Anyway I decided not to do her
myself. You see, to really punish an innocent you have to
get an Other-Worlder to do it. And Siaki was that
Other-Worlder. He knew nothing of real sin. Nothing.
Like all Other-Worlders, he didn't know, like I know,
Tauilopepe, that sin is a violation of one's inner self, of
one's honesty towards one's self: that the Fall in the Book
is only a sugared fable, that the *real* fall is when one's eyes
open inwards and find *nothing*. As Pepe must have done,
and as I've done. I'm worth nothing and, knowing that
since I was a child, I've been able to do the things I've
done without any regrets or guilt. Yes, father — I hope you
don't mind me calling you that — without guilt. I don't
even feel sorry about what I did to the Aiga Falesa. Not an
ounce of guilt. You see I've condensed my whole attitude
to life into these lines: "I gaze into my eyes and, dazzled
by the emptiness I see, know that I am beautiful." Apt
lines, aren't they, father...? You, old man, if you tried
gazing inwards would find only the terror I made the Aiga
Falesa see in the emptiness I made them confront through
Moli. ...'

He continued to bring Siaki for meals. Siaki's advances to Moli become bolder; his hesitant, polite phrases lengthened into tales of his supposed piety, made up specially to suit Falesa's Protestant bias; his cleverly camouflaged glances became lingering caresses. But Moli didn't seem to notice.

'Moli likes you,' he told Siaki one afternoon. 'Would you like to meet her?'

'But Moli is your sister,' Siaki protested.

'I trust you,' he replied.

During the next fortnight whenever Moli wanted a taxi, Galupo got Siaki to drive her. He was in love with Moli, Siaki confessed finally. It was an obsession; he wasn't interested in any other woman — all they were mad about was spreading their legs and getting injected; Moli was different, she was goodness itself. One Saturday Galupo told Siaki to visit Moli that night; he was taking the rest of the aiga to a church meeting and they would be home late. When they returned, even though Siaki wasn't there and Moli was asleep on the settee, Galupo could feel it in the room. Moli said nothing about Siaki. Now she had secrets. Every time the rest of the aiga went out, Galupo arranged for Siaki to visit her. In their meals at home that followed, he sensed the obsessive need between Siaki and Moli. The puppet, his adopted sister, was now craving more pain and guilt. And he, not Siaki, had violated her.

When the mango season started, Siaki's visits became less frequent. Every time Galupo came home without him he saw a frantic look in Moli's eyes. The next pay-day, after Siaki collected his money, he didn't return to work and no one knew where he was. That same morning Malama found Moli vomiting in the bathroom. Moli pushed her away, rushed to her bedroom and locked herself in. When Galupo got home after work he found his aiga in the sitting room and he noticed that the gaiety which usually filled their house in the evening was absent. They told him about Moli. He knocked on her bedroom door and called to her to come out.

She started to sob. 'I've sinned, sinned!' she cried. He called to her again.

Moli's revelation of guilt came loud, clear, and final: 'I'm pregnant. Pregnant!'

Malama gasped and shielded her eyes with her hands as if she was being blinded by a stinging light; Falesa pounded on Moli's door with clenched fists; Tasi just stood beside Malama; and Galupo, who knew hatred so well, recognised it in her. They were suffering the Fall, the descent into the agonising loneliness of flesh, bone, and blood. Pulling Falesa away and shouting 'Bitch! bitch!' he broke in, grabbed Moli, and flung her into the corridor. Malama and Tasi fell upon her. Falesa watched while they ripped off her clothes and bared her beautiful shame to the house which had once throbbed with joy and forgiveness. Innocence is so fragile, Galupo thought.

He went on to the beach murmuring in the darkness. The weeping ended suddenly, and a silence, as for ever as stone, settled on the house. He had revealed to them the secret of life and it wasn't his fault they couldn't accept it. Before he moved on he had one more act to perform — he owed it to the Aiga Falesa.

The sky was alive with stars. The three men brought Siaki out of the club and pushed him into the back seat of the car. Drunk, Siaki muttered unintelligibly as Galupo drove to Mulinuu Point. It had been easy to recruit the three men; they had scores to settle with Siaki: the massive wharf labourer holding Siaki's arms in a vice-like grip owed him for a daughter whom Siaki had seduced and then abandoned; the oldest man owed him for a senseless beating; and the youngest owed him for a girl Siaki had taken away from him.

Galupo drove to the area where the tombs of the Tamaaiga were located and stopped the car. The oldest man checked the fishermen's huts behind the tombs and reported seeing no one. The other two dragged Siaki out. Galupo switched on the front lights. They stung Siaki to a brief wakefulness and he covered his eyes with his arms.

'Don't kill him!' Galupo called to the men. He sat back and watched.

They worked quietly, efficiently, quickly.

365

No woman would want Siaki again: he left the hospital a cripple.

The following evening Galupo sorted through his books and packed those he wanted into an enormous suitcase. He kept the Bible he had stolen from the Protestant church, Camus's *Myth of Sisyphus* and *The Plague*, a paperback copy of Frazer's *Golden Bough*, Dostoevsky's *Idiot* and *Crime and Punishment*, an unexpurgated edition of *Lady Chatterley's Lover*, a collection of pornographic Japanese prints, Dreiser's *American Tragedy*, Norman Mailer's *The Naked and the Dead*, V.S. Naipaul's *A House For Mr Biswas*, Luis Borges's *Ficciones*, and ten volumes of the *Encyclopaedia Britannica*. He locked the suitcase, tore down the bookshelves, and scattered the remaining books and magazines all over the floor. He suddenly realised he was weeping.

'...It was the hardest thing I ever had to do—burning that hut and my books. They had become part of me, like your title and property are part of you, father. But I burnt them. I woke at dawn, doused the place with petrol, and bang! Up it all went! I didn't look back. I went to the wharf and caught the early morning ferry to Savaii. ...Don't look so horrified, old man. I did what I had to do. Did I do wrong by the Aiga Falesa? Is it my fault Falesa soon lost his business and he and Malama eventually divorced? No. I helped them discover their real selves and the real world around them, but they couldn't take it. Like all Other-Worlders they grovelled in self-pity and yearned for a Garden of Eden. No guts, no self-honesty. All you Other-Worlders yearn for is conscience. ...

'I spent five years in a Savaii village I'd better not identify, stealing money from the trading firm I represented. I was a respected storekeeper. I even took a wife for respectability's sake. I treated her kindly and all she didn't have to do was give me children, because children, father, give meaning to the man who sires them and no man is worthy of that. My wife died, by the way. Some people who owed me money said I killed her. But I didn't. I had nothing to

366

gain by killing her. I was even faithful to her till the day
she died. I gave her the biggest funeral seen in that district, picked up my money and other belongings, and
returned to Upolu. And here I am. ...

'At first I idealised my mother's memory, but as my
mind blossomed under the tutelage of my books she faded
into the rightful place of all rat-eaten memories of so-
called "loved ones". She tried to use me, father. She didn't
really care about me. Not that I expected her to — she
didn't owe me anything. The blame for her death is
squarely between you, father, and her. She destroyed herself by letting you use her. It's got nothing to do with me.
So she shouldn't have tried to use me to destroy you. I
don't hold that against her. She didn't know any better.
She was an Other-Worlder through and through, more so
than you others because she couldn't live through anything
but her flesh. She was trapped in it like you're tied to your
property, father. But that isn't news to you. About her, I
mean. How else could you have used her so efficiently and
profitably....

'You may think I've been boasting. But that's very far
from the truth. I'm human, more so than you Other-
Worlders. You're Other-Worlders because you mistakenly
believe you're the centre of our tiny rock. Me, I know I'm
nothing, nobody. And I know nothing belongs to me, not
even the name Moa branded me with which, as you know,
means Wave of the Night. I am more human because I
believe in nothing, but it doesn't terrify me, doesn't send
me to the nearest church to find a conscience and a heaven
to believe in. Or send me scuttling in search of a cause to
die for. Or send me to the rope to put an end to my fears.
Or force me, like you, to spend my days accumulating
money, property, and power to extinguish my fears and
persuade myself I'm semi-mortal. No, father, as I said
before: "I gaze into my emptiness and know that I am
beautiful." ...

'You think, father, that you know why I'm in Sapepe. I
told Taifau — and I do admire that old man — that I'm here
to claim what is mine. I think I've told you that already.
Or did I? Did I tell you I'm here to destroy you? But then

I don't need to do it myself. Your life and all you possess and your power will continue to do so without my help....

'What do I mean by claiming what is mine? I mean this: I want to claim my origins, my identity. I want a name. Yes, father, a name. This is what Sapepe owes me. You obviously don't believe me but that's why I'm here. You may well ask: But why all the theatricals, the planned attack on me, Tauilopepe, crippled king of Sapepe? Why? Because you've turned this land, which rightfully belongs to me and to generations not yet born, into a mockery of what it should be. It is now a caricature like you, father, and all your kind who inhabit Apia. You are the shadows, men without souls. But I don't suppose you understand what I'm trying to say. It's too late. We're years and an education apart and you're just one of the "mimic men", as one writer has put it so aptly.... I don't hate you, father. I pity you. ... My planned attack is merely me playing the respectable game of respectable power for the sake of our respectable Sapepe audience. It's so Other-Worlder. I'm the evil son, you're the righteous king; I'm the villain, you're the fast-gun sheriff, and, as we know from the movies, the sheriff always wins. But, on with the game. Let's give our audience, sadistic though they are, an entertaining show. And I'd better warn you, father, I'm fast and fit. I *stick*. I had stickability right from the womb. Moa couldn't kill me with spokes; the Aiga Falesa couldn't strangle me with what Other-Worlders call "love"; Siaki and that Savaii village were only distractions. I'm what you Other-Worlders call a guilty conscience. I stick and I haunt. And I'm going to win because in relation to you I have guilt on my side, and, as I'm the villain, everybody will expect me to use every dirty tactic imaginable, and I will. You, however, are the hero and heroes are ethical and kill only according to the rules....

'I know what you've planned for me already. I won't tell because that'll ruin our game. I'll let you guess what I'm going to do.

'Because I know everything about you I thought it was only fair to let you know everything about me. That's why

I've described my miserable life to you. If you don't believe a word of what I've said that's your bad luck. Before I leave to resume our game I'd better tell you that I have nothing to lose while you have everything to lose. My mind is also the best, the most devious, the most heartless that papalagi books have produced in our sad country. You've always tried to know and love the papalagi world. But you're an amateur at it. Me, I know the very depths of that world. ... Your move, father. Good night and don't, for your weak heart's sake, spend a sleepless night worrying about what I've told you. You might get another attack and then we won't be able to play our game. *And for all you know, I may have been spending the last few hours lying to you: I may not be your son.*'

15   Bargain, A Little Bargain

You sit in your study, afraid, remembering your only real son, who died unloved. Out of his ashes God has fashioned another son to destroy you. You switch on the main light to try to defeat the fearful gloom clogging your thoughts. You ache to the pores of your being for the fears to go but they cling to you like the cloying stench of mud seeping through the windows. Galupo's voice, ablaze with what you think is madness, continues to stab at you, driving you deeper into the pit of your fears. He was lying, you tell yourself. Lying! But you won't ever be sure. You walk, one, two, three steps to the far wall and gaze at the faded photographs of your mother preserved behind glass, your wife, Lupe, preserved behind glass, your father and Toasa preserved behind glass. Glass, and the yearning gap where Pepe's photograph should be. All gone. Gone. You are fading too. You look at your dead arm, feel the pain in your eyes, and know that you are a mockery of the man you once were. But you refuse to accept death because your second son is unworthy of what you have created — Leaves of the Banyan Tree, this house, the Sapepe you have built alone. Galupo is unworthy because he has no love, no feeling for anyone. . . .

Tauilopepe's thoughts were silver-fish darting among his fears. He ached for a drink but remembered his promise to Teuila not to drink again. He sat down facing the windows, the curtains stirring lazily in the breeze. Two hours or so went by. The room was getting chilly. Outside the dew had settled into the veins of the wreckage wrought by the hurricane. The room grew crowded with the people who had died and the lions and aitu Toasa and Pepe had talked about. With ragged bodies and haunted eyes longing for life, some of them cursed him, others jeered, others simply passed by. But he wasn't afraid of them, he told himself. He sweated even though the air was cold. Toasa had a white mask over his face, his lavalava was open, and he was urinating noisily on to a house of playing-cards, which soon crumpled under the streaming water, while Pepe laughed. Tauilopepe suddenly recognised the pool he was standing beside, watching them. Empty church pews stood in orderly rows before him, and beyond them, illuminated by a slab of light tumbling out of a black sky, was a gleaming pulpit. He went up and sat in the front pew facing the pulpit. Toasa ascended the pulpit steps and sat down. Pepe came and stood at the foot of the pulpit. Like Toasa he wore a white mask.

He sensed that the room was crowded with people but he didn't look round.

'Are you one of us?' Pepe asked.

'Yes,' he replied. Scornful laughter erupted all round him. Toasa raised his right arm and the room was silent again.

'Do you know why you are here?' Pepe asked.

'Yes,' he said, and was surprised when there was no laughter. A loud fart issued from the pulpit. Everyone looked up at Toasa who apologised for committing 'an unpardonable sin'.

'Tell us why you are here since you *know* why you are here!' Pepe ordered.

'I don't honestly know, sir,' he had to say. Toasa guffawed loudly and the audience shouted at him to shut his gob.

'That's an excellent answer. At least you don't know why you are here!' exclaimed Pepe. The audience clapped and whistled and stamped their feet. Extraordinary state of affairs, he thought. No order, no respect for their law and Toasa, their leader. Just a bloody uncouth rabble!

'Do you believe in cowboys?' Pepe asked.

'Cowboys?' he replied wonderingly. Surely he deserved a better question!

'Yes, cowboys. You know, they play guitars and shoot bad fellows?'

'Oh, those. Well, I don't know, come to think of it,' he said. Toasa and the audience groaned with disappointment. 'Come to think of it,' he said, 'I think I do. Yes—I *do*

371

believe in cowboys!' Pepe and Toasa and their unruly gang whistled and clapped and stamped their feet.

When the applause had subsided Pepe asked, 'What about baddies and villains, do you believe in them?'

'No!' he shouted, expecting them to cheer. They didn't.

'Why not?'

'I don't... I don't know why,' he replied. Toasa trumpeted two loud farts which reverberated through the building.

'Surely if there are cowboys there must be villains also?' asked Pepe.

'I agree,' he said eagerly. The applause was almost deafening. Pepe raised his arms and the audience fell silent.

'Now, father....' (It was the first time Pepe had called him father, and Tauilopepe nearly wept.) 'Now, father, who are you — a cowboy or a villain?'

He pondered for a moment, sensing that if he missed this one, he would lose their respect for good. 'I am....'

'Yes?' Pepe encouraged him.

'I am a cowboy!'

'GUILTY!' shouted Pepe, and Tauilopepe knew he had missed for ever.

'Please, listen to me!' he cried. 'Can I change my mind?' But they were crowding round him, clutching at his clothes and arms, and yelling: 'Kill the miserable bastard!'

'Save me!' he called to Pepe and Toasa. The figure in the pulpit rose and ripped off his mask. Tauilopepe gasped. It was not Toasa, it was his father; and beside him stood a grinning Galupo. He screamed into the darkness.

'It's me, it's me!' someone whispered. He struggled against the embracing arms, sobbing with fear, broke from sleep, and sobbed into Teuila's warmth. 'It's all right,' she murmured.

They clasped each other for a long time. Her warmth dispelled the memory of the nightmare and he told her everything Galupo had revealed that night, as if through telling her he would succeed in exorcising his fears.

He also told her what he was going to do about Galupo. Dawn was filtering through the windows.

'I'll help you,' she said.

'We will be doing it for Lalolagi. Lalolagi deserves what I own. Not Galupo. Galupo has no respect, no charity for anyone.'

He sent for Galupo later that morning. He asked Taifau to come too.

As evening fell over Sapepe, Galupo came.

'I wonder how the government is going to feed the population?' Galupo said as he sat down on the settee beside Taifau. 'The whole agriculture of the country is in ruins.'

'Galupo?' Tauilopepe said. Galupo looked up. 'I have a bargain to make with you. How would you like to work for me? No...I mean, how would you like to take over from where I left off?'

'Good idea. After all, I am your son,' replied Galupo.

'As you know,' Tauilopepe said, 'our plantation has been wrecked, and Taifau and I are too old to rebuild it. We, and that includes Teuila and our whole aiga, need you.' He paused and glanced at Teuila who smiled at him, encouraging him to continue. 'I owe you a lot. I cannot repay you for the years you have spent alone — for your mother's death. In my own way I am trying to make up for all that.' Galupo, hands clasped round his knees, was gazing at his feet. 'The plantation, everything, is yours, but before I hand them over you must prove to me — to us — that you can work as hard and as honestly as we have done. I can't give you everything just because you're my flesh and blood; you must earn it, that's the way of the modern world. My father left me only a title but I have made something out of it, an inheritance any son would be proud of. You want to destroy me, don't you? But where would that get you? What would you gain by destroying me? Look at me, I am not worth hating or destroying. I am a sick old man. As you said last night one more attack and I am dead. Galupo, let the attack kill me. You have a future, you are young, and you have what I have earned for you and our aiga. I don't care if you respect me or not. Your hatred of me I deserve. ...' He had to make it abso-

373

lutely convincing, so he lowered his head and pretended to be weeping silently. Teuila, who was now crying, wiped her eyes and told Galupo she was glad he had come home. As he knew, she said, she and Tauilopepe had no children of their own, and if he would let them they both wanted him to be the son they had never had. All they asked of him was to forgive them. She stopped and wept into her hands.

Fully aware of what Tauilopepe was attempting to do, but surprised that Teuila was helping him, Taifau repeated that all they wanted was for Galupo to forgive them; his parents wanted him to help them to give him what he deserved as his inheritance. 'We are all sinners,' he declared, 'but, as Christ's children, we all possess the talent of forgiveness. You must help your father and mother to restore your inheritance. You have said you admire me, so I now plead with you to help your parents. Yes, I, Taifau, who, without Tauilopepe, would never have made anything of myself. You are right to condemn us for trying to act as gods in Sapepe, but it is up to you to show us more just ways of helping our people. You *must* help us,' Taifau ended, and was amazed that he could lie so easily.

Galupo said, with a note of sadness in his voice, 'I accept. I agree. I accept the fact that this is my home. Whether you want me to be your heir, Tauilopepe, is up to you. I make no claims on your wealth or your affections. But I am grateful to be acknowledged as your son. One thing I must correct though — you have nothing to be forgiven for. What I told you last night was all lies. The life history I narrated was mere fabrication. Moa, my mother, died in giving birth to me, my grandparents loved me, there was no such aiga as the Aiga Falesa — I made them up.'

Galupo went on to say that he was a bookish dreamer who had worked as a clerk. One thing he had said was true though — he did love books. That, he supposed, was why he had such a ridiculous imagination. So they had no reason to be afraid of him. He hadn't come to exact a terrible vengeance but to find his roots. His behaviour had been designed to force his parents to acknowledge him as their son. He wanted to be needed by them because he had always admired Tauilopepe. To prove to them that he was worthy of being their son he would rebuild everything. They saw tears in his eyes. 'I'm so happy . . . so happy to be home.'

Tauilopepe looked at Taifau and found him gazing sadly at Galupo. He turned to Teuila: she too was staring at Galupo in that believing way. And he also wanted so much to believe Galupo, but the revelations of the previous night stopped him. He was, however, convinced that he had tricked Galupo into helping them to rebuild Leaves of the Banyan Tree. Galupo, he thought, was a mere novice at the game of leadership, of manipulating and using other people.

'Are you all right now?' Taifau asked Galupo. He nodded. 'Welcome to our aiga.'

'Yes, welcome home,' said Teuila, 'Isn't that right, Tauilo?'

Tauilopepe agreed and then said, 'You will keep the Malo title. It's ours anyway. Better if you continue staying with the Aiga Malo; get them to stop attacking our aiga. It's time our two aiga were reunited. Tomorrow we'll start rebuilding Leaves of the Banyan Tree. You will be in sole charge. Taifau will advise you. I will supply the money and anything else you may need. From now on the plantation is your responsibility. I am sure you can rebuild it in a year. Do you think he can, Taifau?'

Chuckling, Taifau said, 'I think so. Galupo—I mean Malo—isn't like the other useless, gutless members of his generation!'

'By the way, Galupo, the Aiga Malo is your responsibility,' said Tauilopepe. 'You must feed and clothe them out of your pay and your store. You are Malo now.'

Tauilopepe then instructed Taifau to call a council meeting for the next day. At the meeting he would tell the other matai that Galupo was now Malo and that the readmission of the Aiga Malo to Sapepe was accomplished.

'I must write and tell Lalolagi,' said Teuila.

'Who?' asked Galupo.

'Lalolagi. Pepe's son and your nephew,' she replied.

375

'He is coming home for the Christmas holidays this year. Isn't he, Tauilo?'

'I suppose so. I can't keep breaking promises to him,' said Tauilopepe.

'He's going to be a lawyer,' Teuila told Galupo.

'That's good,' replied Galupo, smiling.

16 A New Plantation

On a Monday morning, two weeks before Christmas, the new pick-up truck purred through the plantations on a road still soggy with dew. Taifau was driving; beside him was Tauilopepe; on the back, sitting with their legs dangling over the edge of the tray, were Galupo and Lalolagi who had returned from New Zealand the previous afternoon and who was now a tall well-built eighteen-year-old. Everything about Lalolagi was expensive: the jeans and T-shirt, the immaculate hands clutching the rifle that Tauilopepe had bought him for Christmas, the unblemished face and the stubby nose, and the mouth curving up at the corners in a perpetual smile.

'How long were you in New Zealand?' Galupo asked, trying to sharpen his bushknife.

'About five years. Man, you don't know how glad I am to be back. It's great!' Lalolagi replied in a mixture of English and Samoan. 'You speak English, don't you, Galu?'

'A little.'

'Teuila wrote and told me you could. I'm glad you can. Great to find someone here who can speak English,' Lalolagi said in English.

'Speak English?' Galupo asked in English.

'Yeah. My Samoan isn't too hot any more. You know, spent too many years yakking all the time in palagi lingo. You know?'

'Yakking?'

'Oh, that's slang for conversing. Talking, you know?'

'Oh,' said Galupo. 'Must remember that.' They were both speaking English now.

'Man, the hurricane must have really been something.'

'Yes, it was. But I don't think I'll be able to describe it to you in English.'

'C'mon, try. Teuila wrote to me that you're a bright character. You know — brains, hard work and all.'

Galupo laughed and said, 'Well, the storm blew down just about everything except the coconut trees. But after a year — well, just look around you — everything looks normal and Leaves of the Banyan Tree is thriving again.'

'Thanks to you, *uncle*. You don't mind me calling you that?' asked Lalolagi. Galupo shook his head. 'Man, before Teuila wrote and told me about you and how you were slaving your guts out rebuilding our plantation I never knew you existed. But now I'm here, back home in our beloved country, I'm hell of a glad you *do* exist, uncle. And I'd like to thank you.'

'For what?'

'You know, for helping the old man out. Everything is simply great. Papa looks great, so does Taifau, so does Teuila. Man, I can't wait to see Leaves of the Banyan. Papa's looking forward to it too; he told me last night. He hasn't seen it for about a year, has he?'

'No, I wanted to surprise him.'

Tauilopepe had kept his word to Galupo: he had left him alone for a year, with both the Aiga Tauilopepe and Aiga Malo working on Leaves of the Banyan Tree. At first the Sapepeans refused to believe that Galupo and Tauilopepe could live together peacefully, but when they saw (and heard about) what Galupo was doing to Leaves of the Banyan Tree their fears gradually vanished. In the council, Galupo never once opposed his father, much to the disappointment of the matai who owed Tauilopepe large debts. Galupo also helped each aiga to restore its plantations, sending half his working gangs to work with the aiga twice a week at no cost; he even gave them new crops to plant, and sometimes gave them money and goods from his store. Tauilopepe put him in charge of distributing the food which the United Nations Organisation had sent to help offset the threat of famine. His distribution was scrupulously fair — all aiga, irrespective of status, received equal shares, and he kept none of the food for his own aiga. Some of the high ranking matai objected to this but Galupo, through Tauilopepe, silenced their opposition. Simi, after consulting Tauilopepe, appointed Galupo a deacon, and on Sundays Tauilopepe got him to preach in his place. Galupo's sermons were captivating exhortations praising the virtues of hard work, thrift, and honesty. He practised what he preached: he worked harder than anyone else. Sapepe and Tauilopepe, the Sapepeans started to tell one another, were very fortunate in having such a devoted son.

The pick-up bounced over a rock. The young men heard Taifau and Tauilopepe laughing. 'Happy old jokers, aren't they,' remarked Lalolagi. Galupo nodded and continued to sharpen his bushknife. It was getting hot, the sun was now perched on the heads of the palms. Lalolagi's T-shirt was drenched with sweat. He peeled if off, spread it out on the tray, and started to caress his biceps. 'Taking a body-building course,' he said.

'Body-building?' asked Galupo.

'You know — weight-lifting exercises and all that. Think I'm muscular?' Galupo nodded. 'You're not so unmuscular yourself, uncle. But you should do this course. Some day I'm going to have bigger muscles than Papa used to have. Did you know Papa used to be the most muscular man here?'

'Yes, everyone knows that,' Galupo said. 'They say your father was a big man too.'

'My father?'

'Yes, Pepe.'

'Oh, but let's not talk about *him*. He just bloody well wasted his time and Papa's and everyone else's time.'

'I didn't know that,' said Galupo, running his fingers over the glittering edge of his bushknife.

'Man, I could tell you bloody great things about him. Did you know he was a bloody thief and a hood?'

'Many people here seem to think he was a good man.'

'Who, for instance?'

'No one in particular.'

'Bet you it's Faitoaga and his kind. You know — the uneducated jokers. They go for blokes like Pepe; they don't know any better. Bloody ignorant.'

'I suppose you're right.'

'Bloody right I am. Pepe pulled the wool over the eyes of a lot of uneducated jokers!'

'Pulled the wool?'

'You know—fooled. Anyway let's talk about something else.' And Lalolagi picked up his rifle, took out his handkerchief, and wiped the barrel. 'Must say, uncle, your English is great. Better than most Samoans. A bit more reading and.... Say, do you read?'

'A little, but I haven't read as much as you.'

'That's okay. Now, what kind of books do you read?'

Galupo stopped sharpening his bushknife and said, 'The usual—westerns and gangster stories.'

'Anything else? Teuila told me you've read a lot. Have you read books about politics, for instance? Or philosophy?'

'I'm afraid my knowledge of English doesn't go that far.'

'You can try, man. Look, would you like to read some of my books. I brought a lot home with me. Would you like to borrow them?'

Galupo nodded and said, 'But don't be disappointed if I can't read them.'

'I can help you. You know, explain bits here and there; meanings of words, things like that.'... Bloody hot isn't it? Hey, we're there!' He jumped up and surveyed the plantation. 'Hey, Galu, everything looks as if there hadn't been a hurricane at all! Hey, what's the bloody matter with the old Banyan?' Up on the hill, etched into the flesh of the sky and range, stood the Banyan, bare of leaves, its crippled branches turning brown in the heat. Dying.

'The storm nearly blew it down,' Galupo said. 'We've tried everything we could to save it. Nothing has worked.'

'Anyway it's a useless tree,' Lalolagi said. 'Papa always wanted it chopped down.'

As instructed by Galupo the day before, all the workers were assembled in front of the cocoa dryer, awaiting their arrival. Taifau stopped the pick-up in front of them.

'Man, it's great!' shouted Lalolagi, jumping down. He opened Tauilopepe's door. Tauilopepe leant on Lalolagi's shoulder as he got out. Taifau and Galupo went over to talk to the overseers. 'It's great!' Lalolagi kept repeating.

380

'Galupo's done a great job, hasn't he, Papa?' Tauilopepe only nodded. Taifau and Galupo and the workers fell silent when Tauilopepe and Lalolagi reached them. An overseer brought out a chair for Tauilopepe but he waved it away. Many of the workers surged forward and greeted Lalolagi.

'In case some of you don't know who this skinny fellow is, he is Lalolagi, Pepe's son. He's just returned from New Zealand, so don't expect too much of him!' Taifau introduced Lalolagi, and everyone laughed.

'Now back to work,' Galupo said. And, as the men started to disperse, he called after them, 'By the way, there'll be bonuses for everyone for Christmas!'

'Bonuses?' asked Lalolagi.

'Yes, what's this about a bonus? Can we afford it?' asked Tauilopepe, putting on his sun-glasses. Galupo said that the men had worked hard all the year. 'Well, if you think so,' said Tauilopepe. 'It's a lot of money but you are in charge here.'

They went to the new cocoa and copra dryers. Under the watchful eye of one of Taifau's overseer sons a sweating gang of workers was spreading raw cacao beans across the platform under which a fire was burning in a large furnace. In the copra dryer other men were doing the same thing to raw copra. The air was starting to choke with smoke.

'Great! Great!' Lalolagi called in English to some of the men he knew.

As they inspected the dryers Taifau told Tauilopepe that Galupo had designed them and had also built a viewing platform above them. Leaning on Lalolagi's shoulder, Tauilopepe went up on to this platform. Taifau followed them but Galupo stayed below.

'What a view, Papa!' Lalolagi exclaimed in English. Tauilopepe shuffled over and stood beside him against the railing.

He nodded slowly as he surveyed the plantation which, in a breeze blowing in from the north-west, was rippling like an expanse of green sea. Except for the big mounds of dead trees protruding through the bananas a short distance away no trace was left of the destruction. The bananas had

381

been replanted, the acreage increased, and rows of palms now extended westwards from the road into the valley floor, green and lush. Tauilopepe turned round. Below him, stretching away into the blue morning haze and situated among areas of cacao that had survived the hurricane, were fenced-off blocks of young cacao plants. Workers were weeding between the rows.

'Are you satisfied now?' Taifau asked.

'About the plantation?'

'No, about your son,' said Taifau. Tauilopepe walked over to the opposite railing without replying.

He gazed up at the Banyan. It was certainly dying, he thought. Smoke was rising from Faitoaga's fale under the Banyan's shade. Everything had been restored. God had regranted the blessing He had withdrawn. And he remembered with pride how he had hacked the plantation out of the bush, defeating the giant trees and the webs of liana and creeper and vine. And how the earth had yielded her treasure to him. The haze on the range was lifting, sucked up by a sun which was now a hungry mouth.

'And it's all ours,' Lalolagi said, coming over to him. 'I like Galupo,' he continued. 'He must've nearly killed himself with work.' Tauilopepe didn't answer.

When they came down from the platform they found Faitoaga talking to Galupo beside the truck that was to take them round the plantation. Lalolagi crept up and tapped Faitoaga on the shoulder. Faitoaga whirled round and, with loud joyous laughter, hugged Lalolagi. 'You've not so little and skinny any more, are you, boy!'

'You're not so skinny yourself!' replied Lalolagi.

'Doesn't he look like his father? Eh?' Faitoaga asked the others. No one answered. 'You got a palagi girl-friend yet, boy? Your old man was good with the women!'

'We haven't got all day!' Tauilopepe said, moving to the truck.

They spent the whole morning inspecting the plantation, using the roads and tracks that Galupo had had constructed to separate the different blocks of crops and pasture. They saw the new varieties of cattle, crops, and grasses he had introduced and the modern methods of irrigation, planting, pest control, and fertilising. Taifau explained all of these to Tauilopepe. The new Leaves of the Banyan Tree, Taifau boasted as they came up from the valley, was the most modern, most God-blessed plantation this side of Eden.

Thirsty and hungry, they parked the truck by the dryers and went up to Faitoaga's fale where, after Lalolagi had greeted Faitoaga's wife, they ate a hearty meal of charcoal-cooked chicken, baked taro, and palusami.

After their meal, Taifau offered Lalolagi a cigarette. He glanced warily at Tauilopepe. Everyone laughed.

'Go on,' Tauilopepe said. Lalolagi took the cigarette. 'Will you be allowed to smoke at university?' Tauilopepe asked.

'Yes, Papa. University students are allowed to do anything.'

'*Anything?*' asked Faitoaga, his eyes twinkling mischievously.

'Well, almost anything,' joked Lalolagi. The others laughed again.

Faitoaga's wife brought Tauilopepe and Taifau some pillows and they went to sleep while the others left to work in the plantations. Almost two hours later Tauilopepe woke up and, amused by Taifau's loud, open-mouthed snoring, yelled piercingly. Taifau jerked up to his feet. 'Indians are attacking the fale,' Tauilopepe said, and they laughed.

They smoked and gazed out at the sunlight twinkling on the broad leaves of the banana trees. A large rat dragging a strip of sugar-cane broke from underneath the fale and scurried across the lawn into the bananas. The Banyan creaked above them.

'He has worked hard,' Tauilopepe said.

Taifau glanced at him and said, 'That son of yours is the most conscientious young man I've ever had the luck to work with. (That is, apart from you when you were young, old man). Even Faitoaga thinks very highly of him, and Faitoaga doesn't think very highly of many two-legged creatures. Galupo has earned what you wanted him to earn — the right to be your son and heir.' Tauilopepe said nothing. 'I'm very proud of him, Tauilo,' Taifau continued. 'I don't know why I was ever afraid of him.' He paused and then, almost as if he was thinking aloud, said, 'I wonder what he'll do when he finds out we've been deceiving him?'

Tauilopepe ignored his question. 'I lied to him,' he said, 'because I thought, I was convinced — and you were convinced too, Taifau — that he was out to destroy us. I also needed him to rebuild the plantation.'

'We used him.'

'All right, I *used* him. But, my trusting friend, are you positive he is not using us, eh?'

'In the past year I've worked with him and I am positive he isn't using us,' Taifau replied.

'You are willing to trust him with your life?'

'Yes, with my life, or what's left of it.'

Tauilopepe lit another cigarette. 'I don't know any more. One moment I'm sure he is using us, the next minute I'm equally sure he isn't.' He paused and then said, 'After what I've seen today I *do* want to believe in him.'

'But now the plantation has been restored what is going to happen to him?'

'He stays on.'

'And after that?'

'We will just have to wait and see, that's all.'

They stopped talking when they saw Galupo, Faitoaga, and Lalolagi approaching the fale. Galupo and Faitoaga came and sat down on the lawn in the shade of the Banyan; Lalolagi perched himself on the front steps of the fale.

'I think we should celebrate the new Leaves of the Banyan Tree, Papa,' Lalolagi said after a time. 'You know, go into Apia and have a few drinks. Galupo and Taifau and Faitoaga deserve it. And it's Christmas.'

'Do you drink?' Tauilopepe asked.

'Not yet,' he said, but when Tauilopepe and Taifau gazed sceptically at him, added, 'Well, just a little.' Tauilopepe and Taifau laughed.

'That's a good suggestion. We'll go into Apia and celebrate. Taifau and I will drink lemonade while you fellows can drink all you like,' said Tauilopepe.

Lalolagi stalked out to tell Galupo and Faitoaga.

17   Businessmen and Con-Men Celebrate

As Lalolagi drives slowly through Apia you remember with
a hollow sadness the day you and Pepe sold your first load
of bananas at the market. Your town hasn't changed radi-
cally over the years — a new wharf, a market, more stores,
larger crowds, thicker traffic, the reclaimed area now covering a large section of the harbour, but much is as it was
that day — the dust-caked buildings anchoring the shore to
the sea with a feeling of permanence, the churches' gleaming towers, the urchins peddling vegetables and seafood,
the very feel of the heat, and noise picking at your
thoughts. But you are old now, your dream you think
fulfilled. You could have given Pepe so much. But never
mind, your conscience has been salved: Pepe's son will
inherit your wealth, your name, and the dream. And
Galupo? He is your son but he isn't to be your heir.
Lalolagi will have the education the new Samoa needs. You
remember Lupe and Niu and Vao. You haven't seen your
daughters since they fled from you but you owe them
nothing. You didn't fail them; they failed you. Your father
failed you; so did your mother and Toasa and Pepe. But
you have forgiven them. They did not understand your
dream for your aiga and Sapepe. You loved them, you
want to believe that, but there is only an ache in your
heart; and you don't want to die and become memories
like them. The after life awaits you, but you doubt the
very promise of that life for you have enjoyed this life too
well. . . .

Lalolagi parked the Chev in front of the Samoa Club, got
out quickly, and opened Tauilopepe's door. Faitoaga,
Taifau, and Galupo got out, and Lalolagi went on ahead
with Galupo. It was just past noon.
     This was the first time Taifau and Faitoaga had visited
the club and they felt fearfully apprehensive. Tauilopepe

chuckled as he watched them straightening their clothes. 'Don't worry,' he said. 'No one will bother you. Just act like big shots, you're both very good at that!'

Galupo returned and Tauilopepe asked him if anything was the matter. 'They won't let us in, sir,' Galupo replied. Tauilopepe marched towards the club's front door, the others following him.

'Who the hell do you think you are?' Lalolagi was saying in English to the manager.

'That is enough,' Tauilopepe said to Lalolagi. The manager's opposition dissolved into an ingratiating smile as soon as he saw Tauilopepe. 'These are my sons and guests,' Tauilopepe said.

'I'm sorry, I didn't know.'

'Can we have a table?'

'Certainly,' replied the manager, opening the door and leading them to a large table in the corner near the main bar.

The club was fairly crowded and it was filled with the smell of cigarettes and beer. Men were milling around the billiard tables at the far side of the hall, under the glistening portraits of the Head of State and the Prime Minister.

'Just as a starter, lemonade for everyone,' Tauilopepe told the waitress. Some of the men at the bar waved to Tauilopepe but everyone kept away from their table.

'Nice place,' Taifau said hesitantly.

'Yes,' echoed Faitoaga, looking uncomfortably hot in his white shirt. Tauilopepe guffawed.

'Relax!' Lalolagi said. 'Pretend you're palagi. You're no different from them.'

When the waitress brought them their ice-cold lemonade Lalolagi and Galupo gulped theirs down quickly. 'C'mon, Galu,' Lalolagi said. 'Let's go and win some easy money!'

'Billiards?' asked Tauilopepe.

'I'm not bad at it,' replied Lalolagi, getting up. 'C'mon, Galu, I'll show these locals how to play the game. Got any money?'

'Plenty,' laughed Galupo. 'I finance you, I get the profits. Okay?'

The doors behind them opened. Heely and Ashton

entered and went up to the bar without seeing Tauilopepe. He told Galupo and Lalolagi to wait because he wanted them to meet some of his friends. They sat down again. Tauilopepe told the waitress to bring two fresh glasses, whisky for everyone, and lemonade for him. Faitoaga and Taifau protested but Tauilopepe told them to have just one whisky each. He then waved to Heely and Ashton who came over and lowered themselves into the chairs Lalolagi got for them.

'You're looking good, mate!' Heely said to Tauilopepe. 'Doesn't he look healthy, Ash?'

'Yeah, very healthy!' echoed Ashton.

'You like whisky?' Tauilopepe asked in English.

'You know us, mate,' said Heely, 'whisky men all the way!' The others watched the two papalagi—Taifau and Faitoaga with awe, Lalolagi and Galupo with amusement.

The waitress brought their drinks, and Tauilopepe gave her a generous tip.

'Cheers, mates!' Heely said. Everyone except Taifau and Faitoaga drank with Heely. Galupo elbowed Taifau and Faitoaga who immediately lifted their glasses and took deep gulps. When they spluttered and their eyes filled with tears Lalolagi and Galupo laughed.

Tauilopepe deliberately ignored their laughter and said to Heely and Ashton, 'I like for you to meet mine sons, Lalolagi and Galupo!'

'Great!' chorused the two papalagi.

'Strapping young fellows. You're a lucky man,' added Heely.

'And these two gentlemen?' Ashton asked.

Before Tauilopepe could introduce Faitoaga and Taifau, Lalolagi said, 'They're my uncles. Great drinkers both!' Taifau and Faitoaga grinned as they shook hands with Tauilopepe's papalagi friends.

Lalolagi told the waitress to bring a whole bottle of whisky and jugs of ice and water.

'Which is the son who's been educated in New Zealand?' asked Ashton.

'Me,' replied Lalolagi. 'You're Papa's lawyer, aren't you?'

'I try my best to serve your grandfather, young man,' said Ashton.

'You're not drinking?' Heely asked Tauilopepe.

'My grandfather has been very ill,' Lalolagi said.

'Forgot about that,' said Heely. 'How's the plantation?'

'And the family?' added Ashton.

Lalolagi finished his drink and told Taifau and Faitoaga to hurry up and finish theirs. They did so. Lalolagi immediately refilled their glasses, got up, and went off to play billiards with Galupo.

Tauilopepe talked to Heely and Ashton. Taifau, whose English was better than Tauilopepe's, followed their conversation easily, but Faitoaga, who didn't understand English, continued grinning, and, unnoticed by the others, drank whisky after whisky. When he heard Lalolagi's laughter he got up and went towards the billiard tables. On the way he veered off to the bar, ordered three large bottles of beer, and told the barmaid to charge them to *Mister* Tauilopepe. He opened them with his teeth.

Most people were now crowded around the centre billiard table watching the expensive game between Lalolagi and Thomas Melsop, the club snooker champion. Faitoaga pushed his way through the crowd, ignoring the impolite remarks about these fools from the back who had more money than brains. 'Melsop's teaching them a lesson,' he heard someone say. As soon as he saw the smug grin of the man who was playing with Lalolagi he knew that Lalolagi was losing. He shoved a bottle into Galupo's hand and said, 'Drink up!' He gave the other bottle to Lalolagi. 'Manuia!' Faitoaga said. They took only a few minutes to empty the bottles and Faitoaga belched loudly.

'Another game?' called Melsop. He was the son of a rich merchant and hence had ample free time to practise his game.

Lalolagi nodded. 'How much are we down?' he whispered to Galupo. 'Raise the stakes to forty dollars a game,' he said. Galupo did so.

Melsop won that game too and gave some money to his second, a Christopher Ames, to buy drinks for everyone.

389

Galupo sent Faitoaga to buy some more beer.

'These Apia arses think they've got us,' Lalolagi whispered to Galupo. 'Raise the stakes to fifty dollars a game, and challenge them to a large side bet. Got the money?'

Galupo opened his wallet and displayed a fat wad of notes. 'I'm not worried about the money,' he said. 'Just make sure they don't make fools of us.'

When Faitoaga returned they drank some more beer. Melsop came to the billiard table and called in English, 'Had enough?'

'Make this game fifty and tell your friends to cover our side bet of a hundred,' replied Galupo, thumping the money on to the table.

'I'll take twenty of that!' Melsop's eager second called. Many other men scrambled forward and covered Galupo's bet.

Lalolagi drained the beer remaining in his bottle, picked up his cue, and chalked it carefully. Melsop's second set up the balls. Everyone fell silent.

'Start?' Lalolagi called to Melsop.

'By all means!'

'Now watch this!' said Lalolagi. He leant forward, aimed, and shot hard. The red balls scattered and two of them dropped into the pockets. 'Black.' He stalked round the table to the white cue ball, aimed, shot. The black ball shot into the far-corner pocket. The spectators murmured. Melsop's second claimed that Lalolagi's shot had been a fluke. Lalolagi shot again. Another red into the pocket. 'Black again!' Aimed, shot. Again into the pocket. 'Think we're ignorant villagers, eh! Well just keep watching!' A slow shot this time and the red rolled into the centre pocket. Round the table, another red. 'Black again!' And it went in easily. Deliberately placing the white cue ball in the far corner from which Melsop would be unable to extricate it, Lalolagi called, 'Your shot!' Then he went on drinking with Galupo and Faitoaga without bothering to watch Melsop's shot.

'See if you can get out of that, arsehole!' Melsop said after his shot.

390

Lalolagi saw that Melsop had placed the cue ball in a difficult position. He walked to the table, surveyed the ball from various angles, and said, 'Easy. Watch this!' He aimed the cue ball at the opposite cushion and shot hard. The ball bounced back and slammed the nearest red into the pocket. 'This game's finished,' he said; it had taken him only half an hour to finish it.

Galupo collected their winnings from the scorer's table. 'Another game?' he called to Melsop and his supporters. 'A hundred on the game and another hundred as a little bet?'

Melsop nodded and took out his wallet. This time only a few of his friends volunteered to help cover the side bet and they insisted that Melsop should break.

Lalolagi won decisively.

Galupo went to collect the money. 'Who allowed you into this club?' Melsop's second asked him. Galupo squared the pile of notes like a pack of cards and walked back to Lalolagi and Faitoaga. Most of the crowd were still there. Melsop's second scuttled off to get a committee member.

'You know what's wrong with our country?' Melsop said to his friends. 'The bloody Samoans are ruining everything!'

'Don't ruin Tauilopepe's Christmas!' Galupo ordered Lalolagi as he stepped towards Melsop.

'What did that arse say?' Faitoaga asked.

'Nothing!' Galupo told him.

'These are the blokes, Mr Timms,' Melsop's second said to the papalagi committee member he had brought back with him.

'Any of you speak English?' Timms asked. No one replied. Some of the spectators moved in closer. 'Now, did you take Mr Melsop's money?'

'My nephew beat him in a fair game of snooker,' Galupo replied.

'Gambling is not allowed in this club!' Timms said.

'That's right!' chorused Melsop's second and a few other men.

'Better give back Mister Melsop's money,' said Timms.

'Are you going to make us?' Lalolagi asked.

'I'll ring the police!' said Timms, moving back a few paces.

'What's all this?' asked the manager, pushing his way through the crowd.

'These blokes are spoiling for a fight and they've conned a lot of money off Mr Melsop,' Timms explained.

'I won it in a fair game,' said Lalolagi. 'And any one who says I didn't gets....'

'That's enough!' Galupo stopped him.

'Anyway they're not members and shouldn't be here!' insisted Timms.

'Are you going to get them to leave?' the manager asked.

'Why not? They're only....' began Timms.

'Only what?' a voice demanded. They looked round. Tauilopepe pushed his way through the crowd and stood beside Galupo. 'Only what?' he asked Timms again. 'They guest of mine.' Timms went silently pale. 'My son he win the game, he keep the money.'

'I didn't know who they were,' Timms stammered. He was the accountant of a firm in which Tauilopepe was a major shareholder.

'Don't let this happen again,' Tauilopepe said to the manager. 'These boys, they *mine*.'

On the way back to their table, which was now occupied by three other men, Tauilopepe asked Galupo how much he had won. Only about three hundred dollars. Tauilopepe said that Lalolagi must be really good.

'He's the best,' said Faitoaga, slurring his words and slapping Lalolagi's back. Tauilopepe immediately cautioned Faitoaga not to get stupidly drunk. Taifau was drinking heavily too. Tauilopepe then told Galupo to buy drinks for everyone in the club.

'But why? We haven't stolen their money,' Lalolagi insisted.

'To do business in Apia you must learn to get on even with people you don't like,' Tauilopepe explained. 'And put another twenty on our table. It's your turn to pay!'

Tauilopepe said to Galupo when they reached their table.
'Get me a glass too.'

'But what about your....' Lalolagi began.

'My heart? I'm fit!' laughed Tauilopepe. 'Whisky and
ice,' he said to the waitress. 'Whisky for everyone!'

On Tauilopepe's right was Lefale Maa, a Buddha-shaped
member of parliament, who consumed his drinks with long
guzzling gulps. David Thrall, a hefty afakasi merchant with
a thorough knowledge of the Bible because he was a lay
preacher, sat between Heely and Ashton. Directly opposite
Tauilopepe was the Minister of Public Works, Faletiga
Paumasi, short and compact with a cataract in his left eye
and a booming voice which he obviously loved because he
never talked quietly. Tauilopepe introduced Faitoaga,
Galupo, and Lalolagi. As they talked the waitress had to
work hard to quench their thirst. Galupo rewarded her
with large tips.

Tauilopepe talked to the Minister about the Prime
Minister who, they agreed, lacked the necessary education
for his position; then about the Minister being the only
able member of Cabinet; then about the two new wharves
being a waste of money (Tauilopepe didn't mention the
fact that Faletiga Paumasi, as Minister of Works, had
approved the project); then about the useless Minister of
Agriculture who couldn't tell shit from manure.

Lalolagi and Ashton talked, with Ashton doing nearly all
of it, about Ashton's career and success; then about Ashton's aiga whom, he said, he loved dearly — Lalolagi didn't
know that Ashton had exiled his first wife and children to
New Zealand years before; then about the pill as a cure
for the problems of developing countries. Then Ashton
advised Lalolagi to be honest in all his dealings when he
became a lawyer, to be wary of all judges because they
were a sick bunch of failed lawyers, and to charge fees
according to his clients' incomes.

Galupo and Heely talked about agriculture, with Heely
doing nearly all of it, about manures and fertilisers and
irrigation to turn sick crops into lush crops the size of
Jack's beanstalk, which was a parable; about how plantation

393

labourers must be handled like frisky thoroughbreds — don't overpay them and give them women now and then; about bulls and how Heely, because of his vast practical experience, was always amazed by their prowess and speed — up, in and out, and, bang, a calf.

Lefale, the member of parliament, talked to Thrall, the merchant, about the large debts which most cabinet ministers owed Thrall's firm and how he, Lefale, owed the least because he lived within his modest means. Thrall hinted that ministerial debtors who lost the next election would be sued, but Lefale reminded him that the most powerful minister in the land also owed the most, and of course he, Lefale, was a certainty in the election. They agreed that a loyal and loving wife was essential to a man's career; Lefale didn't mention that he was in the process of divorcing his wife of twenty years, and Thrall, who knew, didn't mention it either because gentlemen didn't gossip, not in a respectable town like Apia anyway.

After his umpteenth whisky, and still with no one inviting him to join in the conversation, Taifau dismissed all the discussions as boring and switched his attention to the buxom waitress. Every time she brought him a drink he thanked her with a series of lascivious pats on her abundant flanks and she dismissed him with a haughty flick of her buttocks, Finally he tried to listen to the rapid dialogue between Lefale and Thrall but his hearing, he found, had turned soggy. He hurried to the toilet, thrust his head under the cold tap, returned with the floor swaying under his feet, sat beside Faitoaga, and started to hum.

Faitoaga, bored by the loud talking in English, tried to defeat boredom by drinking and telling himself that he was the best drinker in the whole country. Later, no longer bored because of the sweet music fizzing up in his head, he heard Taifau's humming and started to sing, at first softly, then, when Taifau started to sing too, loudly. He took the bass part, Taifau the lead, and they both thought they were only whispering.

Preoccupied with their conversation, the other men ignored the singing for a while. But, as it grew louder and harder to ignore, they stopped talking and laughed about it. The rest of the people in the club, happy again because Galupo had bought them drinks, also began to listen. These villagers were quaint. Perhaps they would buy some more drinks. Tauilopepe noticed the positive reaction of the club members and felt relieved. Ashton, Heely, and Lalolagi started clapping to the beat of Taifau's song, and Galupo joined in the singing; the Minister and the member of parliament slapped their knees, and the merchant shut his eyes and clicked his fingers.

> ... There's a theological student
> walking down the road.
> He wears double-clothing
> and his hat is torn.
> He thinks he's smart
> with the pencil over his ear,
> but he's just an oven-cooked
> fellow who can't get a wife.

Taifau, Faitoaga, and Galupo sang in traditional style, the deep chanting sound from the pit of the throat and belly. Eyes closed, Taifau got up and, stretching his arms, started to dance the siva. Lalolagi whooped. Tauilopepe drowned his embarassment with two more quick whiskys and suddenly discovered he didn't care any more about what the other members might think. 'C'mon, warrior!' he called to Taifau. 'We own this town!'

The Minister and the member of parliament were drunk, and in their drunken state they remembered with new-found pride that they too were villagers, so they clapped to the beat and encouraged Taifau to dance. Ashton, Heely, and Thrall were drunk too, and in their drunken state remembered with mounting embarassment that they were papalagi, so they stopped drinking and started to talk to each other, trying to appear to the other club members as though they were not with these loutish villagers.

'Quiet!' Lalolagi said.

'Yeah, you quiet,' said Tauilopepe. 'You watch mine friend dance. He the best. The best!'

Taifau remained in one spot, his lavalava hitched up to reveal his tattooed thighs, his arms and hands turning, curving, hanging in the air like drifting birds, deep grunts issuing from his mouth to punctuate the flight of his hands.

> ... I'm going to give my love
> sweet perfume I got from a town store,
> coming all the way from Eden
> to anoint my love's body....

Thrall was the first to disappear—he went to the toilet and didn't return. When nobody was watching, Ashton crept away and lost his bulky figure among the people at the bar. Heely did the same soon after.

Lalolagi jumped up and started to dance round Taifau, overturning the empty tables and chairs. Tauilopepe laughed and clapped and drank some more. The manager scurried round trying to get a committee member to stop Tauilopepe and his guests but no one volunteered to do so. Timms advised the manager to ring the police but the manager didn't want to lose his job. Galupo sprang up, ripped off his shirt, and danced near Taifau.

They danced until the centre of the hall was littered with overturned tables, broken chairs, bottles, and glasses. Then Tauilopepe called, 'Let's go!' And Taifau, Lalolagi, Galupo, and Faitoaga danced towards the front door, singing:

> We come from a sunny place
> where men eat sharks
> and spit out the bones.
> We come from Sapepe
> where the women are satisfied
> because their men don't wait until night....

Tauilopepe called the manager over. 'Four dozen beer, two bottles of whisky. Deliver them to my house.' He stuffed a fistful of money into the manager's shirt pocket, called goodbye to the two politicians, waved to the bar, and swayed out of the club, laughing. Feeling like a bird about to take flight in a free cool sky. Feeling as if he had been reborn.

18   A Sermon to the New Year

'...People of Sapepe,' Tauilopepe continued his sermon, 'let us welcome the New Year with joyous hearts for our Heavenly Father has been kind to us this past year. He tested us in January, sending a hurricane that devastated our land, but because we passed the test He has helped us rebuild so that soon we will again be enjoying the prosperity we have enjoyed for three decades....' Everything in the church was relaxingly blue behind the sun-glasses shielding his eyes. The whole congregation looked prosperous, with a prosperity that he, Tauilopepe, had brought to Sapepe. '...We have worked hard, as God has wanted us to work hard; we have obeyed His Commandments, as He has ordered us to; we have....' His mind, he thought, was alive with the excitement of original ideas — ideas that were now tumbling off the tip of his tongue clearly, captivatingly. He wasn't old, he wasn't sick, the future stretched out before him across the sunny limitless plains of his hopes, a future as smooth as the flow of his words. As he spoke he thought of his first sermon in the old church: 'God, Money, and Success'; the same dazzling light was flashing through the windows now, mellowing the faces of the congregation; the same atmosphere of profound conviction filling the church; the bouquets of frangipani were in front of the pulpit now as then, and the vases of ginger flower and hibiscus; he could smell the same heady scent of brilliantine and perfume. But with a difference — he was now the sole power in Sapepe; he had arrived, succeeded; he had found God, Money, and Success; his church, his people, his pastor. Where was Toasa's prophecy of doom? Where was Pepe's promise to destroy him?

'...For over thirty years I have struggled, brothers. Why? To make you and our beloved district into something God and our country can be proud of. The New

Year approaches us like an angel of promise....' No one had believed in him, he thought. No one. Not even Lupe. Lost in their ignorance and love of things past, in their fear of the future he had promised them, they had tried to stop him. He had turned his vision into fact: the fertile modern plantations stretching to the range, a modern hospital, a school, a tap-water system, more money in the people's pockets, modern food in their bellies, education for their children, papalagi houses for nearly all the aiga — and this church. Sapepe was the new Samoa, the Progress and Promise which the papalagi had envisaged for Samoa. Ignorance, paganism, superstition, all defeated.

'...We have won the fight, brothers. We have shown our government and the people of this country what can be done when men use their God-given intelligence, drive, and initiative. We have proved that the wilderness can be turned into a Garden of Eden....' He was speaking now to his aiga who were sitting in the front pews: Teuila, vibrant with belief in him and his gift, watching him intently. The full firm breasts like warm milk, the velvet feel of her body. *She* believed in him utterly. Throughout the years she had, with her body and mind and boundless love, healed his disillusionments, expelled the aitu which had haunted him. But God had denied her sons. He had tried — God knew how hard he had tried. No son. No child. Oh, how he loved her!

'...Through our diligent efforts, our children and their children will inherit a proud inheritance. The faa-Samoa is dying, and so it should, for these are modern times and we must, for the sake of those generations coming after us, tune our steps to the times, march as true Christians to the hymn of Godly progress....' Lalolagi in his expensive suit beside Teuila. The new heir. Education. Drive. The son God had denied Teuila. A son to continue his name and line and life. Beside Lalolagi, Galupo in a simple white shirt, a tie, and a lavalava. Can't trust him completely but a good son — loyal, strong, modern in many ways, the link with the future which belongs to Lalolagi. Remembered his will, written and secure in Ashton's safe, to be read when Lalolagi returned from New Zealand with his law degree.

398

Taifau, face wrinkled like the skin of an over-ripe mango, half asleep behind the fan he was holding. The only true friend he had made in Sapepe, a friend who owed him everything — home, education, and jobs for his children. Everything.

His sermon turned to a discussion of friendship. 'Without friendship the peace in our beloved district cannot last. Without friendship marriages cannot last. Without friendship we die alone. Yes, brothers, *alone*. And who wants to die alone? Who? No one. We all want to make our final journey to the Promised Land, with our friends and relatives gathered round us....' As he spoke he observed Simi who was sitting beside Taifau. 'Friendship, as our beloved pastor has told us in the past, is a sharing and a giving of love between aiga, individuals, and nations.' His sermon had assumed a conversational form very similar to Simi's sermons. 'Christ, the Son of God, brought love into our dark sinful world. He left us one Commandment: "Love thy neighbour...."' Simi was gazing up at him, his eyes aglow with belief, Tauilopepe thought. A good pastor, a man of integrity; sometimes too honest but he has learnt to bend a little, become more human like the rest of us. Still an outsider to some of the *uneducated*. Nothing wrong with a Solomon Islander but some people will insist on being bigots. He was starting to feel the heat, sweat was trickling down his back, and the excitement he had felt earlier was beginning to dwindle. He glanced at his watch. Still another ten minutes to go. Some of the children were asleep. He wiped his face with his handkerchief. '...I repeat, if we loved one another there would be no strife, no quarrels between brother and sister, no wars between nations, between black and white. All my life I have tried to live by this simple rule of love. I have failed at times but I have tried. That is all we can and must do. And we will succeed because God is with us. Our reward is the Promised Land....'

He suddenly became aware of the aching in his limbs, the dryness in his throat, the pain in his eyes, and he blamed it on the party at the club two days before. He had enjoyed it immensely and had continued to drink in the car and to laugh at Taifau and Faitoaga who were snoring and muttering unintelligibly in their drunken sleep. When they reached Sapepe late that night, his aiga (and the neighbourhood) had come out to help them into the house. He spent the whole of the next day sleeping and keeping away from Teuila, who was tearfully angry with him for having disobeyed his doctor's orders. Except for the two heart attacks I have never been seriously ill in my life, he thought. He glanced at his watch again. Five more minutes.

'... The New Year is full of promise for us and our children. It will be a year of sweat and toil but it will also be a year of joy, laughter, and love. We have pushed the bush back to the range, and with it we have forsaken things pagan, things belonging to the Darkness before the coming of the Light. God is truly with us now. ...' He raised his voice, exciting images and ideas again gripping him. Then he felt the slight needle-pricks in his paralysed arm and left side. And knew it was beginning. Tried to ignore it by concentrating on what he was saying. 'God will always be with us because our country is founded on God. ...' Suddenly realised he was trembling, his sweat turning cold. Gripped the pulpit to steady himself. Please, Father. Please help me! Continued speaking. Didn't listen to what he was saying. One more chance, Father. Don't want to die! Jabbing needles shooting into his side, jerking him momentarily out of his fear. 'God is merciful... God has led you and me to this Promised Land. ...' Whole left side and arm numb, ringing. Now. And the nightmare trial, when Pepe and Toasa had judged him, filtered into the white tide of his fear. Pepe yelling from behind the white mask, GUILTY! And the image of his past life flashed across the inner eye of his fear, the brilliant years crumbling into evening and the pain beginning again, tearing into his side. Want to live! Live! Dust settling on the grave of his unforgiving father, the man who had denied him; of his mother who had rejected him; of Lupe whom he had — and he didn't want to admit it to himself even now — destroyed; of Toasa, his second father, whom he had denied in his heart as he had pursued the dream; of Pepe, the expensive marble angel on the concrete grave, wings outstretched to

400

catch the evening dew and the tears now obliterating his vision. My son! My son! Why did you deny me? The pain, the claw, was invading the deepest cell of his being in which he was cringing, bringing with it the quick fatal touch of day. At the edge of the pain, behind the grains of dust stinging the skin of his eyes, he glimpsed her. Heard her scream. Scream. Teuila!

19   The Will

Galupo knocked on the door, opened it, and went in.

The room smelt of cigar smoke. Ashton was sitting at his large desk, writing. Galupo sat down in front of him. While he waited for Ashton to acknowledge his presence he flipped through the file of papers he had brought.

'What can I do for you?' Ashton asked, without looking up. Galupo didn't reply. Ashton looked up. 'I'm sorry, I didn't know it was you. How is your father?'

'The same,' said Galupo.

'Any chance?'

Galupo shook his head. 'They've got him in an oxygen tent. A few more days left.'

'I'm deeply sorry,' said Ashton. 'A remarkable man, and one of my dearest friends. A great Samoan. A credit to your race.' Paused and, when Galupo didn't reply, asked, 'Is there anything I can do to help him?'

'I don't think so. But there is something you can do for me.'

'Anything. Helping you would be helping your father and my friend.'

'I would like to see my father's will. I know it's against the law but may I look at it?'

'Can't...I can't do that!' spluttered Ashton. 'What you're asking me to do is against professional ethics!'

'What if I offered you a fair price?'

'No!' shouted Ashton. 'I can't do it. And I never expected the son of my best friend to ask me to break the law. And to bribe me! That takes the bloody cake. You're asking me to *betray* your father. Do you know that? Who do you think I am?'

Galupo placed his file of papers in front of Ashton. Muttering under his breath, Ashton started to read them. 'You're a crook, *Mister* Ashton,' said Galupo. 'A crook who's been stealing my old man's money for years.'

'Hold on. Before you find yourself in trouble with your slanderous accusations let me warn you that these papers won't hold up in court!'

'I'm not one of your scared, ignorant natives,' Galupo said, reaching for the file. Ashton snatched it away. 'Those papers will send you to jail for a long time. Now, hand them over.' Ashton reached for his telephone. 'Go ahead,' said Galupo. 'The quicker we get to the police the better.' Ashton pushed the file towards him.

'Where did you get them?' asked Ashton.

'I have my sources. Yes, very reliable sources.'

'You want to see the will?'

Galupo nodded. 'And at the price it's cheap.'

'Price?'

'Yes, the twelve thousand dollars you've stolen from my father over the last few years. I don't know how much you stole before that.'

Ashton got up slowly. 'It's in the safe. I'll get it.'

When Ashton extended the will towards him Galupo said, 'You read it. I'm not a very able reader of legal documents.' Ashton read it slowly. Galupo told him to hurry.

'Trust the clever, cunning bastard!' Galupo said when Ashton had finished.

'Your father was a very shrewd man,' said Ashton. Like Galupo, he was now referring to Tauilopepe in the past tense.

'Your conscience all right now?'

'Conscience?'

Galupo chuckled and said, 'I didn't think you had one.'

'Oh,' said Ashton.

'Now, from what I understand of the will I get very little. Correct?'

Ashton explained that the Apia house and property, half the money in the bank, and half the income from Tauilopepe's investments were to go to Teuila. Lalolagi was to get the rest except for two thousand dollars which was to come to Galupo. Of the eight village stores two were to be Galupo's, the rest Lalolagi's. The Tauilopepe title, so Tauilopepe recommended to his aiga, was to be conferred

403

on Lalolagi, thus ensuring that Leaves of the Banyan Tree, which was on land under customary ownership, would come under Lalolagi's control. In order to gain the support of the Aiga Tauilopepe and the Aiga Toasa for this recommendation, influential aiga elders were each to be paid a hundred and fifty dollars the week after Lalolagi received the title. Galupo was to administer the estate until Lalolagi returned from New Zealand; for this he was to receive a substantial salary.

'Now for the weakness in his will. Do you see any flaws in it?' asked Galupo. Ashton shook his head. 'There is a flaw, a small one but enough for my — or should I say *our* — purposes. What do Taifau and his aiga get?'

Ashton flipped through the will, stopped, read quickly, and explained that Taifau was to be Galupo's adviser until Lalolagi returned from New Zealand; for this he was to continue receiving his usual salary.

'The will does not guarantee this salary until Taifau dies?' Galupo asked. Again Ashton shook his head. 'And Taifau's sons who were working for Tauilopepe?'

'No mention of them.'

'Just as I thought — the flaw.'

'May I ask how?'

Ignoring Ashton's question, Galupo said, 'Who witnessed the will?'

'Heely and myself.'

'If we made out a new will....'

'A new will?' exclaimed Ashton. 'I can't do that!'

'The price is cheap,' Galupo said. 'You'll do it. Just be yourself.' Ashton bowed his head. 'To keep my aiga from suspecting the validity of the new will which will make me my shrewd old man's main heir I need Taifau's support. No one will question it if, after it is made public, Taifau gives it his support and helps me get the Tauilopepe title.'

'But what about your father's signature?'

'You forge it. You must be an expert at it by now,' Galupo said.

Ashton stared at the blotter on his desk. 'How will you get that other man to support it?'

'He'll do it because, after he's spent nearly all his life helping my father to get rich, my father leaves him nothing. In the new will Taifau and his aiga will be rewarded. We'll just show him this will, written, signed, and sealed by his best friend. Taifau will back the new will because of his aiga.' Straightening up, Galupo said, 'This is what I want you to put in the new will.' Ashton uncapped his pen and opened a large pad.

Teuila was to get the Apia house and property and an annual income of a thousand dollars until she died, then everything would revert to Galupo. (She had done him no harm and she was easy to handle.) The estate was to continue paying for Lalolagi's education and he was also to receive five per cent of Tauilopepe's investments. (A pity Tauilopepe wouldn't be around to see how his spoilt grandson turned out!) Taifau was to receive his present salary plus fifteen per cent of Tauilopepe's investments; when he died his share would go to his wife and children; his children were to continue in their present positions in the Tauilopepe business. Simi Faleula, the most fearless man in Sapepe, was to receive an annual income of five hundred dollars; if he refused it the money was to go to his aiga. Faitoaga, the only other Sapepean Galupo admired, was to continue caring for Leaves of the Banyan Tree and was to receive an annual allowance of five hundred dollars on top of his normal salary. He, Galupo, was to receive everything else. The elders of the Aiga Tauilopepe and the Aiga Toasa were to get a hundred dollars each soon after they conferred the Tauilopepe title on him.

'By the way,' Galupo asked, 'where does he want to be buried?'

'In Sapepe in front of the house in one of those multi-tiered vaults. He's already ordered a gravestone from England.'

'He certainly wants to be remembered. But then most self-made Other-Worlders do. Give him the tomb; after all, it's his money.' Galupo got up, stretched, and yawned. Then he picked up the file.

'May I have that?' asked Ashton.

Grinning broadly, Galupo said, 'Not until you fulfil your part of our profitable bargain.' He went to the door, turned, and added, 'I'll bring Taifau in the day after tomorrow. Make sure the new will is ready. Have the old one here as well. I want Taifau to read it.'

He waved at Ashton and left.

Galupo switched off the motor when they were a safe distance outside the reef. The boat rocked gently in the almost still sea. Taifau baited the hooks and tossed them into the water. Behind them low waves were swirling over the reef and sliding lazily into Sapepe harbour and the island, a blue cliff against the cloudless sky. They sat and watched the lines. Around them the sea sparkled and sucked at the sides of the boat.

Surreptitiously Galupo studied Taifau and asked himself why he felt this sadness, this hesitation over committing the final irrevocable act. All his major acts till now had been clearly planned and coolly carried out; he must not allow emotion, a despicable Other-Worlder trait, to destroy his plans now. He was just going to speak to Taifau when the nylon line tightened in his hand. Taifau had a bite too.

When the two medium-sized mullet were in the basket the men rebaited the hooks and threw them out again.

'Did you visit him yesterday?' Taifau asked.

'Yes. He's still in a coma.'

'I blame myself. He drank at the club because it was the first time he had seen me drinking for such a long time.'

They were silent for a few minutes. The boat started to smell of dead fish.

'Strange man, your father,' said Taifau. 'Always moving, doing things, going somewhere, as if some insatiable hunger is pushing him on. He moved me along too until I felt there was nothing I couldn't do. True, he's impatient, easily angered, intolerant, but that's why he achieves what he sets his mind to.' He paused. 'Am I boring you? The mutterings of old people usually bore the young.' Galupo smiled and shook his head. 'And he finds it hard to trust anyone,' Taifau continued. 'It took him nearly twenty years to learn to trust me, and the Taifau he came to trust was the Taifau he helped to create. It's just the way he is. I think he got it from his parents. Except for Toasa, his father didn't trust anyone. And he had no faith whatsoever in his remaining son. His favourites were the sons who died in the epidemics. That's why Tauilopepe never talks about his father.'

For the next hour or so they brought in fish after fish; the skin on their faces and backs began to sting from the heat.

'You remind me a lot of your father,' said Taifau as they rested. 'The same relentless dedication to hard work, the same uncontrollable urge to build things, the same attraction to women. Too right, boy, your father could have bedded any woman in this country.'

Galupo laughed as he opened their basket of food and handed Taifau some taro and corned beef. They ate and tossed the scraps into the water.

'I'm going to miss him,' Taifau said. 'Thirty years of friendship. He's the only man in Sapepe I learnt to trust and admire and love, so much so that I became his second self, an extension of his flesh and mind and vision. I was grateful for that. I would even sacrifice my miserable life for him....'

'I read somewhere, Taifau,' Galupo broke in, 'that the sea is the only beautiful and permanent thing God ever made. Let me see — yes: "The opposition here is between magnificent human anarchy and the permanence of the unchanging sea." It's by a French writer. Albert Camus I think his name is.'

'Quote me some more. It's very beautiful.'

'Here's another passage: "To feel one's attachment to a certain region, one's love for a certain group of men, to know that there is always a spot where one's heart will feel at peace — these are many certainties for a single human life. And yet this is not enough. But at certain moments everything yearns for that spiritual home." Any good?'

Nodding slowly, Taifau gazed into the horizon. He was

thinking, Galupo sensed, of Tauilopepe and the years they had spent together, and he judged it was the right time to shatter Taifau's faith in Tauilopepe, to expose Tauilopepe's love as another empty Other-Worlder pretence, a sham. He glanced up at the twitching sun and was blinded. He rubbed his eyes and saw Taifau's shoulders rising and falling to the rhythm of sorrow and the sea breathing under the boat and the clouds assuming new fabulous shapes round the sun as everything must have been on the day the first Samoans broke through the horizon's shell into these islands and later into Sapepe harbour to found the Aiga Sapepe. Like all Other-Worlders they had turned the land's and sea's gifts into monuments to their vanity when all that was permanent and true was the darkness within, a darkness as beautiful as this sea, a darkness out of which all truth and power and glory sprang.

'You are weeping for a lie, Taifau,' he said gently. 'He betrayed you; he used you, changed you into a creature of his own making; he destroyed your only gift.' Taifau turned away. 'Look at yourself, Taifau. For over thirty years you have propped up his monstrous vanity, lied for him, destroyed your true self for him. If that is love then it is death.' Taifau was now gazing at him. 'He sold you out, Taifau. He made his will not long after the hurricane and told me what was in it. I never told you because I didn't want to hurt you.'

'Why tell me now?'

'Because whatever wealth or power Tauilopepe has rightfully belongs to you as well.'

'I see,' said Taifau. 'And the will?'

'He leaves you and your aiga nothing,' replied Galupo. Taifau looked away. 'Thirty years, Taifau. A lifetime. Without you and your children he wouldn't have achieved what he did.'

'I was amply rewarded. Without him I wouldn't be where I am now.'

'But where are you now? He's dying. What's going to happen to you and your aiga? You have no title, no plantation of your own. How do you think the other matai are going to treat you? What's going to happen to Nofo and

your aiga?' He stopped, expecting Taifau to reply, but
Taifau said nothing. 'He has left you and your aiga to
Lalolagi's mercy. Can you trust Lalolagi? Do you trust
him? You know Lalolagi for what he is—a spoilt brat.
What's going to happen to all of us—you, me, your aiga,
Sapepe—when he inherits everything?'
'Enough!' whispered Taifau, turning towards him with
tears in his eyes. 'I never expected it from you, Galupo.
Not from you. I've learnt to think of you as my own son.
Now this!'
'I can't lie to you, Taifau. You've watched me work. The
hurricane smashed everything you and Tauilopepe had
built. Who rebuilt it? Me, the illegitimate and despised son
whose mother Tauilopepe used—yes, used—to get where
he is today.' Taifau looked away again. 'You know it's true,
Taifau. Tauilopepe *used* her. And for that alone he owes me
everything. And you owe me too, Taifau, because you did
nothing to stop him from using and destroying her.' He
paused for a moment. 'Compare me to Lalolagi. Who do
you think would serve the best interests of our aiga and
Sapepe?' Taifau didn't answer. 'You won't answer me,
Taifau, because you know in your heart you would choose
me. . . . You must help me help you and your aiga. A new
will must be made out.'
'You're asking me to betray him! I can't do it. Don't ask
me to. Please.'
'I'm not asking you to betray him. I'm asking you to
safeguard our interests and the interests of Sapepe.
Tauilopepe will soon be dead. We have to go on living. He
owes it to you; he betrayed you.' Paused again.
Taifau started pulling in the lines. 'Let's go home,' he
said.
'You'll think about it?' asked Galupo. Taifau wouldn't
look at him or answer. 'I have to know by tomorrow. All it
needs is your public support after Tauilopepe is gone.'

Galupo blew the horn twice. Nofo appeared at the window
and called that he was coming out soon. He waited, and
before long thought he could hear weeping coming from
the bedroom. Nofo? But he dismissed the thought. It was

a fine morning, with the sun hovering above the eastern range. A group of schoolchildren peered into the car; one of the oldest boys asked him if Tauilopepe was getting better. He was much better, he told them. He was feeling completely relaxed because he had slept soundly after the fishing trip. Out of the glove compartment he took Tauilopepe's sun-glasses, put them on, looked into the mirror, and brushed back his hair with his hands.

As Taifau came down the path Galupo saw that he was wearing sun-glasses too. He stopped at the edge of the road and looked back at Nofo who was standing in the open doorway. Galupo raised his arm to wave goodbye to her, then remembered that she was blind.

Taifau said nothing all the way to Apia.

They parked outside Ashton's office and went in. Ashton started to explain the new will to Taifau. Taifau said he wanted to see the old one. He read it quickly, asked for the new one, read that, muttered yes, got up without looking at Ashton and Galupo, and left.

Taifau shuffled up the main street, now filling with people who brushed past him without his caring or seeing who they were and where they were hurrying to; with the dust, kicked up by the traffic and the silent wind blowing in from the harbour peppering his white clothes and glasses; his sandals scraped hollowly across the footpath strewn with discarded ends and nightmares and tragedies. He didn't hear the raucous sound of the cars and trucks that streamed by like monstrous predators in some dark sea, nor smell the rising stench of another town day settling in on the buildings of stone and iron and wood and the monuments and the children peddling away their future in front of glittering display windows. He didn't feel the heat trembling, thawing the hides of the cathedrals upraised like clubs. He walked on slowly for he had a long, long way to go to the hospital and Tauilopepe who was dying.

20   The Time and the Place

I told you, Tauilopepe, didn't I? I warned you that I knew what your next move would be. I let you know who and what I am. But, being the Other-Worlder that you were, you refused to believe me. You didn't even bother to check and see whether I had told you the truth about myself. Now you will never know the truth about me. It isn't important any more that I am not really your son. What is important is that I made myself your son. Who my real parents were and where I came from are totally irrelevant now. Galupo was standing near the head of the bed, gazing down through the plastic oxygen tent at Tauilopepe. The light of the bed lamp made the tent glitter like a butterfly's cocoon. *Does it hurt, father? Can you take the pain? Doesn't matter. Only a few minutes to go and it will be over. I read somewhere — in a medical journal, I think — that a heart attack blows out the cells in your brain and leaves you a breathing husk, a vegetable. So I don't suppose you're feeling any pain. Your wife weeps for you. See her?* Beside Galupo, her face buried in her hands, weeping softly, was Teuila. *She loves you, father, even though you were incapable of loving other people. You couldn't even love your son, Pepe, your friend, Taifau, and all the Other-Worlders you used as steps to climb Jacob's ladder. But you were correct in not loving anyone, in not believing in that sentimental Other-World crap. Love is a weakness.*

A tall doctor was standing on the opposite side of the bed, taking Tauilopepe's pulse. His head was in the darkness above the level of the light so that it looked as though it had been neatly cut off. Next to him sat Lalolagi, half asleep. At the foot of the bed, staring fixedly through the transparent plastic wall at Tauilopepe's almost bloodless face, stood Taifau, his hands gripping the iron bar of the bed; he looked as if he was poised above a chasm. Next to Taifau, and still with grief, stood Faitoaga. Only Teuila's muted weeping stirred the silence. *Look at your ungrateful*

411

*grandson, father. He doesn't really care for you (or anyone else).
You made him that way. He is now what you in your youth
always wanted to be, an imitation papalagi but a caricature:
arrogant, spoilt, selfish, precocious, and with your insanely
inflated ego. Satisfied, father? You tried to make him your heir.
I've saved Sapepe and everyone else from that tragic fate. I've
saved your name and memory by making myself you, even
though we are not of the same blood, as it were. I can play the
part to perfection, and I've decided to do so. In me the Sapepe
fountain-head will come to life again. Perhaps I am Pepesa of
ancient times who, so the myths go, was to return one day and
reunite Sapepe.* The door behind Galupo opened; he turned
to see Simi entering the room.

'Is he...?' Simi asked. Galupo shook his head. Simi
went to the bed, reached under the edge of the tent, and
held Tauilopepe's hand. *I didn't want Lalolagi to take over
because of Taifau, Teuila, Faitoaga, and Simi. Simi is worth
saving, and you would have wanted me to save him. You betrayed Taifau, father, but I've saved him too. So am I evil,
father?* The doctor had drawn down the sheet covering
Tauilopepe's chest and was now listening to his heart. *I am
not evil, father, I am not interested in your wealth and power.
To me, those things are meaningless because they will only give
me value, meaning, and worth in the eyes of Other-Worlders
who mistakenly believe in them. To me, the whole struggle to
recreate one's self in order to be free of the Other-World is the
meaning and the aim. I am a product of my own imagination.
I am also, as another writer has put it, 'a product of our times',
a product of the history and whole movement propelling our
country towards an unknown future. Or, shall I say, I am that
future. If I am evil then our whole history has been a drift
towards evil. I cannot feel what Other-Worlders feel because I
am free of that world. I won our little game because of that and
because of the time and the place.*

The doctor put away his stethoscope and drew the sheet
up to shroud Tauilopepe's face. 'I am very sorry,' he said.
Teuila screamed, and brushed aside the tent and covered
Tauilopepe with her body. Lalolagi and Simi wept with
her. The doctor left the room. Galupo saw Taifau staring
at him, and he went over and gripped his shoulder as the

412

old man wept. 'It's all right, Taifau,' he whispered. 'It is better this way.' Taifau pulled away from him but Galupo didn't notice because he was moving over to Teuila.

He held her shoulders and, lifting her away gently from the corpse, whispered to her, 'He has gone to God, so why weep?' She sobbed into his chest. Tauilopepe's face — the high cheek-bones and sunken cheeks and lips turning blue — was only a few feet away. He bent down and kissed the cold lips, brushed back the hair, and, winding Teuila's arms around Tauilopepe's neck like a necklace, straightened up and walked past Faitoaga and Taifau and out the door.

Up the deserted corridor he marched, his bare feet making squeaking sounds on the tiled floor, his white clothes gleaming in the corridor lights; marched to the outside veranda where the elders of Sapepe were waiting.

He told them that Tauilopepe Mauga was dead. Some of them wept, others offered verbal condolences, one old man told him to be brave. And, as the elders moved up the corridor to Tauilopepe's room, Galupo slipped out the side door into the darkness.

He could glimpse the stars through the tangled branches of the pulu tree which he was standing under; dogs barked from the vicinity of the ovens where they burnt the hospital rubbish; from a nearby ward came the defiant howling of a child; the air felt cool as he breathed it in.

He let the tingling bubble up from the earth into his toes and up into his belly. Then, like sweet coconut milk, it surged up his chest and throat and out of his mouth. And he laughed for the power and the glory was his. Now.

413

Glossary

afakasi	part-European
aiga	family, extended family
aitu	ghost, spirit
ali	wooden headrest
alii	matai with an alii title
ava	ceremonial drink made from roots of kava plant
faa-Samoa	Samoan way of doing things, Samoan way of life
faafafine	effeminate man, homosexual
faamafu	home-brewed beer
fale	Samoan house
fautasi	long boat rowed by oarsmen
fiafia	to enjoy (v.), a feast (n.)
gatae	dadap tree
ietoga	fine mat
lavalava	skirt-like wrap-around garment
lotu	church service, act of worship
luau	young taro leaves cooked with coconut cream
malae	meeting area
malaga	trip, journey; ceremonial visit
malo	exclamation of encouragement
manaia	alii's son—a special position endowed with certain ceremonial duties and privileges (n.), beautiful (a.)

manuia	(be) happy, lucky (v. & a.)
matai	titled head of an aiga
mavaega	last verbal will and testament of dying person
moetolo	person who creeps into fale at night
paepae	raised stone foundation of a fale
palagi, papalagi	person of European stock
palusami	*see* luau
poumuli	hardwood tree
puataunofo	large yellow flower
pulu	type of coastal tree
saofai	ceremony at which matai titles are bestowed
siva	to dance (v.), a Samoan dance (n.)
soifua	goodbye, farewell (polite reference to good health and well-being)
Suipi	card game
taamu	(giant taro), large edible bulbous root
taivai	grass-cutting tool consisting of a metal blade fixed on the end of a wooden shaft
talie	tropical almond, a large tree found near the coast
tamaaiga	title given to the holders of the four highest titles in Western Samoa
tamaligi	tamarind tree, monkey-pod tree
tatau	man's tattoo which extends from the knees to the waist
taupou	female equivalent of the manaia
toonai	Sunday lunch
tulafale	matai who holds an orator's title
tusitala	writer
tuua	senior orator in a village: usually owes appointment to his wisdom and his knowledge of history, genealogy, and protocol
ula	lei, flower necklace
umu	stone oven

416